ROCK BAND FIGHTS EVIL

VOLS
1-3

BAND ON
THE RUN

ROCK BAND FIGHTS EVIL

VOLS 1-3

BAND ON THE RUN

D.J. Butler

WordFire Press
Colorado Springs, Colorado

ISBN: 978-1-61475-388-9

Cover design by Janet McDonald

Art Director Kevin J. Anderson

Cover artwork images by Carter Reid

Book Design by RuneWright, LLC
www.RuneWright.com

Published by
WordFire Press, an imprint of
WordFire, Inc.
PO Box 1840
Monument CO 80132

Kevin J. Anderson & Rebecca Moesta, Publishers

WordFire Press Trade Paperback Edition March 2016
Printed in the USA
wordfirepress.com

HELLHOUND
ON MY TRAIL

CHAPTER ONE

ah wah, ch-ch-chang! The guitar crunched out the end of the chorus with a cymbal crash.

Across the room, the bouncer of Butcher's looked like he was having a bad night. He leaned against the slightly lopsided bar and scanned the thin crowd with contempt, arms crossed over his denim jacket and a semi-automatic pistol visible in his belt. He shook his scarred, buzz-cut head every minute or so like he was trying to knock the sound of the music out.

Mike didn't care what the bouncer thought of the music. He hadn't seen his brother's ghost all day, and he needed a drink to keep things that way. The only reason Mike even noticed the bouncer was that the man was between him and the alcohol. The booze would keep his brother at bay for a little while. Also, after the set, Mike planned to shoot himself, and he preferred to die drunk.

Mike launched into the break, his memory guiding him through the changes. He'd arrived minutes before the show and Eddie had barked at him through the first part of the set, scrawling some notes on a greasy paper bag. It had been enough. After getting his marching orders, Mike had headed straight for the bar—and Eddie had corralled him back onto the stage before he could get his hands on even so much as a warm beer.

The drummer rode with Mike into the break while everyone else fell quiet. *Twitch*, that was the drummer's name, and he hit the skins with a light touch, but perfect timing. Mike nodded and grinned at Twitch and he grinned back as they held down the groove together, Mike boogying with a chromatic run that was probably more jazz than this shabby little blues-rock band was used to, up to the fifth over and over. Maybe he was showing off, just a bit, but it was his last gig. Ever.

The drum kit was a little minimalist, just a kick, snare, one tom, and a high hat. The drummer played with thick sticks that looked more like cudgels than something you'd buy at Guitar Barn. Twitch wore shiny black leathers from head to foot, the kind with studs in all the impossible places, so that he looked like some kind of black and silver sex porcupine. Mike thought of him as a guy, but actually, looking at the drummer now, he wasn't so sure. Twitch could have been a woman with a slightly strong jaw line or a man with a thin nose and eyebrows. Man or woman, the worst thing about Twitch's get-up was that it had a tail, a full horse's tail, silver-colored like the drummer's own long hair, that came right out of Twitch's backside and brushed the floor as he drummed. Twitch looked like he'd whip you, if you paid him.

Then Eddie jumped in, workmanlike power chords chomping over the beat, with the occasional blues flourish curling in the treble. Eddie was a slight black man with short curly hair, in a green military-style jacket with lots of pockets and jeans that had too many holes for any thrift store to take them. Mike had played with lots of guitarists who swanned and clowned and danced, but Eddie shrank back from the edge of the stage. He huddled over his instrument and carefully watched his fingering, which was good, because his playing was okay, at best. The axe Eddie worked on was a crummy red Toronado, a Fender like Mike's P-Bass, but made in Mexico. And discontinued, he thought, because nobody wanted to buy the things. It was red and worn to the wood where Eddie's forearm rubbed it, but the sound, running through a small bank of pedals at Eddie's feet, was crisp.

Eddie had some kind of manager role, too. It had been Eddie who had called him that morning, woken him from a scratchy, uncomfortable sleep into throbbing, painful wakefulness. Eddie had said he'd gotten Mike's card off the bulletin board in a guitar shop in San Antonio, and that there was gig for him tonight, if he could find a crappy little bar outside a crappy little town that wasn't on most maps, on a road that might or might not be indicated as a lumber trail. Bass and amp could both be provided.

That was good, because Mike's amp was in hock.

The crowd mostly ignored Eddie. Hard roadside drinkers that they were, they kept to their seats under the buzzing fluorescent tubes nailed to two-by-fours undergirding the tin-sheet ceiling, sucked their beer and spirits and watched Jim—the singer—like at any moment he might collapse to the floor or take flight. Some of them sent shots up to fortify or reward him, which made Mike lick his lips in anticipation of the first break.

Except there was this one guy, at the little round table nearest the stage, who stared at Eddie the whole time. He was a short guy in a polo shirt and a sport coat and a straw Panama hat, and his shoes were way too shiny for rural New Mexico. He gripped the little table with both hands like he had fallen off the *Titanic* and it was his raft, and he talked the whole time, though he was alone. After staring at the guy long enough, Mike thought he could read his lips. *Tambourine,* he was saying. *Tambourine, Mr. Marlowe, please play the Tambourine.* His face shone with sweat, though Butcher's was, if anything, a little cool.

Marlowe was Eddie's name, Mike remembered. Eddie didn't have a tambourine, he didn't look at the guy who stared at him, and as Mike looked at Eddie, the guitar player spat on the floor.

Then the organ player piled in like a Mac truck. He was loud and had a big sound, like he was playing with all ten fingers and both feet simultaneously, but Mike thought he could hear dropped notes, and the guy's timing was off. Adrian was short and square and dressed in something that looked like a sharkskin suit, but much cheaper. He was dwarfed by his Hammond electric organ, with upper and lower manuals. Other electronic gadgets were piled up around the Hammond, effects pedals and a MIDI controller and a drum machine and other stuff that Mike didn't recognize. Mike was strictly a bass man, really, and didn't go in for toys.

Adrian hit the big climax, flatted sevenths blaring like a rock-and-roll thumb in the eye, and then Jim jumped in with the last choruses.

"Keep your head down," Jim sang.
"Sleep between shows, and watch out
For the punches love throws!"

Jim's voice boomed and echoed surprisingly loud in the small bar. It sounded like it had reverb in it, but Mike couldn't figure out where that might be coming from. It wasn't the mic—that was a plain vanilla SM58, standard issue for bar bands the world over. Mike didn't think it could be the PA, either; he'd watched Harry the bartender set the faders before the show started and then shuffle back behind the bar, and no one had touched the PA system since. The mixer was some eight-channel piece of junk from Malaysia, anyway.

Jim was a tall, broad-shouldered Viking, with long black hair and the kind of pale skin that you got if you never went out in the sun. He looked so rugged and handsome in his long white prairie-style shirt and blue jeans, even Mike noticed, and he was not a man who looked at other men. Women probably loved Jim, Mike thought bitterly. He probably had no trouble at all with the ladies.

Mike amped up the last chorus with the rest of the band, picking up the tempo slightly and then sustaining as Jim belted out the last lines—

"Keeps your eyes on the waves, boy,
Thar she blows!
And watch out for the punches love throws!—"

and then Mike dove into one last round of tonic-sub-dominant-tonic to close out the song, hammering on all cylinders with the rest of the band. He hit his last note short and sweet, then stepped back and ignored the hoots and applause of the crowd, gripping his lovingly polished P-Bass with both hands and staring at the bar.

Butcher's was a real dive, a roadhouse made of concrete with the rebar showing in middle of nowhere, and had a crowd to suit it. Neon spangled the plywood over the bar, advertising mostly low-end beer and tequila, though there was a glowing

Bacardi clock in the middle of it all, to add a little class and to warn the drinkers when closing hour drew near. Mostly the place smelled of sour alcohol and cold air breathed way too many times, but there was a distinct note of piss buried in the stink. Mike hoped it was just because the stage was too close to the restroom.

He was a little bummed to be about to shoot himself in a place that reeked, but not bummed enough to make him change his plans. The gun was in his Impala in the parking lot, anyway. He could just shoot himself out there, or get nice and hammered and walk out into the sand somewhere where no one would notice and the coyotes would eat his body.

In the rowdy crowd were truckers in baseball caps and flannel shirts, Indians wearing cowboy hats from the reservation Mike dimly knew was out in the hills somewhere north of the bar, Mexicans, and two or three hard-bitten, sand-blasted people who might have been local ranchers or farmers, or whatever it was people did to make a living out here in Hell-and-Gone, New Mexico. They were clapping with at least half a heart now, and a slab-faced woman with forearms like whole hams sent another beer up to Jim.

Mike sighed.

His vision swam, just a little. He needed a drink. After years of boozing to keep his brother away, he needed the alcohol not only for Chuy, but for himself, too. He hadn't had a drink since that morning. His throat itched and his belly hurt and he was sweating like a pig in a parka, though the bar was only warmed by a couple of battered space heaters in the corners. He badly wanted to open up a bottle of Jack Daniels.

The bouncer caught Mike's gaze and snarled at him.

Or, Mike thought, he could just go out into the parking lot and shoot himself sober.

It was hard to be sure, because of the tangle of neon that hung there anyway, announcing Miller Light and Budweiser and Jack Daniels and Jim Beam, but Mike thought there was something red and flashing, hanging over the bar. He was pretty certain that, whatever it was, he hadn't seen it there before.

Red and flashing and pouring out smoke.

"Is that a fire?" he stepped sideways and muttered out of the corner of his mouth to Adrian, the guy at the organ, just loud enough for the rhythm section to hear over the buzz of the crowd and Eddie's first choppy chords for the next song. His mouth felt like sandpaper as he spoke.

Adrian shrugged and scowled. "I wouldn't know, there's a light in my face. The blind leading the blind, et cetera."

Mike looked at Twitch; the drummer made a pouty face and air-kissed Mike. Mike tried to smile back, but he was pretty sure it came out as a grimace.

Eddie shambled half a step forward, chunking out a basic rock riff that he half-muted with the palm of his right hand.

"Tambourine!" Shiny Shoes bellowed from the front row. "Please!"

"This next song is called 'Falling Rocks,'" Eddie announced gruffly over his chords. Jim stared at his guitarist while he made the announcement and said nothing; Mike wondered why the singer didn't announce the song himself. "It doesn't have a tambourine in it."

"Key of *G*," Adrian reminded Mike as Eddie squeezed out the first gnarled riff.

"I remember," Mike said. "Also, I'm not deaf."

The bar exploded into red light and fire.

"Duck!" Eddie yelled, and then he and Jim threw themselves left and right, clearing the path between Mike and the lights—

and the *thing* that burst out of the red smear in the air, crashing onto the floor in an explosion of flame. The creature landed front legs first—it was built like a lion in size and shape, but smoke and fire, red and blue and black, licked up from its scaly skin—onto a table beside the bar and shattered it instantly into toothpicks. Drinkers flailed backwards, shouting and spilling their glasses.

The thing snapped open enormous jaws and let out a bellow like a police siren and a train wreck mixed together and over-driven into snarling distortion. Mike felt his own jaw drop open.

The beast swung its head and sent two more tables flying across the room. A man in a checked and yoked shirt with pearl buttons shrieked like a little girl as his shirt burst into flame on contact with the creature's snout.

Mike couldn't think, and he couldn't look away. He stared.

The bouncer lurched into the center of the room, pulling his pistol. The man was brave, anyway. Maybe his buzz cut meant he used to be a Marine or something. He fired, *bang! bang! bang!* and the creature took no notice. Its head, like a dog's, but hairless and scaly, wreathed in multi-colored flame, snapped open. Its jaws were too long, Mike noticed, transfixed and unable to look away. They were like the jaws of a crocodile.

They snapped on the bouncer's neck and decapitated him in a single swift *munch.*

The switchblade in Mike's pocket had never felt more useless.

Mike finally found his voice again. *"Mierda!"* he shouted.

"Get down!" Adrian shouted, and then a spray of bullets snapped past Mike. He threw himself sideways and found Eddie grabbing him by the front of his cracked leather jacket, dragging him off the stage to one side. A gout of flame ripped through the air behind him, singeing the back of his neck.

Mike struggled to break free, out of reflex more than anything else. Eddie knocked his hands aside like he was a child, though Mike had six inches and easily a hundred pounds on the guy, and slapped his face. "Get out of here!" the black guitarist shouted, and shoved Mike off the stage, through the swinging door under the tilted sign that read *PISSOIR.*

The last thing Mike saw before the hallway door swung shut again was Adrian, standing at his Hammond and holding something that looked no bigger than a pistol, but had a really long clip and was firing like a machine gun. And for a split second, he thought he could make out Jim, *somersaulting* forward off the front of the stage with a *sword* in his hand. He looked like Errol Flynn in the old black and white movies, if Flynn were six-and-a-half feet tall and had rock-and-roll hair.

"Die, beasty!" Adrian howled, and then Mike was alone in the hall, with a bathroom door, a payphone missing its handset, and the mixed stink of roadhouse piss and his own fearful sweat.

He staggered to lean against the wall, needing the feel of the cold concrete against his forehead and the solidity of the wall under his arm. The concrete was real. He clutched at the knot of charms around his neck—a cross that had meant a lot to his grandfather, a rabbit's foot, an ankh—he knew it was all junk, it had never helped him before, but it made him feel better to touch it. He pulled out the switchblade and flicked it open. The knife was useless—he'd stabbed other people more than once as a kid, but he knew it wouldn't do anything to the monster rampaging in the bar, and he knew that he didn't have the guts to slit his own throat with it, either.

Then he threw up, all over his own shoes. The gas station tuna sandwich tasted on its way up exactly like it had tasted on its way down, Mike thought, his mind still reeling, no better or worse.

He could hear the rattle of gunfire in the bar, and an enormous animal howling, something like a lion's only more throaty, like the creature had a saw blade in his vocal cords or was a chain smoker. He wiped sweat from his eyes and blinked at the hall he was standing in, looking for an exit.

Chuy stood there. Grinning.

"You gonna knife me, *cabrón?*" Chuy asked. He had Grandpa Archuleta's smile, and like Mike, he'd learned to curse from the old man, chewing tobacco out in the weeds behind the trailer in between long hauls in his big rig. What Chuy had that Grandpa Archuleta didn't, which had broken Grandpa's heart when he had dragged Mike down to the city morgue and forced Mike to help him identify the body, was all the wounds.

Chuy's scalp, long black hair still attached, hung open like a flap covering a pocket, exposing the bloody skull beneath. Blood ran down from the scalp and the flesh around it, but quickly became indistinguishable from all the rest of Chuy's blood. He'd been cut everywhere, not stabbed or slashed but *carved* artfully, like he'd been tattooed or even simply *written on* from head to toe by someone who was an artist. Chuy's throat had been slit—that was the last cut, the police had said, the one that had finally put him out of his misery—all the way to the spinal cord. Every cut bled, and Mike would have sworn he could smell the reek of Chuy's ghostly blood.

It was the stink of guilt.

"No," Mike said weakly. He really wanted a drink.

"Is that how you treat family, Mikey?" When he spoke, blood spilled from Chuy's lips, too. "I mean, you went and left mom alone, now you gonna knife me? Is that what you meant, with all that bullshit about being a man?"

Chuy hadn't aged, after all these years. He still looked sixteen years old, under all the blood.

Mike tried to ignore his brother, though both his hands trembled with the adrenalin and he felt like throwing up again. He wiped sweat out of his eyes again and examined the hallway—no exit, unless maybe the john had a window.

"What, you don't want to talk to me? You feeling guilty, *pendejo?* Maybe what you need is a *woman*, huh? Well, hey, brothers gotta help each other, don't they? When I needed a woman, you got me one … I think I still know where to find her!"

Horrified at the thought of what Chuy might produce next, Mike fled from his brother's ghost, heart racing. He slammed back into the chaos of the bar, elbow first and knife at his hip, ready to jump up and into the belly of anyone getting in his way. Except Chuy, of course. Mike had tried attacking his brother's ghost once, years ago, and the only effect had been to make Chuy even angrier.

Butcher's was on fire. Smoke filled the upper half of the room, so Mike coughed and bent over to run. His gut got in the way, and his lack of stamina, but fear propelled him and he scuttled as fast as he could.

He was so afraid, he didn't even try to grab his bass.

He was halfway to the door, the only exit he knew of, when a new eruption of gunfire and a sheet of flame that spun sideways across the room in front of him forced him back. In the confusion, he lost his grip on the knife and dropped it. He stumbled on something, and when he looked down he saw that it was the bouncer's headless body, jeans jacket scorched to a charcoal gray color.

"Huevos," Mike muttered, but the bouncer had a pistol. Mike picked up the gun. Five seconds of fumbling through the dead guy's pockets were rewarded with a second clip.

The gun was nothing fancy, a simple, straightforward semi-auto, the kind of pistol that cops and guys in the army carried. Mike felt reassured by the weight of the pistol in his hand, though he was no soldier. He gnashed his teeth to bite back a flood of bad memories: gangbanging and robberies and worse.

Poor Chuy.

The lizard-lion barreled across the room in front of Mike. As it reared back, its skull smashed out pieces of the ceiling, bringing a rain of flaming timbers and smoking sheets of corrugated tin. Plunging forward, claws the size of microwave ovens cracked and gouged the concrete into hot gravel. It paid Mike absolutely no attention, but the lash of its long tail—a tail that, Mike now saw, was forked at its tip—nearly knocked him over. Crocodile jaws snapped and fire jetted from its nostrils and it chomped at the singer, Jim. Jim retreated slowly, his white face whiter with fury.

And he fought it back with a sword. With his free hand Jim snatched a bottle off a table as he passed and hurled it at the monster. He retreated over a chair, rising to the top of the chair back to stab down at the creature's face and then tipping heel-first gracefully to the ground, to then hook the toe of his boot into the ladder of the chair's back and snap-kick it into the lizard-like face.

Mike would have laughed, if he hadn't felt sick, exhausted, hurt, suffocated, and afraid of burning to death. The big singer wielded a long, slender sword, like a French or Italian fencing weapon, not that Mike was really in a position to know. He wasn't a sword guy. But it wasn't the big two-handed sword, or better still, axe, that Mike would have guessed based on the guy's build and complexion, and his fighting wasn't hack and slash.

It was dancing. The lizard-lion lunged and snapped, aiming for one of Jim's legs and then the other, and the tall guy stepped neatly back and aside each time, tipping away the beast's head with the hilt of his sword, which was wrapped in a fancy steel basket, or poking it back with the point.

He almost looked like he was having fun.

Except that whenever he stabbed the creature, which happened over and over again, the point skidded off the beast's skin without leaving a mark.

The beast was between Mike and the door, blocking his escape. He raised the pistol, thumbed off the safety and squeezed the trigger. No silly turning the gun sideways to show off now, he just aimed for the big monster's chest and emptied the clip, *bang! bang! bang! bang! bang!*

Actual *sparks* flashed off the creature's hide where he'd hit it.

The creature drew back from Jim and turned to stare balefully at Mike. Its eyes were black and glassy but seemed to dance with flame, and the smoke and fire wisping off its body made it look like the hottest burner in a barbecue. Only moving, and angry.

Jim lunged to the attack once more, stabbing at the flesh around the lizard-lion's black eyes. The thing roared again and turned back to Jim, lunging in a threshing hurricane of long, smoking teeth.

"You can't stay here!" Mike heard yelling in his ear and a hand clutched his elbow. He recognized the voice as belonging to Twitch, the drummer, so he turned to look at the guy—

but there was no Twitch. Instead, a smallish white horse or a pony—Mike didn't really know the difference—stood beside him. The creature had Twitch's coloring, though, and his long silver hair. Mike grabbed the charms around his neck and wondered....

But no, that was crazy. Twitch wasn't a horse. Then the animal tapped one of its front hooves on the concrete floor and held its head low, keeping its mane out of the flames that engulfed the bar's ceiling, and then it lowered its front shoulders, almost like it was bowing to Mike before a dance.

Or inviting him to climb on.

Mike hesitated a moment, and then laughed himself out of it. "Why not?" he asked, coughing from the smoke. Weirder things had happened to him. "Jeez," he dragged himself onto the horse's back, a clumsy and awkward assault for which the animal held perfectly still, "weirder things have happened to me *tonight*."

Besides, after the grisly spectacle of Chuy's ghost and the terrifying force of nature that was the lizard-lion, the white horse looked more ridiculous than anything else, and positively benign.

Mike still wanted a drink.

The white horse plunged forward into the curtain of fire, just before a chunk of the roof collapsed in fiery ruination, shattering into sparks and charcoal on the floor. Mike wrapped his arms around the animal's neck to keep from being thrown off on its second jump, through another sheet of flame, and then he could see the door. It gaped ahead of him like a black spot in a wall of orange and red, and the horse raced for it.

Someone stepped into the door. The horse reared up, like it might attack the person, but then it dropped back onto all fours and galloped past. Mike saw that the person who'd almost gotten himself trampled was Adrian, his suit all singed and tarnished from the smoke.

The horse broke into the cold night air and Mike sucked oxygen into his lungs, coughing as the good air fought with the smoke for possession of the territory. Just as he finally felt he could breathe again, the horse bucked and he fell off, crashing to the gravel strip that served the roadhouse as a parking lot.

Whoosh! All the air immediately left his lungs again and he gasped.

Mike stared up at the sky, seeing the glittering brilliance of the desert at night and a yellowish moon squinting suspiciously over a dark sandstone butte. He heard screaming, the squealing of tires and the sputter of aged car engines as the bar's patrons fled in terror. By the time he could breathe and rolled to his feet again, the horse was gone.

Adrian stood in the doorway of the flaming roadhouse. His guns were put away and he had both his arms raised, like he was saying some kind of prayer. Eddie burst out of the flames first, racing full-tilt past Adrian and toward Mike. Mike almost turned to run, but realized he was standing next to the only car in the parking lot besides Mike's own dented Impala, a big old Dodge van with a bumper sticker reading *I BREAK FOR LAMIAE*, and instead he stepped out of the way.

Eddie jerked the van door open and started rummaging inside for something.

The beast bellowed from inside the inferno. It isn't over, Mike realized, and fumbled to switch the full clip into the pistol.

Twitch rushed out of the smoke and fire next, and Jim ran with him, half-leaning on the shoulder of the much smaller man. That's where the drummer was, Mike thought, and dismissed his silly thoughts of people changing into horses with an ironic snort. Jim still held onto his sword, and as they cleared the door, Jim peeled away, staggering and almost falling, but keeping his feet and bringing his blade up into an *en garde* position, like a Viking Zorro.

ROAR!

Mike raised the pistol.

More of the roof collapsed, sending sparks and flames higher into the silvery darkness of the night.

"Come on!" Eddie shouted, inside the van. "Where are you?"

In the fire, Mike saw movement, and the creature crawled forward. It moved slower now; maybe Jim had wounded it. Maybe *he* had wounded it, he thought, and felt a little pride at the idea.

"Now!" Twitch yelled, but he and Jim didn't move out of the way and Mike didn't have a clear shot at the thing advancing out of the flames.

Adrian shouted something that Mike couldn't understand and waved his hands in front of his face—

and collapsed to the gravel.

"Chingado."

CHAPTER TWO

You're Eddie Marlowe, aren't you?"

"Get away from me, man!" Eddie yelled.

Mike heard the words in one ear and tried to ignore them, focusing on the blazing pyre that had once been Butcher's roadhouse.

Jim jumped into the door of the inferno and slashed at the lizard with his sword, driving it back again into the fire. Twitch slapped at Adrian's face with the back of his hand and tapped him on the forehead with his club-like drumstick, and they were all in the way of Mike's shot. For a split second, Mike thought about just shooting himself then and there. But he was too rattled from seeing Chuy and from the other strange events of the evening, and not nearly drunk enough, so instead he turned to see what was happening at the van.

It was Shiny Shoes. The shoes weren't so shiny any more, and he was scorched from head to foot. He held his hat in his hand, burnt black, and he looked like he was begging. Firelight danced in the high sheen of sweat all over his head, making him look feverish and fanatical.

"Please, Mr. Marlowe, I know it's you. I've seen videos, and I know what you can do. I'm here, look, I'm here even with all *this*—" he gestured at the burning building. "Doesn't that tell you something?"

"It tells me you're crazy," Eddie muttered. "Get the hell outta here."

Mike had to agree with Eddie. With all the insane, impossible things happening tonight, the absolute craziest might just be this guy who stuck around through it all so he could talk to Eddie. What on earth could the guy be thinking? Irritating *maricón*.

"I want to sign you, Mr. Marlowe, I'm an agent. I can book you with the Rolling Stones tomorrow."

Even crazier. Mike shook his head.

The lizard howled again. The sound made Mike's hair stand on end, and his stomach churned like he might throw up again. He didn't know what Eddie was doing, he couldn't help Adrian, he couldn't get at the beast without running past Jim into the fire. He was helpless.

Eddie dove with both hands into a dog-eared cardboard box, rummaging. "I didn't send video to any agents," he complained.

"You didn't have to," Shiny Shoes said, sweating. "Some kid filmed you in Montreal last summer, when you did *Flight of the Bumblebee* on tambourine. They put the clip of you on YouTube."

"Damn Internet!" Eddie gruffed.

"Look, I—"

ROAR!

Whatever it was Eddie Marlowe was trying to do, Shiny Shoes the agent was getting in his way. Mike stepped forward and slapped the pistol against Shiny Shoes's forehead. "The man said *no!*" he yelled.

Shiny Shoes dropped his hat and stared up at the barrel of the pistol, which made him look cross-eyed. "Are ... are you signed with someone else?" he ventured.

"Yes!" Eddie shouted. Only his feet stuck out of the Dodge door now. "Go away!"

"Wh-who?"

Mike pointed his pistol at the sky and fired off a round. "He's signed with *me!*" he shouted, and then poked Shiny Shoes in the cheek with the smoking muzzle.

"Ouch," Shiny Shoes whined, and started to back away.

ROAR!

Mike risked a look over his shoulder. Twitch was dragging Adrian to his feet, but the organist lay as limp as a stringless marionette.

"Got it!" Eddie scooted out of the van, holding up a bandolier—

hung like a cluster of grapes with hand grenades.

Shiny Shoes turned to run. "You haven't heard the last of me!" he called. "I'm not giving up on you, Mr. Marlowe! I'll be back!"

Mike watched the would-be manager run, and movement caught his eye. In the sky, over Shiny Shoes's head. Something shimmering and metallic, but moving through the air. It was like someone was out flying remote control toy airplanes, Mike thought, in the middle of the night on a deserted New Mexico highway.

"Fire in the hole!" he heard Eddie shout behind him as Shiny Shoes disappeared, and then he remembered.

"My bass!" Mike shouted, and wheeled around. Eddie lobbed a grenade neatly over Adrian and Twitch, bouncing it off the ground beside Jim's feet and landing it neatly in front of the jaw-snapping lizard-lion.

Jim spun about and sprinted.

KABOOM!

The beast disappeared back into the flames roaring and spitting, and pieces of concrete launched into the air like mortars—

"My bass!" Mike shouted again, impotently—

crash!—

and a chunk of cheap masonry smashed down in the center of the Impala's roof, crashing through the front seats, driving a hole through the floor of the car and kicking out a cloud of dust and sand as it plowed to rest in the ground underneath.

"My car," he groaned.

"We got bigger troubles than that," Eddie said, jerking open the shotgun door of the van as he threw the bandolier over one shoulder. He pointed into the darkness. "Zvuvim. Keep an eye out for the Baal." From a pocket in the door, he pulled out, of all things, a shotgun. Twelve-gauge, sawed-off. Mike swallowed back the urge to throw up again; a lot of working bands carried some protection, but he'd never seen anyone like these guys.

"Keep my eye on the ball?" he snorted. "What ball?"

Eddie chuckled. "All of them."

Jim raced in the direction Eddie pointed, sword up. Beyond and above him, the things that Mike had thought might be remote control airplanes were coming in. But they weren't airplanes.

They were flies.

Flies the size of Dobermans, with clacking, scythe-like front legs and jaws. They were black and dusty-looking, except for huge eyes that glittered like clusters of Christmas tree ornaments, and enormous jagged mandibles that gleamed like steel and clacked together as they flew.

"*Cagado,*" Mike observed.

"Zvuvim," Eddie said, as if that made any kind of sense at all. "They can be killed."

"They can?" Mike asked weakly. "By what? Giant flypaper?"

"Also, they're kind of stupid until the Baal actually gets on the scene. Twitch!" Eddie shouted. "Get Adrian up now, we need daylight, pronto, or we're dead meat!"

"I'm on it!" Twitch called back.

"Dead meat?" Mike gulped. "I thought you said they could be killed."

"They can," Eddie said, "but there's an awful lot of them." He pumped the shotgun, raised it and fired, blasting one of the giant flies out of the air before it could jump on Jim's back. He stepped forward, pumping the weapon again.

Jim slashed with his sword, backing in a constant quick circle as flies swarmed him like a herd of flying black murderous sheep. He looked like he was trying to scratch them with his blade, rather than impale them, and that made sense to Mike—if the big guy got his weapon stuck inside one fly, the others would pile onto him. A fly zoomed in too close, biting for Jim's knee, and the big guy flipped forward, cartwheeling right over the creature as it missed.

"Twitch!" Eddie called, and aimed at one of the Zvuvim. *Boom!*

The shotgun blast shredded the giant fly like a piñata, throwing black flesh and steel shards in all directions.

Mike looked over at Twitch, and then shook his head to clear it before looking again. He would have sworn that the drummer was a man, but from this angle, Twitch looked more feminine than he … she … did before. And he clearly had breasts.

She.

"Come on, Adrian," she said, and she leaned over the boxy organist and her hair fell around them both like a veil. "There's no one here but you and me, you handsome devil, and I need you to cast a little spell."

Mike shook his head. He'd lived with some pretty odd things in his life, sure. He'd been a gangbanger and a thief as a kid, he'd seen death and he'd caused it, and he'd lived all his adult life with a ghost who tormented him and drove him to constant drinking. That, he knew, was more strangeness and darkness than most people ever encountered in their entire lives, and it was enough strangeness and darkness to push him to the edge of suicide. But the step from his brother's ghost to the events of this evening—the swords and guns, the grenades, the gender-ambiguous drummer, the giant fire lizard, the silver horse, the flies as big as wolves—was a giant leap, like the NASA guys might have said.

But the flies were headed his direction, and suddenly Mike found that he didn't want to die, not really. Siding with the band seemed like his only shot. Mike raised the pistol and started firing.

"Come on, lad," he heard from Twitch.

KABOOM!

Another grenade went off, its concussion waves staggering Jim but throwing a carpet of flies off his body.

Mike heard a chittering and a buzzing sound behind him, and he spun, still firing. He should have counted his bullets, he thought as he plugged a fly right between its thousand-faceted eyes just as it was about to plunge steel mandibles into Twitch's back. Oh, well.

Adrian sat up. "Twitch?" he asked. He seemed lucid, but the way he looked only at Twitch despite the fury and chaos all around him gave Mike the impression that the organ player was stoned.

Bang! Mike blew away another ... Zvuvim?

ROAR!

A loud crash on the far side of Butcher's warned Mike that the big ugly thing inside had probably smashed down the back wall and freed itself. Any moment, it would be in the parking lot and after blood.

KABOOM!

Another grenade exploded, followed by a series of shotgun blasts.

"Ah, Adrian, you big handsome lunk. I've got you alone at last, and isn't it sweet and quiet here in the meadow?"

Mike would have scratched his head in puzzlement, only he was too busy shooting giant flies. He blew away a second, and then a third, and then—

click.

"Fundillo!"

He jammed the empty gun into his pocket, resisting the urge to throw it away. The open side door of the Dodge van caught his eye, and he lurched over to look inside.

"I do like a picnic," Adrian said. He didn't sound dazed or crazy, but his words were totally nuts. Or stoned. "Where's everybody else?"

The inside of the van was a mess, clothes and crumpled food cartons and maps and coffee cups, and in the back he saw the head of a bass guitar poking up behind the seat. And there were weapons.

Lots of weapons.

Mike grabbed the nearest thing, which was a long-barreled silver revolver, like you'd see in a Clint Eastwood film, Mike thought. He spun the cylinder once to be sure it was loaded, then turned—

and a fly crashed into his chest.

He fell backward, slamming into the side of the van and tumbling to the ground. He couldn't aim, but he fired—

Bang! Bang!

The giant fly stank like sulfur and its flesh was dry and gnarled. Cold steel cut into Mike's shoulder as it bit him.

"Aaagh!" he screamed, and tried to bring the pistol to bear on the thing. The gun's barrel was too long, and he couldn't get it properly aimed at the fly, but he managed to jam one elbow up under the bug's mandibles and hurl it away a couple of feet.

It swarmed back at him and he kicked it with both feet, like a mule, knocking it further away.

It rushed a third time and Mike rolled under the van.

"You'll see everyone else," he heard Twitch tell Adrian. "They're all here. Only it's dark, isn't it? Why don't you cast a little spell, nothing hard, just a little light for us to see by, so we can continue our picnic?"

The fly hit the gravel where Mike had been. It bounced off and for a moment he hoped it would go away, but almost immediately it landed … stayed down … turned … and looked at him. He gulped, trying to scuttle backward on his belly without dropping the pistol.

"I can summon daylight," Adrian said. "I'm good at that," he frowned, "so long as nothing interferes."

The giant fly skittered forward. Beyond the fly, behind Twitch, Mike could see something approaching. It looked like it had feet, might even be a man, but if it was a man then he was covered in swarming flies, like bees around a hive.

"And what could possibly interfere?" Twitch asked.

The fly sprang for Mike's head—

bang!

He shredded it, spattering the underside of the van with its withered, husk-like bits. An explosion of bitter black dust, like gunpowder, made Mike's eyes sting and water. He coughed and slapped at his face, trying to clear his eyes, but he kept moving.

Mike rolled out from under the van. He had a bullet or two left, he was sure, and he raised the revolver, blinking away tears as he stumbled toward the fly-covered man.

Only it wasn't a man. It was man-shaped, but at least eight feet tall. It stank of rotten meat, and when the curtain of flies parted Mike could see that its flesh was the dusty black of a beetle carapace, mottled with gray. Its head was three times too large for its body, with fly-like eyes and tusks like an elephant.

It stepped toward Twitch and Adrian. Mike didn't hesitate.

Bang! Bang! Click.

With each shot, the cloud of flies shifted and the monstrosity stepped back slightly, but it didn't fall, and it didn't bleed.

And then it turned to look at Mike.

"Mierda."

"Per Isidem lux!" Adrian called. He sounded cheerful, like he really was at a picnic, and he waved his hands, in one of which he held a bit of glass.

The parking lot was suddenly full of light. It didn't come from anywhere, it just *was*. And it was the warm and yellow light of day, which was really damn weird, since the sky above still glittered with diamond-like stars in a field of midnight black, but Mike's shadow underneath him looked like the shadow he'd cast at high noon. The high sandstone butte above Butcher's that had been a dark shadow before was now a wall of brilliant red.

Raaaaraaaraarrrghhhhh! shrieked the fly-covered giant.

"Isn't that nice?" Twitch said to Adrian, and pulled his head to her shoulder.

The fly-giant staggered back, swiping at the flesh of its own arms and chest with big, razor-sharp talons. Mike rubbed his eyes to make sure he wasn't seeing things—the swarm of little flies on the big guy's body looked like they were *melting off*. He—it—whatever, lurched away, trying to find the darkness again.

Mike stumbled around the van to the open door and looked for something else to shoot with, or more bullets for the semi-automatic or the revolver. He was interrupted by Jim and Eddie running up behind him.

"I'm almost done here," Twitch said, and she sounded drained and weak.

"Load in," Eddie said. The guitarist grabbed Adrian by one shoulder and yanked him to his feet. Mike noticed that Eddie seemed to have a drifting eye, or some kind of nervous fidget. One of his eyes, anyway, seemed to slide sideways as he manhandled Adrian, and then the guitar player shuddered.

"Hey!" Adrian objected. "Twitch and I were having a conversation. A *private* and *personal* conversation."

"Idiot." Eddie threw the organist onto the back seat of the van. "Hold on, Twitch," he said.

Mike looked around the gravel lot. Butcher's burned in a yellow bubble of light. Just beyond that bubble, Mike could now see that the darkness fell, and in that darkness swarmed flies. "Jeez," he said.

Jim leaped into the driver's seat of the van, shoving his rapier in beside the seat.

"Good luck," Eddie said, and grabbed Mike's hand to shake it. "I'd give you your share of the night's take, but I don't have it. By now, it's probably burnt to a crisp. I suggest you hide."

"My car," Mike said stupidly. If they left him, he'd be sober and alone and without a loaded gun. He found that he didn't want to die, but he *really* didn't want to die nibbled to pieces by gigantic flies.

Twitch staggered over to the van and threw herself in, flopping onto the middle seat and swaying back and forth.

"Where we're going, it only gets worse," Eddie said. He said it gently, like he was breaking a hard truth to a kid, but it was still a no, and it still meant Eddie was going to leave him alone in the desert. "Keep your head down here, you might just make it."

"I need a ride," Mike said. "I can't be out here alone."

Jim pivoted in the driver's seat and stared at Mike. His eyes, Mike now saw, were the color of ice, so blue they were almost white. He stared at Mike intensely for several long seconds, and Mike felt that that big Viking was learning something intensely private about him. He felt naked.

ROAR!

Jim nodded to Eddie, held up a hand palm-first and fingers splayed apart, then started the van.

"Get in!" Eddie said, his tone one hundred percent changed, and shoved Mike with his shoulder to help make it happen. The man was all skin and bone, but he had a gift for leverage, and Mike found himself sitting in the van and the door sliding shut before he could say anything else.

And beyond the door, blazing with blue and black fire and jetting tendrils of smoke from its cracked, dry skin, the lizard-lion beast turned the corner of the smoldering ruins, saw the van and charged.

Eddie jumped into the shotgun seat and slammed the door. "Hellhound at three o'clock," he said to Jim, and started cranking down the window to bring his shotgun to bear.

"Hellhound?" Mike asked.

Jim punched the Dodge into gear and slammed on the gas. The van lurched left onto the two-lane highway and accelerated toward the edge of the bubble of daylight. The flies swarming in the darkness massed around and in front of the van, *chittering* and *clattering* at the edge of the light and waiting for their prey.

"Gone," Twitch muttered, and she slumped against the window.

"Son of a bitch!" Adrian yelled. He sat bolt upright, staring at the Hellhound charging across the gravel.

"Keep it together!" Eddie shouted, and leaned out the window to fire his shotgun. *Boom!* One fly exploded, and its neighbors scattered, but the hole in the wall of demonic fly-flesh immediately sealed shut again. The fly-shrouded giant lumbered with long steps toward the asphalt. "Can you move the light?"

"Of course I can," Adrian said. "If nothing interferes." He patted his pockets and muttered.

The Hellhound was getting closer. Mike scrabbled around in the junk inside the van for a weapon and came up with a big curved Arabian Nights-style sword.

"Good!" Eddie shouted at him with an encouraging grin. "Open the door, and when it gets close, let the thing have it right in the eye!" He turned back to shooting at flies. He looked totally calm and relaxed, which contrasted sharply with Mike's own feeling that the world had turned completely upside down.

Mike yanked on the door handle and pulled it back until it caught. The ground whipped past underneath him unnervingly fast. He wrapped one fist in his seatbelt, watching the Hellhound bound closer over gravel and then over sagebrush, while ahead the tusked giant moved to intercept the van on the highway—

thump!—

the van hit something, maybe a big rock, at the edge of the road, and careened off its wheels at an angle—

Mike slid halfway out the door, only catching himself by the hand he'd tangled up—

the Dodge sailed briefly through the air, and—

thud! crashed to the asphalt again. Twitch slid down the middle seat toward the open door and Mike moved to save her, jamming his body in the way. The leather queen bumped up against Mike's hip before she could recover herself enough to grab onto the seat. She smiled at Mike.

She kind of smiled like a man, Mike thought.

"Hey!" Adrian yelled, clinging with both arms to the seat in front of him. "You can't do that to a wizard! Stay on the road, Jim!"

Eddie blasted another fly and shrugged. "What do you expect from a guy born in the sixteenth century?" he laughed.

Adrian's eyes bugged out like he was about to yell something back—

and instead, he passed out.

Like a snuffed candle, the daylight disappeared.

The van raced pell-mell into the seething cloud of flies, the Hellhound snapping at its rear tires.

CHAPTER THREE

The Zvuvim hit the front of the Dodge van like a black hailstorm, cracking glass and ripping away the side view mirrors and the antenna. Only the forward motion of the van itself, and big, awkward swipes of Mike's borrowed sword, kept them from swarming in through the open door. Severed antennae and mandibles and a bit of wing fell into the carpet of detritus covering the floor of the band's vehicle.

For a split second, Mike hoped the fly-storm would stop the Hellhound, but he hoped in vain. The Hound roared again, shook itself to clear off the first swarm of Zvuvim, and then the devil-flies learned it was there and got out of its way.

Boom!

Eddie leaned back almost into the driver's seat, blowing a fly to smithereens in his own window. Two more jammed in behind it, steel mandibles clacketing and grabbing for flesh, and Eddie jammed a foot against them, kicking at them over and over again and forcing them out the window while he scrabbled in his pockets for more shells. Mike noticed Eddie's combat boots, worn and steel-plated in the toes, and the bandolier on his shoulder, still holding a single lonely grenade. The flies looked like they might get Eddie, when suddenly a silver blade flashed into the seething wall of black—

not from Eddie, but from Jim.

The singer's driving, rough already, didn't suffer much as he wove a net of sharp steel around Eddie's feet. He punctured fly bodies and sliced off wings, keeping his guitarist from being snatched out the window. Mike thought he kept his eyes on the road, coming to Eddie's rescue without even looking, much less breaking a sweat.

Then Mike had to look away to focus on the Hellhound.

The beast lunged for the van's open door, crocodile jaws gaping wide. This close, it struck Mike as looking like a dinosaur: teeth like daggers, hind legs a little bigger than the forelegs, tail thicker than a lion's would really be, eyes glossy black. Only it looked like a dinosaur on fire in three colors.

He yanked himself back into the van with his left hand and avoided a swooping bite of those deadly jaws. Cardboard and vinyl and fast food papers erupted in a small cloud around the Hellhound's bite, the oily paper bags and napkins bursting into flame on contact.

The unblinking eyes, big as saucers, were in reach, and Mike swung for them. His heavy saber hit the Hellhound in the face, sending up sparks as if he'd chipped the blade against a ridge of flint, but he missed the eyes. The thing had a head like a horse, or a tyrannosaurus, a bony ridge with eyes fixed on either side of it, and Mike's saber clanged into the beast's ridge. His blow left no mark.

Still, the creature didn't like it.

The Hellhound thundered in rage. It fell back a step as it did, and inside its gaping maw Mike saw nothing but row after row of knife-long teeth, like a shark's mouth, and sulfurous tendrils of smoke. Not even a tongue.

Boom!

"Brace yourselves!" Eddie shouted.

Mike looked over his shoulder in time to see the man-shaped giant hurl itself against the front of the van.

Crash!

Tusks slammed against the front window in the middle of an enormous face that was part fly and part boar. The van swerved, but Jim grappled the wheel as fiercely as any professional wrestler and kept it on the road. Yellowed talons groped at the edges of Eddie's window and he kicked at them, drawing an irritated squeal from the fly-pig-giant. Still without even looking, Jim reached past Eddie and scratched at the giant's knuckles with his blade. The grenade bounced more wildly on the bandolier on Eddie's shoulder as the van swerved, and Mike worried it might fall off and explode inside the vehicle.

The Hellhound lunged again, jaws wide—

and Mike stabbed, not for the eyes this time, but for the open mouth—

And he jammed his scimitar down deep into the fumes and the bristling spikes, feeling it strike solid flesh and penetrate. Fire and smoke erupted from the wound, scorching his hand and forcing Mike to let go of the sword.

The Hound bellowed in frustration and slowed, shaking its head and pawing at the saber.

"Good one, Mikey," Twitch said. He … she … whatever, seemed recovered. He had his thick drumsticks out again and was clambering around Mike, swinging with them to try to help Eddie and Jim with the big gray thing that still dragged along with the van, trying to force its way into the window.

Boom!

Eddie's shot struck the creature squarely in its fly-like eye, but it only flinched and bellowed, sounding more irritated than hurt. Jim stabbed between its tusks, and some kind of black liquid—aswarm with little flies—sprayed over Eddie and the shotgun seat, but the giant didn't give in or go away.

Twitch lurched over the back of the seat, half-climbing on Mike to swing and batter the creature further in its face with his club. It bellowed again, and grabbed for Twitch, but Jim stabbed it in the arm. The drummer pulled quickly out of reach and Eddie kicked it again. Flies—small, normal-sized flies—filled the air around Eddie and tinted Mike's hearing with an incessant buzz.

"What is that thing?" Mike asked. The Hellhound had somehow yanked the sword from its mouth and was circling around to attack again, so he scrabbled around in the slow waterfall of rubbish trailing out the van's open door for another weapon, without success.

"It's a Baal!" Twitch shouted.

Boom!

The humanoid thing squealed and chittered.

"Ball?" Mike asked. He didn't get it. "As in, *keep my eye on the ball?*"

"Baal, as in Baal Zavuv," Twitch explained, without explaining anything. He leaned forward to crack the Baal another time in the face, and Mike was sure he felt breasts press against his shoulder. With Twitch's blow, the rotten meat stink of the Baal got worse, like she had ripped the skin of a decaying corpse to uncover the corruption beneath.

"Do you mean Zvuvim?"

"One Zavuv—"

Twitch pounded a fly-demon away from Eddie's hip with her baton—

"Two Zvuvim!"

She crunched another between the eyes, its carcass falling into the rubbish on the floor.

"Oh." Mike kicked the dead fly out of the van. He wished it were bigger, so its corpse might actually slow the Hellhound down.

Twitch smacked the Baal again, and the firm decisiveness of her attack, and the resulting pleasant jiggles, made Mike very conscious of her femininity. "And their master is a Baal Zavuv."

The Baal swiped at Twitch, and Jim stabbed its wrist with his sword, the blade darting in like a cobra to sting and pull back.

Graaaaraaaaaaaagh! the Baal objected to being stabbed, and Eddie kicked it in the face. Still it hung on, and the van lurched back and forth as it barreled down the highway.

"Baal … you mean *Beelzebub?*"

"Now he gets it," Eddie muttered. Only the speed of the van kept the Baal outside, by forcing it to use its hands mostly to hang on. Still, its tusks snapped at Eddie through the cloud of flies, and Eddie kicked for the center of its face and pumped the twelve-gauge again.

"*The* Beelzebub?" Mike felt sick. He grabbed what looked like a gun, but turned out to be a blow dryer. He looked up to see Jim's blade reaching behind Eddie's seatback and skewering a

Zavuv, pinning it to the wall of the van. The singer snapped his wrist and tossed the fly-demon off his blade and out the door.

"You're not listening," Twitch said. "It's *a* Baal Zavuv."

"You mean there are others?"

"Oh, lots." Twitch grinned.

Mike looked back out the open door and saw the Hellhound, racing closer and opening its enormous smoking jaw. Desperately, he grabbed for the only weapon he could think of—

Snatching the last grenade off Eddie's bandolier—

With a faint *snick,* the pin decided to stay behind—

And hurling it into the Hellhound's razor-pit maw.

"Duck!" Twitch yelled, and dropped into the pile of junk.

Mike grabbed for the door handle and slammed the door forward, as the Hellhound yakked and fussed at the thing in its jaws, like a cat with a hairball.

KABOOM!

Somehow, maybe because it was inside the Hellhound's mouth, the explosion was bigger than the others had been. The van rocked with the impact, tilting up onto its driver's side wheels, and every window on the passenger side of the vehicle cracked. Fire washed up against the Dodge like a tide.

The Baal, caught by surprise in the moment of trying to slap at Eddie with one of its fists, lost its grip. The explosion threw it up and over the van as the van tilted, jerked it free and hurled it into the sagebrush and shadow on the other side. The headlights just caught a flash of it, gray-black and swarming with flies, tumbling down the side of the road, and then the van's passenger-side wheels touched down with a heavy *thump* and the van burst out of the cloud of Zvuvim and into clear night air.

Mike bounced against the back of the shotgun seat and then collapsed. He was sweating and cold, his heart pounded like a jackhammer in his chest, but the stink of the Baal was gone and cold clean air rushed into the van and he felt like he could breathe for the first time in hours. He looked back and saw jets of multicolored flame inside a dark knot of tangled, twisting air that marked where the evening's strange attackers were.

Twitch got back into her seat and Eddie swiveled again into a normal sitting position, winding his shoulder like he was stretching for a pitch.

"Jeez," Mike said. "Who *are* you guys?"

"Like I told you this morning," Eddie chuckled. "We're a rock band."

"On the phone this morning you forgot to mention the Hellhound."

Eddie shrugged. "We're a rock band that fights evil."

Fights evil? "What, like knights of the round table?"

In the dim light inside the van, Mike saw Eddie's bad eye drift sideways again, and Eddie hesitated before answering. "Not like knights," he said. "More like rival gangsters. We're out to get Satan."

"Before he gets us." Twitch laughed.

"Carajo."

"We're your family now," Twitch added. "Jim took you in."

"You've got the Hand on you," Eddie explained.

Mike met Jim's eyes in the rearview mirror. They were shockingly pale, even in the darkness. "The hand?" Mike asked.

"The Left Hand," Twitch said. "It's a bad thing that Jim agreed to let you in."

"No it isn't," Eddie snorted, and began thumbing shells into the shotgun. "The bad thing would have been getting left behind and eaten."

"And going to Hell, poor boy," Twitch continued.

"I'm going to Hell?" Of course Mike knew he was going to Hell. How did Twitch know it?

"No," Eddie finished, "Jim taking you in is not a bad thing. Look, it's like … it's like getting admitted to the hospital for cancer surgery. It's bad that you have cancer, and getting operated on is no fun, but getting admitted to the hospital is a *good* thing."

"Unless you get an infection," Twitch pointed out.

Mike looked around at the rumpled and torn interior of the Dodge and laughed. He felt shaky. "I haven't been in too many hospitals, but none of them looked like this."

"No," Twitch agreed, "I have it on good authority that this is a nineteen seventy-something Dodge something-or-other."

"You want to get anywhere in this world," Eddie said, "you need a good car."

"You saying this is a good car?"

"Nope." Eddie guffawed. "This is a nineteen seventy-something Dodge something-or-other, and a total piece of crap."

"You got anything to drink in this piece of crap?" Mike asked. He rummaged through the junk at his feet. "Other than cold coffee?"

"You got something against cold coffee," Eddie said, "and we might not be able to be friends."

A sign flared on the side of the road in the Dodge's headlights. Jim swerved toward the sign as if to read it better and nearly ran it over before correcting course and getting the van back into the center of the asphalt, over the dashed yellow line.

DUDAEL, N.M., the sign read.

There was no population indicated.

Twitch handed Mike a small bottle. He smelled spirits, and took a sip without investigating further. He tasted cheap whisky, suffered the burn in his throat and stomach and instantly felt much better. "What's the Left Hand, then?" he asked. He met Jim's eyes again in the mirror. "What did you see, Jim?"

"Jim won't talk," Twitch said. "Don't take it personal."

"It ain't you," Eddie tried to soften the blow. "It's because of Isaiah six."

Mike took another sip, trying to puzzle out the reference. He thought of Eddie's combat boots and grenades. "Is that a military thing?" he asked. "Like a code? Are you guys special forces?"

"No, it's in the Bible." Eddie arched an eyebrow at him. "You know what the Bible is, don't you?"

"Yeah," Mike agreed, "but go easy, I haven't actually read it, I was raised Catholic and we had a priest to do the reading for us. But I know …" he took a swig and considered, "I know it's got two halves. And Moses and the Israelites are in one half, and Jesus and the saints are in the other."

"This is the Moses half," Eddie said. Mike offered him the bottle, but Eddie shook his head.

"What does Moses say about Jim not talking, then?"

"'In the year that king Uzziah died,'" Eddie said in a voice that sounded a little bit like a chant, "'I saw also the Lord sitting upon a throne, high and lifted up, and his train filled the temple. Above it stood the seraphim: each one had six wings; with twain he covered his face, and with twain he covered his feet, and with twain he did fly. And one cried unto another, and said, holy, holy, holy, is the Lord of hosts: the whole earth is full of his glory.'"

"Heavy." Mike took a sip, glad he didn't have to drive. "I didn't hear Jim mentioned, though."

"No, Isaiah's talking about the angels in Heaven," Eddie agreed.

"Jim's not an angel."

Mike caught Jim's eye in the rearview mirror and the singer winked.

Eddie and Twitch looked at each other. "No," Eddie agreed, "Jim's not an angel. Here's the thing. The angels in Heaven, what do they do?"

"Holy, holy, holy," Mike said cheerfully. A few more sips of whisky, he thought, and he'd forget the Baal Zavuv, forget the Hellhound, and even, for a little while, forget Chuy. Maybe he'd even forget that he'd wanted to kill himself.

"That's right," Eddie agreed, "they *sing*. They sing in the New Testament ... in the *Jesus half*, too. Luke two, 'and suddenly there was with the angel a multitude of the heavenly host praising God, and saying, glory to God in the highest, and on earth peace, good will toward men. And Job says the morning stars sang together, and the sons of God shouted for joy.'"

"Fine," Mike agreed. He didn't care about any of this stuff. "Angels sing."

"So when angels get cast out of Heaven," Eddie continued, as if he was trying to coax Mike to an obvious conclusion, "what do they do?"

Mike scratched his head. "They rap?"

"They don't sing anymore," Twitch explained.

"They can't even *hear* singing," Eddie added. "They can't hear *any* music. Music is Heaven's gift to the angels, and when they rebel, they lose it entirely."

Mike didn't think he'd had enough whisky to make him stupid, but he still couldn't put his finger on the thread. "Jim's not an angel," he repeated.

"Jim won't speak, because he's worried about being heard by the angels. The fallen angels." Eddie nodded encouragingly at Mike, like this all made sense. "But he can sing all he wants."

"But you guys all talk."

"Oh, the Fallen aren't listening for *us,*" Twitch said reassuringly. "Or for *you,* Mikey. You can talk all you want."

This wasn't a hospital, Mike thought. It was an insane asylum. "Don't call me Mikey," he said, a little sullen.

Eddie nodded. "Almost there," he said. "Better get loaded up." He knocked the glove compartment open with his knee and produced a box of forty-five caliber shells, which he passed back to Mike. "Come with us to stick it to Satan. Or stay here and get stuck. Still have the bouncer's pistol?" he asked.

For an answer, Mike produced the pistol and started loading both clips.

"What happened?" Adrian sat upright in the back seat of the van, shaking his head.

"You fell asleep again," Eddie grumped.

"Ah, but first you and I saved the day, big boy," Twitch elaborated, smiling in a beguilingly feminine way. Mike sipped the last of the whisky, dropped the bottle into the rubbish heaped around his own ankles, and tried to think of an inoffensive way to confirm that Twitch was a woman.

"Remind me, next time I need a wizard," Eddie complained to Jim, "to pick one who ain't narcoleptic."

"I'm not narcoleptic," Adrian said, straightening his tie.

"Oh yeah?" Eddie was unconvinced.

"I'm cursed."

"With what?" Eddie asked.

Adrian looked down at the singed knees of his suit. "Narcolepsy," he muttered. "But only in moments of great stress."

"Right," Eddie agreed. "Only when it counts."

"Why are you cursed?" Mike asked. He tried to keep images out of his mind: of Chuy in the basement of the burnt-out school, Chuy getting high on the weed Mike had scored, Chuy and the girl, Chuy cut to ribbons and bleeding to death.

Chuy in Butcher's, taunting him.

"I stole something," Adrian muttered. "I'm not proud of it, but it was the quickest way to get where I needed to go. Faint heart never won, et cetera."

"Or in other words," Eddie summarized, "you're a thief, as well as a narcoleptic."

"As well as a wizard," Adrian said. "Besides, if I was the kind of guy who followed all the rules, I wouldn't really fit in on this team, would I?"

"Touché," Twitch admitted the point. Mike thought Jim's eyes in the rearview mirror looked like they were smiling.

"We're here," Eddie said, and Jim pulled over. The van was still going five or ten miles an hour when he threw it into Park. Mike nearly fell over as the Dodge ground to a squealing, protested halt.

Mike would have been reluctant to get out of the van, but with Twitch and his (her?) batons pushing him from one direction and Adrian shoving from the other, he had no choice. He yanked open the van's side door and went out gun first, looking for the Baal Zavuv, the Zvuvim, or the Hellhound.

He landed a bit wobbly on hard-packed dirt and heard ... crickets. Overhead, a lid of a million brilliant stars fell screaming to the horizon, where it clanged off the staunch silhouetted shoulders of the hills and buttes of New Mexico. Other than the starlight, and the light from the Dodge's headlights, the night was pitch black.

"Where's the town?" he asked. "Is this all there is?"

The headlights glared yellow on a building. It was a simple brick-shaped rectangle, two or three stories in height, with some kind of a dome on top. The light reflected on many colors in the glass of the high windows. Some of the windows, anyway; as Mike looked, he could see that a lot of the glass had been smashed out. The woodwork around the windows' frames looked chewed to splinters, and the double-wide door to the building was gone.

Not open … gone.

"I guess now we know why the Hound showed up before the Baal," Eddie said slowly. "The Baal came here first, ahead of us."

"The question is why the Baal and the Hellhound got here at all," Twitch noted. "I thought we traveled under the famous wards of obfuscation."

"So did I," Eddie agreed.

"You can complain about my work," Adrian said bitterly, dropping out of the van onto both feet, "when you can do better. He who is without sin, and so forth." He held a green metal three-gallon gas can in one hand, and it sloshed when he moved.

"Are we too late?" Eddie asked Jim, who stalked around the front of the van with his naked sword in his hand.

Jim shrugged and went into the building. Eddie followed him, and Twitch.

BETH RAZ NIHYEH, read a bronze plaque beside the front door, over a single row of characters that Mike guessed were Hebrew; he'd seen them before, anyway, on Bar Mitzvah programs.

"What kind of place is this?" he asked.

"A synagogue," Adrian said.

Mike pointed at the gas can. "You always carry gasoline into synagogues?"

"This is Dudael," Adrian told him, as if that were an answer. He set the can down, spat into the palms of his own hands to slick back his hair, and then picked up the can again. "Where God ordered the archangel Raphael to imprison Azazel and all the other rebel angels."

"Azazel?"

"You know him better as Satan. Lucifer, if you want to be formal about it."

"What?" Mike almost dropped his pistol. "What are we doing here?"

"Jim's looking for something," Adrian said. "Something in the nature of a family heirloom, you could say." He shrugged.

"I suppose you can go back, if you want." Then he disappeared into the building, too.

Mike didn't wait; he jogged in close on Adrian's heels, gun gripped firmly in one hand and the fingers of the other wrapped in the tangle of trinkets on his chest.

The last thing he wanted right now was to be alone in the darkness with Chuy.

CHAPTER FOUR

Wait!" Mike called, stumbling through the door. "What's the Left Hand?"

He found himself in a little antechamber, like a cloakroom or a small lobby, and Adrian had already passed through and gone ahead. Mike stopped to look around and let his eyes adjust—light came in from other chambers, but this entry hall was unlit. Mike had been in more than one synagogue, and here he expected to see, once his eyes grew used to the dimmer light, some kind of social space. Like a board, with community notices, maybe, or items relating to the congregation's history, or ads for used cars.

Instead, the room was stark and bare. Off to his right, the chewed-to-bits remnants of a curtain hung over a dimly lit stairway climbing up. Ahead of him was another doorway containing double doors, one of which hung askew on a single hinge while the other lay flat on the floor. Both doors were heavy hardwood affairs, carved with spiral patterns of square Hebrew letters, the bottom of each had been painted gold. To either side of the doorway stood a single stone pillar, smooth and plain. The pillars ended before the ceiling and had nothing on top of them. In the middle of the lobby sat a square block of stone, waist high, that looked like nothing so much as an altar.

"It'd be nice tonight," Mike grumbled out loud to himself,

"if just *one thing* turned out to be *normal.*"

He kicked himself forward through the door and found himself several paces behind Adrian. The narcoleptic wizard stood beside the can on the floor, shaking a cramp out of his fingers.

"What's the Left Hand, though?" Mike asked the organ player.

"Ask Eddie that stuff," Adrian said, picking up the can again and huffing slightly from the effort. "I'm the guy you ask when you need to turn invisible or curse someone with the plague."

"You saying you don't know?"

"I'm saying it's not my job."

"Right," Mike muttered, and then he looked around inside the synagogue proper and momentarily forgot his question.

Most of the building was a single long, tall room. Rows of pews had once run from the doors up to the front of the room, Mike could tell, but only a few of them were still standing. The rest looked like they had been run through a wood chipper, their stuffing and covering fabric resting on top of the shattered and splintered hardwood like a coverlet of snow over a junkyard. A mezzanine story full of similarly destroyed seating ran around the back half of the room, and around the entire second-story wall, evenly spaced, were tall stained glass windows, many of them smashed out completely. Mike couldn't see well, but he could see because a few incandescent bulbs had survived the general devastation and now shed weak yellow light on the wreckage.

Mike limped up the hardwood floor along what had once been a central aisle among the pews. The walls below the mezzanine and under the windows, he now saw, were hung with long curtains like tapestries. It was hard to see very well in this light, and the tapestries looked faded, but the images he could make out woven into their fabric were weird and old. Angels fought with dragons; serpents threatened a throne sitting on top of a cloud; angels were chained and thrown into a pit.

Thud.

Mike heard something and jumped. He looked around, not

sure what it had been. The entire band was ahead of him, but the noise had come from his left. He looked and saw nothing moving. Rats in the walls, maybe. He shook off an involuntary shiver and continued looking around.

The ceiling overhead was carved and painted, and the cloudy throne was there, too, surrounded by twelve images that Mike at first assumed were the Zodiac. Then he actually managed to make out a few of the faded, unlit signs and saw a ship … another was a deer … a third was a tree branch, and then Mike shook his head. He didn't believe in the Zodiac any more than he believed in the lottery, but he was pretty sure those signs weren't in it. He wrote it off as one more oddity in an already very odd night, and focused back on where he was going.

At the front of the pews and to one side, a platform, like a pulpit with its own stairs, stood astride two steps that climbed to a low dais in front; the pulpit had been gnawed to a misshapen stump. An iron candlestick lay knocked to the ground before the pulpit, its seven arms carved like flowering branches. Beside it were the two shattered halves of a table.

Beyond the pulpit, there was a human body. He was an old man in a dark blue suit, with gray hair and beard, his feet and shoulder jammed against something that forced his knees and head into the air. He was pinned onto the lid of a big wooden chest with what looked like a wooden stake, pushed all the way through his torso and into the wooden container beneath. Death was always ugly, and Mike had seen his share, but he'd never seen it this ugly, or weird. He couldn't see blood anywhere, despite the gaping hole in the man's body. The chest underneath him had two sphinxes carved into its lid, facing left and right away from each other.

The old guy was still moving, though not very much. He muttered something inaudible, just a gasp through twitching lips—

and his skin bubbled. It crawled, and jumped and wiggled like it was loose over the body it covered, and something small, a thousand small somethings, were crawling all over underneath it.

"Jeez." Mike stopped just inside the gnawed-down pulpit

and stared. "Vampire?"

"Worse," Twitch shook her head. "Rabbi."

"Is he alive?" Eddie asked. The five of them stood around the man, several steps back.

Adrian set down the can and whipped a clear glass lens from his suit pocket. He squinted through it at the man in the suit. "No," he said. "But he isn't dead, either."

"Will he talk to us?" Eddie asked. The guitarist held his shotgun at the ready and kept looking around the mezzanine.

"Sure he will," Adrian said. He put away the lens, unscrewed the cap of the gas can and began to back around the man on the chest, pouring a trickle of gasoline on the floor as he went. The petroleum stink snapped Mike out of his reverie.

"How did you lose the last bass player?" he asked. "Speaking of ... you know ... all the crazy stuff I've seen tonight."

Jim walked away from the circle of conversation. He kicked over large boards in the shattered wreckage of the pews and looked around and behind things and generally searched.

"We didn't lose him, big boy," Twitch said. "We know right where he is."

"He died." Eddie's wandering eye snapped spastically in its socket and he closed both his eyes briefly, taking a deep breath.

Mike gulped and tightened his grip on the pistol. "Drug overdose?" he asked hopefully.

Eddie shook his head. "Impaled on his own bass."

"Stand back or get gas on your shoes," Adrian warned. "I need a perfect circle."

"Or what?" Eddie asked. "You might fall asleep?" Jim put a restraining hand on Eddie's shoulder.

"No pressure, Adrian," Twitch said soothingly.

Mike stepped back and watched Adrian finish his circle, then light it with a matchbook he extracted from his pocket. Flames rose from the circle of gas, and when Adrian waved his hand over them, they rose even higher.

"Anyone know the rabbi's name?" Adrian asked.

"Feldman," Eddie supplied the answer.

"No true name? Not even a first name, that's it, just

Feldman?"

Eddie looked at Jim, who was poking around the ruined stump of the pulpit. The singer shrugged and nodded.

"That's it," Eddie said. "No sweat, for a man of your talent."

"Makes you feel better about the tambourine, though, don't it?" Twitch asked Eddie. There was a mischievous glint in the drummer's eye. "The whole incident with the bass, that is. I mean, when was the last time you heard of a tambourine player murdered with his own instrument?"

"A tambourine could be sharpened," Eddie said sourly.

"Murdered?" Mike asked.

"Of course," Eddie snapped. "What kind of idiot would it take to impale *himself* on a bass guitar?"

"If there were such an idiot," Twitch observed, "he'd surely be a member of this band."

"What's the Left Hand?" Mike asked again.

"Don't worry about it," Eddie said. "I'll tell you later."

"It's easy," Twitch said. "At the Judgment, everyone gets sorted. They're either on the Right Hand of God—that's really, really good—or they're on His Left. That's terrible. And people who have the Left Hand on them already in life, why, they're damned. All this, of course, pertaining to humans, and other folk who are judged."

Mike strained to listen to Twitch's voice, trying to fathom his (her?) sex so hard, he almost missed the words Twitch said. "Are you—" he asked, about to guess *a woman*, but then he caught the significance of some of Twitch's words. "Do you mean I'm *damned*?" He knew that he was damned, had known it his entire adult life, but it wasn't anyone else's business and he wondered how Jim could possibly see that. "And do you mean some people *aren't* judged *at all*?" he asked. "What does that mean? And why would Jim want to rescue me just because I'm … because I have the Left Hand on me? What is he, like a priest?"

"Jim has a grudge," Eddie said.

Jim kicked the candlestick, hard; it banged loudly against the floor.

"Against what?" Mike gripped the pistol in his hand, the

sheer solidity of the gun an antidote to all the insanity he was seeing and hearing around him. He could feel the weight of his various charms and holy symbols at his sternum, too, but got very little comfort from that. "Against damned people? Against saved people?"

"Against Hell," Twitch said. "Eddie told you. We're sticking it to His Lowness."

"Shut up," Adrian growled. "I don't jabber at you when you're trying to find the groove, do I? Do unto others, well, you know." The short man straightened his tie, and then waved both hands over the circle of flame, fluttering the fingers of one hand while clenching his other in a fist. *"Per Osiridem te invoco, o Feldman, ad nos veni!"*

The twitching increased. Mike thought he could see individual mites under Rabbi Feldman's skin, like rapidly migrating blisters. He arched his back, pushing off the chest with his heels and shoulder blades, and lifting his body on the spike that pinned him.

"What's wrong with him?" Mike whispered to Eddie, who stood closest to him. "Is that a disease?"

"Shush," Eddie said.

"More like an infestation," Twitch whispered back. She picked up the gas can and held it ready, but ready for what, Mike didn't know.

"Careful," he suggested. "We don't want to burn the place down."

"Not yet," Twitch agreed.

"Veni ad nos!" Adrian repeated. He was making the same arm and finger gestures, but they were getting faster and faster and he looked frustrated. *"Tavo lanu, Rabbi Feldman, bashem hakodesh!"*

Feldman's arms twitched and his legs trembled, like a breakdancer with only one move, and not a very good one. The wooden spike kept him pinned, but his mouth opened and shut fiercely now, so hard Mike could hear his teeth *click*.

Adrian wiped sweat off his forehead with his sleeve. Mike did the same, in sympathy, but the cracked brown leather of his jacket smeared the sweat around rather than wiping any of it off.

"Veni!" the wizard shouted. Veins stood out in his temples and in his wrists, like dancing snakes, and his face was bright red. *"Veni per Yahweh Sabaoth! Per Yahweh Sabaoth Luciferemque te jubeo, veni!"*

He stamped his feet and the circle of flames raced skyward with a huge *BOOM!*—

And then Adrian crumpled to the floor, and the flames snuffed out.

"Huevos," Mike said, though he wasn't sure why. The dying of Adrian's magical fires made the room, if anything, slightly more normal.

"Did you hear that?" Twitch asked. She set down the can and started walking across the room, turning her head this way and that as she went. The horse's tail protruding from the seat of her black leather outfit swished as she walked, and Mike couldn't help watching it for a few seconds, until he remembered that he wasn't one hundred percent sure Twitch was a woman.

Mike jerked his gaze away.

Then he remembered the *thud* he had heard earlier.

"You mean the explosion?" he called to her (he hoped). "I think they heard that in *Dallas.*" She ignored him, peering behind pews and turning over stray boards to look underneath them. "Could be rats!"

Jim returned to the group around the rabbi. He and Eddie stood over the body of the Rabbi Feldman, who continued to writhe spastically. Mike joined them. There was a bad smell about the body that he recognized, though he couldn't immediately place it, and its mouth seemed to be full of something black. Like caviar, he thought. Someone had stuffed the rabbi with moving caviar.

That stank of rotting meat.

"What's with Twitch?" Mike asked. "She thinks she heard something."

"Horses have great hearing," Eddie said dismissively. "You're right, she probably heard a rat."

So she was female, then. Mike shot a guilt-free glance at Twitch's tail again. Then he realized what Eddie had said.

"Wait a minute," he tried to rewind the conversation.

"Horses?"

The guitarist ignored him and talked to Jim in low, urgent tones. "Are you sure the name isn't just a coincidence?" Eddie asked him. "For all I know, *Dudael* is the Hopi word for *Chlamydia.*" He looked around at the shattered synagogue. "Though Heaven knows it looks the part," he said.

The big singer took the rabbi's right hand in his own and turned it palm-up. The old man had a tattoo on his right wrist, bright and black like he'd gotten it recently, and shaped like a candlestick with seven branches. Jim and Eddie exchanged a look.

"We don't have much time," Eddie said. "If that Baal Zavuv found this place before, it's sure as hell on its way here now."

"Let's just leave," Mike suggested.

"Do something useful," Eddie snapped. "Wake up Adrian, maybe."

Mike had just enough booze in him not to take offense. "What kind of thing are you looking for, Jim?" he asked as he crouched over Adrian's unconscious body and slapped the other man in the face. "Maybe I can help."

"Jim's not going to talk to you," Eddie reminded Mike through gritted teeth. "And we're not looking for a *thing,* we're looking for a *place.*"

"Well, did we find it, then?" Mike pressed.

"Over here!" Twitch shouted from halfway across the room. She was poking open the trapdoor of something that looked like an oversized mail slot, built right into the wall. It was about where Mike had heard the noise earlier, he thought.

Jim immediately ran to join her, and Eddie followed at a walk, shotgun at the ready. "What is that, the *genizah?*" he shouted.

"What's a *genizah?*" Mike asked, his head spinning. "And is it more or less dangerous than a Baal Zavuv?"

"It's a cabinet," Eddie said as he broke into a jog, "full of books that are too old to use and too holy to throw away." He called back to Mike over his shoulder, without looking. "Get Adrian up! We need Feldman to show us the way forward!"

Mike went back to the scene of the failed summoning, scratching his head at what to do. Adrian snored gently, so he started by pinching the sorcerer's nose and twisting it sharply clockwise—no effect. He thought of Twitch, and how the drummer had awoken the wizard earlier.

"Come on, big boy," he said awkwardly. "It's just you and me, and everything is hunky-dory." His own words made him feel uncomfortable. He rapped Adrian on the forehead with his knuckle. "Everything is nice and easy, no pressure. Let's have a picnic." Mike cleared his throat and looked around to be sure no one was watching him. The thought that he might see Chuy made him a little nervous, but he guessed that he had enough liquor in him to hold the apparition at bay for the moment. He hoped he did.

The rabbi's twitches were getting more extreme. He flopped around like a live fish on a hot sidewalk, and Mike frowned. What was that black stuff bubbling up between the old man's teeth?

And why had Twitch picked up the gas can earlier? What was it she had said … that the rabbi was *infested*?

Mike stood up and stretched to get a better look at Rabbi Feldman. The substance bubbling inside his mouth was beginning to well up past his lips and spill down onto his throat, and onto the chest on which he lay. It was black as tar, but was formed into discrete globes. Just like caviar, Mike thought, not that he'd eaten much caviar himself, other than what he'd stolen from weddings he'd played at. Only each of the bubbles was quivering, and as they fell and hit the floor, they continued to shake and roll around.

And the rabbi stank of rotting meat.

Just like the Baal Zavuv.

"Guys?" he called it. "This doesn't look very good."

There was no answer. He looked over at Jim, Eddie and Twitch, and saw that they were helping a person—someone really small—a skinny little *kid,* actually, crawl out of a hole they'd smashed in the wall.

He kicked Adrian. "Wake up!" he barked.

Nothing.

How would he light the gas, if he had to? He remembered Adrian's book of matches, pushed the pistol into the back of his belt and got down again to shove his hands into Adrian's pockets until he found it. *GOLDEN DAWN MOTEL*, read the scratched and faded lettering on the little black book, or maybe it was *GOLDEN SANDS*, he couldn't be sure, *AMARILLO*. It smelled like ammonia and the cardboard was fraying, but if the Golden Dawn gave guests matches with their name on it, Mike had stayed in places that were worse.

"Guys?" he called again, and stood up to look at Feldman.

The rabbi's face was covered in a black foam of the jiggling little bubbles. Bubbles were squeezing up around the spike in his chest, too. One of them had bobbled its way down one leg of the rabbi's trousers and quivered beside his ankle, like a tiny little blob of sphinx poop. Mike stooped to look at it.

"Cagado," he muttered.

Inside the bubble, behind a black film that swirled like oil on a puddle, he could clearly see a fly. It was as big as a horsefly and its mandibles glittered like metal.

He kicked Adrian again, really hard this time, and in the stomach.

"Oomph!" Adrian bellowed, and woke up. He curled reflexively, wrapping himself around Mike's foot and tripping him. Mike fell backward—

hit the floor—

and banged the back of his head against the gas can.

"No!" he gasped, scrabbling at the can with both hands—

as it slowly tipped over—

and Mike missed, the can hit the ground and the gas sloshed out. On the hardwood floor it puddled under the sphinx chest and the rabbi's body.

"What are you doing?" Adrian grunted, and clambered to his feet. His eyes widened. "Hey!"

Mike followed Adrian's eyes from where he lay on the floor, and saw that Rabbi Feldman's body was covered in black foam. No, he realized, it wasn't foam anymore. It was a cloud, coalescing and rising off the body.

A cloud of flies.

"Carajo!" Mike yelped. He grabbed the book of matches and fumbled to pull one of them out. The back of his ears felt wet and he wondered if he'd cut his head in the fall. He'd have to check later.

"Per Isidem ..." Adrian intoned, and then staggered back, sucking in oxygen like he'd emerged from long minutes underwater. *"Per Isidem ... "* His eyes rolled back into his head and he struggled not to swoon.

"Help!" Mike shouted, snapped one of the matches into flame—

"Don't!" he heard Eddie yell—

and he tossed the match over his head.

Whoosh!

"Aaagh!" Mike roared in sudden agony and rolled away from the sudden explosion of light and heat behind him. His shoulders and upper back were on fire—literally. He stumbled like a one-legged sprinter past Adrian, who waggled his fingers over his head and tried again to get out a spell.

Water ... he thought. His back and the back of his head burned.

No, a tapestry ... he lurched around, trying to find the nearest wall hanging.

The room exploded into whizzing particles of light, and with a sinking feeling in his heart and stomach, Mike realized that he hadn't stopped the flies, he'd only lit them on fire. Now they raced about the room in all directions, shining with flame and trailing smoke that stank of sulfur, rotting meat and gasoline. They flew zigzag like dandelion spores of light, or like Leonids unconstrained by gravity, racing out in all directions from Rabbi Feldman's funeral pyre.

"Hold still!" Mike wasn't sure who was shouting.

But burning insects hit Mike and stung him, on his legs and his back and his arms, and he couldn't stop running. He smelled a terrible stink and realized it was his own hair and flesh burning, and he kicked and stumbled through the rubble of former pews, trying to get to the wall and a tapestry.

Ahead of him he saw the small silver horse again, and the sight rang a bell in his brain that he was too panicked, and in too much pain, to listen to. A little skinny boy in ill-fitting jeans, white t-shirt and unlaced trainers clung to the back of the animal. He held onto its long silver mane as the horse reared, its hooves trampling a heap of large scrolls that spilled out of a hole in the wall.

Beyond the unexpected horse and its mystery rider, Jim stood with his back to Mike, raising his sword, facing the synagogue door—through which swarmed a funnel cloud of Zvuvim.

CHAPTER FIVE

ot you!" Eddie shouted as he tackled Mike. The guitarist hit him from behind and right on the shoulders and the back of his neck, where he was burning. It hurt and Mike screamed, but Eddie had his jacket in his hands, and as he dragged Mike to the floor he beat at his body, snuffing out flames.

"Aaagh!" Mike screamed again. He pounded his fist on the floor in pain, grateful that at least he wasn't totally sober. He wished he were a hell of a lot more drunk, though.

Then Eddie was up again and shrugging into his jacket. "Incoming!" the guitar player shouted, and brought his twelve-gauge to bear on the swarming cloud of giant flies.

Boom! Boom!

Mike climbed to his feet, feeling fat and fried and chopped to pieces, like a roaster in a chicken rotisserie. The Zvuvim raged in through the front door of the synagogue in a chittering cloud, and the rabbi's burning corpse-flies buzzed forth from the depths of the hall to meet them, a swarm of glittering candle-points that sparkled and winked from within the black mass.

Jim stood in the doorway, heaving the flattened door off the ground with one hand while he slashed at attacking Zvuvim with the sword in his other. He moved like a matador, avoiding flies by throwing every other part of his body out of the way but holding his hand, and the door it pushed up, fixed in place. Eddie charged in his direction, shotgun up and firing, blasting flies out of the air with each squeeze of the trigger. They swarmed so thick now that it was impossible to miss, and the challenge was to hit the one you were aiming at, and not a different Zavuv that got in the way.

Bang!

Mike squeezed the trigger of the pistol, not remembering when he'd pulled it from his belt, and shattered a dive-bombing Zavuv into stringy black fragments.

The silver horse took off at a gallop with the boy on its back, away from the Zvuvim and around the wall of the synagogue.

The kid, Mike thought. It was the kid who had made the noise he'd heard, not rats. Rats would have been less weird, though, than a kid hiding in a ... what had Eddie said? A cabinet full of old books no one could read anymore?

"Get over here!" Eddie yelled.

Boom!

Mike blasted another Zavuv and raced to join Jim and Eddie. Jim had shoved the fallen door back into place and Eddie now held it up with his back, shoving shells into the twelve-gauge and ducking fly attacks. Jim squatted to try to muscle the hanging door up as well, but two Zvuvim clinging to the hardwood slashed and bit at his hands. He bled and grunted and swatted at them with the hilt of his sword, but he made no progress with the door.

Bang!

Mike blew one of the Zvuvim to bits and the other jerked away into the air, *chittering.* Jim got his shoulder under it and slammed the door into place.

"We need wards of sealing here," Eddie said, and Jim nodded.

"It's no good," Mike panted, pointing up at the shattered windows of the second story. The windows were narrow, but only narrow enough that they forced the Zvuvim to crawl through, rather than flying at top speed. "They can get in up there." He fired three more shots, exploding two Zvuvim in the air and a third that crawled rasping along the ceiling beneath the floor of the mezzanine.

"You're forgetting the Baal," Eddie said. "And the Hound. Adrian!" he shouted. "Show me some love!"

Adrian stumbled to the door, batting away burning flies with his left hand. In his right, he held the machine pistol that Mike had first seen back in Butcher's roadhouse. "What's Twitch up to?" the wizard grumbled. "We must all hang together, et cetera."

"Twitch is looking for the way *out*!" Eddie barked. "Your job is to cork up the way *in*!" He took aim at a Zavuv winging in low behind Adrian's back and blew it to kingdom come. The shotgun reports sounded louder under the mezzanine, with an instant slapback echo like a guitar running through a pedal set to one hundred milliseconds of delay.

Mike shook the distracting thought out of his head.

ROAR!

The sound came from outside the synagogue, but it was as loud as the crashing of Niagara Falls.

"Will it help if I tell you we're at a picnic?" Mike offered tentatively.

"Piss off!" Adrian snapped, pushing his pistol into a shoulder holster under his scorched suit jacket and digging two pieces of chalk from his pocket. "And get out of the way."

Mike shrugged. He only wanted to help.

Then he and Eddie peeled aside and stood guard—Jim stepped away from the door but kept one hand up against both panels, pinning them in place as Adrian began to draw pictures on the panels with chalk in two colors, blue and red. Mike took potshots at any Zavuv that got too close to him, but the big black flies seemed to be swarming a little mindlessly. The little flies, at least, burned to extinction one by one and dropped to the floor, leaving the room lit by dim bulbs here and there and the funeral pyre of Rabbi Feldman.

The white horse continued its gallop around the perimeter of the synagogue, plunging under the mezzanine and getting closer to them.

"Don't fall asleep!" Eddie snapped, and threw an elbow into Adrian's ribs.

"Unnh, huh? Hell!" Adrian stumbled and hastily wiped away a long red scrawl down the wood that he had made in the moment of nodding off.

Jim began to hum. Mike couldn't think of the name of the tune, but he would have sworn he knew it from somewhere. It was like one of those songs that you learn as a kid in school, and you never hear again, until you're an old man and you hear some other little kid singing it, and you don't know why you know the tune but you know it.

Adrian nodded and resumed drawing. "Okay, yeah," he muttered. "Wards of sealing. That'll hold them shut for a while."

Mike looked over his shoulder to get a better look at the drawing. It was ornate and in two colors and it covered both doors roughly in a design that looked part spider web, part clock interior, all gears and radiating spokes and here and there a character Mike recognized as being Greek or Hebrew, or didn't recognize at all.

Jim stepped away from the doors, and they stayed standing.

"Now listen to me, my son," Mike heard Twitch say in a gentle, extremely feminine voice, "I need you to show mama your hiding place. The secret one. The secret way out that your father showed you."

Mike was surprised to find Twitch at his elbow again, kneeling and cradling the little boy in his arms. And then he realized that he shouldn't have been surprised, that there was a perfectly logical explanation for Twitch's appearances and disappearances ... only the logic in question was the logic of madness.

The kid didn't look like he could be named *Feldman*—he looked Chicano, like he could have fit in perfectly with Mike and Chuy and all their cousins when they were kids, even wearing the same cheap clothes that were always a little too big because it was cheaper to buy them that way—a skinny little kid under a mop of thick black hair. He looked calm, even blissful in Twitch's arms, like he really thought she was his mama.

"I don't know my father," the boy said.

"Not your dad," Mike said. "Rabbi Feldman."

The kid looked at Mike, his face suddenly contorting into a mask of terror.

Boom!

"Hurry it up," Eddie grumped, pumping the shotgun to chamber another round.

"Hush, baby," Twitch purred, and Mike thought he saw the tail on her rump swish back and forth. The boy calmed right down. Mike wondered whether the kid was scared of him, or he had just broken the spell of Twitch's voice. Obviously, there was something more than just simple soothing words going on, since Mike had seen it work on the wizard and the little boy both. "I meant the rabbi."

The walls of the synagogue shook and the sealed doors bowed slightly inward as something outside hammered into them, hard. Something really, really big and strong. Grains of chalk shook off the door and drifted down toward the ground.

The little kid didn't seem to notice. "Yes, mama," he said, and he started walking back toward the burning corpse of Rabbi Feldman, pulling Twitch by the hand.

"The wards of sealing will hold, right?" Eddie demanded as they all followed.

"They'll keep the door shut," Adrian said. "They can't stop it from getting pounded into smithereens."

Eddie coughed out a bitter laugh. "Remind me to get a competent wizard next time."

"You don't want a *wizard,"* Adrian snorted. *"You* want a *Jedi Knight."*

"Damn straight," Eddie agreed. "Or a Company of United States Marines." He fired several shells at a knot of approaching fly-demons, bursting some and scattering the rest of them in agitated buzzing circles.

"You ..." Mike whispered to Twitch as he followed. "You're the horse."

"Well," she smiled softly and whispered back, "I've never had any complaints from the ladies."

Mike's jaw worked of its own accord for a few long moments, opening and shutting his mouth wordlessly.

"I ..." he finally said.

"Yes, Mikey," she (he?) answered. "It's a big world, full of crazier stuff than you can ever possibly guess. I think your Shakespeare said that."

"He did?" Mike was too astonished to object to being called *Mikey*, and he didn't know what to make of the Shakespeare reference. He had dropped out of school long before they ever got around to William Shakespeare. "I mean, he isn't *my* Shakespeare. He wasn't one of my people."

"Oh, sure he was," Twitch said. "People guess all kinds of mysterious things about that poor young man, but I knew him ... *well* ... and I can assure you that he was very definitely *human.*"

"And you're a horse," Mike repeated himself, feeling stupid.

"No, silly," she said. "Not all of the time."

The little kid stopped, and Twitch and Mike stopped with him. Adrian cleared Zvuvim off to one side of them with long *rat-tat-tat-tat-tat* sweeps of his machine pistol, and Eddie guarded the other flank with his shotgun. "There it is." The boy pointed at the flaming wreck of the chest, with Rabbi Feldman's charred corpse smoldering over wood that had collapsed into glowing coals.

The doors resounded to the sound of another mighty blow, and Mike looked back over his shoulder, through the cloud of swarming demonic flies. Chalk sifted down from Adrian's designs, but the doors held.

"Poor kid," Mike muttered, turning back to look at the kid pointing earnestly at the toasted rabbi. "He's got a death wish."

"What do you mean, darling?" Twitch asked the boy. "Show me."

"Under," the boy told her. His voice was a little dazed, like he might be in shock. "Under the ark."

"Poor dumb kid," Mike groaned, and couldn't help but think of Chuy. Chuy had only been a kid too, really, a criminal many times over but not yet eighteen, when Mike had led him to his death. He hadn't meant to, but he'd done it. "He thinks we're on a boat."

But as soon as the kid spoke, Jim dropped his sword to the floor. The singer grabbed both halves of the broken table beside the pyre, shoving one into Mike's hands and turning to the fire himself.

"Huh?" Mike fumbled.

"Shovel!" Eddie shouted. *Boom!* "Shovel like your life depended on it!"

"It does," Adrian affirmed. *Rat-tat-tat-tat-tat.*

The Hellhound bellowed again, so loud Mike thought he felt his own spine tremble with the sound. The Zvuvim seemed to be getting smarter, and they swarmed in closer, diving and clacking their steel mandibles together greedily. Eddie and Adrian kept them off with a ceaseless chatter of gunfire.

Jim pressed his half-table to the floor like a squeegee and Mike followed him clumsily, feeling fat and slow next to the lean, broad-shouldered giant of a singer. He grunted with effort and proximity to the hot coals, and Jim snorted air through his nostrils, and they fell forward and the weight of their bodies brushed away the stinking inferno—

and Mike saw the outline of a trap door, made of scorched hardwood, with an iron ring bolted into it.

CRASH!

Mike stumbled to his feet and whirled to see the Baal Zavuv, tall and gray-black as it charged forward through the splintered remains of the synagogue door, its cloak of flies buzzing frenetically to keep up. At the demon's heels came the Hellhound, adding blue and black tints to the weird, patchy light inside the building.

"Adrian!" Eddie shouted. "I need daylight!"

"Oh yeah?" Adrian shouted back, blasting a Zavuv away from Eddie's back and slapping a new clip into his gun. "Shall I just set the gun down, then?" *Rat-tat-tat-tat-tat.* "Between the devil and all that jazz!"

Twitch dropped the little boy's hand and jumped to Adrian's side, flailing with a wooden club in each hand and knocking demon-flies away like so many low-hanging apples in an orchard.

Jim grabbed the iron ring and heaved. A groan escaped his lips and Mike saw smoke curl up from around his fingers. The ring, he realized, had to be hot, and the thought of the pain that Jim must be feeling made Mike's back and shoulders and the back of his head ache. He dreaded looking in a mirror.

"Mike!" Eddie yelled, and he realized he was standing in the middle of the action and doing nothing. He drew a bead on the Zvuvim over Adrian's head and started shooting.

In the meantime, Jim had lifted the trapdoor to a vertical position. Stone steps, rough-hewn and worn down really deep in the center of each step, descended into darkness. Jim grabbed the little kid and tossed him down the stairs over a short yelp of objection.

The Hellhound bellowed behind Mike, and with the bellow came a slobbery chittering squeal that he recognized as the Baal's. He spun and fired without aiming, *bang! bang! bang!*

He thought he could smell the Baal's meat-stink from across the synagogue.

"Per Isidem lux!" Adrian shouted, and light exploded from behind Mike and flashed onto the charging Baal Zavuv and Hellhound. It was a palpable wave, like a flashbulb's glare, and when it hit the Baal, the great gray demon lord shrieked in pain and crashed to the ground, flailing and dragging the Hound with it. Zvuvim fell from the sky like volcanic ash, stunned and writhing in surprise.

But the light died in a single flash and Mike knew that the soft *thump* he heard immediately after was the sound of Adrian's body hitting the floor.

"Down the hole!" Eddie shouted. Mike fired off the rest of his clip for good measure, spraying fire all over the tangled knot of demon-flesh without inflicting any damage he could see, then stuck the gun in his belt, grabbed one of Adrian's arms and, with Twitch pulling on the other side, dragged the unconscious wizard through the trapdoor.

The first descent was insane, a sightless stumbling down steps that were irregular in every dimension, and several times Mike stubbed his toes or smacked his head or skinned his knuckles against the walls and ceiling of the passage, or landed bad enough that he thought he had twisted an ankle.

When he was halfway down, the trapdoor above slammed shut with a *clang!* and Mike plunged into womb-blind darkness.

Then he hit a smooth patch, a leveling out of the passage, and he and Twitch and Adrian fell together in a heap.

"Are you alright, son?" he heard Twitch say in the dark. He thought she smelled a little horsey, this close.

Adrian groaned, lying under Mike.

"You can see?" Mike asked.

Then a light snapped on above Mike, and after he blinked away the sting of it he realized it was a flashlight beam. The beam jogged down the stairs to Mike's level as he stood up, and then a second beam snapped on near the first, and Eddie materialized in the white beams of illumination, pressing a crosshatch-gripped Maglite into Mike's hands.

"I don't know how far we have to go," Eddie muttered, "but I know that dawn ain't nowhere near close enough to save us."

"What is that, just a bit of random encouragement?" Mike touched the back of his neck—the skin there felt crisp like cooked pastry dough, and stung fiercely at the contact of his fingers. "Just want to make sure my hopes are set at the right level?"

"Exactly," Eddie agreed. "I've got the back, Jim will carry Adrian and Twitch can lead the boy."

"The boy?" Mike swiveled around with his flashlight and found the kid, staring with big brown eyes at the rock band of freaks and lunatics from out of town that had burned down his synagogue.

"We're not leaving the boy," Eddie explained. "Jim wouldn't have it."

"The boy's got the Left Hand on him?" Mike gulped, wondering what the kid could have done to be in such bad spiritual shape.

But Jim shook his head *no* before he turned and bent over to pick Adrian up and sling the organist over his shoulders. Now that the reek of Rabbi Feldman's pyre and the stench of the Baal Zavuv were gone, Mike could smell the scorched flesh of Jim's hands. Or his own back and neck, he realized.

"Nah," Eddie chewed out the words while stretching his shoulders and neck. "Jim just likes pissing off anything and anyone associated with the Infernal powers."

"You mean Hell?"

"I mean Hell," Eddie agreed. "You take point."

The sound of something thudding against the trapdoor echoed down the stairs and kicked Mike into action, sending him shuffling ahead of Jim and Twitch and into the lead. The ceiling of the passageway was mostly over his head, so he gripped the Maglite in his teeth and thumbed shells into the pistol's clips as he walked. The sound of loud clicks behind him suggested that Eddie might be performing a similar action with his twelve-gauge. Mike felt better when the pistol had a fully loaded clip in it.

He would have felt even better with more alcohol in him. He was starting to feel distressingly sober.

The passage looked like it was a natural cave, to Mike's inexpert eye, but the walls of both sides were honeycombed with large holes of some sort. The puffing of his own breath around the flashlight obscured his vision a bit, as each step he took was into a fog of his own making. His footsteps were loud and crunchy in the darkness. He walked fast, conscious of the demonic things somewhere at his back, and shoved bullets into his second clip as fast as he could manage.

When both clips were loaded and the gun back on his belt he realized he didn't hear the footsteps of the others behind him. He stopped, and then his curiosity finally got the better of him. He took the light in his hand, and poked his head into one of the holes. The depression in the wall was barrel-sized and sank down away from the passage. He shone the light down and looked to see what was inside.

The depression was full of skulls.

A hand from the darkness grabbed his wrist.

"Chingado!" Mike shouted.

"No seas maricón!" Chuy hissed, spattering blood from his lips. "You gonna call your friends, you chickenshit *joto?* You think you can make me do anything I don't wanna do anymore?"

"Jeez," Mike panted, trying not to look at his brother's ghost. Chuy stood in shadow, but Mike thought he could see every cut and every drop of blood on the mutilated specter. "Jeez, Chuy ..."

"You don't get away from me, *hijo de puta, comprendes?* You're blood, and that means you're mine forever, you got it?" Chuy's teeth shone white as the moon behind the sheets and rivulets of blood that fell from them and spilled out his mouth. He looked like a wild beast, feeding. "I'm gonna teach *you* a lesson, this time!"

Mike wanted to pull back but the hand held him. Chuy's face danced in rage.

"Chuy, I ... I never ..."

"You never what, *puto que eres? Me cago en ti!*"

A loud boom reverberated through the tunnel.

Something tumbled into Mike's side, nearly knocking him down. He spun around with his gun and the Maglite, and had his finger on the trigger, about to squeeze, before he realized that the thing in his sights was the mop-headed Chicano kid. He froze, smelling his own sweat and fear.

"Don't walk slow on my account!" Twitch called. "The boy's got his own legs."

Mike turned and stumbled away from the niche of bones, fixing the beam of the flashlight on the ground and not looking at anything else. His heart raced at a thousand miles an hour and the rest of him felt numb.

The passage descended slowly, and as it dropped it opened up, the ceiling rising to twelve or fifteen feet over Mike's head and the walls as far apart. The space didn't make Mike feel any more comfortable. He stared at the pool of light, willing Chuy to leave him alone and hoping not to run into any more giant insects.

And then the passage abruptly ended.

Mike stopped, staring at the wall of yellowish brick and the iron door that barred his way. He pulled at the handle; it turned, but the door didn't open, and Mike saw that there was an antique-style keyhole in the handle's shadow.

"Mab's knuckles," Twitch commented as she and the kid joined him.

"What's the holdup?" Eddie hissed from the back. "This ain't no Sunday picnic, whatever Twitch might be whispering to the narcoleptic!" He caught up with the others. "Damn."

"Can you turn into a—" he almost said *fly*, "worm or something?" Mike asked Twitch.

"Even if I could," she said, "that door's iron."

CRASH!

"What does that mean?" he asked.

Everyone turned to look back. A flicker of colored light told Mike that the Hellhound had finally smashed through the trapdoor and was in the tunnel behind them.

"What it means," Eddie said, "is that we're in trouble."

He pumped his shotgun.

CHAPTER SIX

nyone got anything long and thin?" Mike asked, cold sweat bursting out all over his body. He regretted losing his switchblade in the melee at Butcher's.

"Not at the moment," Twitch snickered.

Mike felt himself blushing. "No, I mean like a bobby pin or a knife." It had been a while since Mike had picked a lock, but in his day he'd picked a lot of them. Jimmied open and hotwired a lot of cars, too, picked a pocket once or twice, and broken a lot of windows and legs. Besides, the keyhole was huge, a keyhole for an old-style warded lock rather than a modern tumbler, which probably meant that the lock was easy.

Eddie slapped a pocketknife into Mike's hand, still shaking from his encounter with the ghost.

"Thanks, Eddie," Mike said. While he snapped the blade open, he heard a ripping sound from the darkness where Eddie stood. He shone his light on the guitarist and saw Eddie strapping his Maglite to the underside of his shotgun with a strip of duct tape.

"You carry a lot of stuff in those pockets," he observed. The sweat on his body was drying and he started to shiver from the cold.

"Man of action has to be prepared," Eddie sniffed.

"Maybe you should MacGyver open the door."

"You MacGyver the door," Eddie chuckled. "I'm gonna MacGyver me a little Baal Zavuv."

"I don't think MacGyver used guns."

Eddie's eye skewed sideways and then he gritted his teeth and blinked. "I don't think MacGyver was ever on Hell's Ten Most Wanted list."

Eddie and Jim turned back to face the oncoming creatures and Mike knelt to look at the lock. "Can you hold the flashlight?" he asked Twitch.

"Son," Twitch said to the little kid, "hold the man's flashlight for him, will you, honey?"

The boy dutifully took the light and shone it on the keyhole, and Twitch went back to slapping Adrian's face.

Mike held the door handle down while he slipped the knife blade into the lock and probed around, feeling for the mechanism. "Where you from, kid?" he asked, and then, in case the boy's English wasn't so good, *"de dónde eres?"*

The kid shrugged.

Boom! The report of Eddie's shotgun was deafening inside the tunnel.

Mike worked faster. Eddie fired again and again. Twitch stroked Adrian's brow and murmur-sang a strange, modal-sounding lullaby. The mode didn't sound familiar, and Mike concentrated on the door, shutting the music out to avoid distraction.

"The rabbi was good to you, was he?"

The kid nodded. "He took me from the sisters," he said, in a high, piping voice. "I helped him around the temple. He taught me to walk in the path of knowledge."

"Oh, yeah?" Mike found a point inside the keyhole that resisted with some spring, but responded to pressure. He thought it might be the mechanism, and he worked on it. If he could get it to turn far enough, even if he couldn't rotate it all the way around, the door ought to open. "So you know the place pretty well? What's your name, so I can stop calling you 'kid'?"

"Rafael," the boy said.

The door in front of Mike face suddenly lit up with orange firelight marred by his own shadow, the source of the light behind him. With the light came a bellow that sounded inside the tunnel like the eruption of a volcano.

The boy trembled and stared up the passage at what must surely be the advancing Hellhound. Mike heard the rasp of metal-on-Hound-hide, and guessed that Jim had entered the fray. He also heard the buzzing of flies, and felt a little sick.

But he didn't see Chuy, and that was good. That was an improvement.

Adrian sat up. "What's going on?" he asked.

"What's always going on?" Twitch countered.

"Right." Adrian dug into his suit jacket as he climbed to his feet and came out with his machine pistol. "The more things change, and you know the rest."

Mike could hear the kid's knees knocking together. "Keep your eyes on me, Rafael," Mike urged him. "Did the rabbi give you that name?"

"The sisters did," Rafael said shyly. "But Rabbi Feldman thought it was a good sign."

"It is a good sign," Mike agreed. He didn't mean anything by it and the name meant nothing to him; he was just making small talk with the kid, to keep both the boy and himself distracted. His fingers were slippery from sweat and he had difficulty seeing through the fog of his own breath.

ROAR! Buzzzzzz!

Rat-tat-tat-tat-tat! Boom!

It sounded like a full-blown battle had broken out behind Mike, Adrian, and Eddie, supporting Jim. Mike resisted the urge to turn around and see how it was going.

"You can call me Rafi."

Click. The door handle popped down several extra inches and the door cracked open.

"What's behind the door, Rafi?"

Rafi shrugged. "This is as far as I've ever been."

Mike lurched to his feet, holding the door. "Well then," he said. "You'd better stand behind me, just in case."

Rafi stepped back, still shining the light on the door. Twitch moved to Mike's side, clubs in her hand. Mike pocketed the knife and palmed his pistol. He nodded to Twitch, then threw the door open.

On the other side waited cold, dark silence. A breeze cooled Mike's already chilled face even further, smelling faintly of some far-away waterhole. Behind him, the battle still raged, squealing and roars and bellows mixed in with the constant coughing of firearms and the gigantic buzzing of flies.

"Rafi," Mike said as gently as he could, "can I have the light?" He took the flashlight and shone it into the darkness ahead. "Stay close behind me," he told the boy.

He moved through the door. Beyond was a broad chamber, its walls of yellowish sandstone brick and its ceiling just over Mike's head. Facing him in the wall were three arched doorways. "Come on!" he hollered to the others, and stationed himself to the side so that he could see both the door he'd come through and the three new passageways. He didn't want anything sneaking up on him from behind.

Twitch pulled Rafi over to one side and perched next to the iron door, clubs raised over her head. "Come on!" she yelled.

Adrian backed through first, wiping sweat from his face and holstering his pistol. "That's me out of bullets then," he said glumly. He rummaged through pockets as he backed away from the door, pulling out bits of string, a stump of a candle, a little bone that might once have been part of a human finger.

Two Zvuvim buzzed in through the door after Adrian, and Twitch leaped to intercept them. She knocked one sideways and into the wall, where it hit with a *thud* and then slid to the ground making a sound that was part buzz and part whimper, but her swing at the second devil-fly missed. She whirled past the creature, overextended and vulnerable. It dove for her neck, buzzing like a power saw—

bang!

Mike splattered black dusty bits and goo all over the wall.

Twitch nodded quick thanks and resumed her position inside the door. Jim backed through next, ducking to get his head in under the doorframe. A Zavuv whizzed clacketing past his guard on the right, and as he stepped into the chamber Jim spun backward with his left hand snapping out in a roundhouse punch. He pummeled the Zavuv with his knuckles, pinning it against the wall.

It bit his forearm, drawing rivulets of bright red blood, but before Mike could get a clean shot, Jim punched the devil-fly in the center of its face with the hilt of his sword. Its eyes burst like Christmas tree ornaments hurled into a brick wall and sprayed thick, sour-smelling fluid on the floor.

Eddie stumbled back into the room, pulling his head down low in the collar of his army jacket like a turtle, and a spout of flame followed him. He tripped and fell flat, hitting the ground hard on his back, and aiming his shotgun at the shadow behind him. The huge black and gray Baal Zavuv rammed its head in through the doorway, its shoulders straining against the top of the frame. Tusks slobbered yellow and thousand-faceted eyes glittered like glass and the Baal bellowed, flies buzzing and swarming around it and erupting from its mouth.

Click.

Eddie's shotgun was out of shells.

Twitch slammed her batons on the Baal's eyes. They looked like glass, but they must be as hard as steel—she bounced off like she'd been kicked back. Jim stabbed at the Baal's neck from the other side; he drew blood, but the Baal didn't pull back.

Chingón. Mike started firing.

Bang! Bang! Bang! Click.

The Baal squealed, straining with its shoulders in the top of the doorframe like it might rip the wall open to get through. Zvuvim crawled through at its feet, buzzing ferociously. Mike thought he could taste his own heart in the back of this throat, even over the horrible rotting stench of the Baal and its horde of flies.

"Per Volcanum ignem mitto!" Adrian shouted.

A hot wind, full of fire and gold-red light, burst from the bit of candle and the glass lens Adrian held in his hand, slamming into the door. The Zvuvim caught in the blaze disappeared instantly into ash and were swept away. The Baal bellowed again and flailed its dagger-taloned hands, trying to bat away the stream of fire, or grapple it, and then the current swept the big demon out of the doorway.

Jim slammed the door shut.

The fire-wind turned off and Adrian staggered. Mike rushed to throw an arm around the shorter man and prop him up. "Good job," he complimented the organist.

"Yeah?" Adrian murmured, yawning and pinching himself. "I thought fight fire, et cetera ..." He yawned again. "Damn this curse!"

"Stay awake!" Twitch snapped at him, and rapped him on the forehead with her baton.

"Ouch!"

In the outer passage, their demonic pursuers still raged. Mike eyed the door nervously, wondering how long it would hold.

Adrian shook himself and stood. "It's not my fault," he said.

"Nothing ever is," Eddie observed, standing and brushing himself off.

"What's the magic?" Mike asked Twitch. "Is it in the stick? Touching him on the head with the stick wakes him up?"

Twitch laughed. "I just like hitting him in the face," she said. "There's no magic. The poor idiot tries to cast spells, especially under pressure, and he gets suddenly very sleepy. You just do what you can to keep him awake."

"But what's the thing with the picnic?" Mike was puzzled. "The whole *we're all alone and it's nice here, Adrian* bit?"

"You're not my mama," Rafi said to Twitch.

"No," she agreed. "I'm too tired to be your mama anymore." She nodded at the iron door as it reverberated with another combined *roar-bellow-buzz*. "But I'm better than any of those things out there, aren't I?"

Rafi nodded.

Eddie limped over to join Jim, who stared at the three passages. Eddie shone his bayonet-flashlight over them by propping the gun in the crook of his arm as he reloaded it. "Does the boy know which door to take?"

"No," Mike and Rafi said together.

"But there's a breeze," Mike said, shuffling over to point at the passageway on the left, out of which he felt the air flowing. "See? This has to lead out."

"I ain't at all sure that where we want to get to is *out.*"
Eddie and Jim looked at the passages further. "You see the glyphs, Jim?"

Jim nodded.

Mike looked to see what they were talking about, and realized that each passage had a symbol scratched over the top of it in the stone, and painted at the bottom with a white coloring, like clay. *Petroglyphs,* he thought they were called, though he'd never been a boy scout and had tried to avoid the deserts of Texas and New Mexico as much as he could. Each passage had a different symbol.

"A serpent," Eddie said. "A star. And what do you think that one might be?"

"A tree," Twitch guessed. It looked like a circle with a line coming down out of it, like a kid's stick-figure drawing of a tree.

"Does it mean anything?" Mike wanted to know.

Adrian shrugged. "They're all in Genesis, aren't they?"

"More Bible?" Mike groaned.

"Everything's *always* Bible in this band, Mikey," Twitch laughed lightly. "More's the pity for those of us who've never read it."

"You *could* call me *Mike*," Mike suggested.

"I could."

"The star is the Host of Heaven," Adrian continued. "The serpent tempted Eve. And the tree is the Tree of Life."

"Knowledge," Eddie corrected him. "The knowledge of good and evil."

"Life," Adrian insisted, and deep inside Mike's fear-chilled and whisky-sodden head, a light bulb went on.

"Knowledge," he said. "We have to follow the path of knowledge."

"You read that in a fortune cookie?" Eddie asked.

Mike jerked a thumb at Rafi. "The boy told me. He's never been down here before, but Rabbi Feldman raised him to walk in the path of knowledge."

The boy nodded. "It's true."

Jim and Eddie locked eyes for a moment. Jim nodded, grabbed Mike's flashlight and started deliberately down the passage on the right, through the arch under the stylized tree. Adrian followed on the singer's heels.

"Let's just hope it *is* a tree," Twitch said impishly, "and not the famous lollipop of creation."

"There aren't any lollipops in Genesis," Eddie grumbled. "Creation or otherwise."

"Really?" Twitch grinned. "That's a shame. I like a good lollipop."

Something heavy slammed against the iron door and it groaned and buckled in response.

"Get moving," Eddie ordered, pumping his shotgun. "I have the rear."

Twitch jogged up the passage, followed by Mike and the boy Rafi, who ran with them now without anyone holding his hand. Mike let himself get distracted by the sight of Twitch's horse's tail bouncing from side to side like a tassel fixed to her leather pants as she ran, until he remembered that whatever she was, she wasn't quite a woman—not *exactly*. For that matter, he wondered now whether the tail really was attached to her pants, or what precisely he would see if she weren't wrapped in leather and spikes.

He cleared his throat and shook his head.

"What's with … the tree?" he huffed and puffed to Eddie, who jogged two paces behind him, and in the light of whose flashlight Mike shuffled along. His heart pounded, and almost immediately he got a stitch in his side. He needed to drop some weight and get into shape.

Couldn't quit drinking, of course.

"It's a marker," Eddie said. "Like a code. Like blood on the doorposts on Passover. Let him who has ears hear."

"A tree?" Mike followed Jim and the others ahead, through a series of quick turns. The passages all looked the same to him, carved sandstone bricks like he was inside one of the pyramids of Egypt, and he had to trust that Jim was on the right track.

"The tree of knowledge of good and evil," Eddie said. "The tree that is the candlestick that is the woman that is the river, et cetera. Not to sound too much like Adrian."

"All that stuff is the same thing?" Mike tried to clarify. "You look for a tree or a river or a light, you're going to see them all over the place."

"Context matters," Eddie said. "And symbols matter. You live long enough, Mike, you realize that there's a whole world underneath the world that we see, and its symbols that tell you how to get around it."

"Who *are* you guys?" Mike asked. "I mean, really?"

Eddie chuckled. "That's a lot of story you're asking about," he said.

A distant bellow echoed through the labyrinth, and Mike wondered if the demons had broken through the iron door. "Can they follow us by smell?"

"The Hound can. The Baal, too, maybe, if our smell is distinctive enough."

"What does that mean?"

"It means through a crowded city, maybe not, but through a labyrinth where almost no one ever goes, yeah, the Baal Zavuv might be able to sniff us out."

Mike squeezed the grip of his pistol once to reassure himself that he still had it. "You're not a rock band."

"Sure we are," Eddie said. "We're a hard working rock band, too. It's how we pay our way, limited engagements, strictly cash. Hell, we're even *good,* in our fashion. New name for the band every gig, of course, so we're harder to track, and that makes it impossible to build up a fan base, as does the fact that we can't record."

Mike rattled down stone steps. "And what's with the tambourine?"

Eddie was quiet for a moment. "Everyone in this band," he finally said, "has a bone to pick with Satan. The tambourine is mine."

Mike almost laughed out loud. "Do you have any idea how stupid that sounds?" he asked. "What does that even mean?"

"It means I'm the best damn tambourine player in the whole damn world," Eddie said gruffly. "Bar none, nobody else is even close."

Mike remembered the agent at Butcher's and the pleading look in his eyes. "I still don't get it."

"What I wanted to be was the world's best guitar player," Eddie said. "I was okay, starting to make a name for myself in some of the bars around Chicago, but I needed to get much better, and much faster than I could on my own. I needed it for my kids, you understand? For my family. It wasn't an ego thing, I didn't want screaming fans or limousines or coke to snort off the backsides of expensive hookers. So I did like all the songs said. I let a hoodoo woman take me down to the crossroads."

Mike stumbled and almost fell. "You mean you sold your soul to the devil?"

"Keep running!" Eddie was quiet again. "Yeah," he continued, "only I screwed up."

Mike said nothing to that. He'd screwed up plenty, himself.

"I told Old Scratch—or his errand boy, anyway, you hardly ever get to meet the poobah himself in person, not on Earth and not in Hell, either—that I wanted to be the world's best rock and roll *musician*. Damn me, if I'd just said *guitar player* it would have been all right. Instead, I sold my soul and just about lost my sanity, and all I got for it is that I'm the world's most amazing genius at rock and roll *tambourine*."

Mike gulped. "Lost your sanity?" he was ahead of Eddie, and after the story he'd just heard, didn't feel really comfortable looking back.

"Out of my left eye," Eddie said, in a voice that sounded like gravel and razor wire, "I see Hell. All the time. And when I sleep, I dream my death."

"Mierda," Mike muttered. He thought of Chuy and shuddered.

"One thing you'll learn quick in this band," Eddie added somberly, "if you ain't learned it already, is that Satan's got game."

Abruptly they caught up to the others. At a final arch, the labyrinth ended, and they found themselves standing on a rough sandstone shelf under an immense stone overhang. Off to their right, Mike could see what looked like a dark-walled canyon, its depths choked with boulders and desert scrub, and a few winking stars peeping down on it from above. The light of the stars and moon was silvery and faint, but it gave Mike more ability to see than he'd had since they'd slammed the trapdoor shut in the synagogue, and he was grateful for it.

In front of them, below the overhang, lay a long strip of packed sand. At the far end of the sandbar, maybe as much as half a mile away, was a brick building. It looked like a cube that narrowed as it rose, like a ziggurat or a pyramid with its tip knocked off.

Mike smelled water.

"That's gotta be it," Eddie guessed, shining his flashlight on the stone structure.

From within the labyrinth, Mike heard the squealing of the Baal Zavuv and the roaring of the Hellhound.

"Let's not stop here," he said, and followed Jim, who was already trotting toward the pyramid.

CHAPTER SEVEN

Jim and Eddie both shone their flashlights around the overhanging stone as they walked, and Mike looked up. The moon- and star-light didn't reach the stone, but what he saw in the splashes of Maglite beam took his breath away.

The entire underside of the cliff was scratched and scarred with petroglyphs. Some formed distinct scenes, and at a walking pace Mike couldn't really figure out what was being portrayed. There were definitely monsters and battles and big beasties inside cages, and some of the creatures carved into the stone were reminiscent of the dragons and angels he'd seen in the tapestries in the synagogue above. He wondered how old the synagogue was, and then he wondered if it really was a synagogue. There was even one picture that looked like an angel riding a dragon underneath a river of water, all done in ancient stick-figure style.

There was writing, too, definitely. Mike was no expert, and he didn't recognize the alphabet, but there was row after row of what could only be words and letters. Some of it, he thought, looked suspiciously like Egyptian hieroglyphs, maybe a little stylized. Zig-zaggy lines, dogs lying down, people with their arms raised over their heads. Someone, a long, long time ago, had spent a lot of time and effort carving this rock.

Below all the writing, greenery clung to the rock, which reflected the beams of the flashlight like it was wet.

Jim stopped at the base of the brick pyramid and the others caught up. The pyramid was bigger than it had looked from the labyrinth exit. A *kiva,* Mike thought they called these things when they were in old Pueblo or the Anasazi ruins. Only kivas were small, like sweat lodges. This was a super-kiva. If Donald Trump built a kiva, it would look like this.

"What is that stuff?" Mike panted, and pointed at the ceiling.

Eddie ran his flashlight across the overhang again. "Writing," he said. "And pictures."

"No kidding." Mike's side ached. "But I mean ... who wrote it?"

"Someone who's dead now." The guitar player ran his light over the structure. A sort of ladder, consisting of a single straight tree trunk with rungs lashed crosswise to it, leaned up against the side of the building, not quite reaching the top. The wood looked as dried out as could be and the lashings were made of dry wiry grass. Mike resolved not to trust the ladder with his weight, no matter what. Under the light's beam he could see that the sides weren't totally sheer anyway, but rose steeply in narrow steps. The super-kiva was climbable.

Jim kept walking, around the base of the pyramid, shining his flashlight at the ground and inspecting it.

"Not necessarily," Twitch contradicted him.

"Looks similar to proto-Eblaite," Adrian squinted. "Or Reformed Egyptian. My guess is it's one of the Primals, though of course you can write with any alphabet."

"You can?" Mike asked.

"Yeah," Eddie agreed. "This is the place."

"What do you mean, one of the Primals?" Mike felt dizzier with each new rush of information, though he was well through the looking glass at this point and no longer questioned anything he was told, not really. With the Hellhound and Baal Zavuv on his tail, skepticism didn't seem likely to contribute to his survival. "What place is this?"

"The Primals are the three original languages spoken on this planet at the moment of the Fall of Adam," Adrian said.

"Really, they're dialects of the same language, but you say potato ... you know."

Mike groped to understand. "What do you mean ... like, Latin?" he asked.

Eddie laughed sourly. "Latin is a late arrival on the scene. Latin is practically *modern*. You can study Latin in *high school.*"

"I mean Angelic," Adrian said, "and Infernal, and Adamic."

"You speak these languages?"

Adrian chuckled. Mike thought his laugh sounded a little condescending, and if he hadn't been so exhausted, he might have bristled a little. "Oh, no. No human being has been able to speak or understand the Primals for thousands of years. Not since the Tower of Babel. We're not *capable* of it, not since we were cursed."

"Nor are *we*," Twitch added. "For entirely different reasons."

"We?" Mike fumbled. "Who's *we*?"

"As for what this place is," Eddie said, "this is the place we came looking for. This is Dudael." He cleared his throat and spoke again in his recitative chanting voice. "And the Lord said to Raphael: bind Azazel hand and foot and throw him into the darkness! And he made a hole in the desert which in Dudael and cast him there; he threw on top of him rugged and sharp rocks. And he covered his face in order that he may not see light; and in order that he may be sent into the fire on the great day of judgment."

"That in the Bible again?" Mike asked. He remembered Adrian had said that Azazel was Satan.

"Nah," Eddie said, "but it should be."

Mike looked up at the overhanging stone, so vast that the super-kiva was almost inside a cave. "That's a rugged rock," he agreed, "and I guess the sun hasn't ever shone inside here." Then he made another connection. "Raphael!"

"A good sign," the boy chirped. He wouldn't meet Mike's eyes and just stood there with his hands in his pockets. Well, no wonder, the poor kid was certainly having the worst day of his life, worse than anything he could ever have imagined.

Like the day Chuy died had been, for Mike.

Then another thought occurred to him and he jumped back from the brick building. "But—Satan! Azazel!"

Eddie chuckled. "Don't worry, His Lowness broke out of this particular hoosegow ages ago."

"So it's safe?"

"Oh, hell no. But you're not going to meet Satan today."

From back inside the labyrinth, Mike heard the roar of the Hellhound and the bellow of the Baal Zavuv. They sounded closer than before.

"Unless you die," Adrian added. "You do, after all, have the Hand on you."

"Thanks," Mike said, and shuddered. "That's cheerful."

"That's our Adrian," Twitch grinned. "A little ray of sunshine. Et cetera."

Mike almost chuckled at Twitch's jab. "Now what?" he asked.

"Now," Eddie told him, "you help us look for a bit of hoof."

"Like a horse's hoof?" Mike looked at Twitch, without meaning to.

"More like a goat's," Eddie said. "A really *big* goat."

Adrian looked up at the overhang, pressing the little glass lens to his eye. "No, there are plenty of wards on the stone here, but they're all broken. We're on a fool's errand. If it was here, just lying in the sand, Satan would have found it long ago."

"Unless there's some other reason Lucifer can't see it." Eddie ambled off, scanning the ground.

"I don't get it," Mike said. He stumbled after Eddie, and the boy Rafael trailed in his wake. Eddie moved slowly around the base of the building, shining his light on the sand and scuffing at it with the toe of his boot. Behind the building, in Eddie's light, Mike now saw that the water trickling down the back of the overhang gathered into a channel, lined with brick, and flowed into a hole in the wall of the kiva. Mike thought hard as he walked, trying to stitch the pieces together in his mind. "It can't be a real goat's hoof. Are you telling me that we're here looking for *a piece of Satan?*"

"In fact, I don't think I did tell you that," Eddie said. "But it's still true. I'm glad you're paying attention. You're much more likely to survive if you do."

"Huevos."

"Pretty much."

Rafi closed in behind Mike and grabbed his free hand. "But … how long has it been here?" Mike asked. "How … how do you know it's here? How … how…?"

Eddie continued moving and examining the ground. The super-kiva, Mike realized as he stood directly under it, was much bigger than he had at first thought. It really was like one of the pyramids, cropped at the top and uprooted into nowhere, New Mexico.

"It's been here since his escape," Eddie said matter-of-factly. "Call it six thousand years, in round numbers. No one realized it because, naturally, His Lowness wanted to keep the vulnerability a secret. Jim found out it was here, back when Jim was in Hell's good graces. Or rather, its bad graces."

"Vulnerability?"

"You heard about voodoo dolls?"

"I watch TV."

Eddie snorted. "Imagine the possibilities."

Mike did, and felt troubled. What could someone achieve who had the power to harm, or maybe kill, Satan? The blackmail opportunities seemed vast. And what if someone with the hoof could do more than that? What if he could actually *control* the Prince of Darkness? Mike gulped. "How can it still be here after all that time? And how can we possibly find a bit of hoof?"

Jim whistled, fingers in his mouth, and Eddie looked up at him. Jim waved an arm at the building and started marching toward it. Eddie turned to look at the brick too, pulling at it with his fingers to test its stability.

Mike heard another Hellhound roar. Eddie seemed not to have noticed.

"It can still be here," Eddie explained, "if for thousands of years, a long line of canny old Hebrew priests has been carefully watching over it, keeping it hidden with wards of obfuscation and other tricks."

"Hebrews in New Mexico?" Mike scoffed. "Thousands of years ago?"

"Those guys get around," Eddie shook his head. "You'd be surprised. And I *don't* expect you and me to find it." He twisted off his flashlight, let the shotgun hang down from his shoulder and started to climb up the side of the building.

"Then why are we wasting our time?"

"I expect *Jim* to find it," Eddie continued. "He's got something of a connection with it, after all. And if it isn't him, it'll be Adrian. Using voodoo doll principles, if he can manage to do it without taking a surprise nap."

Mike gave the boy Rafi a boost, shoving him up the side of the pyramid. He scrambled like a monkey, and Mike followed like a bull, plodding on all fours up the side of the brick. To his surprise, it bore his weight without crumbling or shifting. The solidity of the brick made him wonder a bit about the story Eddie was telling him; he didn't think the super-kiva could possibly be six thousand years old.

Eddie and Rafi were both between him and the curtain of starlight over the canyon below, so they were silhouettes to him, scaling the side of the pyramid much surer and faster than Mike could.

"Why wouldn't the Hebrew priests give the hoof back?" Mike asked, puffing.

"To Satan?"

"I mean to … to Heaven." Mike scratched his head. "I guess that's not really giving it *back*, is it?"

Eddie shrugged. "Maybe they did. Or maybe Heaven wouldn't want it back, like trying to give the White House a chunk of radioactive waste, or a block of kryptonite to Superman. Or maybe Heaven *would* want it, but the priests were too smart to give it to them. Some of this stuff is just beyond me, and I sort of figure it always will be. I'm a practical man, with limited objectives."

"Why would holding it back make any sense?" Mike asked. "I mean, if it's like a voodoo doll, couldn't Heaven use the bit of hoof to trap Satan again? Or have power over him, somehow?"

"I guess that's my point," Eddie stopped to wipe sweat from his forehead. "Maybe it's better for everyone if Heaven *can't* do that. Maybe it's better if there's an opposition, even if it's …" he hesitated, "ugly. But I might be talking out my backside, sometimes I can't tell."

"Don't you want to get rid of Hell?" Mike asked, remembering Eddie's wandering eye and the grim sound of his voice when the guitar player had said he saw Hell out of his left eye perpetually.

"No," Eddie shook his head slowly and spoke with quiet determination. "I don't want to go to Hell myself, but I sure think some people belong there."

All three of them reached the top of the pyramid at the same time as Jim. Rafi and Eddie looked tired and Mike felt exhausted; Jim looked totally unfazed by the climb. Adrian and Twitch still stood at the bottom, Adrian staring at the brick building through his lens and Twitch talking to him.

"What do you mean," Mike asked uneasily, looking from Eddie to Jim and back, "when you say that Jim used to be in *Hell's good graces*?"

Eddie turned to look at Jim; Jim nodded.

"It all has to do with the reason that the rebel angels fell," Eddie explained slowly. He started reciting again: "They took wives unto themselves, and everyone chose one woman for himself, and they began to go unto them. And they taught them magical medicine, incantations, the cutting of roots, and taught them plants. And the women became pregnant and gave birth to great giants."

The stone overhang felt very close, and loomed over Mike's head like it wanted to crush him; the ground below felt very far away, and seemed to be spinning. "The angels had children." He took a deep breath. "With human women."

"Oh, yes."

"Jim's not a giant." Mike gulped, and then glanced quickly at the big Viking-looking singer who loomed over him. "Well, sort of, he is."

"Sort of, he is," Eddie agreed. "And sort of, so is Twitch."

"Twitch?"

Something silver flashed in the corner of Mike's vision. Mike only saw it for a split second, but if pressed, he would have sworn he'd seen a big silver bird, like a hawk or an eagle, swooping to alight on top of the pyramid. Only the eagle, he would have sworn, had a long tassel flying in the wind behind it, like the tail of a horse.

He turned, and Twitch was standing there.

"Yes, Mikey?" she said.

"What *are* you?" he asked. He was so thrown off by the entire conversation, he barely noticed her calling him 'Mikey.' Rafi grabbed his hand and squeezed it.

"Haven't you figured it out yet?" she chuckled, her white tail swishing merrily back and forth. "Some would say I'm one of the fair folk."

"Descended from rebel angels?"

Twitch snorted. "Oh, that's what some of the *Fallen* say, but they say that about practically *everyone*. Everyone who's anyone, at least. Who knows, really? Semyaz goes around tooting his horn that he's Osiris's father, but you don't see Osiris sending the crusty old bastard Father's Day cards, do you?"

"I don't," Mike admitted. "But I'm new to all this."

"Trust me," Twitch elbowed Mike confidentially in the ribs, "he doesn't."

"But what do *you* say?"

"I'm Mab's child," Twitch said lightly. "By Oberon. Whose children *they* might be, they've never told me and I don't care."

"Well how else do you explain it?" Mike asked.

"Explain what?"

"Uh … explain *fairies*? That's what we're talking about, right?" Mike's head was spinning, and he tried to clutch tight to the thread of the conversation. "You're a fairy, aren't you? How do you explain that?"

Twitch snorted. "Explain that I *exist*? How do you explain that *you* exist? Do you have an explanation, or just a bunch of guesses? And since when did everything have to be explained, anyway? I swear, the Enlightenment ruined you humans forever."

"I don't know." Mike felt defensive. He wasn't sure what enlightenment even had to do with anything; didn't that mean people in California sitting in the Lotus position and burning incense? "Stuff should make sense, I guess."

"For that matter, how does Eddie here explain that Jim and I are so different, if we're supposed to be cousins?"

"Different?"

"Do you see Jim changing shape? Do you see him burning at the touch of iron? Or do you see me commanding the legionaries of Hell and biting my tongue all the time for fear my dad will hear me?"

"You're both immortal," Eddie pointed out.

"And you and the chimpanzees both have opposable thumbs!" Twitch snapped. "Do I go about telling everyone you're related?"

"I might be related to chimpanzees," Eddie said, "for pretty much exactly that reason."

"Jim's immortal?" Mike asked.

"Well, he doesn't get old, anyway," Eddie modified his words. "We think he can probably be killed."

"Probably?"

"Well, you never really know until you try, do you?" Twitch pointed out. "And if it was you, would you want to experiment?"

"How old is he?" Mike looked at Jim.

"I've been hearing about him for a good long time," Twitch said.

"He once told me he learned to fence from Cyrano de Bergerac. So what is that, at least four hundred years?" Eddie shrugged. "He might have been pulling my leg."

Mike wasn't sure, but he thought Cyrano de Bergerac might be one of the Three Musketeers. Or the fourth musketeer, maybe, the new guy that got into all the fights. He felt disoriented and afraid, and then Jim put a hand on his shoulder.

The hand calmed him somehow. And in the shadow, poorly lit by reflected light from the stars above the canyon and from the two flashlights, Mike thought he saw Jim smile. It was enough.

He took a deep breath. "Okay. What now?"

Puffing, Adrian reached the top of the pyramid. The space they all occupied was a flat platform, roughly ten feet to a side.

"There's a way in," Adrian huffed. "I can't see it from the ground, but it's up here."

"Everybody step back," Eddie said. "Without, you know, falling off. Look for something that will get us inside."

"It won't be a doorbell!" Adrian snapped. "There are wards."

Mike shuffled back to the edge of the pyramid. From the top, it reminded him not of Egyptian pyramids nor of Anasazi kivas, but of old Maya ruins he'd seen on TV documentaries, late at night and drunk. The connection didn't put his mind at ease at all—he had a dim memory that, according to those same documentaries, the Maya had sacrificed humans on top of their pyramids. Tied them into balls and rolled them down the sides or something. He looked down the slopes of the pyramid into darkness, sweating and nervous.

Rafi took his free hand.

"Thanks, kid," he said.

"What do you see?" Eddie asked.

Adrian stood at the other end of the square platform, his lens held up to his eye. He swept his head back and forth, examining the pyramid. "This thing is warded to high Heaven," he said. "Forgive the pun."

"What kind of wards?" Eddie asked.

"Sealing, for one, and strengthening." Adrian blinked through his lens. "I think the top of the pyramid itself is the door," he said slowly, "only those wards will have to be undone. And that's complicated by a gnarly-looking ward of entrapment."

"Should I go back to the van and get your jammies?" Eddie mocked him.

"Making fun of me doesn't lift the curse," Adrian growled. He was still looking through the lens. "And under all that there are serious wards of obfuscation and silence." He looked up at Jim. *"Serious* wards. Someone wants something inside this kiva to stay hidden, and I'd guess anything inside is undetectable … to anyone."

"This might be it," Twitch suggested. "About time."

Jim nodded.

"Better get going," Eddie pushed the spellcaster along. "You have everything you need?"

Adrian tucked his lens away and grinned. "Of course. I live by the Boy Scout slogan: be prepared."

"That's the *motto,*" Eddie rumbled. "Get on it, then."

Adrian took two pieces of colored chalk from inside his jacket and stepped out onto the platform. He knelt, to begin to draw—

and Rafi suddenly yanked on Mike's arm, hauling him sideways and off balance—

the kid grabbed Mike's gun as they crossed paths in mid-air—

Bang! bang! Adrian tumbled back—

and Mike hit the brick hard, bouncing and tumbling down the side of the pyramid. He threw his arms and legs out, slapping at the brick as the world spun about him and catching himself halfway down, his shoulder jammed up against the top of the super-kiva's pole-ladder. When he stared up again past his own toes and toward the top of the pyramid, he saw Rafi, pointing Mike's pistol at Jim.

"The Hound and the Baal are minor servants of Hell," Rafi said, "and nearly mindless." His voice boomed and echoed, like Jim's had when singing in the bar. He didn't sound like a little kid anymore, not at all, and the giant voice was all wrong, coming out of a kid in baggy jeans and high tops. "They don't know about the hoof, and I won't let them learn. All they want is *you* ... *Jim,* if that's what you want to call yourself ... and as far as I'm concerned, they can have you."

At that moment, Mike heard the squealing bellow and a thunder-like roar.

He craned his head around and saw the Hellhound finally burst from the mouth of the labyrinth, the flames of its body lighting the swarming cloud of flies and the Baal Zavuv that followed closely on its tail.

CHAPTER EIGHT

"How did I not see you?" Eddie demanded, staring at the little kid.

"He's not an Infernal is how," Twitch guessed. "He's something else."

Mike heard the words, but it took a moment for them to sink in. He couldn't turn, and he couldn't stand, so he was letting his body do a slow half-somersault over his own shoulder, grunting and straining in discomfort, to try to get upright. The ladder helped—he gripped it with both hands and hoped it wouldn't shatter. He wondered how sturdy six-thousand-year-old wood could possibly be, and as he asked himself the question, the grasses holding the top rung in place snapped. His somersault rolled downward and forward faster than he meant it, a piece of wood came off in his hands, and he scrambled with fingers and toes to keep his grip.

"I'm not an Infernal," Rafi agreed. The little kid's voice boomed against the overhang and echoed loud in Mike's ears. It seemed deeper now.

"Rabbi Feldman?" Eddie ventured.

Mike got himself upright and looked around. He found himself standing high on the side of the super-kiva, the balls of his feet and his toes wedged onto a shelf barely big enough to hold them. Rafi had his pistol, which left Mike a spare clip, a pocketful of shells, and Eddie's pocketknife. And a chunk of wood the size of a fireplace log.

The Baal Zavuv squealed. Mike could hear the buzzing of the cloud of giant flies.

"Getting warmer."

"You're Raphael," Twitch said. "The angel himself. There's no line of Hebrew priests in Dudael, there never was. Just you, like the book says, keeping vigil here by yourself for thousands of years."

"Very good." The voice was way too big for the little kid, and sort of creepy coming out of his mouth. The gun was too big for him too, and as he waved it at Eddie it looked like a cannon in his hands. "Drop your gun," he ordered the guitar player. "Unless you want to go to Hell right now."

Eddie dropped the shotgun to the top of the kiva, a sour expression on his face.

Jim strained forward at the shoulders, like he wanted to go all Hulk on the guy, shred his shirt and then rip the kid to pieces, but he didn't. He just stood in place and left his sword where it was, hanging on his belt.

Mike was painfully aware of the Hellhound and the Baal Zavuv, racing across the sand toward them all. He didn't know how long they had, but it wasn't minutes—it was seconds at best. He forced himself to keep his back turned to the approaching demons and to keep dragging himself up the side of the kiva, one brick at a time.

Maybe, he thought, I should have shot myself after all.

"I guess you've been switching bodies over the years," Eddie grumped. "Makes sense. Couldn't have people seeing too many full-on fire-of-Heaven manifestations, even out here in the ass end of New Mexico."

"When the Baal spiked you, you already had a new host body, and you just made the jump." Twitch laughed. "I guess it's better to be a little kid than to be an old man full of hatching fly eggs."

The Hound roared.

"It seemed like a random event," Rafael nodded, "and it was. They didn't recognize me and they weren't after my charge. They were hunting you. At first I thought I'd just have to wait out the flies, but then you showed up. Now I'll give you to the Hound and the Baal, and they'll be on their way."

"Or Jim could say *boo*," Eddie countered, "and this little tussle would suddenly have the attention of half the Infernal Council."

"Jim goes back to Hell either way," the little boy said. The light from Eddie's dropped shotgun shone up off the floor into his face, making his grin look demonic. Mike inched a few more bricks up the side of the super-kiva, sweat freezing him. "I'm betting *hope* will keep his mouth shut."

"Heaven's secret weapon," Twitch said grimly. "Pandora's curse."

Mike hefted the wood in his hand, wondering how close he'd have to get before he could club Rafi with it. The thought made him hesitate—Rafi looked a little too much like Chuy for Mike's comfort. Plus, he was just a kid ... or he *looked* like a kid, anyway. What kind of man hit kids?

Mike felt a wave of guilt and shame.

"Don't you think Heaven would be interested in getting its hands on Jim?" Eddie suggested. The Hound and the Baal were close enough that Mike could hear the buzzing of flies and the *whumph-whumph-whumph* of big demon claws in the sand even over the hammering of his own out-of-control heart. "He'd be one hell of a bargaining chip, forgive the pun."

"Don't flatter yourself," Rafi laughed. "Heaven doesn't want Jim. Heaven doesn't want any of you."

ROAR! Graaaaraaagh!

Jim opened his mouth like he was about to speak—

"Unless—" Rafi said. He looked sly and devious.

No more time. Mike took aim at the kid's chest and threw the wood at him.

Rafi took one slight step forward and the throw missed—

Rafi turned and grinned at Mike, and Mike's heart sank—

Plunk!

Adrian rolled over onto his back, both hands out in front of him, and Mike heard a high-pitched *chatta-chatta-chatta* sound.

Rafi's arms and legs danced spastically, he dropped the gun and fell to the platform.

"Taser, bitch!" Adrian shouted.

"Eddie!" Twitch yelled. The fairy moved like a blur, her batons appearing in her hands (Mike wondered where she kept them—they seemed to be in her hands when she wanted them, and then they vanished when she didn't), and as Mike lumbered up to the top of the platform, she met him, shoving his pistol into his hands and then passing him, headed down.

"Watch the kid!" Eddie shouted, then shook his head. "I mean, the archangel!" Then the guitarist slid down the edge of the kiva on Jim's heels, shotgun blasting at the cloud of incoming Zvuvim.

Adrian handed the taser to Mike and brushed himself off. Adrian held the second flashlight, and in its beam Mike saw that filaments ran from the little gray rubberized box in his hand to darts in Rafi's chest. The boy was sitting up, slowly, as if his muscles were cramped.

"Don't talk, you slimy bastard!" Adrian barked at the little kid. "You talk, Mike here zaps you!"

"Yeah." Mike tried to sound tough. He tried to remember that the little kid was really an immortal archangel, and had just thrown him off the top of the kiva like Mike was an unwanted kitten.

"Also," Adrian told Mike matter-of-factly, "zap him if you need to keep him under control so you can get off a shot at the bugs coming in. For that matter, you ought to zap him every once in a while for fun." Adrian grabbed the taser in Mike's hands and pressed down on the button with his thumb.

Chatta-chatta-chatta.

Rafi thumped back onto the platform, heels kicking and head bouncing around.

Boom! Boom! Jim kept the Hellhound at bay, stabbing down from the side of the super-kiva as the beast lunged at him with its forepaws. Eddie rained shotgun blasts at the Zvuvim swarming around his friend. Mike couldn't see the Baal Zavuv, or Twitch, and that made him nervous.

"And don't forget," Adrian said, "he's an archangel. Don't trust him for a second, those guys are in on it."

"In on what?"

"*It.*" Adrian waved his hand around vaguely at the world. "Everything. Believe me, Mike, the joke's on us."

Mike looked down at the taser. "How many zaps does this thing's battery hold?" he asked.

Adrian shrugged, holding his lens up to his eye again. "I've juiced it up a little," he said, "tinkerer that I am. In theory, that should mean bigger shocks and more of them. In practice, well, don't count your chickens, et cetera."

"You saying the taser might fall asleep when I try to use it?" Mike grinned.

"Hey!" Adrian barked. "Don't you start!" He swept the top of the platform with the flashlight beam, then started to chuckle. "Everybody thinks he's a comedian. Even the monkey on the bass."

Rafael opened his mouth to say something. Remembering Adrian's warning, Mike thumbed the shock button on the taser and sent the kid into another round of spasms. "I kinda feel weird," he said. "I mean, I'm standing here tasering an angel. At least I think I am."

Adrian chalked a straight line along one edge of the super-kiva platform, jogging it into a lightning bolt every couple of feet. "Don't feel weird. Feel proud. Get some good licks in for the whole species."

"On *angels*? I mean, *joy to the world*?"

"Yeah, joy to the world, exactly." Adrian squinted through his lens and switched to a different color of chalk. "Joy to the world, *whether you want it or not.* Can't leave the poor shepherds well enough alone. Can't let Balaam just ride his donkey in peace. Can't just let people live decent lives and be happy, can they? Nope, Heaven meddles. Heaven is a bunch of busybodies. Heaven wants to make everybody *better.*"

Mike shook his head, confused. "But what I really mean is that I can't believe it works on him. I mean, he's an angel."

"Yeah, well," Adrian exhaled slowly as he drew a long arc with his chalk. "He's in a body now, isn't he? Anything with a body, you can taser it. Remember Legion and the pigs at Capernaum?"

"No."

"Ha. Well, they can drown, too, when they've chained themselves to human bodies. Doesn't destroy them, of course, but it messes them up and they don't like it. I'm not sure, but I think it's kind of like getting your horse knocked out from under you if you're a cowboy." Adrian stood up, and Mike realized he'd forgotten something.

"Didn't you get shot?" he asked. Adrian looked unscathed.

The organist snorted. "Ward of shielding," he said, as if that explained it. "Stung like the dickens, but didn't break the skin. Stupid angel's been out here on his own in the boondocks so long, he's forgotten how the game is played."

The fight below sounded like a storm, shotgun blasts and the terrifying bellows of demons.

Mike risked a look around and found Twitch. She was on the ground on the far side of the kiva from Jim and Eddie, in horse form, kicking with hind legs at the Baal Zavuv. The big grey and black demon bellowed and squealed and swiped at her with both hands, and there was bright red blood on the horse's flanks. A cloud of Zvuvim buzzed around, clutching with shiny steel mandibles, and Twitch bit back with enormous white horsey teeth.

Mindful of the archangel he held prisoner, Mike squeezed the taser's shock button with his left thumb. At the same time, he raised his semi-automatic in his other hand and squeezed off a handful of rounds, *bang! bang! bang!* pulverizing several Zvuvim in mid-air and even, he thought, landing a shot or two on the big tusked fly-pig-demon thing. It didn't seem fazed by the bullets.

Adrian set the flashlight down on the edge of the platform. "Now," the wizard told him, putting away the chalk and dusting his hands off against each other, "you got the most important job of the evening."

"Yeah?" Mike asked, keeping an eye on Twitch in her strange, circling and kicking dance-fight against the Baal. "What's that, then?"

"You gotta keep me awake."

That got Mike's attention. "How do I do that?" he asked.

"There's something Twitch does with her voice, but I don't—"

"Yeah, she has Glamour."

Mike felt relieved that he wasn't the only one. "Yeah," he admitted, "I guess I think she's glamorous, too."

"Doesn't always work. Nothing *always* works. Just—look, keep an eye on me, and do what you gotta do. Pinch me, shout, hold me up, whatever. Best you don't shoot me with the taser, though."

"That's a nasty curse," Mike said, remembering Adrian's earlier insistence on the fact of his being cursed, and not just naturally narcoleptic.

"And keep an eye on Raphael," Adrian added, rolling up the crisped and burned sleeves of his suit jacket and stepping to the edge of the platform. "Heaven's up to something here. I don't like it."

"Heaven help us," Mike ventured with a grin. "Et cetera?"

"Not very damn likely," Adrian snorted, then turned to his incantation. *"Per Wepwawet Mercuriumque,"* he started chanting, waving his arms. His eyes grew distant in concentration. He was focusing so hard he looked like he was in a trance.

Mike looked away from Adrian just in time to see a big Zavuv that had gotten past Eddie and raced in his direction. He pointed his pistol at it and squeezed the trigger.

Click.

"Huevos."

No time to duck, and barely any time to move at all. The fly rushed for his head, metal mandibles clicking like scythes hungry for the harvest—

Mike swung his fist backhand, pistol-whipping the Zavuv across both eyes—

crash! the demon-fly's eyes shattered and sour, reeking fluid like pus sprayed all over Mike. He flinched, and the Zavuv's body collided with his shoulder, knocking him back two steps and making him teeter on the edge of the super-kiva's platform for long, dizzying seconds. When he had windmilled back into balance, the Zavuv was gone, its body indistinguishable in the carpet of shredded black demon-flesh scattered across the sand around the pyramid.

Mike looked around the super-kiva, checking in on the rest of the band. Jim and the Hound were so close together in their struggle they might have been wrestling. Eddie swung with the butt of his shotgun at the flies swarming around him, ducking and trying to reload. Mike grabbed for his spare clip, meaning to reload his own weapon and clear out some of the Zvuvim assailing Eddie.

"Mike," he heard a voice say.

It was a sweet voice, so sweet he had to listen. It might have been a woman's voice, it was so sweet, but Mike didn't think it was. The voice didn't turn him on, but it warmed his heart and made him feel thrilled.

"Mike," the voice said again, "we can be on the same side."

Some part of Mike's brain knew that he still stood on top of a half-pyramid underneath a rock overhang somewhere in the middle of New Mexico, surrounded by minor minions of Hell and assigned to keep a narcoleptic wizard from nodding off, but that wasn't what he saw. He saw hills, green and rolling under a carpet of flowers, and beyond them a forest and the sea and overhead a brilliant blue sky and all around were fruit trees and friendly wild creatures and birds and butterflies and he smelled warm pollen on the gentle breeze and there wasn't a cloud in sight. And there on the hillock with him stood his good friend Rafael, the little kid who was so funny and brave and charming, and he smiled at Mike.

"Mike," he said, "let's do some good together." And when Rafael said it, Mike wasn't sure exactly what he had in mind, but he really wanted to cooperate.

"Do some good," he mumbled. "Do some good, and go to Heaven."

"Heaven loves those who do good." Rafi smiled wisely and warmly. The kid's voice was so sweet, Mike felt like it was healing the burnt skin on the back of his neck just to hear it.

But behind Rafael stood someone else. Scalp askew, scarred and bleeding, his grudge open on his face, he could have been

Rafael's bigger, terrifying, evil twin.

Chuy.

"Bullshit, *cabrón*," Chuy sneered. "You're going to Hell, and when you get here, you're mine."

"What?" Mike stumbled.

"I know it," Chuy said, jerking his thumb at Rafael, *"he* knows it, and *you* know it."

And Mike *did* know it.

"I'm sorry, Chuy," he said. He felt tears on his cheeks. "I was wrong."

Chuy spat blood onto the stone. *"Vete a la chingada."*

"Mike," pleaded the Angel Rafael. The voice pulled sweetly on Mike's heart.

"Shut up, bitch," Mike mumbled, and he thumbed the shock button on the taser.

Chatta-chatta-chatta.

Then the garden was gone, and Chuy was gone, and the kid Rafi—the archangel Raphael—lay on the super-kiva's platform, jerking spastically again. Mike released the shock button, knees buckling. He shook his head to clear the smell of flowers out of his brain and turned to check in on Adrian—

who lay unconscious on the ground, face-down in the middle of his chalk diagrams.

"Fundillo!" Mike shouted.

He grabbed Adrian and shook him. Pinched. Kicked. Slapped in the face. The buzzing of flies filled his ears, and Rafi groaned.

"Adrian!" he yelled into the wizard's ear.

Adrian snored.

Eddie and Jim backed up the side of the super-kiva. Eddie's shotgun hung at his side and he swung his fists at the Zvuvim, while Jim still slashed and poked. The big man moved like an acrobat, dodging blows by rolling to one side or the other, or leaping into the air and somersaulting over them. Eddie was surprisingly quick, too—he looked like he was using karate on the demon-flies, knifing them aside with the blades of his hand in short, economical motions—but they were still backing up, and getting close to the top of the platform.

On the other side, Twitch retreated, too. She was in human—human-like fairy, anyway—form and her movements looked slower than usual. She was bleeding, and she swung her two batons to keep the Baal at bay, as it lumbered and crashed its way up the side of the pyramid.

"Adrian!" Eddie yelled.

"Adrian!" Mike yelled.

Adrian snored.

Rafi stirred and groaned.

"Cojón," Mike grumbled, but he had an idea. His heart raced and his head swam from the adrenalin, but he remembered that his clip was empty. He managed to switch out the old clip and slap in the full one without dropping either, and then he placed the muzzle of his pistol against Adrian's buttock.

And squeezed the trigger.

Bang!

Blood gushed out onto the diagrams, and Adrian shook awake.

"Ouch!" the wizard roared. "Hey!"

Mike stared at the blood. "I thought …" he said. "You said it didn't break the skin … wards of shields, or something. …"

"Moron!" Adrian roared, and stumbled to his feet. He clutched his backside with one hand, blood welling out between his fingers. "The wards wear off!"

"Well, you're awake, anyway," Mike muttered.

Raphael groaned and twitched. For good measure, and because he felt embarrassed and didn't know what else to do, Mike shocked the angel again, and this time held down the button good and long.

Chatta-chatta-chatta-chatta-chatta-zotzpf!

The taser died in his hand, a shower of sparks scorching Mike's skin.

"Oh, Hell," Adrian said, and whipped his lens to his eye to look at the platform again. Holding his own butt and squinting through what amounted to a monocle made him look almost silly, and Mike started to laugh out loud.

"Is it wrecked?" Mike asked over the roaring of the Hound and the bellowing of the Baal Zavuv, both drawing closer up the sides of the super-kiva.

"I never yet saw a spell ruined by the addition of human blood," Adrian growled, putting away his lens. "Including this one. Stand back."

Mike stepped back, standing at the edge of the platform beside the unconscious boy-angel and pointing his pistol at Rafi, just in case. Rafi stirred, slightly. Eddie and Twitch both backed to within a step or two of the height of the pyramid, batting at the beasts that pursued them and the Zvuvim overhead. Mike was afraid to take his pistol off the prone angel, so he swung when he could with his fist at the fly-demons, batting them away without doing any real damage.

"*In Wepwawet nomini*," Adrian shouted dramatically, despite his funny gimp posture, with all his weight on one leg, one hand waving in the air and the other clutching his own wounded buttock, "*aperiri te mando!*"

The flat space atop the kiva, with all Adrian's chalk markings on it, disappeared. A pit yawned beneath Mike's feet.

CHAPTER NINE

Mike teetered on the edge of the pit, unsure what the others would do. He had expected to see stairs down, and the gaping hole caught him totally by surprise. He flapped his arms like that would keep him in the air and looked for handholds or a rope or anything. He didn't find any, but in his flailing he knocked away the flashlight.

Adrian didn't hesitate. The wizard stepped forward and threw himself into the pit and the darkness. Probably had wards of bouncing, or something crazy like that on him, Mike thought, but the bellowing Baal and roaring Hound and the buzzing Zvuvim left him no choice, and he jumped in right after, clenching his teeth hard so he didn't scream.

He fell—

a beam of light tumbled in after him, spinning around—

looking up, hands pawing at the air, through the square of dimmer darkness above him, glimmering with multicolored flames, he saw shapes pass—

bodies falling—

Splash!

Water closed over Mike's head. So cold, Mike couldn't imagine why it wasn't ice. He fought for air and sucked in water instead, coughing and choking and flailing to get out. He sank, and in the dark water around him he felt other objects hitting the surface and thrashing about, and then beams of light from Eddie's Maglite cut the darkness, and finally, lungs searing with pain, Mike tried to swim.

He wasn't a very good swimmer, had always lived in desert country and had never been a gym rat, but he managed to fight to the surface. He coughed out cold fluid, feeling like a piece of his lung went with it, and kept fighting his way forward. Fists and feet thrashing in the darkness hit his shoulders and back and he tried to ignore them. Someone screamed wordlessly, a sound that echoed huge in the dark space. Mike worried that it might have been him.

After a few long strokes, Mike's hands slapped against something that felt like a brick wall, and he clung to it.

He'd lost the pistol, he realized, somewhere in the pool. *Chingado.* He groaned with effort and dragged himself out of the water. He heard the sloshing sounds of others doing the same, and lots of gasping for air. Mike was dimly aware that overhead, somewhere, danced the strange colored fire of the Hellhound. For some reason, it wasn't diving in right after them.

But it didn't sound very happy, either.

In the dark, he heard puffing breath and muttered curses, and then Eddie shone his light around and Mike could make out a little better what was going on.

The chamber was a cube of mud brick. In the center of the floor was a round sunken pool, and to one side, lying on the ground, was a pole-ladder like the one Mike had ruined outside. Water flowed into the pool through a brick channel from one wall, and flowed out the other. Eddie and Adrian crowded over the channel and looked closely at it. Teeth chattered, breath steamed and drops of water hit the floor off all their bodies while the guitar and organ players examined the sluice, and Twitch flapped in the air above them in falcon form

Above, Mike saw the flame of the Hellhound's body as it shoved its neck into the hole at the top of the super-kiva. It didn't seem to be able to fit, and as it jammed its head into the opening, it shouldered out the Baal. The fly-demon bellowed and squealed in irritation, and the Hound barked and screeched in return. The Baal's minions, the Zvuvim, crowded in through the hole and buzzed in a cloud below it, but didn't descend. Something was stopping all of them from jumping down in the hole after their quarry. Mike cringed at their noises and wondered what was saving his life; whatever it was, he was grateful for it.

"Isn't that just Hebrew?" Eddie sounded puzzled.

"Guys," Mike's teeth rattled in his head as he shivered. "Whatever you're doing, can you hurry?"

Twitch dropped out of her bird form and stood beside the other two. It looked like stretching downward, the falcon's legs growing longer and longer until suddenly the drummer stood there in person. The only thing that didn't shift or change in the process was Twitch's silvery horse's tail.

Mike blinked.

"It's the names of God," Adrian said. "Very old warding, very powerful. The water flows over all the names of God and into the cistern.... Hey! My butt!" The wizard slapped his own backside and Eddie shone the light on it. "No wound!"

It was true; through the hole he'd blasted in the organ player's pants, Mike could see the guy's buttock. No wound, no blood.

Mike felt goose pimples on his arms that had nothing to do with the cold, and he probed the back of his own neck. It didn't hurt, and the skin under his fingers felt soft and new, more like a baby's skin than his own coarse, hairy body.

"Holy water!" Mike blurted. He remembered enough about church to remember holy water. "The names of God must turn it into some kind of holy water. You know, like for healing, I guess. And good against vampires." He trailed off, unsure whether or not he was sounding like an idiot.

"And evil spirits," said a voice in the darkness.

Eddie whipped around and shone his light on the source of the sound. Rafael stood on the other side of the cistern.

"Don't let him talk!" Mike shouted.

"Don't worry, big guy," Adrian reassured him. "Twitch isn't susceptible to the Whisper of Eden. Neither is Jim. If this bastard tries anything, he goes down."

"Maybe I should kill him anyway," Eddie growled, and Mike heard the emphatic *snicker* of a shell being popped into the underside of the shotgun. "Why aren't you wet, you rotten weasel?"

It was true, Mike realized. Rafi was dry as a bone. Twitch was too, but of course Twitch could fly. "This is the pool where the leader of the rebels was imprisoned," Rafi said, ignoring Eddie and pointing at the water. "Of course you know that, it's why you're here. The water was sanctified, and it held him down. Paralyzed by the pain."

Mike scratched his head. The same water that had healed him had kept Satan imprisoned, because it *hurt* the fallen angel? What kind of holy water *was* that?

"What happened?" Adrian asked warily. "He got out eventually, so what was it? Did one of the names erode off? But that can't be it, can it, or the water would be ordinary mundane liquid now."

Rafi nodded. "There was a drought," he said. "When the water got low enough, Azazel managed to kick his way out."

"That's when he chipped his hoof," Adrian concluded. "Guess he was so excited to get out, he didn't notice."

Rafi shrugged. "Or he hurt too much."

Eddie guffawed his derision. "It figures you'd build a prison that depended on water in the *desert*."

Rafi smiled. "There was water enough," he said. "Until the flood. But when the fountains of the great deep spat forth their waters to obliterate the wickedness of the children of men in the days of Noah, the rock seep dried up."

"And in forty days, the prison evaporated." Adrian shook his head. "Serves you right, you idiots."

The demons above raged.

Mike's head whirled among astonishment and curiosity and disbelief and fear, like the spinner of an old Snakes and Ladders game, whizzing in circles while all the players watched to see how many spaces Mikey would get to go, and whether he'd step on the bottom of a ladder or the top of a snake. Mike felt like there were snakes all around him, and no ladders anywhere in sight. He pawed at the cluster of holy amulets on his chest, but they didn't help.

"What do you want, Raphael? You can't talk us out of anything." Eddie's voice had a hard, flat edge to it, and it snapped Mike back into focus on the here and now. "And I have the gun."

"I want to deal," Rafi said. "I want to be on the team."

"No way," Eddie shot back. "I don't make bargains with supernatural forces."

"Once burned," Adrian added, "you know the rest."

"Besides," Twitch threw in, "what do you have to offer us? We're here. We beat you."

"Did you?" Rafael smiled. "Where's the hoof, then? Where's your escape route? Those demons can smell the water and don't want to fall into it, but sooner or later they'll find another way in, or they'll get desperate enough to become reckless and jump anyway. And if they don't, you're stuck here forever. What's your plan to deal with them? And where's Jim?"

The Hound howled bitterly.

Mike realized he *hadn't* seen Jim inside the pyramid—the singer's silence and the darkness had made him forget the man. Eddie spun around, shining his light until he found a wet mass by the side of the cistern, trembling in silence.

"I don't think falling into the water was a very pleasant experience for Jim," Rafi said. "His father certainly didn't like it."

"His father?" Pieces clicked into place for Mike. The rapid pace of events around him had kept him from making all the connections, but now he saw it. "Of course. Jim is Azazel's son."

"Poor bastard." Eddie handed the shotgun to Adrian, knelt by Jim and shook him. "Jim, are you awake?"

Adrian shone the light around the room and scrutinized its walls and ceiling. "Don't get any ideas, angel," he said coldly. "We still have the fairy, and he knows how to bite."

"Where's the hoof, though?" Twitch wondered.

"I needed you," Rafael said. "I have been the keeper of this prison for six thousand years, but I have never known how to open it. I wasn't given any key, wasn't told how. That was deliberate policy, of course, on the part of Heaven. They couldn't have me developing sympathies and betraying my trust."

"Yeah, I know that's what *I* immediately think of when I hear the word *angel,*" Adrian muttered. "How *sympathetic* you guys are."

Mike remembered Rafi almost yanking his arm from his socket as he threw him sideways and stole his gun. "Amen," he muttered.

"I needed you to open the crypt. And now I could just take the hoof and go, but I want to join you. I want to aid you in your quest."

"Bullshit," Eddie disagreed. "Who do you think I am, Sir Lancelot? You don't care about my *quest* one way or the other, anyhow, you lying sack. You have your own game."

"Fine," Rafi admitted. "I have my own game. But we can play our games at the same time. I'll tell you where the hoof is, we defeat the Hound and the bugs together, and then we go put the hoof to good use."

"I don't want to put it to *good* use," Adrian said. "A leopard can't change, et cetera."

"Bad use, then!" Rafi snapped.

And then Mike knew where the hoof was.

"He can't get it," he told Adrian. "Rafi—*Raphael* can't get the hoof. He's frustrated. He still needs us."

"Of course he can't get it," Eddie agreed. He was helping Jim to a sitting position. Jim groaned. Adrian shone the light on the singer and he looked pink, like someone had thrown boiling water on him. "Or he wouldn't be bargaining. But where is it?"

"It's like he said," Adrian added. "Heaven didn't want him to grab the hoof, either." He turned on the angel, shining the light on him and stalking closer. "What is it you want, Raphael? Freedom? Do you just want to lay your calling down and go? Power? Are you hoping you can bargain your way into the Infernal Council? Or maybe get a promotion in Heaven? Who outranks the archangels? The seraphim? Is that it, you want to be one of Heaven's six-winged pool-boys, basking forever in the golden light of the throne?"

"Do you care?" Anger flashed in Rafi's eyes. "Does it matter to you?"

"It matters!" Adrian snapped. "I have plans for that hoof!"

"What do you want?" Rafi asked. "You want to be a real wizard, don't you? You want to cast the big spells, and you don't want to fall asleep when you do it. And Eddie there wants to save his soul. Jim, I can guess. You're like Dorothy and her friends, on a twisted road to Oz to see the wizard. And you're going to trade the wizard his hoof in return for brains and courage and a heart and a return ticket home."

"I guess you get TV reception in Dudael," Adrian chuckled.

"I can get what I want from Azazel," Rafi said firmly. "And I can help you all get what you want."

"No deal," Eddie's voice was flat. He pushed Jim to his feet, his shoulder under the big man's arm. Jim was groggy, and slow to respond. "Not now, not ever."

"We already have someone who can talk us out of traffic tickets," Adrian sneered. "You just don't bring anything to the table."

"I'll tell," the kid said. He sounded petulant, and since the moment when he'd stolen Mike's gun and thrown him off the kiva, he'd never looked more like a little kid.

"Azazel?" Eddie snorted. "We'll tell him ourselves."

"I'll tell Heaven."

"Tell them what, exactly?" Adrian shone the flashlight into Rafi's eyes, and the angel held up his hands to block the beam. "Tell them you went behind their back and tried to cut some kind of deal with Hell?"

Rafi laughed. "Of course not! I'll tell them how you overpowered me and stole the hoof, and where you're headed. And then I'll laugh as Heaven's pool-boys chop you to pieces with their flaming swords."

"Aren't you afraid Heaven can hear you now?" Adrian asked.

"Of course not!" Rafi laughed. "Do you think Heaven wanted Azazel to be able to just call for his friends, and be rescued? This place is warded to silence so deep, nothing can get out. You could set off a nuclear bomb in here, and no one would hear. The screaming of a thousand damned souls wouldn't get past the roof."

Adrian pulled something from his pocket and held it over his head. It looked like a smartphone. *Click*, Mike heard, and then Rafi's voice repeated, *I'll laugh as Heaven's pool-boys chop you to pieces with their flaming swords.*

"You recorded me?" Rafi sounded incredulous.

"There's an app for that," Adrian sneered.

"But ..."

"Don't mess with the gadget guy, bitch!" Adrian spat. The kid stepped back and his face twisted into an expression of anger and fear. "Now stay out of the way, or you'll be the one with his nuts on Heaven's anvil!"

"That doesn't solve our basic problem," Eddie observed. "It's funny as hell, of course, but we still don't know where the hoof is. If it's even here at all."

The Hound howled at them above, as if to emphasize the point. Mike felt goose pimples on his arms and he couldn't wait any longer.

"Isn't it obvious?" he asked, and jumped into the pool.

He wasn't a very good swimmer, and as he thrashed his way to the bottom of the pool, grabbing handfuls of water and pushing them up, exhaling and trying to sink his own weight and wishing he were a little thinner, he wondered what he was doing. He didn't know how deep the water was, he didn't know what might be at the bottom, and he wasn't really sure he wanted to be further pissing off the archangel Raphael, who was already probably irritated at the repeated tasering Mike had given him.

Plus, he couldn't really be sure he was right about where the hoof was.

But he wanted to take a stand. He wanted to show his worth to the team, and he wanted to be part of something. He wasn't afraid of the water, however bad a swimmer he was—it seemed to have healed his burns, and that made him feel that it wouldn't drown him, either. Totally irrational, but that's what he felt in his gut. Besides, maybe, whatever the band was planning to do with the hoof, it could also be used to help him with Chuy. It sounded like they were going to go bargain with the devil. Well, if the devil could make Adrian a real wizard and give Twitch a brain, or whatever it was she wanted, maybe he could set Chuy free, too.

And that might free Mike.

He hit the pool bottom and almost immediately found the hoof.

It was huge, as long as Mike's forearm and curved like a scythe. For a moment he thought it must not be what he was looking for, but Adrian was shining down the light from above now, and Mike could see the bottom of the pool—it wasn't very big, and there wasn't anything else. Besides, the thing he'd found felt like a hoof, like a gigantic discarded nail clipping. He grabbed it in both hands.

Then he saw his pistol. No sense going unarmed, not in all this craziness.

Mike scooped up the gun, jammed it into his belt and kicked off for the surface.

He surfaced from the water, shaking himself like a dog. The first thing he saw when he opened his eyes was a shattered heap of plastic and wire on the brick beside the pool. It was Adrian's smartphone, he realized, stomped into fragments. Looking up, he found Adrian standing in the beam of the flashlight with his hands over his head.

"Who's got the gun?" he asked, and then he saw Twitch behind Adrian, blood on her mouth like she'd been hit. Jim and Eddie stood behind the drummer, the singer still leaning heavily on his guitar player for support. "Oh," he said.

"Slight miscalculation," Twitch told him with a wry shrug.

"I got cocky," Adrian grumbled. "Should have given the gun to the fairy."

"Thank you, Mike," Rafi said. He sounded polite and amused. "Go ahead and bring me the hoof."

"Don't do it!" Adrian snapped, but Rafi's voice was warm and pleasant and anyway, Rafi was Mike's friend. Mike dragged his soggy carcass out of the water. He belly-flopped onto the soft green grass like a beached whale, but his friends wouldn't care, and besides, the sun was warm and the breeze was gentle. He smiled as he handed the gigantic toenail clipping over to his friend Rafael.

"Good job, Mike," the boy grinned, and took the hoof.

"Hell," Eddie said. Poor Eddie, he was always so grumpy, Mike thought. Even when the weather was perfect, like this.

"Not Hell," Rafi said, "Eden. Now, Mike, would you please go get that ladder and set it up? There are some friends I'd like to join us."

"Of course." Mike found the ladder on the green sward and grunted as he tried to pick it up. "It's kind of heavy."

"Adrian," Rafi suggested. "Would you mind helping?"

"Not at all." Adrian and Mike together picked up the ladder and hoisted it up against the ceiling. Except there was no ceiling, there was only blue sky above. Mike's brain skipped like a vinyl record with a scratch on that thought. There was blue sky above, but he had just placed a ladder up into an opening in the sky. Something didn't quite click, and he felt his brain skipping again.

Far away, maybe in the forest over the hill, some big creature made its presence known with a shriek that thundered through the trees and sounded like it would uproot them all by sheer sonic power. It might be a Tyrannosaurus Rex, Mike thought.

"Calling for your father won't help," Rafi said pleasantly. He was talking to Jim, who looked tired and haggard despite the pleasant surroundings, and leaned on Eddie for support. "Assuming you'd want to. But maybe you can play with his servants." Mike heard the buzzing of flies, a small blight on the beauty of the day.

"Jim!" Eddie snapped.

"Phthonos!" Jim shouted, and suddenly the illusion of the garden and the forest and the sunshine and the distant sea snapped to shards like a stained glass window with a brick thrown through it. Jim's voice echoed deep and strong—it *did* have reverb in it naturally, Mike would have sworn—and the inside of the super-kiva returned to view.

But who was Jim yelling at?

The Hound jammed its head through the opening at the top of the pyramid and howled. Jets of blue and red fire crackled from its rows of jagged teeth, lighting the interior like a carnival funhouse ride.

Was Jim calling the Hellhound?

"Jeez," Mike muttered. He felt sick.

The archangel Raphael stood in the corner of the kiva, shotgun in his hands. The pyramid began to fill with Zvuvim and smaller flies, buzzing incessantly in a cloud of clacketing steel and black fly-demon flesh that descended out of the ceiling. The stink of rotting meat choked the air inside the chamber.

Inside the cloud, rattling down the ladder one heavy step at a time and shaking dust as it came, the Baal Zavuv descended into the kiva.

"Phthonos!" Jim shouted again, and something in the big man's voice heartened Mike without any apparent intent to do so. "Attack!"

CHAPTER TEN

Mike charged.

He jerked the pistol from the back of his belt and drew a bead on the archangel Raphael, squeezing the trigger.

Click.

"Huevos!" Mike cursed.

Boom!

He saw the muzzle flash of the shotgun and thought he'd bought the farm, but Rafi wasn't shooting at him. Eddie and Jim tumbled to the ground together, and then Mike crashed on top of the archangel in the body of the little boy.

He raised his fist over his head and clubbed Rafi over the ear with the pistol's grip.

"Ouch!" The kid staggered under the blow.

Mike saw in his mind's eye what would happen next. The angel would blow him to bits with the shotgun, unless he managed to stop it. So he dropped his pistol and threw himself on the bigger gun, wrestling for control.

Buzzzzzz.

A knife sank into his back and then another, and Mike screamed in agony. He felt the legs of the Zavuv on his back and legs and smelled the dry-dust stink of the fly-demon, but he couldn't let it stop him. He grabbed the barrel of the shotgun and threw his weight against it, trying to fall and rip it bodily from the angel's hands.

Boom!

The gun went off, and Mike wasn't dead.

"Get off!"

Rafi backhanded Mike across the face and hurled him across the room—

Buzzzzz! a second Zavuv intercepted Mike in midair, sinking its mandibles into his chest—

Mike screamed again—

"Per Volcanum—" Adrian shouted, and then Rafi clubbed him in the face with the shotgun and he fell like a sack of grain—

Mike landed in the cistern of holy water.

The Zvuvim on his body exploded into flame and he sank, fire burning him before and behind, and at the same time feeling the delicious ice-cool soothing touch of the waters. This was some kind of insanity, Mike thought. Feeling two opposite things at the same time, like loving and hating someone.

Though as he thought of it, he realized that's how he felt about Chuy.

Which, of course, might be madness.

At the bottom of the pool, the smoldering flies fell away from him and he bounced back toward the surface. Mike emerged from the water feeling refreshed and whole.

ROAR—CRACK!

The Hellhound smashed its shoulders against the entrance in the ceiling, knocking loose bricks and dust that fell and peppered the water around Mike. Eddie and Adrian both lay prone and still, and Jim fought the Baal Zavuv.

Jim was a wild man, like a monkey or a comic book character. As Mike stared, Jim ran up the corner of the room like it was a flat surface, dodging a swipe of the Baal's enormous claw. From over the Baal's head, Jim kicked off and flipped backwards through the air, landing with both heels on the Baal's shoulders. The Baal raged and swiped, but Jim dodged, moving from one foot to the other with casual grace, batting and slashing aside dive-bombing Zvuvim all the while.

His balance and speed were inhuman, Mike thought.

Because, of course, Jim *wasn't* human. Jim was the son of Satan.

Twitch dashed around the Baal, landing blows on it as she could with her wooden batons, but mostly smashing Zvuvim to the ground, keeping them off Eddie's and Adrian's bodies.

The archangel Raphael stood back in the corner of the room, holding the shotgun and the hoof of the rebel Azazel and laughing his head off.

"Phthonos!" Jim yelled again.

The Hound answered him with a long, loud hollering cry that was almost mournful.

Mike shook himself. He needed to act.

Adrian was closer. Mike crept forward, hoping that the spectacle would distract Rafael until he could grab the organ player's leg. Fortunately, Adrian was a small man. Mike wrapped his fingers around the wizard's ankle and pulled, dragging the little man into the pool.

As they both splashed into the water, Adrian started thrashing around. Mike grabbed the wizard by the collar of his jacket and pushed off the floor, bringing them both up to good breathable air again—

and staring into the open mouth of the shotgun.

"You've been a lot of trouble, Mike," the archangel Raphael snarled through the mouth of the little kid. "Time to say good-bye."

He pumped the shotgun, pointed it at Mike's head and squeezed the trigger—

Boom!—

Mike threw himself back into the water—

he felt the shotgun slug tear into his chest and felt the flesh healing up behind the projectile immediately, his whole body tingling like electricity.

Boom! He heard another shot while he was underwater, muffled, and felt another slug hit him in the hip. He felt the bone break, and felt it knit again, almost instantly.

Mike came up again spluttering, ecstatic and totally disoriented. Jim and Twitch fought the Baal and its Zvuvim in the background, the flies swarming around them like a curtain, opaque and buzzing.

"Damn you!" Raphael shouted. "Get out of the water!"

"No!" the shout came from Eddie, who had struggled to his feet. Blood ran down his chest from a hole in his shirt and he looked worn and broken, but he broke into a charge. *"You* get *in!"*

Eddie rammed the kid with his shoulder and wrapped both arms around him, launching both of them into the air—

out over the pool—

and *splash!* into the water.

Rafi hit the water and lit up like an incandescent bulb. Light seemed to burn inside him and rocketed from the entire surface of his body as he and Eddie sank. He looked like a living X-ray image—Mike thought he could see bones glowing through his skin, flailing and trembling as he sank. Mike grabbed for Eddie and was nearly blinded by the glow of the kid beside him. He managed to dig his fingers into the guitar player's army jacket and drag the man up, out of the water.

The light streamed up, out of Rafi's body like a bolt of lightning in reverse, a column that shot straight for heaven, through the open top of the pyramid and into the stone overhang above it, and then was gone.

Rafi thrashed as the light left him, then went limp. Adrian grabbed the boy, hauling him up, and Eddie—looking much healthier and moving better—got himself upright. Eddie ducked under the water again and grabbed his shotgun; Mike picked up the crescent of hoof-clipping, floating on the surface, and the three of them moved toward the edge of the pool and the cloud of Zvuvim surrounding Jim and Twitch.

Eddie rested his elbow on the edge of the pool. He pumped the shotgun, aimed into the cloud and squeezed the trigger.

Click.

"I guess it's knives, boys," Eddie muttered darkly. "Unless one of you has that escape plan Raphael was blabbering about." He started dragging himself out of the water.

With a lightning-like backhand, the Baal finally landed a blow on Twitch, punching her with its enormous knuckles in her chest. Twitch hit the wall and sank to the floor in a spray of bright blood. Zvuvim swarmed her.

Mike and Adrian dragged themselves out on Eddie's heels. Adrian was already muttering something. Mike dug into his pocket for a weapon and came up with nothing but a pocketknife.

"Phthonos!" Jim yelled again, his huge voice barely audible under the carpet of swarming Zvuvim. Mike thought he saw the singer, sword in one hand and a pinned Zavuv in the other, parrying attacking fly-demons with the body of their comrade and stabbing at the face of the Baal Zavuv. He looked bloody and tired.

ROAAAR—CRASH!!

With a final lunge, the Hellhound broke through the ceiling. It fell in a shower of bricks and flame straight toward the pool, and Mike scrambled to get out of its way. Adrian didn't move—he struggled to incant something, heaving his chest and shaking his head like he was fighting to stay awake.

Krakkkksh!

The Hellhound landed on the edge of the cistern, its front paws and head out of the water, and its hind legs and tail landing in. It missed Adrian by scant feet, and the wizard stumbled sideways from the shock. Steam gusted up from where the water doused the Hound's flames on contact.

The Hound shrieked and snarled in furious pain.

Grrrraaaaaraaargh! the Baal bellowed in answer.

Jim leaned against the wall. He'd been hit by something, and didn't seem to be able to stand on his own anymore. The Baal towered over him, claws lashing like bandsaws and tusks gnashing at the air.

"Per Isidem—" Adrian collapsed to the floor.

Mike snapped open the puny blade and followed Eddie, charging at the pile of Zvuvim crawling over Twitch. It's over, he thought. This is where I die.

I hope Chuy's not waiting for me on the other side.

He stabbed his little knife into the nearest fly-demon, waiting for his own destruction.

The Hellhound lunged forward, roaring—

and clamped its enormous crocodilian jaws around the waist of the Baal Zavuv.

The Baal howled in fury and surprise. The Hound lifted it off the ground and shook it. Zvuvim buzzed around the two larger demons, whining in to slash with their mandibles at the Hellhound and bursting into flame on contact.

Zvuvim stampeded away from Twitch, nearly knocking Mike over as they buffeted into and past him. The drummer was left in a heap on the floor.

"Twitch," Eddie and Mike said together.

She raised a hand weakly and grinned. "Not dead yet."

"Let's get you into the pool," Mike suggested, and stooped to pick her up.

Twitch slapped away his hands, suddenly animated. "Whoa, Mike, not me! I've seen what happens to immortals who get into that water!"

"Immortals?" Mike scratched his head. "Uh, of course." There was no *of course* about it, though. He had a lot to learn, and he knew it.

Mike turned back to the battle that raged between the two demons. The Hound rushed at the wall of the chamber—

the Baal sank its claws into the Hellhound's shoulder—

"Attack, Phthonos!" Jim yelled—

and the Hound slammed the Baal into the wall, head-first.

CRACK!

Grwaaaaargh!

Blue sparks crackled at the point of impact. Zvuvim swarmed the Hound with angry, frenetic buzzing, which was almost enough to make Mike feel sorry for the beast. When they struck its front half, which still flamed, they burnt and died, but when they attacked its hindquarters they drew blood. The Hound swung about, obviously in pain, managing to stomp on a few of the flies or catch them with its flaming forepaws.

Meanwhile, the Baal Zavuv clawed at the Hound's head. The Baal's flesh smoked and scorched and stank, and with an enraged bellow it tore off one of the Hound's ears.

"Attack!" Jim yelled again.

The Hound charged at the wall again, swinging its head to slam the Baal's skull against the brick. One of the Baal's eyes shattered on impact, spraying thick ichor on the wall and floor in another shower of fizzing blue sparks. The Baal shrieked and sank all its talons into the head and neck of the Hellhound.

Mike noticed the gray pallor of pre-dawn early morning creeping in through the opening at the top of the pyramid. He almost chuckled.

"Attack!"

The Zvuvim swarmed the Hound so thickly Mike couldn't even see its flames anymore, and the inside of the super-kiva was shrouded in thick shadow. The Hellhound charged the wall and smashed the Baal into it a final time—

CRACK!

The wall collapsed.

Brick dust, bricks, and ancient timbers hidden inside the walls exploded in a spray of masonry chaos and waves of blue fire over the struggling demons. Mike staggered back, pulling Twitch with him away from the wall, which continued to tumble, one brick at a time, each brick exploding in blue sparks as it hit the floor. Finally Mike found the corner, coughing and spitting dust on the floor and wiping muddy grit from his eyes.

And then there was silence.

"Twitch?" Mike called. "Eddie?"

He was rewarded with an answering cough. "I'm here," he heard. It was Eddie's voice. "I've got Adrian. He's alive."

"I'm alive, too," Mike heard Twitch say from somewhere very close, and then realized he was clutching her to himself like a scared kid would hold a rag doll. And she felt like a man.

"Uh, sorry," Mike said, feeling awkward.

"Sorry you saved me?" Twitch asked.

"No," Mike answered immediately. He stood, and helped Twitch stand, too. "Sorry, I … uh, I don't know. I don't know anything. Sorry."

Twitch laughed. "Welcome to the band," the drummer said, and kissed him on the cheek.

Mike chose to think of Twitch as a woman, and to enjoy the kiss.

Splash!

The dust was settling enough that Mike could see Eddie dragging Adrian into the pool. When the wizard hit the water he woke up, spitting and cursing.

Then he found Rafi. The boy lay under a fur of brick dust, breathing deeply like he was sound asleep.

"What about Jim?" Mike asked. He approached the pile of rubble, finding himself standing in the weak light of morning among the bodies of what seemed like a hundred giant flies. He could see the tail and back legs of the Hellhound sticking out from under the bricks. There were no flames, and he wondered if the creature was dead.

And then the tail swished.

"Help!" Mike snapped, and jumped back.

But then Jim was there, patting the big creature on its rump and talking to it. "Easy, Phthonos," Jim said in his strange, booming voice. "Easy. Friends."

The Hound shook its big flaming crocodile head free of the rubble, dropping the torn and broken body of the Baal Zavuv into the dust. The front half of its body still burned, and as Mike watched, smoke began to rise from its hindquarters as well.

"You're talking," Mike said.

"Wards of silence," Jim grinned. He was dusty and bloody and his t-shirt was destroyed, but he looked totally unconquerable. Then his grin fell off and he yelled to Adrian. "Please tell me there really are wards of silence in here, and they're still intact."

Adrian rinsed off his lens in the cistern's water and squinted through it at the chamber around him. "Yeah," he said, "it's all still there. But it's starting to fall apart, so you'd better shut up and we'd better get moving. A stitch in time, you know."

"Stay," Jim said to the Hellhound. It made a loud rumbling sound in its belly that sounded like the purr of an oversized lion. "Stay, Phthonos."

"The Hound obeys you," Mike said. He felt numb, and wondered if he was going into shock.

"Some of my father's minions are too stupid to know any better," Jim nodded. "And some have divided loyalties. That's the problem with Hell."

"I don't know," Mike shook his head, thinking of Raphael. "It seems to be a problem with Heaven, too."

"Maybe it's a problem with thinking creatures generally," Jim agreed. "Or maybe it's not a *problem* at all. Maybe it's just the effect of free will. Will you join us?" He stood and held out his hand.

Mike cleared his throat; he wanted to sound professional. "How many dates on the tour?" he asked.

"I don't know."

"Where are we going?"

"I don't know. Probably Chicago, for one."

Mike nodded down at the Hound, purring at Jim's feet. "Are we going to meet more friends like this one?"

"Almost certainly."

Mike thought of his flophouse room in Santa Fe. He thought of Chuy, too, and then he shook Jim's hand. "Sounds like a real crappy gig," he laughed, a little bitterly. "But the alternative is worse."

"That's how I make most of my decisions." Jim smiled. "Phthonos, stay," he repeated, and then he took the hoof from Mike's hands and walked out of the crumbling super-kiva through the hole in its wall. The Hellhound stayed behind.

Freakishly, it wagged its tail.

Twitch followed right behind Jim, in her horse shape, with the boy Rafi slung over her back. Adrian walked next to her, holding the kid in place. He patted Mike on the shoulder as he passed. "Good to have a rhythm section again," he said.

Eddie brought up the rear. "Can you drive?" he asked.

Mike nodded. "I've been a driver before."

"Cab, or limo?"

Mike sighed. "Getaway car, mostly," he admitted.

"Perfect," Eddie laughed.

"I had a rough youth."

"Everybody does. Let's go get the instruments and hit the road, before Fido here remembers that daddy sent it to fetch Jim."

Mike scratched his head and they both walked out of the kiva. Mike shot one last look over his shoulder at the Hellhound, and was rewarded with a lopsided crocodilian grin. A fresh, water-bearing breeze blew into the overhang from the canyon below, and he breathed deep. "Aren't they burnt to cinders?" he asked.

"All the band gear is fireproof and impact-resistant," Eddie told him.

"Wards of instrument insurance?"

Eddie chuckled. "Something like that. Your bass is probably gone, but we have another one you can use."

"I saw it in the van," Mike remembered. "I'll try not to impale myself on it."

"That'd be good," Eddie agreed. "That'd be a real good start."

SNAKE HANDLIN' MAN

CHAPTER ONE

I assume none of you guys has anything against strippers?"

Owen had the dusky olive skin and dark hair that said he was a classic American mutt, some Eastern Europe in him, maybe Serb or Greek, some Latin America, some who-knew-what. He was a heavy man, not in the *this-guy-eats-Twinkies-for-breakfast* way, but in the *this-guy-can-wrestle-a-Peterbilt-to-the-asphalt* way. Also, Eddie had noticed as the man waved at them coming in through the door of the diner, he was packing. It was a big pistol, not particularly hidden in a shoulder holster under Owen's slightly shabby sport coat.

Eddie respected that. He had his Glock in a shoulder holster, too. When the rubber hit the road, of course, he preferred his Remington 870 Express Magnum, a twelve-gauge pump action with its stock shortened and its barrel cut down. He had other guns, other shotguns, even, but the 870 was his favorite. A single slug from the 870 was enough for any human attacker, and most minor minions of Hell. But you couldn't just walk into a diner with a sawed-off shotgun and ask for coffee.

Not even in Oklahoma.

"We ain't proud," Eddie grunted.

"Good," Owen pounded the Formica table with one meaty fist. "It's a small stage, and you're gonna to have to share."

"They have boobs, right?" Mike asked. The big bass player grinned like he was kidding. He was jumpy, but he'd handled himself well in New Mexico, and Eddie didn't mind having him along, even if Jim did see the Left Hand on the guy. For that matter, the fact that he was on Heaven's bad side made him fit in better with the band.

"Mike's no homophobe," Adrian sneered. "Women or trannies, either way. Beggars can't ... well, you know what they say about beggars."

Owen roared with laughter and pounded the table again. Behind the club manager, Eddie saw a sheet of flame. Men hung in it like worms baiting fish, the tips of enormous hooks protruding through their chests. Their feet twitched, gore ran down their bellies and legs, their mouths worked the shapes of tormented howling, but Eddie heard nothing.

He could see Hell, thank Heaven he didn't have to hear it. He rubbed his eyes with the palms of his hands while the vision faded. He'd needed the money, he reminded himself. He'd sold his soul because he wanted to be a good man and wanted his kids to eat bread that wasn't marked down because it was stale for once. The visions didn't come from him, didn't reflect him—they were his punishment for one really stupid choice.

He'd screwed it up six ways to Sunday, but he'd meant to do it for Sharon and the girls.

"This ain't that kind of town," Owen chuckled, "and Correia's ain't that kind of joint. But I got a tip on a place in Amarillo, if that's what you're into. Never been there myself, you understand, but I'm an open-minded guy."

"Jeez," Mike grumbled, elbowing Adrian in the ribs.

"What'll you have?"

The waitress was clean and pretty. She had the look of a self-improver about her, her uniform clean even though it was a horrible orange and brown polyester, her flat shoes shined and spotless even though she'd obviously bought them at PayLess, her hair back in a neat ponytail. Also, she wasn't chewing gum, which was a plus. And she was very pregnant. The plastic rectangle pinned to her chest read *SAMANTHA*.

"Coffee," Eddie said instantly. "Don't bother making a fresh pot."

"In fact," Twitch said, his eyes sparkling across the corner booth, "if you can use water from the urinal, Eddie would prefer it. He likes his punishment self-inflicted."

Eddie harrumphed, ignoring the jab from the fairy drummer. "Chicken-fried steak and gravy for the big guy," he added, jerking his thumb at Jim. Jim nodded quietly and smiled, big pale goth-looking son of a bitch that he was. Big but thin, no matter what he ate. Probably got that indestructible physique from his father, who was Azazel himself, head of the Infernal Council and Prince of Darkness. "And a large Pepsi."

"Ooh," she said, making a tight circle of her lips and exhaling sharply. She rubbed her own belly and then grinned. "He's kicking." She wrote down Jim's lunch.

"Pie, Samantha," Mike jumped in. "A slice of your best. No, one slice each of your two best."

"That would be coconut cream," she said, "and coconut cream. She leaned in close to the bass player, her breasts brushing his shoulder. "The rest of it is Alpo."

"Thanks." Mike laughed.

She nodded and noted the pie on her pad. "You can call me Sami."

"Are your eggs from free range chickens?" Adrian asked.

"Nope," Sami said. "They're from the Costco in Guymon."

Adrian sighed and shook his head. The wizard was finicky. He seemed to think his new age lifestyle was a necessary component of his sorcery; Eddie doubted it but didn't care. The patchouli oil and the incense and the morning exercise routine didn't get in the rest of the band's way, any more than Eddie's visions did.

"Don't fret about it," Eddie told him. "You do enough yoga for you and the chickens both."

"Besides," Mike got in a lick, "free range eggs aren't going to be enough to keep you awake."

"I'll take two eggs anyway," Adrian shrugged, glaring at the bass player. "Scrambled. No toast, unless you have whole wheat without high fructose corn syrup."

"Mmmm," purred Sami, the waitress, in a friendly way, "a man who takes care of himself." Her accent was pleasant and twangy, more deep Texas than Oklahoma, it seemed to Eddie.

"This body is a high performance instrument," Adrian sniffed, "called upon frequently to perform extraordinary feats. You drive a Formula One car, you can't just pull into the Chevron and fill the tank with Unleaded."

"In fact," Twitch said, "if you drive a Formula One car, it turns out that you mostly leave it in the garage. Scrambled eggs for me, too, darling, and I'll have the toast, as long as it's made out of bread."

"Two eggs," Sami noted, "one toast." She frowned a sad frown at Adrian and patted him on the shoulder. She wasn't wearing a wedding ring, Eddie couldn't help noticing. "And for you, Owen?" she asked.

Owen shook his head. "I got a sack lunch in the desk," he said. "You know me."

Sami smiled at all of them. "I'll be right back," she promised. As she turned to go, Eddie got a good look at her swollen belly. She was just about ready to pop, he realized. He remembered when Sharon had looked like that, in the last days of each of her pregnancies. He shut out the memories, concentrated on the table.

"Cash," he said to Owen. "Cash is the important thing."

"I remember," Owen nodded. "No worries."

"Your accountant okay with it? We don't exactly do our taxes."

"I am the accountant," the big man said. "And I'm okay with it. Most of our local traffic pays in cash, so it'll be easy to fix."

"That's what I like to hear."

"I don't get you," Mike said to Eddie, gulping his ice water. One sip of the water had been enough for Eddie; it tasted like sand and chlorine.

"Yeah?" Eddie looked around the diner, staying alert. Cracked linoleum, peeling faux-wood, dirty glass. Ageing donuts and cookies in a bell-shaped glass display next to the khaki-colored cash register, vintage 1980 or older. Posters of Elvis and Marilyn Monroe and James Dean peeling away from Scotch tape faded into yellow visibility. A truck driver scarfing down a foot long sandwich in one corner and two old women yammering over coffee and biscuits. Or maybe it was black tea. And a big wheel, silver-gleaming, on which the bodies of four young women were impaled and spinning. No one else but Eddie saw this last, of course. "What's not to get?"

Mike looked thoughtfully at Owen, which was good. At least the new guy was conscious enough of what he was saying to be careful around outsiders. "I mean, you live so careful, Eddie."

"Yeah?"

"Yeah. If I was you, I'd try the pie. Mierda, if I was you, I'd eat nothing *but* pie. Pie and donuts."

Mike meant: *if I knew exactly when and how I was going to die, Eddie, like you do, I'd go crazy and stuff myself with pie because it wouldn't matter.*

Well, not *exactly* when and how.

"You'd go crazy with the women, too," Eddie predicted.

"Or the trannies," Adrian threw in.

"Hey," Mike objected.

"Probably skydive and mainline heroin and do anything else, right?" Eddie asked. "Smoke like a chimney, drink like a fish. Because you wouldn't give a damn about the consequences."

Mike nodded.

"So what you're saying," Eddie ground out the logical conclusion of Mike's line of thought carefully, "is that if you were me, you'd give up." He realized that he was inadvertently clenching both his fists, and he made a conscious effort to relax them.

"Uh ..." Mike struggled.

Owen scratched his head. "I think he's just saying live a little, man," the club manager suggested. "I mean, coffee? You gotta have more than coffee."

"I do live a little," Eddie said. "Sometimes I add cream."

"You're a wild man," Owen laughed. "Tonight, I'll run your tab at cost. And the first beer's on Correia's."

Crash!

"Help!" the voice was Sami the waitress's.

Eddie jumped out of his seat and Owen jumped with him, shoulder to shoulder as they both whipped out guns. Behind him, Eddie heard the rest of the band struggling with the confines of the circular table and the corner booth. Twitch could become a falcon at will, but he wouldn't want to do it with this many witnesses. Not unless it was really necessary.

"It's okay!" the cook called. He was scrambling out from the kitchen to the area behind the counter, waving at the diner's customers. "She's okay, she just slipped!"

Eddie noticed Owen's gun. "Desert Eagle," he said admiringly. "Fifty caliber?"

"Made by bad-ass Hebrews," Owen agreed. He nodded at Eddie's pistol. "Glock 18? Selective fire?"

Eddie grinned. "Sometimes you just gotta shoot automatic."

"Hey," Owen shrugged. "You can't always choose when you're gonna have multiple assailants. I respect an informed decision."

"I respect a man whose gun can punch holes through brick walls."

"Aw," Twitch sighed. "They're in love."

"Sami?" the cook yelped. He was a burly man in jeans and a greasy white t-shirt, with no hair to speak of on his head and arms covered in burn scars. He stood up and backed away from the spot behind the counter where the waitress must be lying.

"Aaaaaaagh!" she screamed.

"Jeez!" Mike grabbed the bird's nest of superstitious junk that hung from his neck. Eddie holstered his gun and ran for the counter.

He vaulted over the counter as the cook turned and ran, filling the space the man vacated. Sami lay sprawled against a big plastic bag full of Styrofoam cups, legs akimbo and knees up. Her brown and orange skirt was dark and wet, and Eddie's sadly experienced brain instantly identified the cause.

Samantha sat in a puddle of her own blood.

"Aaagh!" she screamed again, throwing her head back and bucking her hips.

"Easy, girl," Eddie tried to calm her. He'd delivered his own first child, on a midwinter Chicago night when the air was frozen so solid the hospital couldn't force its ambulances out the door, at least not when the call came from Eddie's shitty South Side row of tenements. His own car had been broken down, as always, brakes totally shot. He'd never had a car worth owning. He didn't want to deliver the waitress's kid, but he wasn't about to leave her to her own devices, either.

"My baby!" she shouted at him. Her face was red and straining, the cords of her neck muscles standing out like rope.

"Owen!" Eddie hollered. The old ladies had looked up from their biscuits at the commotion. The trucker was staring, too, mayonnaise and barbecue sauce dripping from all his fingers and staining his flannel shirt. "Who delivers babies in this town?"

"Doc Jensen!" Owen snapped, and dug into his pocket for a cell phone.

"Tell him it's the bottom of the ninth!" If there was already blood, Sami wasn't going anywhere to have her baby.

"Aaagh!"

Eddie turned back to the girl.

"You're going to be okay," he promised her. He tried to ignore the river of fire he saw drifting lazily beneath her hips and the skeletal hands that seemed to be reaching up from within it. "Just hold my hand and tell me where it hurts. Focus on breathing." He felt like an idiot. He hadn't been able to do much for his wife when she'd delivered, either, just held her hand and took her abuse and then caught the baby and toweled it off.

"Aaaagh!" Sami screamed again, twisting her neck like she was riding a bucking bronco, and clawing a handful of Styrofoam from the pile she lay on.

"It's okay—"

A snake stuck its head out from under her skirt. A really big snake.

"What the hell?"

Eddie stumbled back, falling onto his own butt. As he did, a flash of movement in the corner of his eye caught his attention.

Eddie had been freestyle fighting champion of his company in Iraq, unofficial but also uncontested. He had lost muscle since then, but his sinews, nerves and reflexes were as good as they'd ever been. He kicked himself back, slamming upward with the blade of his right hand, deflecting the missile darting in to strike his neck—

his blow connected with a heavy *thwack*—

he knocked the missile straight up into the air over his head, where he got a good look at the thing that was attacking him. It was another snake, this one more normal in size, maybe four or five feet long, red and green and vicious.

Only the snake had wings. Leathery bat's wings, and its wingspan was almost as long as the snake's body.

Hisssss!

Then something grabbed his feet. Eddie looked down and saw thick, scaly knuckles tightening their grip on the ankles of each of his combat boots. They dragged forward the thing that emerged from underneath Sami the waitress's skirt, tongue slithering in and out of its diamond-shaped head.

It wasn't a snake. It was a Komodo dragon, or something so similar that Eddie couldn't tell the difference. When it cracked its jaws Eddie saw teeth like shards of glass.

"Jim!" Eddie yelled. "Adrian!"

Another snake popped out from under the waitress's skirt, another flyer that launched itself into the air. She shrieked, a high-pitched, wordless sound of pain that was more like the squeal of a deflating balloon than a noise a human would ever normally make.

Eddie scissor-kicked his boots together, thumping them into the lizard's head behind its jaw, where he hoped the tissues would be soft. His boots were steel-toed and he kicked as hard as he could, but the kick only freed one of his feet, and then the Komodo dragon snapped its mouth at him in rage.

He managed to yank free his pistol as a third flyer popped from underneath Sami's skirt. He felt sick, guessing what was going on under there. She squealed and shuddered like an epileptic. Poor kid.

"Adrian!" he yelled, and pointed the Glock—

bang!—

and shot Sami right between the eyes. Her head snapped back in a flower of bright red blood and then she collapsed, still.

Then the Komodo dragon was on top of him, and Eddie struggled to get an elbow up in front of his face. The thick cloth of his old green jacket saved him from a scratch of the beast's teeth, and then he forced the open mouth away from his face, pinning the jaws between his forearm and the counter's support column under the cash register.

He could still smell the reek of the thing's breath. It stank of sewage.

Eddie heard gunshots as the rest of the band, out of his vision, got into the fight.

"Chingón!" That would be Mike.

The lizard's hind claws scratched at Eddie's hips and pelvis, and again his jacket protected him. Eddie jammed a hand down decisively and grabbed one of the creature's knees. He rolled himself backward, yanking the thing with him—

and hurling it down along the space behind the counter—

crash!—

to where it slammed home against a stack of soda syrup canisters. Like bowling pins, they tumbled around the reptile and rolled in all directions.

Eddie jumped to his feet and thumbed the Glock's selective fire switch to *automatic.* The old ladies screamed and slapped at a snake with handbags. The truck driver clutched at his throat, staining his blond beard with the sauces on his fingers. A snake had bitten him, and the man's face was already turning purple.

Eddie had no time for the dead trucker, but the sight strengthened his resolve not to get bitten himself. He stepped towards the lizard, ducking as he realized that the swarm of winged snakes was thicker than he'd thought, and opened fire.

B-rapp-p-p-p-p-p-p-p!

He squeezed off the entire clip into the canisters and the thrashing body of the lizard. Whatever it was, if bullets could kill it, it was now dead.

The air was full of flying snakes. Adrian chanted something and struggled not to swoon; Jim slammed a pitcher down onto a Formica table top, trapping a serpent under it; Mike swung his M1911 pistol, the one he'd taken off the dead bouncer in New Mexico, looking for a target that would hold still; Owen, the club manager, blasted away at flying snakes with his hand cannon, wearing an expression on his face that might have been *contentment*; Eddie didn't see Twitch. Another winged viper darted at Eddie's head, and he batted it aside with the Glock.

"Oil!" he shouted. The cook peeped out through the order window, wide-eyed and open-mouth. Eddie pointed at him, careful to point with his empty hand and not his pistol. "Oil!" he yelled again. "Now!"

Hissss! he heard behind him, and turned to see more snakes slipping from Sami's skirt. He caught a glimpse of what was behind, and shuddered in sympathetic pain—there was a writhing mass of snakes, and a river of blood.

Eddie heard the pounding of feet and the slamming open of a door. He looked into the kitchen and saw a back door swinging slowly shut, the cook gone.

"Damn!" Eddie raced for the kitchen, slamming the second clip into his Glock and thumbing the fire switch back to *semi-automatic*. As he passed the big lizard on the floor, the one he'd filled with lead, it stirred, slightly. Eddie cursed through his teeth.

A winged serpent whipped out of the kitchen heading for Mike's neck, too fast for him, and he knew he was a goner—

but then a silver wing flashed in his vision and a falcon torpedoed past him—

snatching the serpent from the air with both its claws and crushing its skull with its powerful beak. A long silvery horse's tail snapped behind the falcon like a pennant.

Twitch.

Another serpent hummed in through the order window as Eddie stepped into the kitchen and spotted what he needed—the frying vat, and, under it, a spare jug of oil, like a gas can. The snake attacked, but Eddie saw this one coming, and was ready for it.

He stepped aside, grabbed the snake by the tail and flung it into the hot oil.

Sizzle! A frying meat smell filled the air. Eddie grabbed the handle of a fry basket and jammed it down on top of the winged snake, forcing it deeper into the fry oil in its writhing protest.

"Six piece Quetzalcoatl nuggets," he muttered, "coming right up." He grabbed the handle of the jug, a white plastic five-gallon container, in his left hand, and turned Glock-first back to the fray.

The lizard crouched in the kitchen door, staring at Eddie with beady black eyes. It bled from multiple bullet wounds in its body, but it was moving and it looked pissed.

Beyond, in the chaos of the diner, he saw Adrian drop to the ground. And then the wizard's fallen body was swarmed by flying serpents.

CHAPTER TWO

Eddie threw the oil jug.

He overestimated his own strength, by quite a lot. The jug thudded to a dull halt halfway between him and the lizard, and then the lizard rushed him.

He got the Glock up and into play, squeezing off several rounds and putting at least one of them into the thing before it reached him in an avalanche of claws and teeth. He hurled himself sideways, grabbing for a big squeegee on a pole and jamming it between his own body and the reptile, fending the beast off like a caveman with a sharpened stick. Stab, retreat, stab, retreat, catching the creature on the end of the pole and trying to push it further away. The squeegee's rubber strip tore into shreds under the lizard's assault, leaving a dull tip at the end of the hard pole.

Eddie jumped back to avoid a snap of the jaws that got past his stick. He felt a sudden burning sensation on his own backside, and realized the lizard had forced him so far in reverse that he was sitting on the edge of the grill.

"Damn it!" he shouted, and shoved back on his stick. He got his shoulder into it, scooped the lizard backwards several feet, and then he switched into a staff-fighting stance. He spun the hard wood in an arc that lodged one end of it firmly in the crook of his elbow, and with the other end he battered the lizard in the face with a quick succession of blows.

The creature pulled back, spitting with rage.

Having bought himself a little space, Eddie raised his pistol, aiming the Glock a little higher—

bang!—

and shot a hole in the jug of oil.

Glug, glug, glug, the contents slurped out, filling the kitchen even more with the cloying, dull smell of vegetable oil.

The lizard pushed forward and Eddie jammed the squeegee pole into its face. The beast kept pushing, Eddie shoved back with a fierce snarl, and the makeshift spear snapped in two. Eddie staggered forward and so did the monster and suddenly the big lizard was in his lap, clawing at him and snapping with a mouth like a blender set to *liquefy*.

Eddie jumped back. He fell onto the grill, smelling the scorch-stink of his jacket and feeling the heat intensely, especially on his already burned and stinging buttocks. Above him, gray-white feet hung flaccidly dripping blood, a dozen corpses dangling, each with its neck drilled through by a saber-like tooth in the mouth of a grinning scab-faced fiend. Eddie heard the gunshots and shouting and the zipping of winged serpents through the air behind him like a soundtrack to the infernal carnage he saw overhead. The stink of winged serpent flesh frying past the point of edibility filled his mouth and nose.

He shuddered and kicked.

He caught the lizard square in the center of its face with both his boots and threw it back into the puddle of oil. It hit hard and slipped back, sliding across cracked and mildewed tile in a puddle of canola. Eddie rolled back on his feet, backside and elbows burned and the back of his neck too warm for comfort, but he still held his pistol in his hand and reptilian death in his heart.

The lizard thrashed to regain its footing and scrabbled to try to launch itself at Eddie, jaws gaping. Its maw opened and closed loudly, teeth champing against each other and groping for Eddie's flesh with visible hunger. Eddie didn't waste time shooting it again.

He shot a hole in the fryer, and as the hot oil sloshed out and into the mess on the floor, he kept firing at the metal of the vat.

Bang, bang, bang—

and on the third shot, he got a spark and the hot oil ignited. A sheet of flame like a grassfire sprang into being, rushing across the floor in all directions, and heat and light exploded up at the ceiling in the fryer. The lizard squealed and paddled backward as the fire overtook it, hissing with pain and rage.

Eddie jumped out of the way too, planting one hand in a tub of shredded iceberg lettuce and vaulting up onto his feet on the grill. He could feel the heat of the cooking surface, but the vulcanized rubber soles of his boots kept him from being burned. For the moment.

Eddie had never owned a decent car, but he'd never let himself be without a good jacket and boots. If only he had had a sheet of vulcanized rubber in the seat of his pants, he thought, he wouldn't be feeling the sting of the grill now. He knew Chuck Norris sold rubber-crotch jeans for karate enthusiasts; maybe he sold fireproof-seat pants, too. Really, everyone in the band could probably use a pair.

His speculation was interrupted by a flying serpent whizzing in through the order window. Eddie grabbed it with his left hand, feeling scratchy, shuddering wings inside his clenched fist as he swung the thing around—

and brought it down hard, impaling its head on the order spike. It wasn't much in the way of justice, but it cheered him up a bit to see one of the serpents twitching out its last snake breaths over Mike's double order of coconut cream pie.

Across the kitchen, the burning lizard flailed into a tall set of shelves. They swung forward and crashed to the floor like a hammer, dropping paper-wrapped stacks of paper towels and stacks of toilet paper and cardboard boxes full of paper napkins hurtling through the oil-fire and across the room into its corners. A pile of rags under a big metal double sink burst into flames. Jugs of cleaning chemicals bubbled and tipped over, and thick smoke started to fill the top half of the room.

Heat seared Eddie's lungs. He crouched and jumped, throwing himself headfirst through the order window, tumbling down full-length onto a narrow table behind the counter. He hit the diner's two coffee machines and bounced, all the breath knocked out of him and his body hurting. He struck the floor at the same moment as one of the coffee pots and it shattered, spraying him with hot black coffee.

With his luck, he thought, the one that hadn't shattered was probably the decaf.

Eddie groaned and dragged himself up onto his elbows, patting the puddle of hot coffee to find his pistol again. When he managed to get his eyes opened, he found himself looking at the ruined body of the poor waitress, Sami.

Flying serpents whizzed and hummed about her in a cloud, gnawing the flesh off her body. He fought back a vomit reflex. Probably nothing in his stomach but coffee grounds, anyway.

"Damn snakes!" Eddie jumped to his feet, feeling the heat of the blazing kitchen on his head as he did. He realized that he had shards of coffeepot in his hands and face, but he had no time for that. He grabbed the surviving pot—it was the regular, after all—and tossed its hot contents on the feeding monsters.

They hissed in anger and rose from their interrupted meal, spinning like hummingbirds to face Eddie. And then he heard the teeth-clacking hiss of the bigger reptile behind him, and smelled the stink of oil-charred serpent.

"Ah, nuts," he muttered. "I thought you were dead."

Before and behind him, the waitress's deadly reptilian brood lunged at Eddie.

He dove over the counter, shattering the glass bell full of donuts and cookies with his boots and heading for the floor shoulder-first, trying to come up in a roll.

He hit the tiles next to jeans and boots that he recognized as Jim's. The big man jumped over Eddie as Eddie rolled, and looking up, Eddie saw Jim swinging one of the diner's trays like a club, smacking aside two of the winged snakes with a lunge right, slamming a third onto the countertop with his backswing, and then spinning like a gymnast on a pommel horse to squash another with the back of his boot.

Jim was a swordsman, really. And of course he didn't wear his sword into small town diners, any more than Eddie carried his shotgun. But he was a crazy Cyrano de Bergerac sort of swordsman, as much an athlete and an acrobat as a guy that stabbed with a pointy stick, and he took the battle to the snakes with gusto.

Eddie bumped into Adrian on the floor and stopped his roll. Adrian was turning purple in the face, the livid purple bordered with streaks of yellow that marked an ugly bruise in the height of its flowering. He gasped for air, and he locked his bloodshot, bulging eyes on Eddie's own and choked out a few words.

"Three hours," Adrian managed, and then, "*per Hypnum dormito.*" His body went limp and his head fell back, cracking on the tile.

"Adrian!" Eddie shouted, and pressed his finger against the wizard's neck. Adrian, who was also the band's organ player, often fell asleep in the middle of trying to cast a spell—he was cursed—but he didn't usually look like he was at death's door when he did so.

He shot his eyes around the room as he checked Adrian's vitals. The Komodo dragon scrambled to try to get out from behind the counter, but Twitch wouldn't let it. The shape-changing fairy was in his big pony form and stood with his hindquarters to the lizard, kicking it over and over again. It squealed and tried to get around Twitch, but there was no room and the fairy was quick as lightning, and then he kicked the lizard back into the inferno of the diner's kitchen. The lizard shrieked and disappeared.

Mike fired his M1911 and plugged a flying serpent right through the cross of its wings, breaking the beastie in half and dropping it to the floor. Next to him, Owen the accountant held another snake pinned to the table with his meaty fist. It squirmed as he sawed off its head with a steak knife. Jim smashed a snake to the wall with his tray, the last that Eddie could see, and then he threw his shoulder against the tray and squashed the reptile into paste.

Adrian had a pulse. He was breathing, too.

But his breath was ragged and shallow, his heartbeat was intermittent, and he didn't look very good.

Eddie took a deep breath and let it out. His own heart raced like a train and he felt adrenalin surge through him. He held still and tried to let himself calm down.

"That was hilarious," Twitch offered.

"Jeez," Mike said, and he laughed a shaky laugh. "You guys ever go anywhere that you don't burn to the ground?"

"What?" Owen was astonished. "You mean this kind of thing happens to you a lot?"

"It isn't on purpose," Eddie growled. He sat up, trembling. "And I wouldn't say that it happens *a lot*." Through the order window, in the burning kitchen, he saw a row of men wearing helmets, hanging from the neck by nooses and dancing in the fire. "But it has happened once or twice *lately*."

The horse disappeared and Twitch was there, head to toe in his usual spiked leathers, with his ever-present horse's tail dangling behind. "How's Adrian?" he asked.

Eddie shrugged. "I think he put himself into a coma," he said. "Anyway, you can see he looks like death warmed over, and then he cast some sort of spell and passed out."

"So, business as usual?" Mike joked.

"Maybe." Eddie shrugged again. "But he said something that might have been *Hypnos* in his incantation. Isn't that the god of sleep? I think maybe he knocked himself out before the poison could kill him."

"Spell?" Owen said. He held his big fifty caliber Desert Eagle again, carefully pointed away from everyone, like an experienced and safety-trained shooter. "Incantation? God of sleep?"

"Owen," Eddie said, feeling stiff and sore, and his scorched butt hurting him, "I just watched you saw a flying serpent in half like so much ribeye. You gonna quibble about incantations now?"

"Nope," Owen chuckled. "I guess not. But if this kind of thing happens a lot, maybe there's a market opportunity here. Have you thought about making a business out of it? I mean, monster pest removal, or something?"

"Sounds like a winner of an idea to me," Eddie agreed. "It's all yours."

"So, what?" Mike asked. "We find a cure for the poison before Adrian wakes up?"

"Or his wards of sleeping wear off. Or he just dies," Twitch agreed. "Humans are so fragile."

"Humans?" Owen asked, and then he shook his head. "Never mind."

"Adrian told me three hours," Eddie shared. "That doesn't sound like very much time to me."

"That'd just about get you to show time," the big club manager observed.

"Perfect," Eddie grunted. "Our sound really depends on those big organ chords. You got cops in this town?"

"No, but it ain't that big a county," Owen said. "Sheriff could be here sooner than you'd think."

Eddie nodded and climbed to his feet. Standing, he saw the dead trucker, and beside the trucker, the corpses of the two old ladies. They were all swollen and purple in the face. The heat scorched him, making his burned cheeks throb sympathetically, but he dragged himself around behind the counter and looked down at the corpse. At Samantha's body, he forced himself to say.

Poor girl.

At least the gnawing fangs of her unholy serpent children had hidden the mark of Eddie's bullet hole. He sighed and dug around in her pockets. Sometimes this could be the world's worst gig.

"Car keys," he announced as he found them. "Nothing else."

"We gotta get Adrian's body," Mike said, "I mean, we gotta get *Adrian* out of here."

Owen stooped to one knee and picked up the wizard in a quick, practiced fireman's carry. Eddie liked the club manager— he was a practical, can-do sort of guy. "I'll carry him across the street to the club," Owen offered. "At least until the ambulance gets here."

"No hospital is going to be able to help our organist, poor boy," Twitch observed. "Unless you mean a nunnery...? There are orders of sisters still passing down the old healing arts, though I didn't know there were any in Oklahoma."

"No, I ... what?" the accountant looked puzzled.

"Never mind," Eddie told him. "If you can take him to the club, that would be great. Don't tell anybody he's there, and don't let the EMTs get him, if you can help it. With Adrian's luck, they'd just undo his wards and kill him. We're going to have to look into this poison ourselves, and find a cure." He looked pointedly at the flames licking up along the ceiling and headed for the door.

The burly club manager pushed out the door first, not even breathing hard from his burden—Adrian was a solidly-built guy, but he was short. Mike followed, then Twitch, then Eddie, holding the car keys. Jim exited last, looking around the diner as the flames charged out of the kitchen and into the rest of the building, as if daring more snakes to show their scaly heads.

Jim was no paladin, but the guy really hated evil, and had a jones for whupping its backside whenever he could.

Speaking of backsides, Eddie's hurt. He limped into the gravel parking lot next to the diner, looking for a car in the pale afternoon sun. Pale, but really hot. Eddie would have been pathetically grateful for just two minutes of Chicago winter.

"I'll have him when you're ready," Owen grunted, and headed across the street for his club.

The town wasn't much more than a crossroads, Highway 56 and some nameless county road that cut out at right angles through the fields of dryland wheat. Everything out in this part of the world was right angles, it seemed to Eddie. Showed a lack of imagination. There wasn't a rise of land higher than six feet in sight, and the enormous watery-blue sky was broken at the margins only by about a dozen buildings. The diner was nameless, a third-rate imitation of a Denny's built entirely of plywood and now burning. Correia's across the street looked like it might once have been a barn, built of corrugated steel and windows covered in iron bars and chicken wire. The two neon signs in its windows read *BEER* and *GIRLS*. Past the bar was a combination gas station / mini-mart and then a long low building with a boardwalk and a sign that read *FEED AND SEED*. Further beyond that, past a quarter mile of weeds, Eddie saw some bulkier building, like a smallish big box store. Finally, there were other buildings scattered here and there whose uses Eddie couldn't immediately identify—houses or municipal buildings or signless businesses. They all looked like prefabricated sheds, square and ugly.

And that was the whole town.

It was easy to find Sami's vehicle. Other than the band's hammered brown Dodge van, the dusty little Camry was the only car in the parking lot.

"Start the van," Eddie told Mike. The big Mexican piled into the driver's seat and got the engine growling; Jim and Twitch followed Eddie to look at the waitress's car. "Crank the AC up as high as you can!" Eddie yelled over his shoulder as Mike ground his window open with the old-fashioned crank-style handle.

But there was nothing in the Camry. A bent pine tree freshener, a purse with a few dog-eared bucks in it, a credit card and a driver's license, and a book so creased in the spine it almost fell apart as Eddie picked it up: *Chicken Soup for the Waitress's Soul.*

"Nuts," Eddie muttered. "Check the trunk," he called to Twitch and pushed the button that opened it.

He sat in the driver's seat and leafed through the *Chicken Soup* book. It was full of stories about cute animals, and people helping each other, and good folks ground down by life who had faith and therefore things eventually went their way. Optimistic bullshit, all of it. Buy my book, because I will tell you what you want to believe, that you can change your life with the pure and holy power of your hope. Eddie snorted, but not too hard. He didn't really disdain the book, any more than he disdained its readers. He almost admired them—they were trying to put a good face on existence, trying to live happy lives.

Really, it was better that they didn't know the truth.

Eddie rummaged through the glove compartment. A compact mirror, a stub of lipstick, a ballpoint pen without a cap.

Nothing else.

"Hell." He got out of the car.

Bam, bam, bam! Mike pounded on the outside of the van's door with his fist. "Come on, man!" he shouted. "Adrian's *dying!*"

"I remember," Eddie muttered.

"Nothing in the trunk," Twitch reported. "Unless you think antifreeze will help our boy." The fairy held up a sloshing blue jug and grinned.

"Nothing in the car, either," Eddie reported. "We may be out of luck." Then he found the bookmark in the middle of *Chicken Soup*—it was a pamphlet, printed cheap on a photocopy machine on a single sheet of paper. "Hold on."

Jim loomed over him, leaning in close.

"What is it?" Mike called.

"That doesn't look Christian," Twitch observed. "Not that I'm an expert, but don't you people usually put Jesus on your pamphlets?"

Twitch was right, it didn't look Christian. *First Church of the Redeemer Nehushtan* was the title printed on the front of the pamphlet, over an image that looked like a caduceus, a snake twisted around a tall cross. Under the serpent-cross was the name *Phineas Irving, Preacher.* "Yeah," Eddie agreed. "We do."

He flipped open the pamphlet to look at the inside. There was an address and a short quotation that Eddie knew immediately: *"And these signs shall follow them that believe; In my name shall they cast out devils; they shall speak with new tongues; They shall take up serpents; and if they drink any deadly thing, it shall not hurt them: they shall lay hands on the sick, and they shall recover."*

"Mark sixteen," he said. "The pamphlet's Christian. I think."

"Bible?" Twitch asked.

"They shall take up serpents," Eddie read out loud. "They shall lay hands on the sick, and they shall recover."

"That sounds fitting," Twitch looked at the pamphlet, nodding as if he could read.

"It's Bible," Eddie said, and Jim nodded.

"It's Bible again, Mike!" Twitch called out to the band's bassist. "Wouldn't you know it?"

"Chingado," Mike grumbled. "Moses half or Jesus half?"

"Jesus half," Eddie said. "But does it matter?"

Mike shrugged. "Just saying I should have read that when I had the chance. Instead of all those comic books."

"Yeah," Eddie shot back, "you should have. But you ain't dead, so it ain't too late."

"Too late for me," Mike shook his head.

"It ain't too late," Eddie disagreed. "It ain't too late for anyone."

"Not even for the damned?" Mike asked. It wasn't an academic question, not for any of them, but Eddie let it hang. It was only mid-afternoon, and he'd already had more than enough hell and damnation to last him the day. "But what good does it do Adrian?"

Eddie noticed some scribbling at the back of the pamphlet and looked closer. *APEP*, someone had written. Next to a squiggly line. He frowned, feeling an uncomfortable nervousness at the base of his spine.

In the distance, he heard sirens. Could be the fire department, from some bigger town, or maybe the county owned fire trucks. Could be an ambulance. Could be cops. None of those would be much of a problem.

He held up the pamphlet for Jim to see. Jim shot his ice blue eyes over it quickly, and nodded.

"Come on," Eddie said to Twitch, and he climbed into the shotgun seat. Jim and the fairy got into the back.

Eddie set his chunky watch to a two hour, forty-five minute countdown.

"Where are we going?" Mike asked.

Eddie flipped back to the front page of the pamphlet and picked up his sawed-off shotgun. "This is your lucky day, Mike," he said. "It ain't even Sunday, and we're going to church."

CHAPTER THREE

"Who's the redeemer Nehushtan?" Mike asked. The bass player was driving, but he rolled slowly through town, a little directionless, and he spared a glance for the pamphlet. "I know there's a lot of saints, but I don't think I've heard of that one. Is he one of the weird ones, like he sat on a pole for forty years or had his skin peeled off or somebody forced him to eat his own ears?"

They rolled past Correia's just as the big manager, Owen, shuffled through the bar's front door with Adrian slung across his shoulder. He winked and waved before he disappeared.

"The Nehushtan ain't a saint," Eddie said. "It's an object. Book of Numbers."

"Who knew that memorizing the Bible would be such a useful thing for the guitar player in a rock and roll band?" Twitch smirked.

"I haven't *memorized* it," Eddie grumbled. "I've just *read* it." Hadn't memorized *all* of it, anyway.

"Fine," Mike surrendered. "Next time we stay in a motel nice enough to have a Gideon in the drawer, I'll steal it. Happy?"

"Not really."

"So what is it?" Twitch asked. "Is it a snake?"

"And where are we going?" Mike asked.

The sirens and flashing lights ahead drew closer. It looked like a couple of sheriff's deputies in a pickup. "Let's ask Officer Friendly," Eddie suggested.

"Uh … what?"

Eddie leaned over from the shotgun seat, enjoying the squirt of conditioned air hitting his face from the slits in the dashboard, weak as it was, and jammed his hand on the horn. Mike braked, the van shuddering to a halt, and the truck slowed to meet them.

"Twitch," Eddie warned the fairy he was at bat.

"Got it," Twitch said.

Mike and the driver of the sheriff's truck both rolled their windows down. The deputy was a sour-faced man with thick eyebrows.

"You got something to tell us about the fire, son," he said gruffly to Mike, "you'd better not leave the scene." The truck was in neutral but he revved the engine, making the point that he was on official business and in a hurry.

Twitch leaned over Mike's shoulder, taking on a more feminine look. It had taken Eddie a good long while to get used to the way the fairy shifted back and forth between male and female, and then was sometimes an animal, but he thought nothing of it anymore.

"We're not going anywhere, deputy," Twitch said. "We're parked right here, waiting for you." He winked.

"Right," the deputy grunted, pleased. He pulled up the truck's handbrake. "And what do you know about the fire?" He seemed to have completely forgotten that there actually was a fire, even as he was discussing it. Whatever training should have sent him to the conflagration to rescue people in peril, direct traffic, or whatever, evaporated under the direct assault of Twitch's Glamour.

"The snake did it," Twitch smiled. "A snake in the kitchen."

"Did you manage to get your hands on the snake?" the second deputy leered. He was heavier, and wore a cowboy hat and a mustache.

"Easy," Eyebrows objected. "She's a lady." Eddie almost laughed out loud at that one. Whatever the deputy was seeing, it wasn't the silver-haired drummer in black leather and spikes. And he definitely wasn't seeing the horse's tail.

Jim shifted impatiently.

"Address, Twitch," Eddie muttered from the shotgun seat. "Adrian's dying, remember."

"I'm new to town, gentlemen," Twitch said to the two lawmen, "and I'm looking for someone. His name is—" he took the pamphlet from Eddie, "Phineas Irving, and his address—"

"Crazy son of a bitch," said Mustache.

"You one of his weirdos, then?" asked Eyebrows. "I mean, parishioners?"

"We get complaints," Mustache said darkly. "Snake worshippers, or some crazy nonsense like that, and laying on of hands," he practically slobbered at the words, "I think we all know what *that* means."

"He's my cousin," Twitch lied smoothly. "I'm just visiting."

Eyebrows jerked a thumb over his own shoulder in the direction of the big box store. "Turn right at the Sears," he said. "Nothing else out there but your cousin and the rattlesnakes."

"You've been very helpful," Twitch batted his eyes at the deputies. "I'm sorry you won't remember anything about me."

"Me, too," Mustache grinned, thinking he was still flirting.

Eddie tapped Mike's shoulder. "That's your cue," he whispered, and Mike put the van into gear. The deputies waved like excited little kids as the Dodge rolled forward and they disappeared from view.

"Ugh," Twitch flopped back onto his seat. "Two men at the same time is so exhausting."

Mike gulped and kept his eyes on the road.

"Only two?" Eddie chuckled. "It looked to me like you had Mike here going, too."

Twitch yawned and stretched himself. "That's our Mikey," he said. "Excitable boy."

"Mike," the bass player muttered. "Call me Mike." He looked a little grumpy, and Jim slapped him on the shoulder to cheer him up.

Eddie turned from his band mates, saw the Sears—

and was stunned.

Ice swept the ground around the blocky retailer, thick and bleak as a Minnesota lake in winter, with bodies stuck in it. Faces emerged from the ice, hundreds of them dotting the frozen plain like geese on a pond. Blue lips moaned soundlessly, and a bitter wind ripped through and around the heads, whipping up crystal flurries of snow and ice, tearing at their ears and noses and ripping away bits of flesh.

Eddie was grateful for the burns on his bum. Their grinding pain reminded him that the vision was just a vision.

"Damn," he shuddered and looked away, rubbing his eyes.

"Where do I turn?" Mike asked, and Eddie had to look back. "There's only a parking lot."

He still saw the sheet of ice and the tortured heads. The sight of it hurt Eddie, and it frightened him. His glimpses of Hell were constant, but they were rarely sustained. He saw a person or a small knot of people being tortured by Azazel's minions and then his vision passed on. He never saw this many, and he never held a vision this long.

"Am I the only one seeing this?" he asked.

Mike shrugged. "What, the crappy run down Sears with the dirt parking lot and no right turn?" he asked, and then he understood. "Oh."

"I'm the only one," Eddie said.

"*Carajo*," Mike said by way of expressing sympathy.

Eddie couldn't look, and he couldn't really keep from looking. He would have sworn the heads were looking back at him, and he felt naked and guilty. He saw the damned all the time, but the damned never saw him. What was this vision? What was this place? He shrank within himself, and then he realized something was tapping on his shoulder.

It was Jim. The singer reached past Eddie now and pointed. Out his Infernal Eye, Eddie saw only the glacier of the damned and the wind that gnawed at their heads, but if he concentrated on the other eye, he thought he saw a dirt road exiting the parking lot at its far end. He pointed too, hesitant and uncertain.

"I see it," Mike said, and turned the van into the lot.

The heads stared at Eddie as he drove through. His vision was silent, but the frost-furred lips and bluing flesh were so vivid, he imagined he could hear the crumbling, terrified moans of the damned souls. Eyes sunk deep into black pits, their lashes ripped away by the frozen wind, rolled in their sockets to stare at him as the Dodge trundled across the parking lot. They were so close, and so many, and had been there so long, that Eddie began to feel *cold*.

And then they were gone, and the van was back in the griddle-hot and griddle-flat desert of the Oklahoma panhandle, rattling along a dirt road between two fields of burnt-brown wheat stalks.

Eddie sucked in a deep breath and let it out slowly.

"What the hell is wrong with that Sears?" he asked.

"I dunno," Mike shrugged. "Jeez, you tell me."

"I … I …" Eddie groped blindly. "I don't know. There was something really bad there." He kneed open the glove compartment, took out a box of bullets and started reloading the Glock's emptied clips. The ammunition ritual gave him a little tactile comfort, but no distraction. He wished he had a cup of hot coffee to sip.

"Is it following us?" Twitch asked.

Eddie looked back over his shoulder, past gig bags, amps and stacks of Adrian's electronic gizmos and through the rear windows. He saw only desert.

"No," he dropped himself into his seat and sighed. "Forget it."

"Yeah," Mike agreed, "forget it. Tell me about the Nehushtan."

"It was a snake," Eddie spat out, trying to block the images of the frozen damned from his mind's eye.

"Following us?" Twitch asked. "A snake at the Sears?"

"No," Eddie said. "I mean the Nehushtan. You're right, Twitch, it was a snake. A snake on a stick. The Israelites in the desert, they were bitten, the Bible says, by a bunch of fiery serpents."

"Moses half," Mike said, like it was an important insight.

"Moses half, the Israelites after they left Egypt. Like with Charlton Heston. And Moses put a snake on a stick and raised it up, and when the Israelites looked at it they were healed. That snake was the Nehushtan."

"They were healed of their snake bites," Mike concluded. "Adrian was bitten by a snake."

"And this guy's church says it's the church of the Redeemer Nehushtan," Eddie said. "It can't be a coincidence that it's here. It can't be a coincidence that the waitress … Sami, it can't be a coincidence that she had this pamphlet in her car."

"Could be he's the one who knocked her up," Twitch suggested cheerfully.

"Could be she was going to him for help," Mike had a different take. "What was that Bible bit you read on it? People holding snakes and not getting bitten, or something? Lay on hands and heal people?"

"Either way," Eddie growled, "it's the right place to start looking for a cure. Or maybe it's the right place to start looking for the problem, which is sometimes the same thing. Only I don't know what this other thing is." He turned the pamphlet over and read the end of it again. "Apep."

"Oh, that's easy," said Twitch. "That's not from the Bible."

"I know that," Eddie rumbled. "So what is it?" He saw a row of naked men, pinned to the road in front of the Dodge with long jagged wooden spikes like thorns through their bellies. The van rolled over them with the same bumping it made on the dirt road, and Eddie was glad for the new vision of torment—it was brief, and it almost helped him forget the frozen Hell-Sears.

Almost.

"Apep is one of the Egyptians," Twitch said lightly. "He's a snake, as it happens."

"Or maybe not just *as it happens*," Eddie countered. "*Snakes* seem to be the order of the day."

"*Mierda.*"

"Right." Twitch considered. "Well, that's not good. He's not thought of as one of the good ones, not even by the Egyptians, and you know how crazy they can be. Bird-headed men and dogs with aardvark snouts and all that crazy mixing up of forms." He grinned mischievously. "Hilarious."

"What does he do?" Eddie asked.

"Ah …" Twitch thought. "I don't know. Eats people. He's a giant snake, what do giant snakes do? Shed giant skin? Dance for giant flute players? Live under giant sheds?"

"So we got an Egyptian snake god on a pamphlet printed by a guy who preaches under the sign of the snake, which we found in the car of a woman who gave birth to a bunch of snakes that ate her alive." Eddie grabbed the Remington 870, checked its magazine and shoved a handful of shells into his pocket. "That about sum it up?"

"And Adrian was bitten by a snake," Twitch reminded him.

Jim pointed again. At the top of a very slight rise sagged a dilapidated yellow and blue double-wide trailer. Above it, a tilted rusty weathervane rooster dawdled lazily back and forth, and to one side, half-collapsed and leaning right up against the wall of the trailer, slouched a big dirty canvas tent. At the start of the dirt track that turned off and led to the trailer, a sheet of plywood hung nailed to a lashed tripod of two-by-fours. On the plywood was painted a ragged cross, and a long snake coiled around it, meeting the viewer's gaze with beady eyes and flickering tongue.

"Friendly," Mike joked.

"Cheerful!" Twitch added.

"Better than Sears," Eddie shot back. "Best park the van here. We don't want to go in guns blazing, in case we need this guy's help."

Mike stopped the van and they piled out. Jim took his sword this time, buckling its belt around his waist right over his jeans. Twitch looked unarmed, but he was always able to produce those wooden batons he used both to play the drums and to pound the minions of Hell over the head. Mike had the .45 semi-auto he'd picked up in New Mexico tucked into his belt; as an afterthought, he grabbed a knife out of the driver's side door pocket and stuck it in his pants.

It was Eddie's van, more or less, and he tried to keep it full of weapons. It was easy enough, when you didn't really have to worry about questions from the cops.

Eddie carried the Glock in its shoulder holster and the Remington hanging off a sling. His old green jacket's pockets were stuffed full of things that could be useful, too, though most of them weren't weapons per se—pocket knives, a compass, string, a deck of playing cards, matches, duct tape, that sort of thing. The duct tape especially came in handy when you played in the kind of band where your gear was always falling apart. He had a couple of odd knick-knacks that really just had emotional value, too, he could admit to himself, like a plastic cup full of jacks and a red bouncing ball. In a pinch, he could kill a person with any one of those things, if nothing else, by stuffing them down the poor bastard's throat.

Even the jacks.

Giant snake gods, he was less sure about.

The afternoon sun hammered down hot, despite a stiff desert breeze that came and went, thick with the scent of sagebrush. "I got point," he told the others, "and Mike's got the rear. Keep an eye on the van. Twitch, get overhead and give it a look." He turned and headed out.

He heard Twitch's sharp cry as the fairy sprang into the air, and the silver falcon's horse's tail brushed Eddie's head as he took flight, racing up the gentle slope and towards the trailer. Twitch was pretty—though kind of weird—as a bird, but Eddie had seen it before, and kept his attention focused. For all that he didn't want to kick in the door, he didn't want to get caught with his pants around his ankles either, so he walked with the Remington in his hand, pointed down at the ground but ready to pull up and shoot if he needed it.

Eddie was calm, and normally he trusted his own judgment and coolness. He still felt a bit shaken by his vision of the backcountry Sears, though. He worried he might see frozen heads sticking out the ground and feel like he had to shoot them.

Instead, he heard a hiss and a rattle off to his right. He turned, brought up the stubby nose of the shotgun and almost fired, anyway.

But Jim got there first. With a loud *snick!* his sword jumped from its scabbard and the head of the rattlesnake snapped off and went flying into the brush. The snake's body, scaly yellow-brown and surprisingly long, danced spastically before collapsing into the dust.

And then suddenly there were two more snakes lifting their heads from the dust to threaten Jim. The big singer kicked one incoming with his boot, sending it sailing into the back of the church's plywood sign with a loud, meaty *thud*. The second lost its head like its companion.

"*Huevos!*"

And then there were a dozen.

"Twitch!" Eddie yelled.

So much for the quiet approach. Eddie pumped the shotgun and waded into the hissing curtain of rattlesnakes.

Boom! went Eddie's shotgun. *Snick!* followed Jim's sword. And then Mike finally got his gun out of his pants and joined in, *bang! bang! bang!*

"I don't like this!" Eddie shouted, stepping over spattered snake meat to take aim at another serpent, blasting it to oblivion.

Jim nodded and pointed up at the trailer by way of answer. He skewered two rattlesnakes with a single deft stab of his blade and then scraped them off with the instep of his heavy boot.

Mike saw Jim's gesture and led the way, jogging up the track towards the trailer. He got ahead of Eddie, who took a couple of seconds to turn around and follow, but Eddie could tell by Mike's continued shots, and the plumes of dirt that exploded into the air around the bass player, that he was still threatened by attacking snakes.

Jim brought up the rear. Eddie didn't worry much about him, and worried even less when Twitch swooped down suddenly from the blue sky to snatch up a pair of snakes, one in each claw.

Mike, though, looked like he was in trouble. Snakes closed in on him from behind, and on both right and left, as he staggered over a cattle guard and between two driftwood fence posts. He fired again and then dug into his pocket for his second clip.

The big guy stumbled—

Eddie whipped up his shotgun and broke into a run as snakes swarmed out of the tall dry grass and sage, slithering towards the bass player on the ground—

and then a wave of gray-brown fur washed over Mike. Something like a dog—several things that looked like dogs, or maybe foxes, it was hard to tell at this distance—scurried over Mike's back and legs and threw themselves at the snakes.

Something was helping Mike. That gave Eddie the breathing room he needed to blast a couple of rattlers out of his own way, and then he was on top of the bass player, grabbing Mike by his elbow and dragging him to his feet.

"*Cojón!*" Mike shouted. Jim caught up with them and they raced for the double-wide. Bouncing blue and yellow in his jogging vision, the little building didn't look cheerful at all—it looked ominous and false, like a clown's greasepaint smile. The trailer sat on blocks, Eddie saw, and was hugged by a rough wraparound plank porch. Under the trailer was darkness, and he wondered if there were more snakes lurking. And if there weren't, what was lurking inside? Was Phineas Irving, preacher, some kind of snake-summoning warlock, sending his minions at them by mind control?

But zigzagging lines were chopped into the planks of the porch, and though Eddie saw snakes coiling and sliding on the ground right up to the edge of the wood, he noticed that none of them actually so much as touched the planks.

"What are those things, badgers?" Mike shot at another snake. "Ferrets?"

"You'd have been a great farmer, Mike," Eddie laughed. Jim swiped with his sword and swept three snakes out of the way, clearing a path to the porch. Eddie and Mike charged through, with the singer on their heels, and then they spun to look at the field of snakes behind them.

Twitch the falcon snatched another snake from the ground, tearing it in half with his talons and shattering its skull with his beak. The gray-brown things, whatever they were, played havoc with the snakes. They had long faces and bodies and tails but stubby little ears, and they were quick as bullets, slipping out under every rattler's strike and then biting snakes through their windpipes, killing them instantly.

"Weasels?" Eddie guessed. It had been a long time since he'd earned his Mammals merit badge. Whatever these things were, he hadn't seen any in Chicago. Or Iraq. He kept the Remington trained on the snakes nearest him—just because they hadn't come on the porch yet didn't mean they couldn't or wouldn't do so now. But the rattlers hissed, shook their tails at him, showed him their long, curving fangs, and stayed back.

Twitch alighted beside the three of them, melting into his human form. He chose his female shape, which Eddie assumed was for Mike's benefit and the amusement it gave the fairy, because Mike saw Twitch and did a double-take. "Whatever it is," Twitch hazarded, "it isn't cats."

"Cats?" Mike asked.

"Mongoose," said a voice Eddie didn't know, and he realized the colossal screw-up he'd just committed. "Hands up."

Eddie relaxed his grip on the shotgun, letting it dangle by its strap from his right shoulder. He raised his hands over his head, his companions doing the same, and they turned to look at the source of the voice.

The man was tall and wiry, the kind of wiriness you got by living in the desert and not taking in enough water or calories. The skin of his face and his big knuckles was sunburned and rubbed raw by the wind, and a shock of bristly yellow hair made his head look like a scrub brush. A once-nice gray wool suit jacket hung off him like a trench coat off a scarecrow. He squinted down the barrel of an M1917 Enfield into Eddie's chest. That would be a .30-06 cartridge, Eddie knew, and it would blow a hole in him the size of a pineapple.

"You Phineas Irving, by any chance?" Eddie asked.

Chapter Four

I'm the owner of this land," the scarecrow spat out. "And you're trespassers." His elbow was a little jittery, but his aim didn't waver.

"Mierda."

"Easy," Eddie said. "We didn't come looking for a fight." Jim looked poised to stab the guy; that he hadn't done it yet probably meant he took seriously the threat that the homeowner would kill Eddie.

"You have guns out," the blond man pointed out. "You're shooting."

"At snakes!" Eddie snapped, exasperated. "Didn't you notice you're surrounded?"

The gunman dropped his elbows to his sides and seemed to relax, just a little. The gray-brown animals bounded up onto the porch and cuddled around his ankles. "Yeah," he said, "but the fact that you're carrying them at all makes me nervous. And your friend has a sword."

Jim's nostrils flared menacingly.

"He's old-fashioned," Eddie said. "And this is Oklahoma. Aren't we required by law to carry guns?"

The man grunted and considered. "I'm Irving," he admitted. "What do you want?"

"Can we talk?" Eddie suggested. Irving hadn't shot him when he had the chance, which made him think the preacher might not be a bad guy. "We're just looking for a little information."

"Put down the guns," Irving countered. "And the sword. And if the fairy talks, I start shooting."

Eddie was a little unsettled that Phineas Irving had spotted Twitch for a fairy. It probably meant that he had seen Twitch transform himself from falcon form. And it definitely meant that he knew enough about the real nature of the world not to be freaked out at the thought of fairies. And he knew that if Twitch talked, he might pull out the Glamour.

But he unslung the shotgun and laid it on the planks, and Mike and Jim followed his lead.

Eddie didn't mention the Glock.

"You preach under the sign of the serpent," Eddie observed. "But it's the raised serpent, the one that heals snakebite."

"Oh?"

"The Nehushtan."

"You know your Old Testament," Irving conceded. He kept the rifle pointed at Eddie's chest. "Or you read the signboard. Good for you. How did you find me and what's the information you want?"

"If I could just reach into my pocket?" Eddie waited for the preacher's slight nod, and he pulled out the church brochure. He unfolded it and showed it to Irving.

"You friends of Sami's?" There was a note of concern in the man's voice. "How is she?"

"How did you know that was Sami's?" Mike sounded impressed. "What, did you only print one of them?"

"I only *wrote on* one of them." Irving nodded at the squiggle and the name *APEP*.

"You got the drop on us," Eddie noted calmly, "and either way we need your help. Maybe you'd better tell us whose side you're on."

Phineas Irving chuckled bitterly. "Choose you this day," he quoted.

"Joshua," Eddie said. "Moses half," he added, for Mike's benefit.

"As for me and my house," Irving nodded at the plywood sign of the Nehushtan, "we will serve the Lord."

"And Apep?" Eddie asked.

"Sami had a … a problem," Irving said. "She came to me, and I tried to help her."

"I think she gave birth to her problem," Mike grunted. "And it ate her. Not to mention a lot of other people, almost including us."

"Dammit."

"Yeah," Eddie agreed. "Flying poisonous snakes. *Dammit* is right."

"And you?" Irving asked. "The snakes wanted to bite you, so you're not one of theirs. Whose side are *you* on?"

"Mostly," Eddie told him, "we're on our own side. But we have a problem, and I think we need your help."

Irving looked at the four of them, his inspection lingering on Twitch. "Are you telling me the fairy's pregnant?" he asked.

"Ew!" Twitch snorted.

Irving failed to make good his threat, and shot no one. Eddie noticed the omission, and relaxed a few degrees.

"I'm telling you that our buddy … our organ player, actually, got bitten by one of … one of Sami's problems."

"When?"

Eddie checked his watch. "About half an hour ago."

"Then your friend is dead."

"He might be," Eddie agreed, "but he might not. He's a wizard, and he put himself into some kind of magical coma right after he was bitten. I think he meant to slow down the poison, and I'm hoping it worked. But it won't mean anything if we don't find a cure."

"You're hoping that because I have the Nehushtan raised over my church that I can cure your friend," Irving finished the thought. He didn't bat an eye at the word *wizard*.

"Yeah," Mike said.

"Pick up your weapons," Phineas Irving said, "and come inside."

"Can I talk now?" Twitch asked impishly.

"Depends on what you say," Irving answered. He patted the stock of his rifle affectionately, like he was patting a baby's bum. "I'm still armed."

The inside of the trailer was an unholy mess, but not the kind of mess Eddie expected. There was no sign of drugs or booze or personal filth, and it smelled okay, but the trailer was full of books and papers in total disarray. It was like a library-meteorite had hit inside and exploded, scattering handwritten notes and diagrams all over the place. The linoleum countertop and the plastic coffee table and the sunken-centered couches fraying at the shoulders were all barely visible under snowdrifts of paper.

"Read much?" Mike asked.

"Not enough," Irving said grimly. He gestured at the couches. "Shove that stuff onto the table. Coffee?"

"Please." Eddie meant it. He and Jim shoveled papers aside so the band could sit down. He sat on the nearest couch and sank deeply into it—the couch was ugly, but worn to the perfect point of comfort. But for the scorched skin of his backside, the couch might have put him to sleep.

"I'll put on a fresh pot."

"Screw that," Eddie said. "Gimme the coffee. Black."

"I'll take sugar, cream, whatever you got," Mike added.

"When my brother and I fell out," the preacher recounted, pouring coffee into chipped mugs, "it was over a woman."

"Isn't it always?" Mike grunted.

"I totally wanna hear your life story," Eddie said. "It sounds like country music, and I am definitely a fan of Nashville. First, can you tell me how to help my friend?"

"I'm telling you now," Irving said, shuffling slowly across the scabby shag floor with mugs in his fists. He was a little shaky, but he managed not to spill. It didn't escape Eddie's notice that he'd left the rifle in the kitchenette. "It's the woman. And *fell out* is something of an understatement."

Eddie took the coffee. It smelled bitter and the warm mug stung his burned hands at the touch. He took a sip and felt strengthened. "Ah," he sighed, "acid for the battery. Go on."

"Her name was Miriam," the preacher said. He drew up a three-legged stool and settled his lanky frame onto it. His pets flopped down on the floor next to him and wrestled each other. "Maybe it still is. I loved her very much."

Jim snorted. It was a cynical sound.

"Don't talk much, do you?" Irving asked the singer.

"He's cursed," Eddie said. It was sort of a lie, but it was much simpler than trying to explain the whole story. "So this woman of yours, Miriam, she can heal snakebite?"

"Jeez," Mike muttered, "you don't know how to tell a story. Get to the part where something happens already."

Irving ignored both of them. "I was an Egyptologist," he said, and then he chuckled wryly. "Who am I kidding? I was a grad student at Penn, studying to be an Egyptologist. I was going to be to the next Flinders Petrie. I was doing physical archaeology, potsherds and garbage heaps. Miriam was in my program. She was doing the sexier stuff, the Coffin Texts and Old Kingdom demonology. She was young and beautiful and I fell in love. I thought we both did. We got engaged."

Eddie saw a man and a woman, naked, standing behind the preacher. They were emaciated, their hair falling out. Each held a jagged saw to the other's abdomen and yanked back and forth on the handle. Blood gushed down, drenching their legs. He resisted the urge to make fun of the man for the romance in his story. "Go on."

"My brother Aaron was studying theology," Irving continued. "He became obsessed with old gnostic documents about apotheosis, the divinization of man. Crazy stuff, all about men becoming like the gods, or becoming angels."

"Yeah, crazy," Mike muttered.

"And it was all in Coptic, so he and Miriam spent a lot of time together."

"But in these gnostic books," Eddie probed, "in the Coffin Texts or whatever, Miriam learned how to deal with these flying snakes? Where is she? Is she in town here?"

"She's close," Irving said dryly. "While we were engaged, she and Aaron became lovers. When I … found out about it, when she told me about it, you know, she said it had nothing to do with love, and nothing to do with me, it had to do with the ritual."

"So you called it off," Mike concluded. "Sent the skank packing."

"What ritual?" Eddie asked.

"They wanted to summon Apep, but there were steps they had to take before that, to become his true worshippers. To get his gifts. Apep's a snake god—well, a snake *devil*, really—and his worship is orgiastic, so they ... they became involved."

"Isn't that your family, Jim?" Twitch asked. "I mean, aren't you all cousins or something, according to Eddie? Family reunions must be so entertaining."

Jim glowered at the drummer and drew his sword partly out of the sheath, exposing six inches of sharp blade.

"But why on earth would they want to summon the big snake?" Twitch asked, ignoring the bared weapon. The fairy looked more curious than shocked. "There are easier ways to commit suicide."

"Power, I think," Irving said wearily. "And immortality."

"The snake sheds its skin, born anew each time," Eddie whispered to himself. "Are they crazy? Can they possibly be right?"

"I think both," Phineas Irving said. "I found out on our honeymoon. I woke up in the middle of the night in the hotel and she was gone, so I rang her cell phone. When I heard it in the room next door, I broke in and found them." He stopped talking and his eyes glazed over. His face was drawn and pale.

"Orgiastic, you said." Mike fidgeted. He stared at the mongooses, tussling and tossing each other about on the trailer's shag carpet. "Does that mean what it sounds like?"

"What does it sound like?" Twitch winked.

Mike hesitated. "Like *orgy* plus *fantastic*."

"You mean like *ginormous*," Eddie snorted. "*Giant* plus *enormous*."

"Yes," Irving whispered, and looked down at the floor. "That's about what it means."

Eddie respected the other man's pain and waited.

"There were snakes everywhere," the Egyptologist said slowly. "And incense, a cloud of it so thick I couldn't see or breathe. And then I saw a light ... like a gap in the air, and on the other side of it was lightning. And when the hole was gone, there was a crowd of people chanting and shaking rattles. And in the middle, there they were. Only ... only ..." He couldn't seem to get it out, whatever it was.

"Only they were snakes," Twitch guessed. "Snakes and humans at the same time, all mixed up, like the Egyptians like to do."

Eddie felt sick. "Monsters."

Irving nodded miserably. "Aaron's arms were gone, and instead he had snakes growing out of his shoulders. Once the incense cleared and the light was gone, I could see it clearly, because he was naked. And Miriam ..."

"Miriam got what she wanted," Twitch said. The fairy's voice was gentle. Eddie thought that was pretty generous of him, since only a few minutes earlier Phineas Irving had threatened to shoot Twitch if he opened his mouth.

"Miriam is a lamia," Irving told them. He couldn't meet their eyes, and just sat staring a hole into the carpet.

Mike looked baffled.

"Lower half of a snake," Eddie said. "Upper half of a woman. Ugh. Sorry, man. I didn't know you could *become* one."

"Jeez, I really gotta read the Bible one of these days." Mike shook his head in amazement.

"Snakes for hair, too," the preacher said. "Aaron and their ... cultists ... wanted to kill me, but Miriam stopped them. She told me what she'd been doing, and let me go."

"And *then* you divorced the bitch," Mike said. "'Cause a snake ... Jeez ..."

Phineas Irving shook his head. "She spared me. Besides, I was in love with her. I'm still in love with her now." He dug into the pocket of his jacket and pulled out a creased and folded letter envelope. He shook out its contents, and a single gold ring, heavy and dull, fell into his palm.

"Did they summon Apep, then?" Twitch asked.

"They're still trying," Irving said. He clenched his fists together in a big ball of knuckles around the wedding ring. "And I followed them here to try to stop them."

"That's why you're penned in by snakes?" Mike asked. "They know you're here?"

"They know I'm here," Irving agreed. "I keep the snakes at bay with my mongooses and my jerry-rigged charms. I preach against them, but the county thinks I'm crazy, so they send deputies and social workers to harass me. Almost no one listens, anyway. I try to help people I can—people like Sami, who get involved with the cult and then want to leave—and I try to figure out how to stop the summoning. They don't care. They sit just down the road and laugh at me."

"Down the road?" Mike asked.

Jim sat up, suddenly alert and looking curiously at Eddie. Even the mongooses stopped wrestling, and their stubby round ears perked up.

The hair on the back of Eddie's neck prickled. "Sears," he said. "Tell me they're not in that old shitbucket Sears we passed."

Irving just nodded.

Eddie felt a thick lump at the back of his throat. "I was hoping you'd say that you can raise up the Nehushtan on a pole and Adrian would look at it and be cured," he said. "Like in the Bible. Now you're telling me that your ... wife ... is a lamia, and she knows the cure."

Irving shook his head. "She doesn't *know* the cure."

Eddie scratched his head. "Then my memory's shorting out on me, or I just don't get it. You said *it's the woman*."

"She doesn't *know* the cure. She *is* the cure."

"There's no Nehushtan?" Eddie pressed. "You just put up a signboard to announce that you're a snake hater?"

"There's a Nehushtan," Phineas said, and he jerked his head at the back door of the double-wide. "It's in the tent, and it might even be *the* Nehushtan. But I've never cured anybody with it. I've got enough juice to keep snakes out of the tent, and that's about it."

"Juice?" Twitch asked.

"The Nehushtan is powered by faith," Irving said. "Faith's not my strong suit." He put the ring back into the envelope and jammed it into his pocket again. "Snakes do stay out of the tent when I'm preaching, though, so that's good."

"Huevos."

"So what's the cure?" Eddie asked, slightly puzzled. "Is this some kind of voodoo thing, like the snakes are her offspring and so you can cure the children's bites with some of the mother's blood? Hair of the dog?"

"They're not her children," Irving grouched. "They're Aaron's."

Eddie felt sick. "You mean it's still an orgiastic cult," he said. "And girls like Sami …"

Irving nodded. "Young girls, girls alone who need jobs and help," he finished. "They get taken in and … they get taken. Boys, too. By Aaron, or by someone else in the cult. They're all monsters, or they want to become monsters. And some of the kids escape, I try to help if I can. But if they don't, then their bodies are consumed by their children. And by the other worshippers of the snake."

Mike looked shaken.

"What do you mean, you try to help?" Eddie demanded. "How did you *help* that poor girl? She was still stuck in this town, right next to the temple of the snake. Why didn't you get her out?"

Irving buried his face in his hands. "She was going to leave tomorrow," he muttered, and ran his fingers through his bristly hair. "Collect her last paycheck and leave. And I thought I had hexed her womb, killed the snakes inside. I thought she'd get to her aunt's house in Dallas and be in for a terrible shock when she delivered dead snakes … she'd make the *National Enquirer*, but she'd be alive."

"She didn't know," Eddie realized. He remembered how delighted Sami had seemed when she thought her baby was kicking. "She thought her baby was just a normal human kid. She wanted a boy."

"Should I have told her?" Irving had despair in his face. "Would you want your daughter to know that she had snakes in her womb? I did what I could, and I thought I had done enough. I thought the danger was controlled."

"Your hex failed," Twitch said sharply. It was an awfully direct statement from the fairy, Eddie thought, and unusually judgmental.

The mongooses hissed. They chased their own tails and looked skittishly into the corners of the room.

"Jeez, are there any wizards who actually know what they're doing?" Mike asked.

"Not me," Irving said. "I'm no wizard, I'm just an Egyptologist. Not even that, I'm ABD, never got my degree. Whatever I know, I learned by reading the old monuments, execration texts, second millennium B.C. medical treatises. Or from folklore. Some of it works. I think the hex I put on this house works—anyway, the snakes don't come in."

"Anyway, it ain't a house," Mike grumbled. "It's an advertisement for meth lab tenants."

"And the Nehushtan?" Eddie asked. "You get the instructions for that out of a book?"

"I stole it. The University had it in its museum collection, and I had access because of the work I was doing on the Wadi Hammamat grave finds. I took it with me when I left. I don't know if it's authentic or not—neither did they, it was a recent acquisition and they were still examining it. But it works. At least, sort of."

"You and Adrian have a lot in common, really," Mike mused. "You a napper?"

"What?"

"What are you doing to stop the summoning?" Eddie asked. He knew this was a distraction, and that he should be focused on his real challenge—Adrian, the ticking clock, and getting the wizard cured—but the thought that some sort of snake-worshipping sex cult was trying to *summon* its demon-deity caught his attention. "Was that the idea behind stealing the Nehushtan?"

"Yeah," Irving looked depressed. "But I can barely get it to flicker. It's the real deal, all right—but I'm not. Funny thing is, if our positions were switched, Aaron could probably use it like a flamethrower. He was always a believer."

"Still is," Eddie pointed out. "Just in the wrong stuff."

Irving nodded. "And the spells. The summoning—I *think*—is a sort of group performance and incantation. I only saw it the one time, of course ... on my honeymoon ... but some of the kids I've known have told me that the same kind of thing is what they experienced. I think I have some ideas about how to throw a monkey wrench into it, but I'd need to have access to their props and scripts beforehand. Well," he chuckled uneasily, "or else I'd need to be present at the ritual."

"Would that be another orgy?" Mike asked.

"Boobs," Twitch said cheerfully. Mike turned his palms up in an innocent shrug and Jim shook his head in mock frustration. "We all know what you like, is all I'm saying," the drummer added.

"Yes," Irving answered. "And at the end of the orgy, Apep is supposed to appear. Surviving worshippers will be touched by him—like Aaron and Miriam were touched."

"You mean they'll turn into freaky snake-mutants," Mike interpreted. "Dare to dream."

"Surviving?" Eddie asked.

"Most of the worshippers will be eaten."

"And what do you get out of all this?" Eddie asked. "Don't go quoting the Book of Joshua and telling me you're on the Lord's side. What is it you want here? You think this gets you to Heaven?"

Irving shrugged and looked down at his feet. "Maybe," he admitted. "If there is a Heaven. Or maybe I get my revenge. Or maybe I get my wife back."

Mike whistled. "Really? Don't you just hate her too much now?"

Eddie shook his head; he understood Phineas Irving all too well. "Says the man who ain't never been married. Love and hate ain't opposites," he told the bass player. "They're pretty near the same thing. The opposite of *both* of them is just not giving a crap."

"I give a crap," Irving agreed, but he couldn't look up.

The mongooses darted across the room and through a doggie flap in the trailer door. Jim stood and stared at the animals, his hand on his sword, but the preacher waved him down.

"They're going after snakes," Phineas Irving said. "There are always snakes."

"I'm glad you care," Eddie said, and he meant it. He hoped Irving succeeded, but he was concentrating again on his own immediate problem. He wanted to get Adrian back on his feet, play the evening's gig, and get clean out of Oklahoma. "But I'm on a clock and you still haven't answered the question I care about. How does the lamia ... Mrs. Irving ... cure snakebite?"

"Milk," Irving said. "Lamia's milk is a sovereign remedy against the bite of any snake."

Twitch laughed. "Boobs," he said again.

CRACK!

The trailer shook.

CHAPTER FIVE

Eddie spilled his coffee on his lap.

"Dammit!" he yelled, and jumped to his feet. Now he was burned front and back.

Jim was already standing, and the big man whipped out his sword and raced for the door. Twitch would have been on his heels, but the drummer got tangled up in Mike, whose knees knocked the fairy down and slowed them both. The snake preacher fell off his stool with the shuddering of the trailer, and then turned and scrambled for the kitchenette, going for his Enfield rifle.

Eddie grabbed the Remington and pumped it.

The trailer shook again.

Jim opened the door and jumped back—

a snake head jammed itself at the singer, a snake head the size of a whole ham, with a tongue as long as a human arm.

Eddie saw his shot and took it. *Boom!* The Remington's slug bit into the hinge of the serpent's jaw with a small splash of blood, and the snake pulled back.

"Is that Apep?" Mike yelled. The bass player pushed the sofa over onto its back and crouched behind it, drawing his pistol and covering the windows. From the yard, Eddie heard a surprisingly loud hissing sound.

Twitch flashed into a silver avian blur and swooped out the open door. Jim fended off a second lunge of the enormous snake's head by sliding his backside up onto the kitchenette counter, kicking with the heels of both boots. Eddie scooted to the front window of the trailer, trying to get a better look outside.

The preacher came over by the kitchenette sink with the .30-06 and looked through greasy Venetian blinds at the yard. "No," he said. "Apep should be much, much bigger. Also, I think Apep should be a straightforward serpent."

Eddie brushed aside dingy cotton flaps that served as curtains with the nose of his shotgun and threw a glance into the yard. "Hell," he said.

A shambling crew of monsters rammed themselves against the porch. The mongooses stood on hind legs and hissed a protest, but the furry little snake-eaters were out of their depth here, because their foes weren't simple snakes. They were *snake-men*. The big head that shoved at the trailer door trying to get in sprouted from the shoulders of heavy-bellied human body in denim overalls. A second monster looked like a mass of snakes, an entire hedge of them, sprouting out of a brown gabardine skirt and a pair of shapely legs. A third beast was a snake the size of a Christmas tree, with three sets of muscular human arms sprouting out of its scaly flanks and a human head. There were more, but Eddie stopped cataloguing and started shooting.

Boom! Boom!

He shattered the window and put as many slugs as he could into Overalls the snake-headed man. In the yard, Twitch harassed the other serpent-thugs, but he wasn't very effective in falcon form against creatures so large. He did manage to pluck several heads off Lady Legs the bush of serpents, but either Lady Legs grew them back immediately, or she had so many to start with that the loss of a few made no difference.

Mike crawled over to join Eddie, while Phineas Irving smashed out the window over the kitchenette sink and poked the muzzle of the Enfield out through the hole. Jim slashed and stabbed at the creatures, making Overalls bleed from several chest wounds and reducing Many Arms to One Arm Less, but the monsters didn't seem to care. They grunted and hissed, and snapped at Jim and the mongooses when they had a chance, but their focus was elsewhere.

They rammed themselves against the porch, and grabbed at it with both hands, lifting.

"They're trying to break apart the trailer!" Eddie barked, seeing the danger. "They're not getting past your hexes, so they're just going to tip us over or smash us to bits!" He leveled the Remington at a man who looked totally normal, and wore a blue-green-colored jumpsuit like he was a plumber or some sort of appliance repairman. He was squatting to get his hands under the lip of the porch, trying to rip planks out directly. Eddie got a good enough look at the man to see that the name on his chest read *Bob* and that his belly writhed, and then he squeezed the trigger. Blood spattered the porch, the khaki fabric ripped open and a mass of hissing serpents sprang from Bob's belly. Bob stumbled back, arms windmilling. Eddie glanced around the yard and guessed there might be fifteen or twenty of the snake-man-monsters besieging them. "We need another way out!"

Phineas fired three quick shots, brass shells spinning out of his bolt-action rifle like rolling dice between each *bang*. "Only other door's the back!" the preacher shouted. His face was slick with sweat and his voice quavered a little. "Through the tent, past the Nehushtan and on down the hill!"

"Chingones might be on that side, too!" Mike pointed out. The bass player emptied his clip into a bearded man whose lower body was a hissing knot of snakes—the inversion of Lady Legs—and knocked him back into the sand. Gray-brown mongooses jumped onto Snake Legged Man and bit at his snapping serpentine lower body.

"Have faith!" Eddie bellowed back, and shoved more shells into the magazine. "Jim! Out the back!" he yelled at the singer, and then he jumped into the kitchenette, grabbed Phineas Irving by the shoulder, and spun the preacher around to head him in the other direction. "Lead the way!"

Overalls rammed his snake head in through the kitchenette window; Eddie pointed the Remington at the flickering tongue, as long as Eddie's forearm, and squeezed the trigger.

Boom!

Then Eddie stumbled back through the trailer, on the heels of Irving and Mike, with Jim close behind them.

A tiny hall ended in a scratched dark brown door with a flaking plastic knob. Irving pulled at the handle and the door didn't budge. "It sticks!" he exclaimed.

The trailer shook and its wood groaned.

"No time!" Eddie shouldered Mike aside, pointed the shotgun at the doorknob and *boom!* blew it to pieces. He muscled past Mike and Irving both, pushing himself first through the door.

He hopped down a cinderblock step and into the tent, leading with his weapon. There were a few benches, rough-cut and dirty. The tent was propped up on four poles and some cross-beams that connected them; one side of the white canvas sagged to the ground, but there were no snakes. An iron tube sunk into a poured puddle of concrete served like a flag stand, and stuck into it was a wooden pole. The wood looked so ancient it was almost petrified, and nailed to the top of the pole, coiled around a stubby crosspiece, was the desiccated body of a snake, six feet long and a brilliant red that managed to gleam through layers of sand and dust. Eddie could smell the antiquity.

He blinked and tried not to focus on the infernal feast he saw at the back of the tent, haggard women ladling soup from a huge cauldron into bowls that they handed to a line of equally haggard men. The soup, Eddie saw, was thick with tiny fingers and toes.

"Clear!" he shouted, and stepped forward.

The trailer shifted again, and the other three men stumbled in behind Eddie. Twitch must be outside still, Eddie thought. He hoped the fairy was okay. He'd hate to have to find a new drummer; your choices were limited when you only let damned men join.

"Get the Nehushtan!" he barked to Irving.

"I … I can't," the preacher fumbled. "I … you're a man of faith. You carry it!"

"It won't work if I hold it," Eddie growled, "trust me."

Irving turned to Mike.

"It won't work for any of us!" Eddie snapped. "You said you could make it flicker, that's better than nothing! Pick it up and let's go!"

The trailer shook again, and Eddie heard a loud *CRASH!* inside it. He imagined the porch torn to toothpicks, and Overalls and Lady Legs trampling the shag carpet.

Phineas Irving flinched, gulped, and slung the Enfield over his shoulder. He bent to pick up the Nehushtan. "I've never tried this against … against things like those," he said. "Just the little rattlers. Just keeping them out of the tent so I could preach a little."

Eddie shrugged and stepped to the tent flap. The sagebrush and sand beyond wiggled and danced with a sea of snakes, but they stopped a few feet from the canvas. Eddie locked eyes with a particularly angry-looking diamondback and hissed right back at him. "Apep can crap 'em out big," he guessed, "and he can crap 'em out small. It's still all the same shit." He hoped he was right.

"Carry the tent," Irving pleaded, and he stood up with the Nehushtan on his shoulder.

"What?"

Twitch touched ground and shifted from his falcon to his humanoid forms, looking very feminine. "They're coming around this way!" the fairy gasped, and slipped his fighting batons into his hands. His long silver hair and matching horse's tail bounced with his own edgy footwork.

"I don't know if I can do it without the tent," Irving explained. "I think I can make it work with the tent."

"Jeez," Mike said, but he jumped over to one angle of the tent and picked up the pole supporting that corner.

Eddie was tempted to shoot the preacher. "What do you mean, like it's a force field made out of tent canvas?"

Irving shrugged, trembling. "I know I can keep snakes out of the tent," he muttered. "I don't know what happens if I leave the tent."

Jim nodded to Eddie, arched his eyebrows, and positioned himself at a second tentpole.

Faith, Eddie grumbled in his head. If creation had been up to him, he'd have chosen an instrument that was less finicky. "Fine!" he snapped, and grabbed one of the sagging poles. He hoisted it up onto his left shoulder, ripping a couple of tent pegs out of the ground as he did so. Twitch grabbed the fourth, and they began to shuffle forward. "I know you can do it, Reverend Irving," he said, trying his hardest to sound encouraging. Warm and supportive was not Eddie's strong suit.

The corner of the tent flapped around Eddie, sometimes obscuring his vision and sometimes not. He was at the front of the tent, with Mike, and they walked forward towards a trembling jumble of serpents.

Idiot, he thought, this is not going to work. He tightened his grip on the Remington, made sure the shoulder strap was in place so that when he'd emptied the magazine he could drop it and pull out the Glock instead. He only had one hand to work with, now.

But the snakes hissed and pulled back. Only scant feet in front of Eddie and Mike, and drawing back in parallel to the tent's advance. They weren't afraid, Eddie realized. They weren't fleeing. They were being *forced* back.

It was *working*.

He heard the crunch of Phineas Irving's feet on the sand behind him, and then the preacher began to sing.

"Onward, Christian soldiers, marching as to war,
With the cross of Jesus, going on before."

"I'd take the cross of Jesus going on before," Mike said. The bass player grunted and sweated and looked nervous. He held the pole against his shoulder with both hands, and his M1911 in one fist. "I don't really like being in front, and I'm not crazy about having a snake at my back, either."

"Don't shoot yourself," Eddie warned the other man, and then he looked back at Phineas Irving.

Irving looked like he was praying, like he was concentrating so hard he might be in a trance. And above him, nailed to the high cross, Eddie would have sworn that the serpent was *moving*.

Eddie blinked, trying to be sure he wasn't seeing a vision of some damned soul.

The snake moved. Its red scales flashed like rubies; dust and sand shook off its flanks as it coiled around and around in a spiral on the tall pole. Eddie met Jim's gaze, bringing up the rear with a tent pole on his shoulder, and saw that the big singer had noticed it, too. They both raised their eyebrows.

"Huevos," Mike said, and Eddie whipped his head back around.

Ahead of him, blinking in and out of his vision as the edges of the tent waved up and down in the desert breeze, he saw a slope down to the van, parked on the track where they'd left it. To his left were Mike and, beyond the bass player, the edge of the trailer as they slowly coasted around it. Between the van and the trailer in Eddie's intermittent field of vision came a horde of snake-men, shambling around the trailer's shoulder and hissing in rage. Eddie raised his shotgun.

Irving sang louder:

"Christ, the royal master, leads against the foe,
Forward into battle see his banners go."

"They're back here, too!" Twitch shouted.

Eddie heard the clash of Jim's sword on something hard, and then the dull thump of Twitch's batons coming into play. He wanted to risk a look back, but he couldn't. Overalls was charging straight at him, enormous head goggling in the air like a living antenna with jaws the size of a tire clamp.

The Nehushtan wasn't keeping the monster back. Or at least, it wasn't keeping it back enough. It would be no comfort if the artifact stopped the creature from entering the tent, if it could rip Eddie to pieces while standing outside.

Boom! Eddie shot the snake-man. Overalls staggered sideways, and Lady Legs rushed up behind to fill the gap.

Bang! Bang! To his left, he heard Mike taking pot-shots, too. The tent swerved and sagged as Mike adjusted his grip, but the big guy managed to still hold his end up.

They were past the trailer now and headed down the slope. Cutting across the desert in the straightest line, Eddie's combat boots tromped down on crackling sagebrush and crunching pebbles. Mercifully, he didn't step on any snakes; the little ones, rattlers and whatever else they were, continued to wiggle back from the advancing tent.

But the big mutant buggers rushed at the men holding up the four corners.

Onward, Christian soldiers, marching as to war,
With the cross of Jesus, going on before.

Boom! Eddie fired again. A handful of the pinwheel-spinning snakeheads erupting from the gabardine skirt exploded into pulp and gore, but the others kept coming. He fired again, and again, and then Lady Legs was on top of him—

whoosh!—

something sprang past Eddie.

He slipped back and rocked on his heels, his vision flashing sideways like he was on some Six Flags Chicago rollercoaster. He saw Mike swinging his pistol like a club, hammering Many Arms in the face over and over while the hands grabbed at Mike and tried to rip away the pole. Mike was taller and kept the pole out of the monster's reach, but he was being inexorably dragged down.

Then Eddie's toes hit Overalls, who rolled on the ground, and Eddie fell. He squeezed his trigger as he fell—*click.*

He hit the sand shoulders-first, hard, and lost all his wind. Vision spinning, he tried to keep his grip on the tent pole. He could see that the white canvas overhead was sagging quickly towards him, but he pushed up, hoping against hope that Overalls wouldn't bite his head off in the meantime, and kept the tent from collapsing.

And Overalls didn't bite him. Overalls rolled out of the way, squirming to get out of the tent.

Eddie lurched to his knees, climbing the pole like a ladder. He let the shotgun down to his hip and whipped out the Glock. The tent was down and blocking his view, but he knew his friends were all behind him or to the side because the tent was still up, so he pointed the pistol at the canvas, thumbed the selective fire switch to automatic mode and squeezed off two short bursts.

The gun bucked pleasantly in his hand and punched two streaks into the white cloth. When the tent opened again in the breeze, Eddie saw what had sprung past him—

the Nehushtan, the red serpent on the cross, had joined the fray. It slithered ahead of the lurching tent, throwing wide jaws that were impossibly elastic. A huge snake, thick around as a tree trunk and with a gaping mouth at each end of its body, rose hissing to contest its right of way.

The ruby Nehushtan swallowed the human-sized snake monster in a single bite.

"Holy Moses," Eddie muttered, but he saw the path to the van opening ahead of them. "Run!" he barked, and then he remembered the tent: "I mean, jog!"

They hustled down the hill. The van was two hundred feet away, and Eddie emptied out the Glock's clip at a thing with two heads. One hundred feet, and Mike tripped over a hole in the ground, like the entrance to a prairie dog's warren. He slipped and fell to one knee, and Jim dragged him to his feet.

Fifty feet and the tent fell away. It just slipped right off the crossbeams and bounced to the ground behind them like a bride's thrown veil.

Irving stopped singing and shrieked. Eddie looked over his shoulder, afraid he'd see the preacher lying on the ground. To his relief, and prodded by Jim, the man was still running, and he still held the cross on his shoulder.

But the Nehushtan wasn't eating snakes anymore. It was slithering towards Phineas Irving like it wanted to get back on its pole. Despite all it had eaten, it was the same size as it had always been and moved quick as thinking.

Behind it, in a wall, the mutant snake-people and the rattlers rolled down the hill towards them.

"Start the car!" Eddie yelled. "Reverse!"

Mike was surprisingly fleet of foot with an army of snakes on his tail, and the big man beat Eddie to the Dodge, throwing himself into the driver's seat and gunning the engine to life. Jim grabbed the preacher by the scruff of his neck just as the rubescent serpent slithered back onto its perch and hurled the man and the artifact both into the back seat of the van. Twitch didn't waste time or risk a bottleneck, simply changing shape into his falcon self and bursting into flight over the crappy brown van.

"In!" Mike yelled. The mongooses scrambled into the van as if taking his orders.

Eddie stepped into the back seat of the van and grabbed the hand strap behind the shotgun seat. "Go!" he roared, and jammed his second clip into the Glock. Still set to automatic fire, he squeezed the trigger into the wave of descending serpent flesh, letting the snakes have it as Mike threw the Dodge into reverse and slammed backwards down the road towards town.

Rat-tat-tat-tat-tat!

Eddie dropped Many Arms in his tracks, if only for a moment, and sent Snake Legged Man lurching sideways behind brush for cover. As he ran out of ammo, Jim joined him from the back seat, firing with one of the pistols lying on the floor of the van. Phineas Irving's Enfield stayed silent, though. Eddie spared him a glance and saw that the man was shaking. He was conscious, and looked lucid, but he looked scared half to death. His mongoose guard dogs slunk around his feet in the trash that cluttered the van's floor.

They retreated from the rise, the preacher's trailer disappearing with the mob of snakes. When Mike swung the van around in a quick turn where the road was a little wider, Twitch flashed in through the open door, hitting the grease-stained seat beside Eddie in his leather-clad drummer shape.

"That was amusing," the fairy said.

"It was unexpected, that's for sure," Eddie muttered. "Hey, Irving, what happened back there?"

Irving shook his bristly blond head and shrugged. "You mean with the Nehushtan?"

"Yeah," Eddie said, feeling irritated, "I mean when the Nehushtan turned into a live snake and went and ate all the other snakes."

"That's in the Bible, too," Irving said. "I think."

"Yeah, but not the Nehushtan. That was Moses's staff when he fought the magicians of Pharaoh—unless maybe those are the same thing." Eddie looked back to be sure the pursuit was out of range, and then slammed shut the side door of the van. "Hey, what do I know? But what I mean is, did you know the Nehushtan was going to get down off its cross and start taking names?"

Irving laughed, nervous. "No. I only knew that it kept snakes out of the tent, better than my hexes."

"Maybe the big red snake will heal Adrian after all," Mike suggested, looking at Eddie in the rear view mirror. "Maybe we should go pick him up and heal him and get outta this town."

Eddie looked at Irving and saw the fear in the man's eyes. "Nah," he said. "Faith don't work that way. We gotta go get the lamia. Still, the Nehushtan will probably come in very handy." The snake was dormant again, dimly red under its furred coat of dust.

"I'm going to guess Mike will volunteer for the milking job," Twitch sparkled.

"Hey," Mike objected.

Jim reached past Eddie and pointed forward.

Eddie had been resolutely not looking ahead, afraid of what he'd see, but he looked now. There again was the frozen field of ice and the wind-gnawed heads protruded from it, groaning soundlessly and staring at Eddie.

"What?" Eddie mumbled.

"I think he means the cars," Mike said. "Look how full the lot is. It was totally empty before."

"Maybe there's a sale," Twitch chirped.

Eddie grunted. He tried to shake away the vision of ice, failed, and then tried to squint past it. The parking lot around the three-story building was full of cars. Also, ahead of them, the sun inched into late afternoon.

"I would have preferred an emptier house," Eddie said. He felt tired. His burns hurt. There were two hours left on his watch's timer. "You up for this, preacher?"

Phineas Irving shook, but he gripped the Nehushtan with both hands and nodded. "I want to help your friend," he agreed. "And I want to stop Apep."

"Load up," Eddie told them all. He reached over the shotgun seat for the ammo boxes he kept in the glove compartment.

CHAPTER SIX

Eddie knew that to everyone else, he looked like he was walking drunk. But the others couldn't see the frozen heads, and he couldn't bring himself to just walk through them. In his rational mind, he knew that the sun, dropping towards the horizon now, was still fierce, but the cool desert breeze bit into his flesh like a piranha. He shuddered under the black-eyed stares of the damned and tried to stay focused on the crumbling brick cube ahead of them, even as he stumbled from side to side through the obstacle course of frozen heads.

Jim put a hand on Eddie's shoulder and Eddie looked up, catching a quizzical look from the titan of a singer.

"Same old bullshit," Eddie lied, shaking himself. "A little worse than usual, maybe, but nothing new."

"What do you mean worse?" Mike asked.

"What is it, your job to ask all the dumb, irritating questions?" Eddie chomped at him, but then he felt guilty. "I don't know," he grumbled. "Something bad happened here, I'm guessing. Some kind of terrible sin, maybe."

Twitch laughed lightly. From someone else, it might have sounded like mockery, but it lifted Eddie's spirits a little. "Sin," the fairy giggled, "is for humans."

"Yeah, it is," Eddie agreed.

Metal shutters had been dropped over the storefront windows of the Sears. It seemed a little extravagant for a box store in the middle of nowhere, but maybe that's why the Apep worshippers had chosen it. As Eddie and the band stalked around the edges of the gravel parking lot, he saw a couple who looked like small ranchers, wearing boots, yoked shirts and blue jeans, walk in through the swinging glass doors. Eddie didn't see any guards.

That made him uncomfortable.

"How trained are your mongooses?" he asked the preacher.

Phineas Irving shrugged. "Like a dog, I guess," he said. "Not as much as that, really. They fight snakes by instinct. Fortunately, they have really good instincts."

Eddie had hoped he might be able to send the animals in as scouts somehow. "I'd give a lot for a decent wizard right now," he said, thinking of Adrian and wishing he could turn invisible.

"Sorry," Irving muttered.

"Never mind." Eddie spotted something at the side of the building. "Twitch," he told the fairy, "I'm glad you can fly." He pointed and then set out at a jog.

It wouldn't pay to forget that Overalls, Lady Legs and the other mutant snake-men were somewhere out behind them, and coming their way.

The building's shadow should have given Eddie relief from the heat as he rolled to a stop underneath a fire escape; instead, it added to his sensation that he was freezing to death. He gritted his teeth, forced himself not to shiver, and looked up. The iron ladder bolted to the side of the building as an emergency exit only ran halfway down its side, but then it had a second half on tracks, that could be unlatched and pushed down from above.

Twitch hit the top of the fire escape in falcon shape and immediately became the spiked, leather-bar-garbed drummer. He skittered down the ladder like a monkey and kicked open the latch.

"Easy!" Eddie hissed, but too late. The ladder bumped, rattled and squealed like a hinge that needed oiling, but it dropped. Jim stepped forward and caught it easily before it hit the bottom of its descent, cutting off what might otherwise have been a very loud noise.

"Thanks," Eddie said to the singer.

Jim shrugged, slid the ladder easily down to its full extension, and started climbing up.

"I'll go last," Eddie told them, and sent Irving and Mike up the ladder ahead of him. Mike climbed reasonably well, for a big guy, but Irving moved slow, humping the Nehushtan on one shoulder and the Enfield on the other as he went. Then Eddie climbed up the rungs. Halfway up, he grabbed a bit of rope that was knotted around the top rung of the sliding half and pulled it up after him, latching the ladder back into place and then joining the others on the gravel-strewn rooftop.

There were air conditioning units, a small water tower and a gas generator on the rooftop. The way inside was a door at the top of a staircase. Eddie pulled at the handle and found it locked. "Mike?" he said.

"Sure," Mike said, no problem. The bass player had grown up running in gangs and had some useful skills. "I just need a credit card."

"Credit card?" Eddie snapped. "Do you think we're here to go *shopping*?"

"*Chingón*," Mike laughed. "I can open this door, but I need a credit card to do it." He looked around at the band. "Nobody? Nobody's got a credit card?"

The band stared back dully. Eddie shrugged. "Bad risks," he deadpanned. "I guess when Satan got my soul, he dinged my credit score, too."

Phineas Irving shoved the Nehushtan into the crook of his neck and shoulder and rummaged in his pockets. "How about this?" he asked, and held out a driver's license.

Mike took it. "It's expired," he noted. "Pennsylvania."

Irving nodded. "I'm kind of on the lam," he said, and pointed at the big red snake on his shoulder.

"Isn't everyone?" Twitch cracked wise.

"Stop reading the damn thing and open the door," Eddie said gruffly. He took the Remington in both hands and stood watch.

Up here on the rooftop, at least, he didn't see the frozen heads. Just the metal hulks of building machinery and the dusty blue sky, slowly deepening.

Click. Good as his word, Mike opened the door. "Easy," he said. Eddie wished he felt as confident as Mike sounded, and resisted looking at his watch.

"Do we have a plan?" Irving asked, as Eddie headed first into the gloom-shrouded stairwell.

"Sure," Eddie quipped. "We find the lamia. Then Mike milks it." The stairs under his boots were concrete, and he shuffled slowly, trying not to trip himself. Under a glowing green exit sign, he hit a landing and turned.

"I do?" Mike asked.

The door at the top of the stairs slammed shut, and the stairwell plunged from shadow into darkness.

"What's the matter, Mikey?" Twitch asked. "Boobs are all fine and good until you actually have to touch them?"

"Don't call me Mikey," Mike complained. He sounded like he was at the end of the line. "And don't leave me. I think I'm alone back here."

"No matter what you may say," Jim sang from somewhere behind Eddie. He sang in a whisper, but in the stairwell his voice boomed, anyway.

"I always will be true.
No matter how far away,
I'll always be with you."

Eddie chuckled. "You in love, Jim?"

"You said he was a mute," Irving squeaked.

"Nah, I said he was *cursed*," Eddie reminded the preacher. "Strictly speaking, that wasn't quite true, either. He's just trying to avoid unwanted attention."

"By singing?" Irving asked. "Like *that?*"

"Why don't you do it more often?" Mike asked. "We could have, like, conversations, instead of you just pointing and looking serious and then Eddie talking all the time."

"Do you have any idea how hard it is to have a conversation entirely by singing?" Twitch demanded.

Eddie bumped his toes into a door at the bottom of the stairs. "Hold on," he urged the others. "Slow up."

"He could make up his own words and put it to music," Mike suggested. "Kind of scat-singing. Like," and the bass player burst into sing-song, *"hey, Mike, how about you pick this lock for us?"*

"That's cheating," Eddie said. "It's just talking with pitch, and it don't count."

"Why?" Mike pushed. "I mean, if they can't hear music?"

"Who's *they?*" Irving asked.

"Uh … Satan," Mike said. "And those guys."

Eddie felt something brush against his feet. He jumped almost out of his skin, and then realized it was probably a mongoose. "Just having a pitch to it doesn't make a sound music," Eddie said. He found the door handle, and pulled. This one was locked, too.

"It doesn't?" Twitch asked.

"Rhythm section," Eddie muttered. "Mike, get up here and open this door."

"This from the world's greatest tambourine player," Mike grumbled, but down he came. There was grunting and huffing as he stepped on toes and finally tumbled down to the bottom of the steps. "I still have the card," he said.

Eddie guided him to the door's handle.

"If just pitch or rhythm was enough to block a sound from the Fallen's hearing," he pointed out, "they wouldn't hear machines working, or animal calls, or just about anything else. They'd be practically deaf. It's gotta be *music.*"

"He could have code songs," Mike persisted. "Like 'Beat It' could mean 'run away'. Or he could sing 'Eye of the Tiger' to mean 'attack.'"

Eddie shook his head. "I'm gonna let you think about that one on your own, Mike, and tell me why it's a terrible idea."

"I don't understand," Irving groaned.

"You don't have to," Eddie said. "Hang on tight to the Nehushtan, and remember how it drove away those crazy-ass half-snake bastards back at your trailer."

"Got it," Mike said, and pulled open the door.

Eddie dragged Mike with him and slunk out onto the top floor of the Sears. They found themselves behind a mock-up of someone's front room, with a three-part sofa and chair set and an oval glass coffee table. The floor was dimly lit, only a few sections of its fluorescent tube lighting turned on, and no windows.

"Home sweet home," Mike sneered at the furniture and drew his pistol.

"Don't knock it," Eddie shot back. "I miss this stuff." He saw bodies stacked three deep on the couches and on the floor between them, oozing red from thousands of tiny perforation wounds. They lay in puddles of their own blood, white and drained like slaughtered chickens, but they weren't dead. They were wiggling.

He looked away.

The others filed out behind them onto the floor.

"Why is the top floor Furniture?" Mike asked. "That just means they have to bring all the floor models up two flights of stairs."

"No one impulse buys a bed," Eddie pointed out. "Or at least, anyone who throws around that kind of money doesn't shop at Sears."

Mike shrugged. "Maybe they got an elevator, anyway."

"I hear something," Twitch said. "It's rhythmic, so it must not be music."

"Does it have pitch, too?" Mike snarked.

"Ah, now you're asking really sophisticated questions, and I'm just the drummer." Twitch sprang into the air and took flight as a falcon. He flapped his silvery wings and shot across the Furniture section of the Sears, dropping into a wide double-stairwell in the center of the floor.

Jim followed, and the others trailed after the singer. At the stairwell, Jim stopped and looked down. Eddie looked with him, and saw a stack of inflated, life-sized, bowling pin-shaped clowns standing guard over a table of woodscrews. He guessed it might be the junction of Toys and Hardware.

"Of course I thought he had to be a fairy when I saw him," Irving muttered. "But thinking a thing and actually seeing it are very different." The preacher shifted the Nehushtan on his shoulder, looking very out of place in the department store. Eddie chuckled. They *all* looked out of place.

"The fairy's not your problem," he told the other man. He patted the pole, freeing a falling sift of sand from the ancient wood. "Your problem is that you are our biggest gun. When the fight breaks out, we need to get you into position and unleash the power of your weapon."

"We're not in a tent," Irving said hesitantly.

"You kidding?" Eddie gestured at the floor displays all around them. "What is Sears, what is any big box store, if not just a big tent in a bazaar? And you know that the Nehushtan can rain Hell down all over these things. You don't *think* it, you *know* it, because of what you've *seen*."

"Faith seems complicated," Mike said. "I'm glad it's not me." He shifted from foot to foot, carefully checking all the corners of the floor as they waited for Twitch to come back.

"Nothing simpler," Eddie lied. "And the good news is that we've got us a powerhouse here, a man whose faith is true and weapons grade."

Mike snorted. "Weapons grade?" He laughed. "Mierda."

"It's true," Eddie said. "For your faith to be effective against evil, it's not enough to believe in God. You have to believe in evil, too, and you have to believe that your faith will protect you."

"So ... vampires ..." Mike said slowly.

"A cross ain't enough," Eddie explained. "On the other hand, a cross in the hands of someone who believes in the cross, and believes in vampires, and believes the cross can stop the bloodsuckers ... well, sayonara, Nosferatu." He patted the Nehushtan again. "The Reverend Irving here believes in snake-mutant sons of bitches, and he knows from personal experience that the Nehushtan is an ass-kicking weapon of heavenly vengeance against them, so his faith is exactly the kind we need."

"Huh." Mike scratched himself.

"Of course, we don't want you to kill the lamia before we milk her."

"I'm not really a reverend," Irving said.

"Well, you're not a Ph.D., either, so I can't call you *doctor*." Eddie snorted. "Besides, I kind of like *reverend*." Irving looked shaky, and sounded none too confident. Eddie wanted to shore up the man's faith before they got back into the thick of it, but he didn't quite know how.

"You do it," Irving said.

"Can't."

"Why not?" The preacher tried to push the Nehushtan pole into Eddie's hands and Eddie resisted. "You saw it work just like I did. You know it works. You carry it and I'll shoot the rifle."

Eddie grabbed the pole and shoved it onto Irving's shoulder, hard. "I'm damned, don't you get it?" he hissed. "It doesn't matter how much I believe or what I've seen, I sold my soul, and I can never have the gift of faith."

Irving looked at Mike.

"Yeah," Mike said. "Me too, I think."

Phineas Irving sighed heavily.

"It ain't that bad," Eddie urged him on. "Everything I said is true. We know you've got faith, and we know what you can do with the Nehushtan."

"I choked when the tent fell off," Irving reminded him. "And suddenly it stopped working, and we were almost eaten."

"This time you won't choke," Eddie reassured him, and then he pumped the Remington. "Besides, we're here with you, and we're armed to the teeth."

"I'd still rather it was you holding the pole."

"Believe me," Eddie laughed harshly, "I'd trade places with you in a heartbeat."

"What are we going to milk the lamia into?" Mike asked. "I mean, Adrian's not here, so he can't ... you know ..."

"Breastfeed?" Eddie asked, grateful for the change of subject. Too much thinking wasn't going to help Phineas Irving at all. He stepped over to a display of kitchen furniture and took a green pebbled plastic pitcher off the top of a finger-smudged black table. "That'll do," he judged. "We get that much milk, we can donate the extra to Johns Hopkins or the VA."

He heard a clicking sound and looked up. Standing at the top of the stairs, dim light washing his face from the story below, Jim snapped his fingers and hissed in Eddie's direction.

"Uh-oh." Eddie rushed to join the singer of the band.

Jim pointed.

The floor of the story below was awash in snakes. They were the normal-sized ones, rattlesnakes and whatever else, but there were hundreds of them. They hissed and slithered over each other and tied themselves in knots like living pretzels, batting the inflated clowns every which way and knocking showers of woodscrews to the floor.

Eddie felt tired.

"Dammit," he sighed. "All I want to do is keep us alive until we can get to Chicago, get a little help from the hoodoo woman, and save our souls. Why's it have to be so hard?"

The snakes began to climb the stairs. No sign of the big freaky mutant ones, though. Jim braced himself and Mike came around to join them, pistol ready.

"Irving," Eddie hissed, "get over here!"

Phineas Irving stumbled around to the top of the stairs. He looked like he was in shock, and the Nehushtan on his shoulder shook. "Maybe we should shoot the snakes," he suggested.

"Maybe they ain't heard us yet," Eddie countered, "so we should try something a little more quiet."

"Even Peter sank into the water," Irving pointed out.

"Just once, though," Eddie said optimistically. "The second time out, he was gangbusters. Should we sing a hymn? It's gonna have to be soft if we do. Plus," he pointed at Jim, who stood resolutely pointing his sword at the advancing snakes, "it'll mean Jim gets to join us, and it'll make him feel included."

"I ..."

"*Onward, Christian soldiers,*" Eddie started in a whisper, "*marching as to war....*"

Irving closed his eyes and moved his lips along with the music.

Come on, Eddie thought, you can do this.

The Nehushtan began to loop and slither on its pole. Eddie crossed his fingers.

"I'm taking the safety off," Mike said. "They're close."

"You've still got the safety on?" Eddie snapped, incredulous.

The Nehushtan shook off a veil of sand and coiled like a spring. It stared at Eddie, and its black, beady eyes glittered.

"You're doing great, Reverend Irving," he told the preacher. "*Christ, the royal master, leads against the foe....*"

"*Forward into battle see his banners go!*" Jim joined in. The boom of his voice filled the Furniture section, even whispering as he was.

Eddie heard the *whoosh* of wings, the angry *hiss* of a snake and a tiny *crunch* as a serpentine skull was cracked open. Twitch the horse-tailed falcon tossed a bloodied scrap of former snake to the floor and then landed in his human shape, batons in hand.

"They're getting ready for a party down there," the fairy said. He turned and joined Jim, both of them swiping with their weapons at the slow flood of snakes. "An orgiastic one."

"Where's down there?" Mike asked. Jim and Eddie continued to sing softly, as the song reached its chorus. Eddie kept his eyes locked on the preacher's face, communicating all the faith and confidence and trust he could. Out of the corner of his eye he saw the twinkling red of the Nehushtan's scales as it shifted about, and he tried not to let himself get distracted.

Onward, Christian soldiers, marching as to war,
With the cross of Jesus, going on before.

"The basement," Twitch answered. He and Jim were hard pressed by the snakes, slapping them aside and skewering them and stomping them flat. "Kitchenware. Apparently, Apep's a domestic goddess."

Ding!

"What's that sound?" Eddie asked, and stopped singing to listen. He looked into the depths of the floor where he thought the sound had come from and saw a light appear, sliding into visibility as the door concealing it opened.

The elevator door.

"Uh oh," he muttered. Over a cluster of bookshelves and a wardrobe he saw the waving, jaw-snapping head of the mutant snake-man Overalls. He couldn't see the other monsters yet, but from the sound of many feet that Eddie heard, he knew that Overalls wasn't alone.

Then Overalls turned his head in the direction of Eddie and their eyes met, man to snake.

"Hell."

"What?" Phineas Irving gulped.

The Nehushtan froze.

CHAPTER SEVEN

Eddie hurled the pitcher at the mutants. It was a pointless gesture, except that it freed his hands for the shotgun.

Jim leaped into combat in his crazy Zorro way. In two steps he was stomping on the springy center of a little kid's bed set, grinding his heel into the eye of Fuzzikins the Slumber Bear, and then he hurtled himself upwards.

Eddie didn't wait for Jim to come down. He took three steps to the side to get a clear look at the elevator and raised the Remington.

"Believe!" he shouted, and squeezed the trigger.

Boom! He missed Overalls and shattered all the glass in the windows of an ornately scrolled but gaudy china cabinet. Shards flew in all directions.

Jim skipped like a flat rock over water across the top of a high wardrobe, coming down through the air, boot heels first, on the other side.

Bang! Bang! Eddie heard Mike start unloading behind him. He didn't see what happened with the bullets, so either Mike was missing big-time, or he was shooting at the snakes on the stairs.

Jim kicked down into the grinning human head of Many Arms, flattening the mutant's ear in a spray of blood and knocking them both sideways in opposite directions. Eddie saw that all the snake-man thugs from the Church of the Redeemer

Nehushtan were here—no, not quite, since the ones the Nehushtan had actually eaten hadn't reappeared, but in the meantime, the survivors had picked up a few new friends. He also saw they looked fresh and uninjured; the limb he had seen chopped off of Many Arms was now small and stubby, but it was visibly growing back.

At least with this many of them coming, he couldn't really miss. Eddie pumped the shotgun and fired.

Jim hit the ground on his shoulders and slid on the smooth floor, like a human toboggan skidding backwards and head-first. When he rolled to his feet, he came up swinging a blue lava lamp by its cord. The singer jumped back into the fray alternating swooping strokes of the lamp and sharp, quick thrusts with his saber.

Overalls lurched at Eddie, jaws gaping open and down at Eddie's head. Eddie found the creature's persistence irritating, more than anything else. He jammed the shotgun into Overalls's maw with his left hand, muzzle against the back of its throat. The mouth clamped shut, and Eddie narrowly missed losing his arm—the monster's teeth sunk into the thick fabric of his jacket sleeve. The mutant snake-man's beady black eyes glittered and he hissed. Having his fist inside the creature's mouth made Eddie feel like one of those TV veterinarians on some PBS show, sticking his arm inside a cow to deliver its calf. He felt wet snake-slobber on his fist and a bad stink clogged his nostrils.

Eddie squeezed the trigger.

The back of Overalls's big serpentine head blew out in a shower of red blood, white bone fragments and black and yellow scales. The velocity of the slug carried the monster back with it but didn't open its jaws and, with a sharp tearing sound, Eddie's sleeve ripped right off at the shoulder.

Eddie had no time to mourn for his jacket. Snake Legged Man rushed at him, his snakes for feet hissing in protest as they were thumped against the floor. At his side came a barechested guy in a John Deere cap and corduroy pants who had a mass of snakes sprouting from his back and shoulders like wings. Eddie grabbed his Glock with his free hand, whipped it out, and started entertaining the company.

Meanwhile, Jim whirled his lava lamp like a bola, tangling it around the neck of Many Arms and jerking the snaky son of a bitch sideways and off balance. Bob the repairman grabbed for Jim, trying to drag the singer and pin him against the nest of snakes writhing on Bob's chest. Jim sidestepped and lopped off the entire bush of serpents in a single swipe—

they dropped to the floor and kept swarming.

The Nehushtan, Eddie thought. He needed the snake-on-a-stick to push some of these things back.

"Why do I not hear singing?" he barked. "*Onward, Christian soldiers!*"

"Cagado!" Mike shouted back, like that was some kind of answer.

Eddie threw a look over his shoulder in between shots and saw that the Nehushtan leaned against the railing around the stairwell, and Phineas Irving worked his Enfield rifle, slamming .30-06 bullets alternately down the stairs at the snakes or past Eddie at the mutants. Mike had stuck his M1911 back in his pants and swung a club that might have been a table leg originally. He and Twitch swiped at the snakes that raged hissing up the steps, not making any progress. They might have already been overwhelmed but for the preacher's mongooses, which bit through snakes' heads with terrible efficiency and kept a frightened circle of serpent flesh milling away from them.

"Twitch!" Eddie yelled. "Get us a way down!"

"I already have one!" the fairy howled back as Eddie turned away to pay attention to the horde that rushed him. "It involves you turning into a bird!"

Lady Legs charged, a hurricane of snakes. Eddie didn't let himself get distracted by the biting mouths, and calmly aimed for one of her knees instead. *Boom!* The 870 chewed a coconut-sized hole right through the gabardine and punched the knee out backwards. Lady Legs toppled to the ground writhing and kicking, her half-disconnected leg spinning red out like a centrifuge.

A white horse flashed in the corner of Eddie's eye.

And then John Deere piled into Eddie like a freight train.

His fists were cinder blocks, and they both connected to Eddie's jaw before Eddie really even saw them coming. Snakes bit at him and he shoved the Glock into John Deere's belly—

bang!

John Deere slipped and fell in the gore, and as he dropped, one of the snakes on his back grazed Eddie's bare arm with a fang. Cold terror lanced through Eddie's heart and he leaned into his pistol, pushing it like a knife into the mutant's belly and squeezing off several more muffled shots. John Deere flailed and shrieked, the sounds coming out of his mouth sounding more animal than human.

Jim appeared, a television in his hands. The device dragged an extension cord behind it and its screen was jagged with rolling horizontal lines of static. Eddie looked up and saw that Jim had cleared a space the length of several wounded and shuddering mutants' bodies. John Deere howled and clawed at Jim's legs, and his snakes bit harmlessly at Jim's boots as Jim raised the TV—

smash!—

and brought it down in a final hammer blow that threw sparks in all directions and obliterated John Deere's head. The barechested mutant kicked his feet in one final moment of agony then was still.

And then the silvery horse flashed past Eddie again, headed for the stairs.

It pushed a bed, its chest pressing against the high headboard.

"Go!" Eddie yelled. He switched the Glock's selective fire mechanism to *automatic* and strafed the surging crowd of mutants with everything left in his clip. It didn't last long. "Go!" he yelled again, then holstered the pistol, grabbed the Nehushtan where the preacher had laid it down and jumped onto the bed.

Mike and the not-quite-Reverend Irving stumbled in with him. Jim threw his shoulder against the headboard and then vaulted over it as the bed tipped over the stairs—

and began rattling down like a big sled.

"Five little monkeys!" Mike hollered, his teeth rattling.

It occurred to Eddie too late to wonder how high the bed's legs were—if they were too tall, he thought, they might hit a step and tip over forward. He heard and felt the squishes of snakes being run over as the bed ba-ba-ba-ba-bumped down the stairs at a trot.

Twitch whizzed over the bed and ahead of it in falcon form, wings spread wide.

"Four little monkeys!" Mike laughed.

Eddie turned to look behind them and saw Lady Legs and Many Arms and a swarm of their friends lumbering after them. Including Overalls, dammit! How many times did these things have to be killed? He raised the Remington to add a few to the score before remembering that both his guns were empty.

And the second story was coming fast.

He shoved the Nehushtan into the hands of Phineas Irving and started singing. Jim joined in:

"Onward, Christian soldiers, marching as to war!"

Eddie switched clips on his Glock and shoved shells into the Remington as fast as he could without dropping them, watching the floor rise up to meet them and praying, though he had no right to pray, that Phineas Irving would just *believe*. Clowns with fixed maniacal grins bobbed back and forth, and Eddie felt like they were mocking him. He twisted around as the stairs were coming to an end and let off three quick slugs into the ravening crowd on their heels.

"With the cross of Jesus ..." Irving's voice rose to join his and Jim's in a warble.

CRASH!

The wood of the bed splintered on impact, throwing splinters in all directions and hurling Irving out of the bed. The lanky man rolled forward into a hissing wall of snakes, clutching the Nehushtan on its pole—

and the snakes parted.

"Three little monkeys!" Mike laughed, short of breath. A bobbing clown with two buck teeth in his yawning mouth bowed low and touched foreheads with the bass player. "Mierda!"

Eddie jumped off the bed and staggered to drag Irving to his feet. "*Mierda* is right!" he yelled. "Run!"

Sheets of blood ran down the walls and Eddie's combat boots stepped on a floor of heads. Damned souls stood beneath his feet, stacked shoulder to shoulder like sardines, so tightly that they made a solid floor. The flesh on their heads was worn from treading feet all the way down, exposing cracked and oozing skulls under the tatters of hair and skin that remained.

Eddie ignored them. He jammed the muzzle of his 870 up the stairwell and squeezed off a couple of rounds, and then he half-dragged, half-kicked Phineas Irving into the Toys Department.

Mike was right on their heels. Jim jumped from the demolished bed to the banister of the stairs. Out of the corner of his eye, Eddie saw the big dark-haired man slash three times at the pell-mell mutants before leaping over a shelf of sagging plush giraffes to join them, landing on his feet light as a cat.

Twitch touched down in man-shape as they raced through a depressing junkyard of dusty fire trucks and no-name action figures, but immediately took to the air again as a falcon. Eddie saw why and pumped the shotgun. "They're bad enough when they stick to the ground," he muttered, and pulled the trigger.

Two flying snakes in the way of the Remington's slug exploded into shuddering meat. Two out of a thousand.

Phineas Irving sang louder and he sweated rivulets of salt, but he was still singing.

The wall of flying snakes hit the Nehushtan's bubble of faith—

and bounced back.

"Yee ha!" Eddie shouted. "Onward, Christian soldiers!"

They rounded out the back of Toys at the top of the next flight down in a no man's land between shrink-wrapped wire crates of fake plastic food labeled to look like off-brands on one side and a pallet of two-by-fours on the other.

"Down!" Eddie barked, and pushed Irving and Mike forward, after the flashing horse's tail of the falcon Twitch.

He joined Jim at the back. The singer ducked under and wove around a hedge of snakes that snapped and hissed at him from the floor as well as from the bodies of the mutants—Lady Legs charged at him, along with Bob the repairman and others Eddie hadn't yet bothered to recognize.

Eddie squeezed the trigger of the 870, letting off several rounds into the horde and setting them back a few paces.

"Don't mind us back here!" he yelled to Irving, retreating from the serpents in a quick skipping shuffle down the stairs. "Everything's under control!"

"*Forward into battle ...*" came the indirect reply.

They hit the ground floor, and it was ice. Heads protruding from the ice surrounded Eddie, and he was close enough now that he could see the words they were mouthing.

Save us, they said, and *I'm sorry*, and *Soon you too will join us.*

Eddie turned with Jim to see the late afternoon sun through the glass doors. He saw more heads out in the parking lot, but he saw cars, too, and with half his heart, he wanted to ditch Adrian and run like the devil.

Then the snakebite he'd got from John Deere's wing-snake itched, fiercely. It stung. Eddie scratched at it, and saw that Mike and Irving were hesitating, too. "Go on!" Eddie bellowed, channeling his Inner Sergeant. "The basement, Twitch said!"

They ran through racks of brassieres and panties. Mike's choice, Eddie thought. Guy can't stop thinking about tail, even when he's getting shot at. He could hear the sound that Twitch had been talking about now. It was a chanting, with a drumming mixed in, the shaking of metal rattles. If it counted as music, he thought idly, it did so only barely. It sounded like the crap he'd played for Sharon back when she was in college and he was just back from Iraq, and he wanted to impress her with his sophisticated interest in things African.

Bullshit, he snorted now. Gimme a fuzzed-out, wailing guitar solo any day. That's the music of my people.

He forced himself to ignore the freezing heads, and charged straight through them. They flinched as he struck them, but of course he didn't feel anything. They were ghosts, figments in a vision. Still, it was strange that they seemed to see him back. By a rack of underpants printed with fading images of Space Ghost and Quick Draw McGraw they turned again, and charged down towards the basement. Eddie wasn't sure what to expect, and whatever it was he might have imagined, it wasn't what he saw.

He stopped, several steps from the bottom, and stared. The basement was thronged with people. It might have been a Kitchenwares Department once, but the shelves and tables of merchandise had all been shoved to the walls to make a great empty space in the center of the floor. In the center of the floor lay a dog on a low-end kitchen table, a charcoal barbecue grill full of smoldering incense, and two figures.

The mongooses stood beside Eddie on the steps, rearing up and hissing.

Miriam was unmistakable.

She towered above him, voluptuous and dark and naked. Eddie gulped, trying to concentrate and not be distracted by the sheer lush sexual power that oozed out of her full lips and breasts, her thin neck and large eyes. It helped that from the hips down she became a huge, blue-scaled serpent. Her human body was ordinary in size, he realized; it was the serpent half that coiled up and pushed her off the floor, made her tall and menacing and monstrous. Her hair helped bring him back to his senses, too—it was a sleepy, rustling mass of blue snakes. In her hand she held a long flake of glassy black stone over the dog, like a primitive surgeon about to cut into a patient.

Aaron was almost as easy to identify. He looked like Phineas, a tall, gaunt, blond man wearing a trench coat. Only where human hands should have protruded from the sleeves of his coat, Aaron had snakes' heads instead.

The ceiling was a sheet of ice, and white, naked bodies hung from it by their necks. A buffeting gale that Eddie could almost feel chewed at their flesh and made them sway back and forth like human wind chimes.

The two lovers stood in a central space empty but for the dog on the table. Surrounding them was a crowd, chanting words Eddie didn't recognize, beating small hand drums and playing sistra. A sistrum was a brass rattle from ancient Egypt that looked something like the hollow metal head of a hairbrush with loose rods jammed through it. Eddie knew what they were because of Bible class, way back when, and he knew what they were because they were related to the tambourine.

Damn tambourine. Should have said *guitar player*.

At the edge of the crowd, standing in four points that approximately made the four corners of a square, were totem poles. They were wooden and crude, and each had only one figure carved on it. The nearest looked like a monkey's head, and, taking them in at a glance, Eddie thought he saw a dog and a bird and a human. They looked vaguely Egyptian, or at least they looked like someone's bad imitation of Egyptian art. All of them had long strips of cloth bandaged around their eyes.

Eddie's arm really hurt, and he didn't know why.

The dog on the table whined, and only then did Eddie register what was actually going on in the scene in front of him. The dog was alive, but its ribcage was cracked open, exposing heart, lungs and other things Eddie couldn't immediately identify, in a soupy mass of blood, organs and living flesh. Ropes held the dog to the table, but it might also be sedated—it wasn't struggling. A row of stone bowls lay on the table beside the animal, and each bowl held a little puddle of meat, like sorting bowls for a butcher.

Miriam—the lamia, Eddie forced himself to call her in his mind—stooped and grabbed the heart out of the dog's chest, severing the connecting arteries with a single swift slice of her stone knife.

"Ayayayayayay!" she wailed, and in a single gulp she devoured the heart while it was still beating.

The dog's whine became a yowl, but then Aaron leaned over it, the snakes' mouths that served him for fingers snatching what must be a heart out of one of the bowls and massaging it into the cavity from which the dog had lost its natural organ. The replacement seemed to fit, and the dog still moved, though its new heart looked smaller to Eddie's eye.

It's a snake's heart, he thought. Were they replacing all the dog's natural organs with a snake's parts?

"We consecrate thee Wepwawet, opener of the ways," Aaron chanted. "Thy heart is pure in the ways of the serpent. Thy breast nourishes all his words."

The sistra exploded in a burst of noise. It wasn't chaotic, Eddie realized. There were various sections of sistrum players, and they were playing different rhythms. But all the rhythms hit a crescendo together as Aaron finished his short dedication. The swaying legs of the damned dangling from the ceiling looked perversely like dancers.

And then, over the heads of her congregants, the lamia saw the band.

"Infidels!" she shouted, pointing a long-nailed bloody finger. "Enemies of Apep! Unbelievers!"

"Huevos," Mike muttered.

Then Eddie realized that he'd been standing and staring like an idiot while Jim, behind him, kept the mutants at bay. He turned to help and saw Jim slashing at three of them, but Lady Legs and Overalls and Many Arms, hiss though they might, weren't attacking. They hopped back and forth and raged within a cloud of flying serpents, similarly angry and similarly harmless. Jim and the mongooses picked off many of their number, but the well of enemy serpents seemed bottomless.

They were all being held back by the power of the Nehushtan, and the faith of Reverend Irving.

The preacher still mouthed hymns. He was pale and sweaty and he trembled, but he nodded slightly to acknowledge Eddie.

"Good job," Eddie patted Irving on the back and raised his shotgun, pointing at the mass of cultists in front of him.

They were a mix of ordinary human-looking folks in rural Oklahoma outfits and people with minor mutations—gifts of Apep, Irving had called them. A boy with a perfectly ordinary face stared at Eddie out of unblinking snakes' eyes. A girl near him had human eyes, but a face that was scaly and lacked nostrils around the slits of her nose. Elsewhere forked tongues slithered between human lips, and under a white cotton dress, Eddie heard the sound of a rattle. The worshippers pushed forward, but the Nehushtan held them back, too. The ones in front grimaced in pain. Eddie didn't know if they were getting pushed too hard by their friends behind them, or if the Nehushtan itself was burning them. Either way was fine with him.

He pumped the shotgun. "We don't give a rat's ass about Apep," he called over the heads of the crowd.

Phineas Irving chanted hymns at his side; the other guys in the band stood at bay, weapons out and pointed at the snake-people.

"This is a free country, and if you want to go to church with snakes, that's your own business." He tried not to cringe back from the pallid, frozen feet hanging directly in front of his face.

"What are you doing here?" Aaron Irving demanded. "You've wounded many of my people!" He didn't move from beside the mewling dog, and the sistrum players stayed in place and kept up their rhythm. What had he called the dog? Opener of the ways? That sounded like the kind of thing Adrian was always working into his incantations. This was no ordinary worship, Eddie realized. This was a magical ritual.

This was the summoning.

He felt warmer than he thought he should, and wiped a scalding dew of sweat from his brow before it dripped into his eyes. "All I need," he said slowly and deliberately, trying to radiate calm strength like he was talking to an unhappy dog, "is a few moments of cooperation from the lady. Nobody else has to get shot or bitten."

His arm hurt.

The lamia straightened until she nearly scraped the ceiling, the snakes of her hair coming to life and hissing at Eddie. "Phineas," she called in a voice husky with lust and treason, "why do you want to hurt me?"

Beside him, Eddie felt Phineas Irving collapse to the floor.

CHAPTER EIGHT

Pump and squeeze, pump and squeeze, pump and squeeze—
spent cartridges chunked onto the stairs and Eddie's
shotgun blasted ragged holes in the attacking crowd, but after
three quick shots the Remington was ripped from his hands.
Knuckles plowed his eyes and his jaw and angry fingers dragged
him to the ground so boots could kick him, over and over again.

"Don't kill them!" he heard the husky voice of the lamia cry.
"Apep likes his meat fresh!"

Then something stabbed Eddie in his arm, really hard, and he
lost consciousness.

● ● ●

Eddie's hands were empty. He wanted a knife, or a roll of
tape, or anything. A gun, especially. Not that it would have done
him any good.

Sharon and the kids were on the ground in front of him. Not
the ground, the floor. They lay on a red carpet, tied and helpless.
Sharon was dressed in a suit like she'd wear to work, and seeing
her made Eddie wonder for the thousandth time what on earth
Sharon, a gorgeous girl with a college degree and then an
aggressive and successful investment advisor, had ever seen in a
guy like him. Marriage was the most important investment of her
life, and she'd screwed it up. I screwed it up for her, Eddie

thought. The girls were dressed for school, in modest plaid skirts, knee-high socks and maroon sweaters. All three were disheveled and battered, like they'd been run over or mugged. There was fear in their eyes.

They were afraid of Eddie.

Fire licked up the heavy curtains all around them; they were in a palace, or something that was furnished to look like one. Above him, a heavy chandelier swung uneasily on its chain, throwing shifting yellow light onto Eddie. Sweat poured down the guitar player's entire body, but it did nothing to cool him.

You want out? Rumbled a dark, heavy voice behind Eddie. Terror kept him rooted in his spot, and prevented him from looking around. He felt hot breath on the back of his neck and he smelled goat-stink. *Pay the price.*

"No," Eddie said, like he'd already said a million times. "They're innocent!"

The voice laughed. *No one is innocent*, it laughed. *Especially not them. Especially not her. Pay the price, or you're a dead man, as well as damned.*

"I'm unarmed!" Eddie roared, feeling flames crackling about his ankles.

You didn't need a weapon when you decided to kill my child, Eddie Marlowe, the voice boomed. *Use your hands. You are your own most dangerous weapon.*

"No, dammit!" Eddie yelled.

The fire engulfed them all.

◗　◖　◗

Eddie opened his eyes to the sight of dangling feet and a sheet of ice. He felt weak and sluggish. "Where am I?" he muttered.

"The ass end of the universe," Mike told him. "In Nowhere, Oklahoma. At Sears. Locked in Customer Service."

"Soon to be the belly of Apep the snake-god, though," Twitch added cheerfully. "They say that a change is as good as a rest."

Eddie's arm ached and he was dripping with sweat. He sat up. His head pounded relentlessly, he was feverish, and his tongue was enormous and dry. He felt like he had a whole potato in his mouth, and the potato was covered in sand.

"What happened?" He saw that the other sleeve had been ripped off his jacket and the sturdy green cloth had been torn into strips and made into a bandage. No, not a bandage, a tourniquet—in his lean, wiry arm, Eddie saw the X-shaped cut under the tourniquet through which someone had sucked out the poison from his snake bite.

Some of the poison, anyway. Eddie felt like hell. He wondered if being a thin man was a disadvantage, where the poison was concerned. Maybe a bit of fat in his arm would have slowed the venom.

"You ain't been out long," Mike reassured him. "They locked us up is all you missed, and then we cleaned you up a bit."

Eddie realized that part of the pounding in his head came from the noise of the chanting, the drums and the sistra, which he could hear loud and clear. The Customer Service room was split in half by a counter, and Eddie was sitting on top of it. Three walls ran all the way up past a thicket of pipes to the concrete ceiling, and there was a metal grate like a garage door on a prison cell, walling off the fourth direction. The music was really, really loud. He stepped down off the counter gingerly.

"Thanks for making my sleeves match," Eddie cracked. "You know how particular I get about fashion."

The Nehushtan lay in the corner of the room, but at a quick glance Eddie could see that no one was otherwise armed. Phineas Irving crouched in a black office chair, face on his knees like a whipped dog. He had one mongoose on his lap, and the others tumbled around the wheels of the chair. They were bloodied and maybe injured, but still hyperactive. Maybe the blood all belonged to the snakes they'd killed. Twitch perched on his heels on the edge of the countertop. Mike stood and Jim paced. They all looked worse for wear, but especially Jim, who had bruises on his face and cuts on his arms; the big guy must have gone down swinging.

"They tried to break that thing," Mike said, seeing Eddie eyeing the Nehushtan. "They couldn't do it, so they threw it in with us. I don't think they liked touching it. It was like it burned them."

"So we got one weapon, anyway," Eddie muttered. "Too bad Moses didn't heal the Israelites in the wilderness by raising up a decent submachine gun." He patted his pockets and found they hadn't stripped them of any of the usual clutter. "Maybe I could duct tape them to death."

He stepped over to the chain link wall and looked through. The wall was bolted down by a thick padlock running through its bottom edge and a ring in the floor. Beyond was a short hall with men's and women's restrooms and a door marked *EMPLOYEES ONLY*. Janitor's closet, maybe. The hall ran right into the main area of the basement.

Eddie knew they were in the basement, of course. He could still see the legs of the damned dangling above him. He wondered why the vision of the field of ice, the heads sunk into it and the flesh-stripping wind was so persistent. He didn't remember anything about that in the Bible, but of course the Bible saw Hell mostly as fire. Tares were pulled up and thrown into the fire; trees that didn't bring forth good fruit went into the fire; death and Hell were cast into a lake of fire, the second death of the Revelation of St. John.

That wasn't quite how Eddie saw Hell, though. Fire would have been clean and quick and merciful, compared to what Eddie saw through his Infernal Eye. Of course, he saw more than just visions of Hell through his damned eye. He saw Infernals themselves, when they were present. Maybe that's what he was seeing here—though the people trapped in the ice field didn't look like demons.

Jamming his head into the corner between the wall and the bars, he could make out the backs of worshippers and the corner of the nearest totem pole. None of the cultists paid any attention to the short hallway at the rear, or to the prisoners in Customer Service. And why should they? Eddie's heart sank as he contemplated the poverty of his chances.

"That big tube up there runs air," Twitch said, and pointed at an accordion-like flexible conduit. Eddie saw a rip in the tube's fabric and guessed that Twitch must have already examined it in bird form, and torn open a hole. "But it would never support the weight of a man, and it's full of snakes."

Jim pointed at the mongooses at the preacher's feet.

"Yeah, but then what?" Mike asked. "Unless those mongeese ... mongoose ... mongooses, whatever ... are ninjas, too, getting them out ain't gonna help us any." He licked his lips.

"Nervous, Mike?" Eddie chuckled.

"I'm not excited about going to Hell," Mike admitted.

"You shouldn't be," Eddie grunted. "But don't give up yet." He considered. The music was thunder in a box, loud enough that he could barely hear the yelps of the vivisected dog as tiny chirps, nearly inaudible accents over the throbbing, droning wall of sound. He almost grabbed the earplugs out of his breast pocket and popped them in, like he'd do onstage, but decided he'd better risk the hearing loss.

Eddie shook his head, clearing fog out of his vision. He felt like throwing up.

"We can stop the summoning," Phineas Irving suggested. "If we can get out, anyway."

"How's that?" Eddie focused on Irving's words and clutched the bars of his prison, trying to fight through the vertigo and stay conscious. He was poisoned, he knew. He was dying.

"The columns around the circle," the preacher said. "They represent the four sons of Horus. They're present at the ceremony for the purpose of being blinded. Blinding them is a magical ward that prevents the gods from seeing the summoning of Apep, and stepping in to put a stop to it."

"Nope," said Mike, "now you're talking crazy. You're saying that the Apep worshippers summon the sons of Horus first, and then they blind them so they can't see that they're summoning the big snake second?"

"Yeah," Irving agreed, "that does sound crazy. But that's not what I'm saying." He thought carefully. "Look, don't think of it as religion, right? This isn't church. It's a magic spell. And the sorcerers don't want attention, so what they do is include in the spell an element that will hide it."

"Okay ..." Mike said slowly.

"This is all just sympathetic magic," Irving sniffed. "James George Frazer? *The Golden Bough*?"

"Nope," Mike frowned. "You're talking to the wrong guy. The guy you want got bit by a snake and is lying in a coma in a topless bar."

"Look, it's simple. Like produces like. So if you don't want the gods to see, you set up their images and you blind the images."

"Why the four sons of Horus?" Mike asked. "What about all the other gods, like … uh, Odin and Odysseus?"

"The four sons of Horus stand for the four cardinal directions," Irving said thoughtfully, "and the four seasons. They represent the whole universe."

"*All* the gods," Mike said. "I get it. So we take off their hoods and then what? The gods see and step in?"

Irving shrugged. "I don't really know. I think these things are all intricately tied together, so hopefully if we take the hoods off, it crashes the whole summoning. Or maybe, yeah, whoever it is that put Apep in his cage in the first place jumps in to keep him there. Ra the Sun God in some stories, or Bast, who had the head of a cat."

"Don't like *her*," Twitch tsked.

"See?" Eddie snarled. "I knew I should have gone into Egyptology."

"Really?" Mike asked. "'Cause what I really wish knew more about is guns and kung fu."

"What do the ancient Egyptians say," Eddie hazarded a question, feeling a little drunk, "about people frozen in a lake or a glacier, with only their heads sticking out?"

Irving frowned. "The Egyptians?" he considered. "Nothing. Isn't that Dante?"

"Dante? You mean, the *Inferno?*" That sounded a propos to Eddie.

Irving shrugged. "I'm not a lit guy, but yeah, I've read Dante. I think that's one of the circles of Hell. Uh … traitors, maybe."

"And they're ripped apart by a nasty, nasty wind?" Eddie added.

"I think that's Dante, too." Irving frowned. "Different sin though, I think. Maybe … usury?"

"Could it be lust?" Eddie suggested.

"Could be."

Eddie looked at Jim, and Jim nodded confidently. Eddie snorted. Jim ought to know; he'd lived all over Europe for a long, long time, and probably knew Dante personally. Lust and treason, though, that made sense, for a description of a bunch of orgy-happy cultists who wanted nothing more than to betray their own kind to snakes. So what was he seeing? The souls of the mutants? Their future punishment in Hell?

"Kung fu is overrated," Eddie opined. He felt dizzy. "Stick to the guns."

Jim cleared his throat.

"We ain't here for the ritual, though," Eddie reminded the others. "We're here for the lamia milk."

"We could run," Mike suggested. "Just get out, rip off the blindfolds and run like the devil."

"And Adrian dies?" Twitch asked. He looked like a woman now, and Eddie wondered if he was getting ready to Glamour Mike into cooperation.

"No, I mean … maybe the Nehushtan can cure him. Isn't that what it did in the Bible?"

"Good point." Eddie didn't think the Nehushtan would heal Adrian, any more than he thought it would heal *him*—neither of them, he thought, was entitled to any of the gifts Heaven bestowed on men of faith. He knew the Left Hand was on him, but he was dying now anyway, and anything was worth a try.

Eddie was woozy, but he started towards the Nehushtan. Halfway across the room, he collapsed.

"Cojón," Mike commented.

Jim picked up the Nehushtan and handed it to the preacher. Gold glinted on Irving's hand, and Eddie realized that, weird as it was, the preacher must be wearing his wedding ring again.

"Believe," Eddie croaked, his face pressed into hard gray industrial carpet squares. Dragging himself up onto his elbows, he repeated himself. "Believe!" He wasn't entirely sure who he was talking to.

Irving didn't look like he believed, but he looked like he wanted to.

"Come on!" Eddie snapped. "I'm dying!"

"I believe!" Irving hissed. "I believe in God and the power of the Nehushtan, anyway, I just … I'm not sure I'm the right man." He wrapped both his bony hands around the Nehushtan's pole and closed his eyes.

Jim stood behind the preacher and sang something, but over the ringing in his ears and the drone of the ritual, Eddie couldn't hear it. He stared into the snake eyes of the Nehushtan, begging it to get off its pole and … something. And heal him. This couldn't be how he died, Eddie was sure of it. He had been seeing visions of his own death since that fateful night at the crossroads, and this wasn't it. His death was to come by fire, in a palace, together with his family.

That was most of the reason he'd stayed away from them— they couldn't die, none of them could die, until the moment came that Eddie always saw in his dreams, when they were all together. That was the ultimate terrible irony of Eddie's failed bargain with Hell; he had done it to provide for his family, but the result forced him out of their lives. At least for now, and maybe forever. He just couldn't risk bringing the events of his terrible repeated dream to pass, even if, stubbornly, they were inevitable.

Unless his recurring dream was a trick. Staring at the Nehushtan, Eddie started to laugh. His mouth was dry and sweat ran down his face, but the thought that he had pinned so many hopes, and lost so much time he might have spent with his family, on what might be nothing more than a lie punched him right in the cynical part of his sense of humor and once he started laughing, it was hard to stop.

After all, Old Scratch had tricked him about his gift, giving him amazing tambourine chops when he wanted to play the guitar … why not give him false visions of death, too? Forcing Eddie away from his family for nothing struck him as just the kind of practical joke that would appeal to the head of the Infernal Council. Maybe separating him from his family was Eddie's real damnation.

"You okay?" Mike asked. "You all right, or did you go crazy?"

Irving's knuckles were white with effort and Eddie's eyes hurt from staring, but the snake remained frozen in place. Finally, Eddie collapsed forward onto the floor. His burned buttocks hurt, and his snake-bitten arm and his belly. His muscles all felt like rubber and he had the mother of all fevers. He'd never felt worse in his life.

"Yeah," he muttered into the carpet. "I ain't cured, but I'm all right."

He dragged himself to his feet with the counter, and Twitch jumped down to help.

"Mike," he said. "Have you looked at the lock?"

Mike nodded. "No big deal, just the same kind of thing you'd put on your storage locker, but I got nothing to pick it with."

Eddie dug into one of his pockets until he found a hairpin and a paperclip. He untangled the latter from a folded stick of gum. "Either one of these work?"

Mike grinned and took them both.

"Here's what we're gonna do," Eddie laid it out. "Mike picks the lock. Irving takes the snake-on-a-stick. We arm ourselves out of the janitorial supplies—hopefully that's what's across the hall, since it's probably too much to hope that the manager has a gun locker. We rush the first totem pole and rip its hood off. Then we do whatever we can to get to the lamia."

"Ah," said Twitch, "so it's a sophisticated plan."

Eddie shot him the evil eye. "You wanna bolt," he said, "now's the time. Fly on outta here and spend the rest of your long, fairy-ass life alone."

Twitch was quiet.

"Or stick with us," Eddie continued. "Next stop for this band's Chicago, where we got a little business to take care of." He straightened his jacket and cleared his throat. "We just gotta get through a minor obstacle first."

Twitch was a man again. He smiled, bowed slightly, and plucked his fighting batons from thin air.

"You need the milk, too," Irving said quietly to Eddie.

"Yeah, I do," Eddie admitted. "But it ain't lack of faith on *your* part that makes the Nehushtan not work on me. It's lack of faith on *mine*. I'm a damned man, I told you, and I can't have the gift. But *you*," he clapped the preacher woozily on the shoulder, "you've got it up the wazoo. So you're the key part of the plan, got it? Without you working the mojo of the Moses snake, we ain't gonna get to the totem pole."

"I have faith," the preacher said. He said it so confidently that Eddie almost believed him. "If we die, but we stop Apep, we won't have died in vain."

"I ain't gonna die," Eddie said, willing it to be true. "Not today. Someone promised me that once, and I'm gonna hold him to his promise, come Hell or high water. Mike?"

"Done." Mike picked himself up off the floor with the open padlock in his hand.

Eddie grabbed the chain door and hoisted, but his strength was sapped and he couldn't budge it. Jim, big pale rugby-looking lunk that he was, stuck two fingers into the gate and raised it up over his head in a single gesture.

"Damn showoff," Eddie grumbled, but he shot Jim a grateful look.

If anything, the noise of the magical ritual throbbed even louder in the hall. It was almost groovy, the complex rhythm that the sistrum players had going, though it was too complex to be easily danceable. That kind of rhythm took practice and real coordination. The *EMPLOYEES ONLY* door was locked, so Eddie stepped aside and stood guard while Mike worked his magic on it.

"We consecrate thee Wepwawet, opener of the ways," he heard Aaron's voice over the noise. "Thy brain is purified by the fire of the serpent. Thy vision is free of taint."

Idiots, Eddie thought. At least the ritual wasn't over yet. He kept an uncomfortable eye on the backs of the cultists. They danced and pressed forward, humans and mutants and actual snakes all alike, as if they were watching the concert of their lives. Like the Rolling Stones and Led Zeppelin were playing on the same tiny stage.

Hadn't Irving said that Apep was going to eat some of them? What kind of stupid religion was that?

Of course, he and his comrades were supposed to be the appetizers now. Eddie wished he had a gun.

"Open," Mike said, and stepped aside. Eddie tried to pick up a jug of cleaning fluid and a box of lye flakes, but found he couldn't heft either. He settled for a straw broom and stood aside, leaning on it, while Mike and Jim loaded up with chemicals and box cutters.

"Here we go," Eddie said softly. He looked at his watch just in time to see the countdown slip below the one-hour mark. He really hoped Adrian hadn't been too optimistic in his estimate of the time.

BOOM!

A dazzling light suddenly burst into the dim basement of the Sears, accompanied by the stink of sulfur. Eddie staggered and caught himself with his broom, then looked toward the ritual, shielding his eyes with his hand.

The sistrum players had changed rhythms, but continued, their patterns as complex as before. The worshippers at the back of the circle, nearest the band, still faced into the center, but now they were beginning to step out of their clothes. Fine, Eddie thought. Naked and disarmed was better. The incense cloud was thick in his nostrils.

In the center of the circle, beside the makeshift surgical table, there was a hole in the air. It looked like a streak of starlight had been painted onto nothing at all, or an invisible curtain had parted and directly behind it was a lighthouse, blazing at full power. Eddie blinked against the strength of the light and tried to keep his attention on the figures in the middle.

With a final slash of the stone flake knife, Miriam the lamia freed the dog from the ropes that still tied it to the table. Eddie saw that its chest was stitched shut now, but of course, the dog couldn't possibly be alive, not after all its organs had been replaced.

But as he watched, the dog—Wepwawet, opener of the ways?—rolled over. It rose quite steadily onto all fours, sniffed at the air and jumped to the ground.

And then padded forward quickly, disappearing into the blazing gap of light.

CHAPTER NINE

No!" Phineas Irving yelled.

Eddie wanted to punch the preacher in the face. The cultists nearest the band stopped in the last stages of their disrobing and turned to see the source of the noise. A bald man, with sagging flesh, wiry gray curls of hair all over his body and ridges on his skull like a lizard, met Eddie's gaze and hissed in disapproval, showing a row of needle-like teeth and a preternaturally thin tongue.

"Screw you," Eddie muttered, and jammed the end of his broom into Ridge Head's eye. The fat man jerked back from the blow and doubled over in pain.

Something orange flashed past Eddie and spun out over the crowd. It was a box, Eddie saw, like a large box that baking soda might come in, and it shed big white snowflakes as it flew. From the shrieks that erupted from those that were hit, he guessed that the flakes were lye. The worshippers clawed at their faces and cringed and Jim launched into them like a vengeful comet, box-cutter spinning without mercy.

"Sing!" Eddie shouted. "Or pray, or whatever!"

Ridge Head lurched forward, grabbing with both hands for Eddie's throat. He felt weak, but he managed to stumble under the attack and avoid it, probably because Ridge Head's face and eyes were already red from the lye and the broom handle, and he was blinking out too many tears to see straight. The lizard-man's nudity and blindness made his testicles an easy target, and Eddie launched a knife-hand of knuckles into the soft tissue, twisting and tearing and dropping the mutant to the floor in a spray of blood and shrieking.

Twitch whizzed past on Jim's heels in falcon shape, and then Mike lumbered by. Eddie saw that the singer was already bogged down in fighting the crowd. He pushed off one man's shoulders to springboard with his boot heels into another's chest; he grabbed a snake-legged woman by the hair and cracked her forehead-first into the nose of a heavy bearded man with snakes' heads dangling limply from his clavicle; he sliced with the box cutter, eviscerating in a single blow two men rushing him with knives; he grabbed a snake-headed freak by the ankles and hurled his feet toward the ceiling, dropping the monster onto its face on the floor. But there were just too many of them. They grabbed Jim by the elbows and shoulders and pulled him back, swinging and kicking, to the ground.

Mike threw a gallon jug of something orange on a knot of them and they hollered and hissed in protest. A second gallon, colorless, smashed into their faces as they looked up, and then the big bass player plowed into them, bellowing like a bull and cursing like a Mexican pimp.

They were both still several rows back behind the sistrum players. In the center of the room, worshippers rushed forward into a thickening cloud of incense. Without being able to pay much attention to it—and sure as hell without *wanting* to—Eddie noticed that the surgery table had become an altar-bed. Phineas's snake-armed brother, naked now, savaged one prone woman with his hips while others rushed to embrace and caress the coiling monstrosities that sprouted from his shoulders. The lamia Miriam rose beside the shimmering gate of light, singing, while men and women alike pressed themselves to her sides, stroking her body with their hands and mouths. Most of the snake-snakes and the winged snakes in the room clustered around the table and the lamia, pressing to get into the action like so many detached, living organs. In their frenzy, they pushed each other against the incense brazier-charcoal grill, and the stink of their scorched flesh added a new note to the reek of the ritual chamber.

Above them all, the legs of the frozen damned twitched and shook in a frenzy of restrained motion.

"This is just wrong," Eddie grimaced, and limped forward into the fray.

"Onward Christian soldiers," he heard Phineas Irving trying to sing behind him, but the preacher was timid and quiet, and then he faltered.

"Come on!" Eddie barked. "Louder!" He grabbed Irving by the lapel of his jacket and stumbled forward into the crowd. He looked up at the Nehushtan to see if Irving was having any success.

The snake stayed coiled on its pole. It looked still and dead.

Ahead, Twitch landed on top of the nearest totem pole. The fairy shifted from falcon into human form as he touched down, and squatted on all fours above a big carved monkey's head. Baboon, maybe. In his leather-and-spikes outfit, Eddie thought, Twitch fit right in with this crowd. He crouched low and reached down with his hands, trying to get at the blindfold over the monkey's eyes.

Three young women had Mike knocked to the ground and stood over the bass player, scratching at him with their long nails. Mike wore his cracked old brown leather jacket and it protected his arms and chest, but there were bloody furrows on his neck and the backs of his hands. He held his box cutter, but he wasn't fighting back very effectively, just raising his arms and cringing.

Mike was not the right guy to bring to a fight against naked women. He had plenty of hate and fear in him, but it wasn't directed at women. For women, what he mostly had was a slack jaw and a dumb grin.

But Eddie had enough bitterness in his heart for both of them. He swung his broom as hard as he could like a bo staff, cracking it against the temple of the nearest girl. She stumbled away, shrieking in outrage and grabbing her head. Eddie continued his charge and rammed with his shoulder into the second young woman's side. She fell squirming and breathless.

Phineas Irving stabbed the butt end of the Nehushtan's pole between the shoulder blades of the third.

"Aaaaaararaaaaagh!" she shrieked, a piercing cry that cut through the drums and the chanting. Her skin where the pole touched her charred instantly to black, like a Satanic cattle branding, and the stink of scorching flesh filled Eddie's nostrils, overpowering even the billowing incense. She crumpled to the ground and Mike staggered to his feet, just in time to meet a slithering charge from the mutant Many Arms.

This guy, Mike had no trouble attacking. Head down, he rammed the fingers of one hand into the mutant's throat while he slashed with his janitorial knife at the thing's long, scaly and exposed chest.

"It works!" Irving laughed. "It's working again!" He raised the pole like a spear and jabbed over Mike's shoulder, poking Many Arms in his human face with the butt of the pole. The mutant roared with rage and slithered back, bleeding from the cuts Mike inflicted on him and slapping at a charred mark on his face the size of a silver dollar.

Jim was back on his feet too, and crashed through a writhing pile of sex-inflamed worshippers, scattering them right and left and almost forcing open a path to the center of the circle. Eddie looked into the light—no sign of the dog's return yet, or of any giant snake. Any *more* giant snakes, anyway.

"Twitch!" he yelled.

The fairy lay on the totem pole's head on his belly, booted feet and tail hanging over one side while his arms dangled over the other. "I'm working on it!" he shouted back.

A small cloud of winged serpents rushed towards Twitch from the focal center of the orgy. "Faster!" Eddie called, and he swung his broom, smacking serpents left and right. He sucked in the sex-reeking, serpent-fouled air, wishing it were colder and cleaner and willing his head to stop spinning.

He heard the hiss of a snake at his ankle level. He spun to face it, fearing he was too late and that he was about to take a second dose of venom, but gray-brown fur flashed between him and the snake and then the snake collapsed, headless.

The mongoose kept moving, bounding off between the wrestling bodies in search of more prey. Its fellows raced around the melee with coordination, striking down serpents by the charcoal grill, around the totem poles, on the stairs, under the altar, and even low in the air.

"Got it!" Twitch yelled triumphantly. He hooked two of his unnaturally long, slender fingers into the rough cloth of the blindfold and ripped it away. Eddie held his breath.

But nothing happened. Underneath the blindfold, Eddie saw that the monkey's head didn't have eyes, anyway. It had had them once, big and bulbous, but they'd been hacked into splinters, as if by hatchets, and then burned by fire. The Apep worshippers weren't going to take any chances.

"Rats."

Eddie knocked another flying serpent away, staggered and almost fell.

Stay focused, he told himself. Get to the lamia.

He looked into the center of the rite again. Still no dog. Snakes swarmed all over the frenzied multi-participant coupling on the table, and on the swaying mass of the lamia's body. There were lizards too, he now saw, things the size of iguanas and bigger, nastier monsters, like the thing he'd battled back in the diner kitchen ... that seemed a decade ago now. Worshippers of every kind pressed themselves against the lamia like piglets against a sow, writhing and squirming with ripe urgency.

Could he just slip in there with them and ... feed?

The thought made him feel sick. Miriam was voluptuous, but there was an unhealthy tinge to her skin, and the snakes in her hair and her lower half made her a monstrous thing. She was blue, dammit, and more than half a snake! Some men would have been aroused—some men clearly *were* aroused—but the naked Eros of the lamia's body just made Eddie think of Sharon and curse his luck even more.

And he had to get milk for Adrian, he reminded himself. This wasn't sex, this was grocery shopping.

Besides, he'd never get in there, not with all the worshippers pressing around, not unnoticed. And he wouldn't be able to collect milk casually in a container without being spotted. He had to stop the ritual, somehow immobilize the lamia.

He just didn't see how.

"Come on." He shanghaied Phineas Irving, pulling the preacher away from a four-person pile-up that now stank of burned flesh as well as of lust and viscous body fluids, dragging the rangy man with him towards the center of the room. Where were his guns, anyway? He wondered, his vision slipping like an old filmstrip on a jerky projector. He'd give a lot right now for his pump-action, twelve gauge Remington 870 Express Magnum shotgun, fully loaded with three-inch shells.

He'd give even more for a fifty caliber M2, a pile of sandbags and a high vantage point to shoot from. Clean out this nest of snakes in thirty seconds.

Jim had opened a path through into the center of the room. He held the box cutter in his left hand now and fought with a long hunting knife in his right—he must have taken it from one of the cultists while Eddie wasn't watching. Overalls lunged at him, snapping and biting, and Lady Legs charged from another direction—

and from a third came John Deere. The man's head was still gone, a ragged bloody stump of a neck sprouting from his shoulders, but the snakes waggling from his back seemed longer and angrier, and he held a long metal pipe in his hand like a club. At least he didn't have a TV on his shoulders, Eddie thought, and then he wondered why he thought that would be any worse.

Jim fought like a dancer, weaving in and out, feinting, dodging, stepping under. The mutants tangled with each other, missing, and chased him in circles. But they were getting closer, and Jim had nowhere to go. The smaller serpents, ground-stuck and flying ones as well, began to close in on him too. The mongooses wreaked havoc among serpentkind, but they were slowing down. If they weren't injured, they had to at least be exhausted.

Eddie dragged the preacher out into the circle. "*Onward, Christian soldiers, marching as to war.*..."

"*With the cross of Jesus going on before,*" Jim joined in. The guy had serious lungs on him, to be able to sing and fight at the same time.

Eddie spun with his broomstick club, knocking aside serpents, and then Twitch flashed through the central circle in falcon form, snatching two more flying snakes out of the air. Mike backed into the circle, too, his box cutter in his hands slashing half-heartedly to fend off the bare-fisted advances of two women. One had a perfectly formed womanly body but a snake's scales on her cheeks and forehead, and the other had a fine, clean young woman's face but snakes erupting from her chest instead of breasts.

Mike circled back to keep out of both their reach, but mostly he stabbed at the latter.

The sistrum players changed rhythm suddenly.

"O Wepwawet!" Aaron Irving's voice boomed suddenly from beneath a shuddering pile of women and snakes. "Wepwawet returns! The opener of the ways, behold, he comes!"

Eddie really wished he had guns.

Christ the royal master leaders against the foe,
Forward into battle see his banners go.

Overalls and Lady Legs and the others hesitated at the fringe of the Nehushtan's bubble, but Phineas Irving's voice sounded like it was losing some of its intensity.

Eddie looked around for anything else at hand that he could use—a gun, a knife, a torch, a charm, anything that might be more effective than a broomstick.

Nothing.

A dim outline began to take shape in the light of the pulsating rift. Eddie saw that the sistrum players nearest to him were just outside the space cleared by the Nehushtan. He staggered towards them, a plan spinning into being in his feverish brain. It was half-baked and half-assed and wholly insane, but what was the point of being the world's best tambourine player if he never used his chops?

Lady Legs rushed at him hissing—

and the sparkling red Nehushtan sprang from its perch, intercepting the hedge of woman-legged snakes and snapping it into its gullet in a single bite.

"No!" bellowed Aaron Irving. He sat up on his altar-bed, scattering scaly nymphlets and ecstatically hissing serpents with his sudden movement. The Nehushtan struck again, devouring John Deere whole. Freed of some of his assailants, Jim leaped spinning through the air, crashing into one of the totem poles and knocking it flying.

Eddie squinted at the pillar of light, fearing it was about to disgorge Apep himself, but the shadowy shape coalesced into a discrete form and emerged. It was the mummy-dog, Wepwawet, and it padded out calmly, looking totally normal apart from beady black eyes and a long snake-like tongue wagging from between its jaws.

And what would happen if Apep himself came out? Could the Nehushtan swallow the Egyptian god whole like it swallowed his minions? Somehow, Eddie doubted it.

Eddie shuffled and kicked his way into the row of sistrum players and snatched sistra away from them. As he plucked the instruments from their grip, some of the players kept playing, shaking their empty hands intently as if they were still making sound. Others stared at where the instruments had been in surprise.

He wondered if they were in trances. Or ensorcelled. Or high, although people who were stoned shouldn't be able to make such a complicated, coordinated sound together. Or maybe there were just enough of them playing together that they were individually trapped in the collective groove.

He thought he'd grab all the instruments and silence them, but there were too many of them, and then the rest of the worshippers lunged his way. He looked over his shoulder for help, but the others were distracted with their own problems.

Aaron Irving was standing, snake arms raised high and chanting as nude women crouched around his feet like feral cats. His brother faced off against him, staggering forward one step at a time like the Nehushtan was a boulder and he had to push it.

Eddie grabbed a handful of the instruments and retreated. Whatever it was that drove the sistrum players, he hoped they still had free will. He hoped they could see and hear, and be distracted.

Eddie, who was as good as stoned on snake venom, shouldn't by rights be able to play anything at all. The crowd loomed huge around him, naked and sweating and full of breasts and totem poles, and the room spun. But he was the world's best tambourine player, dammit. The world's *best*.

He jammed a sistrum handle into the top of each combat boot. He pinned a handle in the crook of each elbow by bringing his fists up to his shoulders, and he held two more in his two hands.

And he started to dance.

Not that he was much of a dancer, not in any formal kind of way. Sharon had paid for lessons once and he'd gone; the Foxtrot he'd been able to handle, and the Waltz, and even the Rumba, which was just the Waltz in four-four with a bit of Latin booty-shaking mixed in, but that was his limit. When he'd tried the Tango, he'd literally fallen down. Eddie didn't dance, he led the dancing from the stage.

But this wasn't a dance, not really. The sistrum was just a funky old tambourine, shaped like a hairbrush. Loaded up with six sistra, Eddie wasn't dancing—he was putting on the world's first one-man-six-tambourine performance.

He skipped in front of the section of sistrum players in front of him, trying to distract them. He needed to be the Pied Piper of Tambourines now, the most fascinating thing a sistrum player could ever see, and accidentally follow. He built up a rhythm in layers, and he built it up fast. He moved on his left foot in a slow hop, with his right shuffling and slamming down in a syncopated, ankle-twisting rattle quickly after every other front beat. He swung his left arm in slow circles, getting a steady *chink-chink-chink* out of the elbow rattle and shifting, ever-so-slightly-out-of-sync rasp on the back beats with the sistrum in his left hand. It looked sort of like a cross between St. Vitus' Dance and the Funky Chicken.

And with his right arm, he really went to town. His right elbow played sixteenth notes in an almost study drumming, deliberately omitting the third, the seventh, the eleventh and the thirteenth in every measure. The right hand played the rhythm of the melody to the song that he could hear Jim and Phineas Irving and even Mike now still singing.

"Onward Christian soldiers, marching as to war,
With the cross of Jesus going on before."

Eddie didn't need the sistrum players to follow his lead; he just needed to put on a wild enough show that it would snap them out of their pattern. Hopefully Irving was right, and the whole summoning was bound together in a tight interlocking pattern so that Eddie could put a stop to it by throwing off the rhythm.

Some of the players faltered, staring curiously at him. Eddie looked around the chamber. His friends sang and fought around the Nehushtan pole in Reverend Irving's hands in the circle. Snake mutants and flying vipers and ordinary rattlesnakes threw themselves against Eddie's friends and were thrown back by the ancient Israelite artifact, or chopped down with box cutters and cleaning supplies, or trampled by the hooves of the fairy, who now fought in his silver horse form. The ruby serpent itself was off its pole and inflicting terrible damage on the cultists, snapping up snakes and worshippers and mutant snake-worshippers with equal relish, and looking unstoppable.

Jim and Twitch and Mike, though, looked tired.

And Eddie felt exhausted. He was drained and sick, and only the Satanic power of his curse-begotten prowess with the tambourine kept him going. The sistrum players near him faltered and slowed, puzzled. They stared at him and some of them fell silent, but the overwhelming rhythm of drums and sistra and chanting continued, driven by the dozens of worshippers who didn't join in the combat. The racket was now supplemented by the squelching and grunting sounds of the further dozens who neither made music nor entered the fray, but piled upon each other in frantic animal lust all around the periphery of the room.

The chasm of light still shone in the middle of the room, and between it and the charcoal grill full of incense Aaron stood and chanted something Eddie didn't understand.

The lamia, Miriam, moved forward, shedding her more insensate micro-lovers as she went, sliding across the floor to intercept the Nehushtan.

"He comes!" Aaron Irving roared. "Behold, Apep comes!"

The mummy-dog sat obediently by the snake-armed sorcerer's side. Aaron flung his serpent arms wide like a carnival barker, and Eddie saw that something dark and very, very tall was inside the rent space full of light.

Eddie worked faster.

He hopped forward to the next bank of sistrum players. He didn't know what else to do—he had no gun, no wizard, and almost no hope. He clung to the recurring nightmare of his death, telling himself that he couldn't possibly die in the basement of a Sears in Oklahoma today, because his wife and daughters weren't here, there was no chandelier, no carpet, no curtains, no fire, no palace.

Unless that was all a lie.

The Nehushtan moved like a thing with intelligence, like it was reading Eddie's mind and trying to help him. It cleared his path, swallowing John Deere and a woman swinging a hatchet without slowing down.

Jim rushed Aaron Irving, with Mike and Twitch behind him, but a wall of snakes forced them back.

Eddie looked at Phineas Irving and saw that the preacher had dropped the Nehushtan pole. He stared at the column of light and backed away from it and snakes began to swarm in his direction.

The Nehushtan stopped, turned, and slid back towards its fallen perch.

"Oh no," Eddie muttered. He found the bank of sistrum players and shook his booty for them, knowing in his heart it was over. "Run!" he yelled feebly to the others. He was a dead man, and so was Adrian, but the others might still escape. "Run!" He knew they couldn't hear him.

"He comes!" Aaron Irving shouted again.

In his normal sight, Eddie still saw a moving shadow within the light. The shadow was immense. With his Infernal Eye, he saw a towering giant man with the head of a cobra, wearing sandals and a kilt and holding a curved scimitar in each hand.

Then another shadow rose over him, and he realized it was Miriam, bearing upon him to crush him with the coils of her body. She still held the obsidian knife, raised high overhead like she would follow the crushing body blow with a slashing attack.

"No!"

The shout was in the voice of Phineas Irving, and then the preacher slammed into Eddie, knocking him out of the way.

The lamia came down hard, square on the body of her estranged husband, with a sickening crack.

Eddie stumbled and fell to his knees, nauseated and burning, directly in front of the gate of light.

CHAPTER TEN

Nooooooooo!"

The lamia pulled back, bucking and rearing and scattering her lustful worshippers like a suddenly-charging rhino might scatter the birds feeding off its back. Lizards and snakes and snake-people staggered away in all directions.

Eddie shook himself, cracked an eye in the direction of Phineas Irving, and saw that the man was dead. Not just dead, totally squashed into a stain. His legs still existed, and one of his arms, and part of his head; the rest was a puddle of meat-pulp and blood.

But on the hand of the arm that hadn't been totally flattened, Eddie saw Irving's wedding ring.

Miriam saw it, too. She stopped for several long seconds, staring down at the bloody band of gold.

"Nooooooo!" she howled again and spun around.

Her tail was the thickness of a horse's chest where it joined her woman-shaped hips and tapered out maybe twenty long feet, covered in bluish scales. It was smooth except, Eddie now saw, twisted little fins of flesh near the end. The fins looked like bits that had once been legs and were in the long, slow process of withering away or being absorbed into the snake-flesh.

As she spun, the lamia thrashed her tail through a bank of sistrum players, killing them, knocking them out, knocking them over, and totally silencing their rhythm. The totem pole with the dog's head toppled too, falling into a writhing knot of naked worshippers with a wet cracking of bone. There had been mongooses in and around that writhing knot, Eddie thought dimly, and he wondered if the creatures had escaped.

He turned back to the gate of light, hoping it would now slam shut. It didn't. Either the ritual was a lot more tamper-resistant than Phineas Irving had imagined, or it had gone beyond the point of no return before Eddie and his friends intervened. The shadow, and the serpent-headed Infernal, loomed large in the brilliance. Lying directly in front of the gate, Eddie smelled sulfur and snake.

"Stop!" Aaron Irving cried. He stood naked before the charcoal grill, snake arms flailing. Incense billowed around him a cloud like he was being fumigated.

"We agreed!" the lamia howled. Her tail flicked right past Eddie in a blow that surely would have crushed him into jelly if it had hit him.

"It was his choice!" Aaron shouted to her. "We spared him once! He should have left us alone!"

Eddie saw Jim sweeping snakes off Mike's body with a broom, and dragging the bass player to his feet. Twitch, in his falcon form, snatched serpents from the air around the big singer's head.

Miriam darted forward and snatched her priest-lover by the throat. Their torsos were the same size, but her tail made her loom over him, and she evidently had superhuman strength, because she hoisted the man off the floor with one arm.

"*We* should have left *him* alone!" she hissed in a voice of a thousand rattles.

Eddie staggered to his feet. The worshippers were scattering, so he had a clear run at the lamia, but nothing to do once he got there. He patted his jacket pockets for something to hold lamia milk in and found the plastic cup full of jacks. That at least was something.

"He's not the first to die and he won't be the last!" the sorcerer hissed. "Besides, *you* killed him, not I!"

The lamia emitted a long, drawn-out wail, like a police siren. The chanting, the drums and the sistra were falling silent here and there around the room as the players fell victim to the spreading chaos, but Miriam's howl was louder than the musicians had ever been, and more piercing. And sad.

The gate of light stayed open.

"I killed him!" she shrieked, and then Eddie saw the back of the hand in which she held the obsidian knife.

And saw that she was wearing a wedding ring, too.

"Eternal life!" Aaron Irving choked out around the long-nailed fingers on his throat. His feet kicked helplessly off the ground and he was starting to change color to a deep purple. "Have you forgotten?"

The lamia raised him over her head and slammed him down on the table, hard. He groaned.

The mummy-dog Wepwawet barked at her and snarled. Without so much as a look of disdain, Miriam snapped her tail and threw the creature across the room. It sailed over the heads of scattering, confused orgy-goers and hit the stairs. Its body burst at the stitches on impact, scattering blood and a macabre collection of tiny organs on the concrete.

"*Love!*" the lamia shouted back at her consort, all the snakes in her hair mad and dancing with aggression. "Have *you* forgotten?"

Aaron Irving attacked her. Lying prone on his back, his snake-mouthed arms bit her flank and her neck, teeth sinking into her flesh. She didn't flinch, though blood ran down her chest and over her scales onto the floor, and sank the obsidian knife into Aaron's belly.

The priest-sorcerer arched his back, spitting blood from his mouth and nostrils. His snake arms bit Miriam again and again, on her arms, on her face, on her belly. His legs thrashed, the frantic activity of his body hurling blood in all directions. "Too late!" he shouted wetly. "He comes!"

With a last slash of the stone knife, Miriam chopped off the sorcerer's head. It bounced to the floor with a wet thud—

she swayed, lurching this way and that—

and crashed to the floor.

"Eddie!" Mike yelled, pointing at the gate.

Eddie looked down at the flattened body of the Reverend Irving. *If we die*, the preacher had said, *but we stop Apep, we won't have died in vain.*

"Hell."

Eddie grabbed the stone knife from the lamia's relaxing fingers; at least that was some kind of weapon. He blinked sweat from his eyes, stepped over her twitching tail—

and walked into the gate of light.

The basement of the Sears and the cleared-out Kitchenwares Department disappeared. The totem poles were gone, the sistrum players, the drums, the serpents, the fallen Nehushtan, the flattened Egyptologist, the altar, the dying lamia, Eddie's friends, all of it, disappeared in the blink of an eye.

Eddie still felt like total shit. His body burned and trembled and he sweated.

He stood in a long hall. It descended smoothly before him in a ramp, the floor of which felt like stone and was covered with sand. The air was warm and close and stank of snake. The ceiling of the hall disappeared in darkness, and the walls were ribbed with stone columns, with flickering oil lamps set into the stone between each pair. He heard a low humming sound, like a far-away engine idling.

He couldn't see the bottom of the passage. Below and ahead of him, he saw Apep. With his Infernal Eye, Eddie again saw the gigantic man with the head of a serpent. Apep wore an Egyptian-style headdress and simple white kilt, he had sandals on his feet, and he held a curved sword in each hand. And he was massive— maybe fifty feet tall, though the darkness and the distance might be deceptive.

Through his normal human eyes, Eddie saw an enormous cobra, hood flared—

headed his way.

The flake of sharpened stone in his hand now seemed totally inadequate. He really wished he had a decent gun. Or hand grenades.

No, he needed another kind of solution. What had Irving said? Sympathetic magic, like produces like. He was inside the ritual now, inside the summoning spell. He needed to do something to stop it, like producing like.

He realized that, out of reflex, he was patting his pockets. What did he have? The usual stuff. No hand grenades, sadly. His fingers found the plastic cup with the game of jacks in it. He'd bought the game at a gas station because the girls had liked jacks when they were younger, playing it on the stoop of the apartment building when they were supposed to be doing homework, and it had given him something to stare at and reminisce.

He pulled out the cup and ripped the top off. Could this possibly work? Or was this more insane than his Funky Chickenesque six-part sistrum performance?

Only one way to find out.

Eddie hurled the jacks down the passageway in a single handful, and the little red rubber ball with them. Some kind of incantation seemed appropriate, too, since that's what Adrian always did, only Eddie didn't know any magic words.

"Piss off, Apep!" he shouted. "Go back to where you came from! You ain't welcome anymore!"

It wasn't poetry, but it would have to do.

Apep stumbled. The giant stepped on the first of the spiky little metal jacks and winced in pain, tripping and crashing against the wall. He landed on his knee, one shoulder against a column, and stared up the hall at Eddie.

Who are you, mortal? he bellowed.

Oops.

The enormous, echoing voice sounded oddly familiar, and Eddie pegged the familiarity immediately—Apep sounded just a little bit like Jim. The thought of what that might mean made Eddie's skin crawl.

Eddie carefully put the cup and its lid back into his pocket. He planned to get out again, which meant he planned to need the cup. He didn't dare look behind him to see whether the hallway had an exit, and what it might look like.

Apep rose slowly to his feet again. *I will eat you first!* he roared, and started moving forward again, taking careful steps and watching the floor for more jack-caltrops. *I will eat you all!*

Eddie needed something else. Flashlight, pocketknife, compass, cigarette lighter, he couldn't imagine how any of it would help him. Then he grabbed the duct tape.

"Oh yeah," he said to himself.

Like produced like. Eddie fastened the end of the duct tape to the column to his left and quickly ran it across the passageway to the opposite column, where he tore off the strip and anchored it.

"I bar the way to thee, Apep," he intoned, doing his best dramatic spellcaster voice. The *thee* was a nice touch, he thought. Sharon would have been impressed, or at least she would have pretended to be impressed. Adrian would have mocked him.

No! Apep lurched forward, raising a scimitar in objection, but his feet came down on more jacks, and the giant fell to his knees, roaring.

That seemed like a good sign. Eddie ran across a second strip, cross the first at an angle. "I forbid thee passage!" he added.

Apep scrambled forward on gigantic hands and knees. Eddie could see the giant's blood smeared on the sandy stone floor of the tunnel. The swords flashed in the lantern light like a terrible two-tusked death machine, getting closer.

He ran a third strip across. Third time's the charm, he thought, and he ran it at a contrary angle to the second, so that the three strips of duct tape met in the center of the passageway like a big asterisk. A lucky star, Eddie said to himself, feeling a little panicky as the giant crashed towards him. Star light, star bright.

He wedged the stone knife into the tape for good measure, right into the center, turned so that its sharp edge faced down the passage towards the onrushing demon.

"I place this blade against thy heart, O Apep," he chanted, feeling himself getting a little carried away in the theater of the moment. "Thou shalt not pass."

Then he turned to look for a way out. Behind him rose a solid stone wall with a painting of an open doorway on it. To one side of the painted door image, to his shock, was a painting of Aaron Irving, the snake-armed man, and on the other was a picture of the lamia, Miriam. All the images were painted in what Eddie would have called, without any expertise whatsoever, ancient Egyptian style—they looked flat, with their shoulders both pointed to Eddie and their feet (Miriam's tail) all pointing inward at the door. They were dressed in what he thought of as Pharaoh-garb, too: cobra-crowns on their foreheads, kilt and sandals for Aaron, lots of eye make-up for them both.

It was troubling to Eddie to see his foes represented in tomb art. What did that mean? Was he in some real Egyptian tomb, where paintings of Aaron and Miriam showed Apep the way to escape? Was he in some magic dream-space, created only by the ritual?

But what troubled Eddie even more was the fact that the doorway was only a painting.

Wait! Apep thundered. *We can make a bargain!*

Eddie looked back and saw the snake-headed giant crouching in the hall above him. He was in easy reach of Eddie with his enormous swords now, but he stayed back, squatted in the hall with blood on his knuckles and running down his knees. In snake form he swayed from side to side, his hood flared wide and his fangs bared.

"Oh, hell no," Eddie shot back. "You got nothing I want."

He hoped.

Like produces like. Eddie turned and fell against the painted doorway, his strength gone—

No! Apep bellowed, shaking the tunnel so hard that sand fell from the ceiling onto Eddie's head and neck—

and then Eddie was through the doorway, collapsing to the ground in the basement of the Sears. Light shone on him and past him from behind, but even as he fell through, he could feel that he was being pushed, that the gate was closing shut behind him.

BOOM!

And then the light was gone, and he smelled snake and incense and saw by the blue-gray light of fluorescent tubes. At first, he just saw smears of blood on the concrete floor against which his face was pressed.

"Eddie!"

He lifted his head enough to see boots and shoes splattering through the gore in his direction. Sand fell off him as he moved, dusting the blood with an improbable yellow. His body trembled and he tried to point at the lamia, where she lay on her side next to the table, on a pile of the bodies of her worshippers and minions. "You might need to hold her down," he mumbled, and started crawling.

Jim picked him up and carried him, and Eddie saw that Jim's sword was belted around his waist again, and Mike bristled with guns.

Eddie half-expected the lamia to break him in two, but she didn't resist at all. She raised her head to meet Eddie's gaze as Jim set him carefully on his feet, nodded once and relaxed her neck again.

"Mierda," Mike muttered.

Eddie crawled into the embrace of the lamia. Her flesh was warm and she smelled as much of woman as she did of snake. Her torso, certainly, was all woman, dusky and voluptuous. If he hadn't felt on death's door, Eddie might have been excited to be this close to a beautiful woman. The danger, the fear that any moment she might rise up and smash him flat, only added to the thrill of the moment. Shaking like a bad drunk with the DTs, he curled into her arms, attached himself like an infant, and drank.

The blood that poured from her many wounds and trickled onto Eddie was as hot as his own. The snake heads of Miriam's hair hissed at him gently. It sounded like voices shushing a baby. Eddie listened to their voices and almost slipped into oblivion.

But then he felt the burning and the weariness and the trembling of his limbs fall away. He didn't feel refreshed or rejuvenated—he felt exhausted and beat up, but the effects of the venom were gone. He didn't feel like he was on the brink of dying anymore.

He dug into his pocket for the cup. It felt strangely intimate and invasive to lie beside the lamia and milk her, but it would have felt even more wrong to kneel and treat her like an animal. She had made terrible decisions, but she had paid for them, and in the end, she was as much a person as Eddie was. Eddie's heart roiled with all sorts of feelings, and he found to his surprise that one of the strongest was gratitude. As respectfully as he could, he filled the bottom of the jacks cup with the warm bluish milk of the lamia Miriam. When he had what he thought was probably enough, he put the cap back on the cup and stood.

He met her gaze one last time through lidded eyes.

"I forgot," she hissed simply.

Eddie nodded solemnly. "I know," he said. "I won't forget."

Then her last breath rattled in her throat and the lamia was gone. Eddie didn't feel bad for her—she'd killed way too many people, and done worse, to arouse his compassion. But he didn't hate her. In the end, he didn't even really find her monstrous.

He took a deep breath and stepped back. When he was sure he could face the others without tears in his eyes, he surveyed the damage.

It was total. There were bodies all over the room, snake, lizard, and human, and mutant combinations of all stripes. Eddie saw mongoose corpses, too—none of the preacher's furry allies had survived. The dog was smashed to pieces, the headless priest bled out, the preacher smashed into sanctified marmalade, the totem poles knocked over. The Nehushtan was either pulverized or hidden in the wreckage. Still, there was something about the room that nagged at his perception, something positive, something that made him feel almost happy.

Mike handed him his guns. Eddie checked to see that both weapons were loaded, snapped the Glock into its holster and reattached the Remington 870 to its shoulder strap while he thought about what it could be. It felt good to be armed again.

On the other hand, the junk in his pockets had been surprisingly useful.

"You okay?" Mike asked.

Eddie snorted and cut away the tourniquet with his pocketknife. "All things considered," he said, "not too bad."

Then it hit him.

The legs were gone.

He looked up and saw an ordinary concrete ceiling, undergirded with pipes and fluorescent lights, spattered with blood, but with no sign of the field of ice and the dangling legs of the damned that had previously haunted his vision.

Eddie took a deep breath and let it out slowly. "Yeah," he said. "I feel good."

Twitch looked around at the mess. "No amount of bleach is going to clean this up," the fairy chuckled.

Jim shook his head and bent to pick up the charcoal grill of smoldering incense coals by its struts. Eddie watched as the singer walked slowly around the carnage, shaking coals out onto fallen totem poles and into puddles of cleaning fluids, throwing the last of them indiscriminately into the janitorial closet. By the time he was done, the basement was on fire.

Eddie started towards the stairs. In front of him a rusty iron chain ground slowly from right to left at his chest level. Severed human arms, legs and heads hung pinned to the chain like so much laundry on a clothesline. The mouths of the severed heads opened and closed and their eyes bulged in Eddie's direction like they were calling to him.

Eddie shook his head and walked right through the chain. He ached and he was exhausted, but he was alive and free.

Did that mean, he wondered, that his vision of death in a burning palace was a true one?

Or had he been inspired to fight on by a false vision, thereby making the vision true? Or at least, preserving the possibility of its truth?

He shook the thoughts out of his head as he crossed the ground floor towards the glass doors. Really, he knew, he wouldn't know the answer to anything until it was all over.

"I hope Adrian made it," Mike muttered.

Eddie checked his watch. "We still got fifteen minutes," he said. "We'll get there in time. How are your fingers?"

"Fingers?" Mike opened and closed his hands experimentally. "Fine. Why?"

"We got a gig," Eddie reminded him. "Unless you got cash you ain't told me about, we gotta play or we don't have enough money to get out of Oklahoma."

"*Cagado.*"

"That's about the size of it," Eddie agreed. He pushed open the doors and he and Mike walked out into the cooling air of the early evening.

CROW JANE

CHAPTER ONE

Jane looked with eyes that had seen many things. She had watched the Holy League sink the Turk at Lepanto. She had seen Spartacus and his six thousand revolutionaries nailed to crosses on the Appian Way. She had witnessed the falls of Troy, Ugarit, Ebla, and Babel, when she had still been recognized by the children of men, and known by the name her mother had given her. It had been a long, long time since anything had truly delighted Jane's eyes.

This rock and roll band certainly didn't. They tried to make up in enthusiasm what they lacked in finesse, but their efforts left her unsatisfied. Time was infinite, mankind was a huge, flowing river, and Jane had heard it all before. Still, she had followed them all the way from New Mexico, and this was her first actual glance at them, so she paid close attention.

"Ten thousand miles of motorway tar," the singer roared.
Maori girl and a Japanese car,
Picking a living on this old guitar,
I gotta go.
I gotta go."

He was tall and lean, with the broad-shouldered, muscular physique of a rugby player or a Myrmidon. He looked the part of a rock and roller, pale and intense, with eyes like ice and black hair to his shoulders. There was something familiar about him too, something Jane could not quite place. His wide mouth nearly swallowed the microphone, and his booming voice threatened to shake the brick walls of the bar.

"I loved you well but from afar,
Picadilly or Zanzibar?
I gotta go."

The crow flapped directly over the players on the tiny stage, mocking her with its enormous black wings. She couldn't avoid seeing it, but she resolutely avoided paying it any conscious attention.

"Enjoyin' the music?" a voice asked at her elbow.

Jane turned and saw that it had come from the man behind the bar. "Layers of sound piled on top of each other do not necessarily become music," she told him, "just as a series of events is not necessarily a story."

"You don't follow the band, then?"

"I don't."

"Too bad," he said, "I'se hopin' maybe you could tell me their names. I coulda swore when we booked them yesterday they were The Racket Club, but tonight they're callin' themselves Laughing Jack and the Sons of Bitches."

"Maybe they're on the lam."

The bartender chuckled deferentially. "If they are, I reckon they're not the only ones in the room. That's quite the set of tattoos you're sportin'," he said.

Jane looked at him more closely. She didn't particularly care for the bartender, and it had been centuries since she'd had a conversation with a human being that was anything other than dry dust and hollow words, but she wanted a distraction from the crow. Also, the fact that he had noticed her at all caused a tiny spark of surprise to flash in her mind—he must be a keen observer, and she must have let herself drift too close. "And you have quite an accent, barkeep. You're not from here."

"I ain't from Kansas," the bartender agreed. He was a tallish man with a shock of silver hair and a twinkle in his eye. He wore jeans and a checked shirt, and Jane could see in the *Wild Turkey-*branded mirror behind him that he stood within easy reach of a sawed-off, double-barreled shotgun under the bar. "I wandered the hills of North Carolina in my youth, and I reckon in my old age I jest started wanderin' a bit further. Name's John," he grinned. "What're you drinkin'?"

Jane was already bored. No amount of wandering could compete with hers. She looked back at the stage again and saw the crow perched on the guitar player's amplifier. He was a wiry thin black man in torn blue jeans and a green military jacket, bristling with pocket flaps, the sleeves of which had been crudely ripped off. He played a worn red guitar and stared down at it with intense focus. Behind him lurked the bass player, a tall, slightly paunchy man with thick black hair. If any of the band was a real musician it was him—he threw improvised little flourishes into the turnarounds like he too was bored with the song, and was trying to liven it up—but he looked shaky, and barely under control. Drugs, Jane thought, or some deep-seated fear.

The burning sands of the hippodrome,
Slick my hair back, polish my chrome,
One final battle, one final poem,
I gotta go.
I gotta go.

"Call me Jane," she said. "And pour me rum."

"Got a bit of an accent yourself, don't you?" John asked, pouring black liquid out of a bottle with sea monsters inked on the label.

"I was young in another time and place," she said. "I only learned English as an adult." When she was a child, no human foot had yet trod upon the forested knob of land that would one day become England.

"I wouldn't want you to feel I'se pryin', but I'm guessin' the South Pacific … am I right?" John asked.

Jane threw back the rum. She'd learned to like the drink while sailing Spanish treasure galleons, centuries ago now. It seemed like yesterday to her, but a yesterday from which she was separated by a yawning gulf of infinite tedium.

"I mean, from the tattoos. Ain't a lot of people get tattoos like those, are there? Big swirlin' patterns on the face and all? That's distinctive."

"They were put on me as a mark," Jane said, the word *mark* bitter in her mouth. "They were meant to be distinctive."

"Plus your complexion's that nice caramel color," John said. "I don't mean nothin' rude by it—chalk it up to my age if you're offended, or the hits to the head I took in Nam—and I think you're pretty. I'm jest sayin' you look Polynesian. Or Latina, maybe, or some kind of mix. Am I right?"

I know I told you I was born to roam,
But now I'm burning to get back home.
I gotta go.

At the back of the stage with the bass player were the electric organ and the drums. The organ player was a boxy little mesomorph with brown hair, a thin black tie and a neat blue suit, tight at the wrists and ankles. He was nearly invisible under piles of electronic devices and cable and his sound was huge, but patchy.

The drummer, by contrast, sat at a very spare drum kit and played with two wooden sticks that looked like fighting clubs. She wore spiked leather from head to toe and had the androgynous facial features and animal tail that marked her as one of Mab's folk. That, Jane thought, was almost interesting. What was one of the fey doing playing in a crummy rock and roll band in Dodge City, Kansas? The Legate hadn't said anything about that, and it made her take a second look at the other members of the band. What were *they* hiding?

"Men have always found me pretty," Jane agreed. "That's the root of the problem."

The song ended in a predictable clash of cymbals and some modest scattered applause. The guitar player shuffled over to the singer and took the microphone. Jane noticed their footgear—the singer's looked like what a horseman might wear to ride, and the guitar player had combat boots.

"We'll take a break now," the guitarist announced, "but we'll be back on the stage in a few minutes."

"Another?" John asked cheerfully.

"I've had enough," Jane said. She slapped a bill onto the bar and stepped away into the crowd, her spurs jingling slightly.

Her wards of dissembling made her hard to notice, and she let the sweaty, alcohol-breathed herd swallow her. Wellman's wasn't full, but it was full enough to give her space in which to be inconspicuous, despite the ankle-length black duster she wore and the black broad-brimmed hat, the knives strapped to her belt and boots and forearms and the swirling tattoos that covered her entire face as they covered her entire body. She had given up cursing those angels who had held her down and marked her millennia ago, but only because her curses were pointless. If she ever saw one of them, she'd kill him.

That was why she'd come to Kansas.

Not that her knives would work on an angel. Of course, the knives weren't her only weapons. Deliberately, she brushed the pistol holstered on her hip, the Horn. And that was why the Legate had come looking for her.

That, and the fact that he had something to offer her that she couldn't refuse.

The crow flapped slowly in circles in the high space above the bar. The drinkers, primarily college kids but including a few self-consciously hip-looking older people, went about their business and mostly ignored the band that stepped off the stage into their midst. The big handsome singer got offered a few beers and took one, nodding and smiling as three college girls asked for the blessing of his presence, but saying nothing. Was he shy? The others were left to their own devices. Three of them headed for the bar, the heavy bass player in the lead and walking fast.

The fairy moved off alone.

Wellman's had been built in a structure that had once housed a railroad station. Its walls were two stories tall and made of brick, and its windows and ceiling had a Gothic look about their arched apices. Bare light bulbs hung in straight rows from very long wires, and the crow wheeled slowly around them. A length of track still ran along one wall in a bed of gravel, terminating at either end in blank brick. The restrooms squatted off a short hall tunneling out perpendicularly from the bar, over a bridge of planks that had been nailed into place to limit the tripping opportunities for drunk patrons with urgently pressing bladders.

The fairy skipped over the bridge and headed into the restrooms.

Jane followed. She prepared as she went, slipping an iron knife—not steel, *iron*—into her right hand and a digging a small glass vial from the pocket of her duster with her left. She checked the vial visually as she passed under a light bulb to be sure she'd grabbed the right one—the glob of quicksilver inside slid back and forth and she smiled without pleasure.

The wards of dissembling were her general travel disguise because they were so simple to erect and so costless to maintain and they did the job—mostly Jane didn't bother people. She just didn't want to be noticed. Unfortunately, the wards of dissembling would lose effectiveness if she walked directly up to the fairy. As the drummer stepped into the mouth of the restroom's hall, she cast a long, pale shadow by the hallway's lights. Jane stepped firmly onto the shadow and spoke a few words.

If anyone in the hall had heard the words, they would have been unable to decipher them, or even remember the sounds, two seconds later. She had spoken in the tongue of her birth, a language that hadn't been spoken on earth for millennia, and which most humans were no longer able, by divine fiat, to understand. The language was Adamic, and Jane understood it because she had been born before the Great Tower, the Confusion of the Tongues, and the First Scattering. She was subject to the Fall of Adam—indeed, she was its firstfruits—but not to the Curse of Babel.

She spoke her spells in Adamic because it was one of the Primals, and a powerful language for magic. As soon as she had spoken this one, and willed some of the force of her *ka* into it, some of the fire and energy that was the power-component of the collection of spiritual things most mortals knew as their *soul*, she became invisible. Everything looked the same to her, but she knew that to any other observer who had been able to see her at that moment, she would have vanished into the fairy's shadow.

The shadow pulled her now and she walked faster, padding behind the long silver hair and silver horse's tail of the drummer. The fairy pushed at the *GENTLEMEN* door first, found it shut, and then opened *LADIES*. Jane followed her in, nimbly slipping through before the door thudded shut.

The fairy latched the door and Jane drifted out of the way, tightening her grip on her weapons. She wanted the creature fully distracted when she made her move, and she could afford to wait.

Then the drummer turned to the mirror over the sink, looked into it with a fierce eye and spat on the glass. That move piqued Jane's curiosity, and as the fairy filled her hands with blue-foaming soap from the dispenser over the sink and then smeared it all across the mirror, she considered. Was the fairy an outcast? A criminal? An exile?

What was she doing here? Jane wondered.

And could she still enter the Mirror Queendom?

She had been waiting for the fairy to be distracted, she realized, and instead she had distracted herself. Jane whispered several more words of Adamic and willed into place wards of silence. As the silver-haired drummer shook foam from her hands, splattering it on the broken red tile of the floor, Jane attacked.

She struck with the iron knife first. She didn't stab, because she wanted the fairy alive, at least for the moment. Instead, she leaned forward with her elbows and forearm, leading with the blunt edge of the blade. The first notice that the fairy had of the attack was Jane's iron knife suddenly pressing into the back of her neck.

The iron burned her at the touch. Smoke and a burning smell—not the bitter stink of burning flesh, but a woody odor, like that of a tree on fire—filled Jane's nostrils.

"Aaaaaaaaagh!" the fairy howled. Jane heard her perfectly well, but she knew that as long as she kept physical contact with the creature, no one else would be able to hear her. The fairy jerked and twisted, but the pain sapped all the bite out of her resistance. Jane fell forward with the creature, slamming her face into the soapy mirror and then pinning her to the sink.

"Who are you?" the drummer shrieked, kicking back wildly. Jane cracked her forehead against the white porcelain of the sink and then spun her around, keeping the blade pressed to her white flesh.

"I'm the Marked Woman," Jane growled. "Don't your people teach their cubs and kits about me anymore?"

She said it to instill fear, and because it couldn't hurt her that the fairy knew. Then she slammed her other hand against the drummer's exposed clavicle, shattering the glass of the vial and grinding the quicksilver into the fairy's pale skin.

Wings sprouted from the side of the fairy's head like ears, flapped once and disappeared. A horse's legs exploded out of the leather-bar-style clothing the drummer worse, and then her face became a horse's long, bony phiz, and then a falcon's. She exploded into a shrieking, flailing, formless and many-formed abundance of shapes. She kicked and writhed and twisted but she didn't escape, because Jane didn't let her.

All the while, Jane pressed down with the iron knife and smelled smoke.

And all the while, the elusive, ever-present crow of her death perched on top of the paper-towel dispenser and stared down at her with a sour yellow eye.

Then the animal forms were gone, and the man and woman shapes, too, and Jane held the fairy against the sink in her true form.

She was a female, two feet high, with leathery gray skin and eyes that were completely yellow. Her belly and her dugs sagged, her cat-like ears and whiskers trembled. The one remnant of her more beautiful self, her silver horse's tail, flapped soggily in the running water of the sink.

"What shall I call you?" Jane pulled the knife away, keeping it still in her hand and visible, but she held the quicksilver pressed to the fairy's flesh. It would keep her from changing shape, or attempting to use her Glamour.

"I'm a fairy," she croaked back. "I don't have a true name, sorceress."

Jane stared coldly down at the creature and flared her nostrils. "Don't repeat the mistake of thinking I'm stupid, child of Mab," she said. "I will happily release you from your exile with my iron blade."

The fairy hissed through gapped yellow teeth. "How…?" she wrinkled her nose, looked at her own handiwork on the mirror, and slumped in defeat. "Twitch," she said. "Call me Twitch."

"Very good, Twitch," Jane gave her prisoner positive reinforcement. "Now listen to me closely. I'm going to ask questions. You're going to be tempted to evade them, or to lie. The first time you choose not to answer fully and honestly, I'll cut you." She held the iron knife in front of the fairy's eyes as a reminder. "The second time you do so, I'll kill you. Do you understand?"

The fairy nodded.

"Use words, Twitch." Jane smiled.

"I understand," the drummer agreed.

"Several days ago," Jane began, "something was stolen in New Mexico. Something that Heaven considers very valuable, that had been in its keeping and hidden for thousands of years. The keeper fled." No point identifying the keeper as the angel Raphael, or Jane's real errand, or the bitterness of her feelings. "The thieves escaped. I have tracked them here." No point explaining about the Mare, either. "Are you following me so far, Twitch?"

"Yes," Twitch nodded.

"Now," Jane said slowly. "I'm going to ask you the question that you are going to try to lie about. Remember this, child of Mab. The first time, I'll only cut you."

Twitch gulped.

"Where is the hoof, fairy?" Jane asked.

Twitch hesitated. "I ... I don't know," she ventured in her bullfrog voice.

Jane nodded, affecting a sad face, and stabbed the drummer in her arm.

"Aaaaaaaagh!" Twitch shrieked again, a horrendous, piteous cry. She thrashed and wiggled on the sink, but Jane held her pinned, and kept the quicksilver firmly pressed to her chest.

Smoke billowed from the wound rather than blood, and stung Jane's eyes.

"Stop! Please, stop!"

Jane pulled the knife back and regarded the fairy with stern eyes.

"I told you," she reminded the ugly creature, "the first time I would cut you. Do you remember what I'm going to do the second time you choose not to answer me?"

The fairy's eyes rolled desperately in her head. "Kill me," she hissed through chapped and shuddering lips.

"Kill you," Jane agreed. She turned the knife so that its sharp edge now faced the fairy, and gently touched the blade to her neck. She heard a *sizzle* and smelled faint burning. "Now, are you ready to try again?"

Twitch said nothing, only shivered. The crow stared down impassively. After thousands of years and thousands of failed attempts, Jane still had to suppress the urge to throw the knife at the crow instead, to make a heroic lunge and grab the bird with its terrible, joyous burden, tearing into its flesh and feathers with her teeth and devouring it whole, drawing it into her body's permanent embrace.

She blinked and exhaled, driving away the thought.

"I know that you and your friends stole Azazel's hoof from the well in Dudael," Jane said. "Understand me clearly: I *know* it was you. Unless you are content to die here and now, Twitch, child of Mab, tell me where the hoof is."

Twitch swallowed hard and stared into Jane's eyes. "Jim has it," she said.

Good. Once the stone started rolling down the mountain, the fairy would be hard pressed to stop it. "Which one is Jim?"

"The singer," Twitch said, and closed her eyes pathetically.

"Where does he keep it?" Jane asked.

"On his body," the fairy admitted. "He keeps it taped ... taped to his belly."

Jane nodded. She wouldn't have let it away from her person, either. "Is that where the hoof is now?" she asked.

Twitch hesitated, but only for a second. "He hasn't let go of it since we got it," she said. "It's his."

"What do you mean, it's *his?*" Jane asked. "Is he your leader?"

"Yes," Twitch said instantly. "The hoof belongs to his family. Really, his father." Now that she had started talking, she couldn't stop. "Jim is Azazel's son."

This thoroughly mediocre dive-bar band was quickly becoming the most interesting thing Jane had seen in a century. "What are you doing with the hoof?" she asked. She rationalized the question easily: she needed to gauge how much resistance would be put up when she took it, and whether Jim would try to take it back and thereby interfere with her plans. Really, though, she was curious.

"We're going to Chicago," Twitch said. Tears leaked from her yellow eyes and streamed onto the bathroom porcelain. "Eddie knows a hoodoo woman there, and we're going to contact the Infernal powers and make a deal."

"Eddie?"

"The guitar player. He sold his soul and he wants it back."

"And what does Jim want?"

Twitch sobbed openly now. "He wants to be … he wants peace, I think."

"And you want back?" Jane nodded at the foam-covered mirror. It felt strange to indulge pure curiosity. Strange and sort of pleasant. "Somehow, you can strike a bargain with Azazel that will let you back into the Shadowless Palace."

Twitch nodded and shuddered. "I need his forgiveness," she wept.

That was a queer thing to say and prompted more questions, but Jane shook herself mentally; enough games. Time to take quick action. "Do you know who I am?" she prompted the creature.

"You're the Marked Woman," Twitch nodded. "You're Qayna, the one the humans call *Cain*."

Jane raised the iron knife to plunge it into the fairy's body.

Bam! Bam! Bam! came a hammering at the boor.

"Twitch?" called a man's voice.

CHAPTER TWO

T witch, we're on in three. You in there?"

Jane hesitated a split second, considering whether she should hold the fairy drummer hostage and demand the hoof of Azazel in exchange. In that split second, she realized that the voice at the door didn't belong to Jim the singer, and remembered that he had sat down, grinning, to drink a beer with the table of co-eds, so the person knocking must be someone else in the band.

In that same split second, Twitch bit her.

Jane cursed in Adamic (her native tongue had few true curse words, but they were very strong—Jane's curse splashed cold water around the room as if she had punched her fist into the sink) and pulled back her hand. It was the hand with the bead of quicksilver cupped in it, and the fairy had craned her neck at an impossible angle to sink her yellow teeth into the flesh of Jane's wrist.

She only pulled the hand away half an inch, but that half inch was enough.

A silvery falcon exploded into being beneath Jane's hand, a broad-winged, beautiful bird that was instantly recognizable as a fey creature, and as Twitch, by its possession of the same long silver horse's tail. With a powerful flap of its wings, the falcon snapped out of Jane's hands and up to the top of the paper towel dispenser. It shrieked, a sharp and piercing cry, and then Twitch was again a lithe, androgynous drummer wearing leather and spikes. The crow gazed dully at them both, unfazed that it had to share its perch so long as it wasn't sharing with Jane. And the fairy, of course, didn't see the crow at all.

Twitch struck the wall with her heels and kicked off. Her drumsticks leaped into her hands in mid-air as she soared over Jane's head, striking with a drum major's *rat-tat-tat* of hard blows.

"Twitch? What's going on, *chingón*?" the voice at the door insisted.

Jane blocked several blows of the fairy's batons with her forearm, ducking as the other woman sailed over her. She had an instant's regret that she had let herself be distracted, but then decided that this was a development she could use.

"Mike!" the fairy shouted, landing lightly on her feet by the cracked toilet. "Help!"

She was outside the wards of silence, and Mike heard her. "*Huevos!*" Jane heard him shout, and then a shoulder was thrown against the door.

Jane let the wards of silence drop and kept fighting.

She gained space for herself with a series of sharp thrusts. The fairy parried and retreated until she was forced to hop up and stand on the toilet seat itself, back against the old lead plumbing. Then Jane whirled, throwing her duster up behind her like a cloak to impede and distract her fey combatant. With a swipe of her forearm, she cleared the mirror of foam and then finished her spin arms first, catching and deflecting another flurry of blows from the fairy. She kept her right fist closed around the lump of quicksilver, and the iron blade in her left.

The crow watched, unmoved.

"Hold on!" Mike shouted. "Eddie! It's Twitch!"

Reinforcements were arriving. That suited Jane just fine, so long as they didn't include Jim.

Bang! Bang! Bang!

The doorknob burst inward and clanked to the floor, and then the latch flew off its screws.

Jane forced the fairy back again with the cold bite of her iron knife, muttering an Adamic incantation as she did—

then turned and leaped for the mirror.

254

The bass player shouldered into the room, leading with his pistol and following with his burly frame. Behind him came the guitarist, shorter and wiry and also holding a gun.

"Are you leaving so soon?" Twitch shouted, and Jane felt the creature strike her in the back, wrapping long fingers around Jane's shoulders as the surface of the mirror faded, became translucent and then transparent, revealing behind it an endless maze of stairs and corridors and two surprised faces—

"Dammit!" someone yelled behind her in the restroom—

and then Jane felt the cool veil of the mirror's unsubstantiated presence pass over her like a film of water and she was through.

But she had come with a passenger.

The fairy bit her again, in the neck.

Jane hit the ground rolling forward, onto her fingertips and the top of her head and then she slammed down onto her back on the stone floor, hard—

smashing Twitch.

"Oomph!" the fairy grunted.

"Halt!"

Two girl-boyish fey faces loomed over her—the faces of Queen's Rangers, no doubt—over spears pointing down. One had flame-orange hair and a fox's tail and the other was striped, head and tail, like a badger; both wore leather jerkins and greaves, the breastplates carved and painted with Mab's emblem, the tree and lightning bolt. Their spears were entirely wooden, their tips sharpened by fire.

The Queen's Rangers were scouts, warriors and sentinels; they patrolled the infinite maze that was the Outer Bounds of the Mirror Queendom.

Jane ignored the Rangers and stood; Twitch was too stunned by the impact with the floor to stop her. The Outer Bounds stretched around her in all directions, an explosion of halls, staircases, shafts and pits with glass windows in every flat surface. This was a defense mechanism, Jane knew, a classic maze to disorient and deter outsiders. Any ordinary human who managed to stumble in through a gate would find himself bewildered and lost, and the fairies could easily kill him or, if it so struck their puckish senses of humor, let him wander forever.

Jane was no ordinary human, and she knew how to make her way.

"I say again, halt!" cried Foxtail in a shrill voice that whistled through his nose. "Friend or foe, and state your business!"

"My business is my own," Jane said coolly. She sheathed her iron knife, but slowly, making sure that the fairies saw it first.

It had the intended effect; they both shuffled back a step and tightened their grip on their spears.

Jane kept the quicksilver in her fist—she'd need it to get through the Bounds, anyway—and deliberately doffed her broad-brimmed hat, letting her long black hair fall out behind her in its loose plait and allowing the Rangers get a good look at the tattoos all over her face. "And I'm no one's friend. I'm a fugitive and a vagabond ... hadn't you heard?"

Both Rangers gasped. "The Marked Woman," Badger growled uneasily.

"Let me pass," Jane told them, replacing her hat. "You have no choice, anyway. You can't kill me, and if you get in my way I'll surely kill you. This one, though," she turned and kicked Twitch hard in the belly, "this one is one of yours."

She straightened her duster and walked on. She knew that she had the initiative, but she would only retain it if she kept moving.

"How did you even get in here, Outcast?" she heard Badger grunt behind her, and then came pummeling sounds that boded ill for Twitch.

Light shone in through all the windows around Jane. Each window let in luminescence of a different quality—noon's blaze here, starlight there, and in a third place a fluorescent flutter—resulting in a dim and shifting patchwork of illumination in the maze Jane now traversed. Nowhere was there darkness, but nowhere was there any light a traveler could trust. She whispered instructions in her birth tongue to the drop of quicksilver, infused it with her ka, and then followed its directions as it strained within her hand.

The fey were overwhelmingly convinced of their own cleverness, but a little insight and a few basic tools were all one needed to handle them.

Before she'd activated the quicksilver, the crow had sat on a high step and stared at her. Now it preceded Jane up a staircase, across a needle-thin bridge, under a series of arches so low Jane had to stoop, across a vault the size of a football stadium and into a warren of twisting halls only a cubit wide. At her every step she heard the muffled swishing of things moving, just out of her sight, not quite in sync with the metallic jingle of her spurs; Jane ignored the sounds. The crow stopped at the window she was looking for, the gate she had willed her quicksilver guide to locate.

With a single word, Jane cleared the frosted surface of the window and looked through. She saw what she expected and hoped to see: the silvered back of the bartender John's head, a row of bleary-eyed college boys flipping cups at the bar, and beyond them, a table with a circle of giggling young women chattering at the tall singer, Jim.

Azazel's son. Azazel had had another son.

And Jim had the hoof.

Jane didn't have an empty vial. She drew the FN Model 1910, the Calamity Horn, the weapon Heaven had loathed and now coveted, and fired off a round into the maze. *Bang!* the discharge echoed loud, but there was no mortal in earshot to be driven mad by it. The sound that Jane was looking for was the tinny rattle of the brass shell as it hit the floor. The noise might discombobulate Foxtail and Badger, but she was indifferent to their concerns.

Jane holstered the gun. She stooped, picked up the shell, and poured the quicksilver bead into it. She tamped a bit of wax from a candle stub in her pocket into the top to seal it; that would have to do for now. She pocketed candle and shell again and turned to face the window. She stretched to look down at the floor at John's feet, watching his movement and his shadow. When he stood to calmly refuse another beer to a buzzcut boy who looked like he was on the verge of throwing up his last one, she cast the opening spell—

stepped through the gate, still mumbling in Adamic—

and touched down in John the barkeep's shadow, safely invisible.

John stiffened, straightening his back and looking around him. The Appalachian wanderer knew too much; Jane stepped quickly away from him, exiting the print of his shadow and slipping out of his arm's reach, letting the wards of dissembling take over again. She crouched quickly, stepping under the hinged flap in the bar leading out onto the floor at walking speed.

She looked back from the other side. For just a moment, she thought the bartender was looking directly at her.

Jane frowned, but then John's eye wandered away, and the crow flew out through the mirror and soared above the tables.

She looked to her right, at the restroom hallway. The guitarist came hustling out of the ladies' room with the bass player on his trail. They were headed directly for Jane, not seeing her for her wards of dissembling.

"Hey!" the heavy bass player called. That was *Mike*, then, the one who cursed in Spanish and looked like a drunk.

"Don't be such a damned coward!" the black man hissed back. "What do you think's going to happen if you're alone for a minute?"

"You have no idea, Eddie!" Mike shook his head. The guitar player was *Eddie*.

Eddie grabbed the short organ player at the corner of the bar. He was dressed like an extra on an eighties television show, but he drank like a yogin—the glass in front of him had an egg in it, as well as fibers that might be some kind of grass, and it smelled like vinegar. "Adrian!" Eddie snapped. "In the can, pronto! It's Twitch!"

"A friend in need," Adrian chuckled, "and so forth. Especially Twitch." He gulped his egg mess in one swallow, pulled his sleeves down to his wrists, and turned to follow his friends.

"Jim!" Eddie yelled, waving across the bar at the singer as they went.

Then Adrian stopped. Jane had a sense of foreboding and stepped into the edge of a booth full of men in cheap suits chattering over mozzarella sticks and olives. She hid her body behind the wooden column that formed the corner of the booth and peered around it.

Adrian pulled something from his pocket and held it up to his eye. As it touched his face, Jane saw it glint and realize that it was a piece of glass, a lens of some sort. She ducked back further into the booth, chanting quickly in Adamic to throw up the deepest, strongest wards of obfuscation and seeming she could. Her ka raged indignantly within her at the suddenness with which she tapped its strength, and she ignored it. Its fury felt like bad indigestion or a heart attack, but she knew it couldn't kill her.

Then she held her breath.

Long seconds passed in which nothing happened, except that her omnipresent crow dropped onto the high seat of an adjacent booth and stared at her.

Soon enough, she thought, but she kept her mouth shut.

When she looked back around the column behind which she was hiding, she saw the organ player—the *wizard*—Adrian, moving with Eddie and Mike towards the restroom, and concluded he must not have seen her. They were going to rescue Twitch; Eddie and Mike needed their spellcaster Adrian to open the gate into the Outer Bounds. Jane was still acting, the rock and rollers reacting.

She relaxed a touch and released her wards.

"Holy shit!" the man nearest her spat out. He had big hands, a brush-like brown mustache and a slumping cigarette clamped between his teeth. "What just happened to me? Did I black out?"

"What happened to *you?*" asked his friend, a burly man with tomato stains on his blue shirt. "Jeez, I think I had an aneurysm! You all disappeared!"

A third man pulled a plastic cylinder from his pocket and tapped several white pills into his hand.

Jane almost laughed out loud at their collective confusion. In her haste, she realized, she had thrown wards over the entire table, and the men sitting at it had been blinded for the duration.

Not her problem. She saw Jim crossing the floor towards the restroom, a flock of young women around him, and she moved to intercept. He didn't look fey, nor Angelic, so she drew two long knives, muttered up a quick ward of seeming to make herself look innocuous, a drunk and stumbling fraternity buffoon, in a stained baggy t-shirt and expensive jeans.

"I get it, I get it!" one of the girls giggled. Her jacket was a shell of sequins around a bubbling core of young fluff. "This is like Calvin Coolidge, right? Isn't there some story about Coolidge not talking much?"

Jim arched an eyebrow and nodded in the direction of the restrooms. Jane didn't relish the idea of stabbing Azazel's son; nor did she relish the thought of another six thousand years of lonely wandering.

"Silent Cal," her friend agreed. She had big hair that looked like it would coordinate well with the suit and tie of the wizard Adrian. Fashion, like everything else, was a boring, unstoppable cycle.

"And at this party, right? This woman comes up to President Coolidge and says 'I bet my friend I can get you to say more than two words.'" She seemed proud of herself for remembering this banal story about a dead, unimportant president.

Jane remembered Calvin Coolidge; the best she could say about him was that he didn't have delusions of grandeur. Which, on reflection, was an unusual quality in a politician.

Jim smiled politely and kept walking towards the hallway. He clenched and unclenched his fists, which Jane read as a sign that he was itching for action and wished he had a weapon in his hand. She was happier, of course, that he didn't.

She stumbled onto the tracks a few feet away, feigning drunkenness, as Jim reached the railroad tracks and the little plank bridge. She saw clearly now that he had something under his shirt, against his belly.

"What was Coolidge's answer?" Big Hair looked like she was on the edge of her seat.

"'You lose,'" Jane said, and she stabbed Jim with both knives.

She'd heard the story, too.

Jane's knives were not enchanted, but they were good sharp steel and they cut flesh effortlessly. Jim yelped and fell back, and Jane grabbed for his belly—

but Jim wasn't *collapsing*, he was *rolling*, and as Jane's fingers brushed fibrous, sticky bands on the hard, flat stomach of the bar-band singer, he was gone, out of reach. Her two knives went with him, one in his hip and one in his side, and she narrowly avoiding getting kicked in the face.

Hot red blood spilled onto the planks, unhidden by Jane's wards.

Big Hair shrieked first, but Sequins screamed louder.

Jane rushed forward to close the gap, whipping smaller knives from their sheaths on her forearms and slashing overhand, trying to cut the big man. He moved like an acrobat, though, staying just beyond the glittering razor edge of her blades. His first tumble backward landed him in a handstand, one hand on each of the metal rails of the abandoned train track that ran across the floor of the bar, and then he sprang further away again, landed on the tips of his boots, and shuffled backward immediately. The spurting arc of blood trailing behind him spattered across Jane's duster and, from the suddenly ramping volume of the shrieking behind her, might also have ruined the girls' outfits.

Slash, slash, duck and dodge, and then suddenly Jim snatched two beer bottles off a table as he passed and hurled them at her. Jane batted one aside with an elbow and let the other hit her in the shoulder. The crow swooped between her and her target in a cruel and taunting maneuver, obscuring her aim for a moment and pricking her in one of the few remaining sensitive spots in her soul.

In the fraction of an instant during which she hesitated, Jim pulled the knives from his own body and charged to attack.

The yelling was more general now, and Jane could hear the voice of the bartender in the tumult. "Everybody cool it!" he barked in his Appalachian twang. "Now!"

Boom!

That would be one barrel of the man's shotgun. Jane wasn't at all worried about the firearm, nor was she too concerned about the bartender himself, despite his unusual perceptiveness, but she didn't want the rest of the band to come back out of the restrooms and interrupt. Especially the wizard, but in a band whose drummer was an Outcast from the Mirror Queendom and whose organ player was a sorcerer, who knew what other hidden talents and threats might lurk?

Besides, the singer Jim was amazing. He met her every attack with a parry or a sidestep, and he fought like the furniture and people around him were a third weapon constantly at his disposal. He flicked tumblers at Jane with the tips of her own knives, and kicked stools in her direction, and when a scar-faced man with a bandanna covering his shaved head—maybe a bouncer—moved to intervene, Jim tripped him and kicked him into Jane's way like he was rolling a barrel down a gangplank.

Time to take decisive action.

Jane launched her effort with a fierce counterattack, genuinely hurling herself at the singer's jugular and crotch with staggered, alternating blows. She did her best to cut his flesh, but she was unsurprised when his lightning speed and panther-like athleticism kept him out of harm's way.

Nor was she surprised when he stabbed her, sinking her blade into her belly.

She let herself go slack and stare.

The screaming of the college girls was very loud in her ears.

Jim sank the second blade into her back, between her shoulder blades. Jane felt it bite deep into her heart, and she grimaced in pain.

Jim stared at her fiercely. His lips mouthed words: *"Who are you?"* This close, she knew his face. He looked so very much like his brother.

How odd, Jane thought. How very nearly amusing.

She let the hammering pain force one of her knees to buckle, not losing contact with the big man's gaze. He caught her from falling and repeated his lips-only, silent query.

"Easy with the lady, mister," Jane heard, and in the corner of her vision she saw the bartender, John from North Carolina, arrive. He held his shotgun leveled at Jim, and the singer frowned. "I saw as it was her who attacked you first, but I reckon it's time for all the stabbin' to be wrapped up."

Jane grabbed the strapping on Jim's belly with one hand and cut at it with the knife in her other. It was duct tape, and as the tape and the object wrapped in it came away in her hand, she head-butted Jim the rock and roll singer in his handsome face.

Jim staggered back, blood spattering down his face from his nose.

John turned to object and she ran him over, knocking him to the ground with her shoulder in his midriff. Unexpectedly, a rush of feeling coursed through her. Searching her memory, she recognized it as glee. With any luck, she thought, she might be dead by morning.

And she'd take that angelic bastard with her.

She shouted the Adamic incantation of her spell as she vaulted over the bar, spraying blood on everything she touched. The crow flapped its wings and plunged into the *Wild Turkey* mirror ahead of her—

and then she jumped again, into the glass and gone on the tail of the black bird.

CHAPTER THREE

Qayna—who, millennia later, would be known as Jane—came home from her fields and found Abil waiting.

He was cleaned up, out of his customary kidskins and leggings and instead wearing a white tunic and sandals. His hair was oiled, and he smelled of flowers rather than of the herd. The whole family stood behind him, Father, Mother, Shet, the younger children. Behind the family, towering above them and crackling white, stood one of the Messengers, his six wings flapping steadily behind him as if to keep him in flight, though his feet appeared to touch the ground.

They were all waiting for her.

Qayna had been in the fields because she worked, as everyone worked. She never felt unsafe, however long she was alone—the beasts, for the most part, didn't molest her, and there were not yet any other people besides her immediate family—and she accepted the work. Her mother, though, in hushed tones when they were alone together under a comforting moon, had often told her of a time when all their kind had been only two, and there had been no such thing as work and no risk of starvation or any other kind of death, only love and tending the plants of the garden. Mother's stories of discovering the infinite variety of life and nurturing it so that it could blossom to its fullest thrilled Qayna's heart in a way she could not make Abil understand, and she tried to be like Mother in her daily tasks, her contribution to feeding and clothing the family.

Abil chose instead to work with Father. Qayna was the oldest, but Abil was second, and he was nearly Father's height and serious when the rest of the children were a gangly troop of monkeys, always on the heels of cheerful young Shet. Abil worked with the herds, which was a labor of long hours. He milked ewes, cared for injured animals, chased away wolves, sheared the flock before lambing every spring, and, when one of the herd was to die to feed the family, it was Abil who chose the animal to make the ultimate gift.

Abil's was a lonely work, and Qayna didn't envy it. Besides the long hours he spent leaning on his staff in the fields, it was Abil who moved the sheep into warmer valleys when the winter winds came. At those times, Father stayed with the family, which was good, because Father's first task was to oversee the instruction of his children.

On the same day the herds went to the winter pastures, Father would retreat into his own private tent for hours, and then the Messengers would come. Jane knew why they came, because she had crawled as a child under the tent flaps and listened to Father's rhymes, the names he had given the Messengers in them and the odd words he used to conjure them. And the summoning was not the end of Father's responsibilities; the Messengers came from the towers in the west bringing lore and learning, but it was Father's job to make sure his children were prepared and to repeat their lessons with the family over and over until they were taken fully to heart. If his children didn't learn and live the teachings of the Bearers of the Word, Father told them, then the Bearers of the Sword might come in their stead. All this was well and good, and, Qayna thought, the proper order of things.

Still, it meant long, cold nights for her brother, huddled over a small fire with his flute and his wallet of dried lambs' flesh.

Qayna, meanwhile, combed the forests and the fields for herbs that were edible, good for body and spirit, and she brought them to the family. As Father taught the children the Way and

Mother whispered lessons to Qayna of the Garden, Qayna in turn taught the plants. With example, with firm, dirt-fisted persuasion, with patience and with love she taught them to stand in rows, to grow upright, to be nourishing and cheerful, and to beautify the hillsides above the family's dwellings of skin and stone. On winter nights, when her grain slept in silent furrows, waiting for the spring to rise and bud, she stooped under the lintel to return to her Father's fire in the evenings and spared a thought for her brother in the hills, a thought that was loving and compassionate.

Loving and compassionate, but nothing more.

During this most recent winter, a tall Messenger with an expressionless face taught the family about the Bond. The Bond was the tie that connected Father and Mother and all of them together, and the First Precept was that man and woman should enter into the Bond, be fruitful and multiply. Qayna had found it amazing, and though she had shushed the tittering of the younger children, she had found it embarrassing, too, and she was vaguely relieved that Abil wasn't present. But late at night, when Father and the six-winged Messenger stood on the brow of the hill and recited the names and deeds of the stars above them, Mother whispered to Qayna that it was all true.

Not only was it all true, she confirmed, but Qayna had to prepare herself. She was to be the first woman to enter into the Bond east of the Garden. This was the Way for her daughters to keep the First Precept, ever since Mother's own choice, a mysterious fork in the path to which she only alluded and only in hushed tones, but which sounded like a decision freighted with dread, rebellion, and regret.

Qayna expressed doubt.

Her body was ready, Mother explained patiently; it was time. In the same way, Qayna prepared the earth before she filled it with seed, enriching the soil with the castoffs from the family's table, so that the seed could flourish in it and grow into tall stalks of wheat or fruit trees, Qayna had been preparing her own body.

Qayna denied it.

She was outraged. She had participated in no such embarrassing pursuit, and besides, there was no one for her to marry. Would the Messenger take a rib from her side and make a companion for her? Would he form a man from the dust for her convenience and pleasure?

Mother insisted. She had prepared her body without knowing, feeding it and exercising it and making it strong. And Qayna's body had responded; the changes in her flesh that had sent her once under each moon into Mother's private, separated tent were a clear sign that her body was ready to fulfill its purpose, to achieve the task designated for it by its creator. Mother had told the Messenger about these changes, she admitted to Qayna, and that was why the Messenger now taught the family about marriage.

Besides, the First Precept was inexorable. There was only the family, and if the family did not multiply, then there would be no more people, only a wide world, empty but for the Towers and the Messengers. And the Bond, cruel as it might seem, would tie her and a mate together for their own protection, and the protection of their children.

What children? Qayna asked. What mate?

It was time, Mother explained, and there was a companion.

There was Abil.

Qayna fled. She didn't want Abil, not as anything other than her brother. She wasn't sure about the First Precept and the Bond generally, but she knew that she wasn't ready yet, and maybe never would be. Horrified and sickened at the thought of what was proposed, angry at the base treachery of her mother, she began from that day to carry a knife.

Abil returned with the warmer weather, as green tendrils started cautiously to poke their heads out of Qayna's furrows. He was tall and worn by the weather, his jaw becoming straighter and his arms and legs longer and more muscular, like Father's. Qayna couldn't look at him directly, and neither could she avoid looking at him when she was in his presence. Mostly she tried to avoid him, dunging and pruning the orchard and the field and searching his face, when she could do so without being noticed, for any sign that he, too, had spoken with the Messenger this winter.

She wondered if he *knew*.

Shet and the others, meanwhile, seemed to follow her even more closely than they always had, giggling and pointing at her whenever she caught them peeking around a corner or peeping up from behind a rock. The little children pointed and giggled, anyway. Shet just stared.

Until the day when she came back from watering her farthest field and found the family gathered in front of their dwelling.

Abil stood in front of Mother and Father, perfumed and oiled. He was dressed in a fine white kilt Mother must have woven and sewn for him, and tooled sandals that had obviously been cut, stitched and dyed by Father. Her parents held up more clothing, she guessed for her, and they smiled.

Behind them rose the Messenger. He was tall, far taller than Abil or even Father, and his skin, his robe, and his six wings all glowed crackling white. His hair danced and snapped like flames in the spring breeze, and there was a smell about him that was unnatural and unearthly. He had a strong, imperious brow and piercing eyes that seemed perfectly clear and bottomless. Qayna had never felt totally at ease around this Messenger or any others of his kind, but she was especially uncomfortable now.

"Come," Mother said.

"Come," Father repeated.

Abil smiled. It was an ugly smile, a smile Qayna had never seen before on a human face, a smile that looked like it belonged on the bristling muzzle of a wolf.

"It is time," the Messenger boomed. His voice was like lightning in the far hills in Autumn, a thundered utterance that was impossible to misunderstand and that brooked no dissent.

"No!" Qayna cried, and she fled.

Qayna bathed in a spring beyond her orchard, in private and in secret. The spring was her own special place, a canyon of young stone and crystal water she had discovered while chasing fluttering spores in a dry summer storm the year before. She ran to the spring now, not directly because she feared pursuit, but by a circuitous route. She dropped below the fields into a gully, crossed a river, climbed a hill, and then finally came to her spring by traveling downstream from its sources.

She undressed, trembling from shock and rage, laying her tunic and sandals on a large rock beside the stream and setting her small knife carefully on top of them. She threw herself into the water, gasping from the sudden cold shock.

The spring was deep, and with the chill of the water prickling her skin, Qayna sank to the bottom. The solid reality of the rock beneath her bare feet and hands reassured her that the earth and its limits were unchanged, and when the pressure on her lungs became so real that it began to pain her, she surfaced.

Abil stood above her at the water's edge, and behind him waited the Messenger.

"Am I so bad then, Qayna?" Abil asked. The look on his face was petulant and wounded, a look such as Shet might wear if a prized toy had been taken away from him. Something else lurked in the expression, too, a note of violence that Abil could not entirely hide. "Am I so bad that you will not have me?"

Once Qayna and Abil would have played together freely, naked and thoughtless. Now she stayed in the water, trying to keep her body from his eyes and unable to think of anything but the strange and terrible revelations the Messenger had delivered the previous winter about Mother, Father and the First Precept. As if he were thinking of the same thing, Abil couldn't keep his eyes off her body, and stared at the water in front of her and the rippling, distorted images it bore.

"Am I a beast?" Qayna replied. There was no word for *slave* in the tongue of her birth, as there was yet no one to enslave. "Am I a mere thing that has no say in its own use? Am I a garment to be worn and cast aside, a tool with which to harrow up the earth, a lamb to be slaughtered?"

"It is the First Precept," the Messenger intoned. Between the canyon walls that enclosed the spring, his words rolled like the cracking of the heavens. He hesitated. "Do you choose to disobey the will of Heaven?"

"You would not have me choose at all!" Qayna shouted. The heat of the anger warmed her against the water's cool bite. "You would have me only lower my head and submit! That is not the joy of the Garden, that is not the path of my Mother!"

Abil crouched beside the water, beside the stone on which she had laid her things. Perhaps he meant it as a way not to appear threatening, but it brought him closer to Qayna and that felt like an invasion. Besides, squatting on his heels, he opened his tunic and exposed his body in a way that reminded Qayna uncomfortably of the fact that he, like she, was no longer a child, and that his body, too, had prepared to obey the First Precept.

"Let's choose to obey together," Abil said, grinning. "We could choose to do otherwise together, but let's choose to obey."

"Obedience is sacrifice," the Messenger trumpeted. His voice was loud and brassy, but Qayna thought she heard the faintest note of compassion in it. "To obey is to sacrifice the other things you might have done, the other possibilities you might have enjoyed. If those other possibilities were always and in all respects bad, obedience would be painless. Every commandment is a summons to obedience, a call to sacrifice on the altar."

The horrible, ineluctable tone in which the Messenger spoke, and the tiny trace of warmth in his voice, only made the content of what he said completely unacceptable, even though, Qayna realized, the words were true.

"I'm not ready!" she cried, treading water. "Not now! Can I not wait?"

"It is the First Precept," the Messenger repeated. "You must choose now." The gigantic being's voice softened considerably. "I, too, have no choice."

"Come on, Qayna," Abil splashed into the water after her. He was laughing, but Qayna didn't think there was anything to laugh about, and his mad chuckle did nothing to break the rising wall of tension in her breast.

She backed away from him, towards the edge of the spring.

"You know me. You know the Messenger's teaching, and the Way, and what Father and Mother have done." He swam towards her.

She splashed out of the water on the far side, staring down at her brother. He stared up at her, his eyes on her naked body, and now his look truly became the hungry stare of a wild animal. Qayna felt vulnerable and threatened, the more so when she realized that the Messenger was staring at her, too.

And the Messenger's eyes, always so patient and mechanical and full of rote wisdom, were now full of something else. Something animal, something that burned.

Abil splashed for the bank. He was a fast swimmer, faster than Qayna, and her heart and mind raced in fear. She ran around the edge of the water, brambles and sharp stones cutting into the work-toughened skin of her feet, running for her clothes.

"Stop!" the Messenger roared, but he didn't move to intervene.

"Stop!" Abil cried, and he sloshed out of the water on her heels.

Qayna scooped up her scant belongings in both hands and kept running. Along the bank of the spring she raced, into thickets of long-spined thorn trees that grew where the stone raced above the water higher and higher in narrow ledges and steep slopes. Abil had longer legs than she did, and heavier muscle, but she thought she was more nimble and might be able to evade him if she could get to where agility would make a difference.

Abil caught her in the trees. She dropped her clothes as her brother slammed her against a stone wall cluttered with dried tree branches. Stray thorns dug into the flesh of her belly and thighs and her blood marred the virgin rock. Though her sandals and tunic fell into the thicket, she kept possession of the knife, and as Abil pounded her against the stone again, she tightened her fingers around it.

"Stop!" the Messenger cried.

"This is the First Precept!" Abil raged, and threw his body against hers. He was awkward and animal and he approached her from behind and butted her, like a ram subdues a recalcitrant ewe.

"I ..." the Messenger hesitated.

Qayna fought back with her ankles and elbows, and Abil pushed her harder against the rock.

"Obey!" he snapped wolfishly.

She wiggled around and pushed him away with both feet, feeling the rough stone abrade the skin of her back with the force of the blow. "Abil!" she cried. She was trapped by the thorn trees and the stone, and the knife in her hand seemed both pitiably small and laden with doom. "I am no beast!"

"You *must!*" Abil snarled. "It is the will of Father and Mother! It is the will of Heaven!"

"It is not *my* will!" she shouted back.

The Messenger was silent, and Abil threw himself forward—

Qayna swung the knife fiercely, aiming for Abil's chest, willing the blade to wound and subdue her brother—

but the weapon had darker plans.

The point of the small knife sank into his throat and Abil's blood gushed over her, surprisingly hot on her water- and wind-chilled body. Abil thrashed and jerked, and pulling himself off the blade only opened the wound and caused his blood to spill faster.

Qayna stared in shock as her brother, and would-be Bond mate, staggered away from her clutching at a gaping hole in his neck, fell backwards into the embrace of a tree of thorns, and crashed to the ground.

Qayna still held the knife, slick and warm. For long seconds, it was all she could do to focus her entire will on not fainting.

Slowly, she looked up at the Messenger, uncertain how he would react. The Messenger looked back at her, and in his clear, translucent eyes she saw deep reserves of will and sudden, terrible insight.

The Messenger drew himself up to his full height, like a mighty oak tree, and suddenly he opened his robe. His glowing body was even more finely-muscled than Abil's, as if it were the light and the original at the same time, and Abil's newly-acquired man-body were merely a shadow.

"And now … daughter of Eve?" the Messenger rumbled. He spoke slowly, but as he spoke he picked up speed, as if he were making up his mind. "Now what do you choose, since you have learned the unstoppable power of your own free will? You are a rebel against the First Precept. Will you rebel with me?"

Qayna fled again, scrambling through trees that clutched at her and tore her flesh. She scrambled up the stone and way, staring back at the Messenger behind her. "Who are you?" she demanded. Mother had taught her the First Precept, and though Qayna feared and rejected it, she knew that it didn't mean that the Messengers were supposed to mingle with the mortals entrusted into their care. "You defy Heaven, too!"

"I am Azazel," the Messenger called back, smiling brilliantly, "and you teach me that I need not care."

"I want nothing from you!" she cried at the terrible, naked figure.

"Remember me, mortal!" the Messenger bellowed, his rumbling voice rebounding against the sky itself.

Then Qayna tumbled out of the top of the canyon and left the Messenger Azazel behind.

She ran naked and bloody, holding nothing but the knife that had killed her brother. That night, she butchered lambs from Abil's herd and hid from the eyes of Father and Shet, who wandered the hills crying her name and Abil's. She wondered what had happened to the Messenger Azazel, and why he had not reported his own failure, or Qayna's crimes.

She traveled at night, taking comfort from the rebel moon and nursing the thought that if she was a disobedient child, she had learned from a Mother with a similar streak. By day she lay in the hollows of rocks, ate the flesh of her stolen lambs and chewed on roots she dug out of the ground. When she slept, she dreamed that the stones around her were the grinding, merciless arms of her dead brother, Abil.

On the third day, they found her.

It was Shet who was staring at her, wide-eyed, when she awoke.

"They found Abil," her younger brother said. "And your clothes."

She stood, dropping the last of the uneaten carcass and the tiny, guilty blade.

Then came Father, the sternness of his brow trembling in hint of softer feelings behind the facade, and with him a company of Messengers. She expected them to bring Swordbearers, but there were only the blue-white, six-winged giants she had always seen. She searched the faces of the Bearers of the Word—the first time she had ever really done so—wondering whether she might see Azazel and almost hoping that she would. She had witnessed terrible things in his eyes, a rage to possess and to destroy, but at least when she had looked into his eyes she had seen *something*, and not just the blank tables on which were inscribed the long list of Heaven's mandates.

But she was disappointed; Azazel was not among them.

"I'm sorry," Father grunted, grabbing her by her shoulders and throwing her down.

"I deserve it," she said. She didn't really mean it, but she hadn't intended to cause Father grief.

"This world is a hard and fallen one," he said, tears streaming down his cheeks. "That is not your fault."

The foremost of the Messengers bore down upon her, a clay pot in his hand. Qayna stared at the Messenger's face, imprinting it upon her memory. "This dye," the Messenger thundered, "is the blood of Abil. His blood cried to heaven to witness your guilt, and now it will cry to all your family and their descendants as an eternal witness."

The Messenger dipped a shard of bone into the pot and scraped its jagged edge across Qayna's face. She screamed and twisted, and Father held her down.

"This stylus is the bone of Abil," the Messenger continued. "You would not make an acceptable sacrifice, and instead sacrificed your own brother's flesh and bone. Now the bone records your sin."

The Messenger continued scratching her, running curving lines about Qayna's face and all over her body. Qayna bucked and screamed and stared at each Messenger, memorizing their faces. One day, she swore, it would be her turn to witness, and the Messengers would be the ones screaming in pain.

Father wept, but did not relent.

Shet only stared.

"These words that I write upon your face," the Messenger finished, "are all the names of Abil. "As you have blotted out his name from among your family, so shall your name be blotted out. As you have taken from him his life, so do I now take from you your death. You shall be a fugitive and a vagabond upon the earth, until the end of time."

The Messenger arose and stood away, but the pain did not subside. As Father stood and turned away also, pulling Shet with him and abandoning Qayna to her pain, she rolled over and curled into a ball, sobbing.

She lay a long time. There was no one to find her or to be disturbed.

When she was done weeping, hours had passed and her pain had subsided into a stinging that covered her entire body. She stood gingerly and picked up the bloody knife where she had dropped it. She picked it up because she needed a tool of some kind in the great empty world into which she had been cast, and she picked it up because was hungry to someday, somehow, get her revenge.

And then she saw, perched on an outcropping of stone above her, a large black crow.

CHAPTER FOUR

Millennia later, Jane leaped through the *Wild Turkey* mirror behind the bar in Wellman's.

She landed in the Outer Bounds expecting to hear its usual soft-swishing silence. Instead, the halls and arches echoed to the sounds of shouting.

"Let go of her, damn you!" The voice belonged to the guitar player, Eddie. He sounded like he was just around the corner, but Jane knew that sound could carry a long, long way in the Mirror Queendom. Especially in the Outer Bounds.

"She's an Outcast in violation of the terms of her exile!" squeaked an excited fairy voice that might have belonged to Foxtail. "You have no right to talk to the Queen's Rangers like that, and you have no permission to be here!"

"We don't need *permission, cagado!*" That would be Mike. "We have *guns.*"

"And don't go imagining our bark is worse," the organ player snarled, "et cetera. We also have fireballs."

Jane pulled her knives from her own body, carefully wiping each on her duster before sheathing it. The hoof was as long as her forearm and looked like a gigantic toenail clipping, polished and smooth. It was the right size to be Azazel's. Of course, when she had first known him, he had had feet.

The hooves—and the wings—had been *his* mark, but they had been his own doing.

"You'll risk the wrath of Mab and Oberon," *thud!* "for *this* wretch?"

"If Mab and Oberon ain't pissed off with us already," the guitar player laughed out loud, "they're just about the only ones."

As Jane removed the blade from her heart, a sudden gush of hot fluid spilled out, but she felt the flesh of the pierced organ knit together almost instantly, and then the wound shut and the blood stopped. An ancient ward kept any of her blood from staining the duster, so it dripped onto the floor instead.

She took the shell-rigged-into-a-makeshift-vial from her pocket, removed the wax and poured the blob of quicksilver out into her palm.

BOOM!

The sound of an explosion deafened Jane for a moment, and shock waves knocked her against the wall. When she stood again, moments later, she could hear animal yelps, the scrabbling of paws on stone and a pair of running feet.

"Twitch!" Eddie hollered. "We're on!"

"You think I care about the *show?*" Twitch called back. "I'm going to kick that bitch in the forehead!"

The wizard muttered something Jane couldn't hear.

"Are you sure?" Eddie asked.

"Go!" Adrian yelled.

Then the pair became a crowd of feet, and the rattling hoof beats of a horse.

Jane incanted in Adamic and followed the silver bead in her palm. Its movements were subtle enough that she had to keep an eye on the wiggling drop, and couldn't rely on her sense of touch alone. Staring into her own cupped hand slowed her, but even worse was the fact that the bead led her backward, straight into the teeth of her pursuit.

Wondering how many fey eyes had already examined her and seen what she was carrying, Jane slid the hoof into the inside pocket of her duster. She pinned it with her elbow against her side to keep it secure, and drew the pistol.

The gun was an FN Model 1910, a mediocre old semi-automatic pistol at best, vintage turn of the twentieth century. This particular pistol, though, was unique. Its serial number was

19074. It had been purchased by the Black Hand and its owner, the Serbian enthusiast Gavrilo Princip, had taken it at midnight, on June 27, 1914, to a shadowy crossroads outside Sarajevo. There a *vestica* with the face of a young girl but the hands of a crone had anointed the gun with boiled fat extracted from the body of a murdered priest and pronounced over the weapon a dreadful curse.

Jane had been watching from the shadows.

The next day, young Princip had killed the Habsburg Archduke Franz Ferdinand with this same pistol, and started World War I. The gun, famous to those who followed it as the Calamity Horn, was a killer of kings; that was its blessing, and the purpose for which Princip had wanted it. There was no creature its bullets could not wound, Angelic or Infernal, cursed or anointed.

It could even wound Jane. But it couldn't, as she found out on the third day after the vestica had done her work, kill her. Not even with a bullet through the temple. So all Jane's tedious labor in training the vestica and in nurturing the nationalistic madness in young Gavrilo had gone to waste. Her scheme to end her life had failed, and instead millions of others had died.

The madness that the gun caused was, apparently, an unintended side effect of the witch's enchantment.

The quicksilver bead in her palm tugged Jane to the right into a square room several paces across, with a circular shaft in the center of the chamber and a ceiling that was so far away it was invisible. At the same moment that Jane saw the bead, she heard the horse clatter into the room in front of her. She looked up and fired three quick shots.

Bang! Bang! Bang!

The echoes were infinite and deafening, a wave of sound that crashed out of the cursed gun and blasted along the passageways in all directions. The horse reared in surprise and went down in a tangle of hooves and wings and bright-splattering blood.

Right behind the horse rushed in the three rock and roll musicians, and the wave of sound struck them full in the face. For a moment, they seemed to hang suspended in mid-air and their faces contorted with sudden insight and anger.

Then Mike turned, raised his pistol—

and fired on his companions.

Eddie ducked, roared and fired back.

Jane veered right, skirting around the pit at her feet. Out of the corner of her eye, she saw movement within the pit, the rustling, quaking tremble of many-limbed things that were climbing inside, but then she was past it and gone.

"*Selenen abiuro!*" Adrian shouted, throwing a pocketful of ground and powdered something into the air—

Jane smelled an herb that might have been oregano—

Mike and Eddie dropped their guns, horrified looks on their faces—

and Adrian himself collapsed to the ground, unconscious.

Jane fled the room at a run, gun pointed at the ceiling and hoof under her arm. The Model 1910's magazine held seven rounds, which left her only three shots. Really, she had not been thrifty with her ammunition. One shot would have been enough to induce madness in the rock and rollers, and the only reason she had fired more was the presence of the fairy.

The gun's bullets injured fairies and could kill them, but its sound did nothing to their minds. This, Jane guessed, was because fairies were already insane.

A net struck her, flung from a passage to her right, and bowled Jane sideways. The snare was woven of something elastic and slightly sticky, and weighted with what looked like giant acorns. Under the force of the attack, Jane slipped to her knees, but she managed to avoid dropping anything.

"What is it, what is it, a big ugly outsider!" Three thin-bodied persons in leather armor sprang from a shadowed alcove and raced in a circle around Jane, shaking wooden spears over their heads. One had a skunk's tail and coloring, one a monkey's, and a third kept shifting back and forth between a humanoid shape and the shuffling, wheezing form of a small brown bear. "Outsider, topsider, flatworlder!" they chanted, not in unison. "Big-footed, ugly, smelly human!"

Beyond them, the crow settled onto a head-sized knob at the bottom of a staircase banister and glared at her.

Jane listened and thought she could hear Adrian chanting. Whatever had knocked the wizard out, his friends had him awake again, and he was probably dealing with Twitch's injury. She also heard the pounding of many feet, and flapping wings.

Dragging the weight on her shoulders, Jane stood. The three fairies stopped and staggered back at the sight of her.

"Do you not know me?" Jane demanded slowly. "I am the Marked Woman."

A horse whinnied behind Jane, in the maze of the Outer Bounds. The fairies before her slipped away, fear and embarrassment on their faces.

"We're the Queen's Rangers!" Brown Bear gruffed.

"Vengeance rides in my wake," Jane added, beginning to get irritated, "sevenfold and hungry." She shook the net with her hand and found that the fibers clung to her skin and the fabric of her duster and hat.

"We can't!" Skunk squealed. "We can't do it!"

The fairy raised his tail in excitement and his comrade Brown Bear grabbed it and yanked it back down with a look of warning on his face. "Duty!"

"Release me," Jane said flatly, "or die." She heard the horse Twitch coming after her again.

The fairies scattered. "It's spider silk!" Monkey called over her shoulder as she scrambled under an archway no bigger than a cupboard door. "We can't release you! You're stuck until it melts!"

Jane muttered in Adamic and poured her ka into the spider silk net, burning it instantly into ash. She strode forward in the falling curtain of cinders, regretting the low, drained state to which she had reduced her ka and kicking herself for having been caught in an ambush set by fairies, of all creatures.

Gunfire erupted behind her, but her ears didn't pick up the popping and snapping of bullets passing her, so she guessed the shots must be coming from the guns of the rock and roll band, and they must not be shooting at her.

The fairies were attacking them, too.

She picked up the pace, jogging. She was surprised and a little annoyed at how long it was taking her to get to her destination, though of course distance on earth and distance in the Mirror Queendom bore no correlation to each other. She wondered if she might have been better off just running out the front of Wellman's in ordinary mortal space, but cut off the line of self-doubt immediately. She'd had no way of guessing the rock and rollers would be this persistent, and once she shook them, passage through the Outer Bonds would be a good first step to shaking off pursuit. Besides, she hadn't been foolish enough to leave her ride in front of the roadhouse.

It occurred to her that it was strange that they were following her. Maybe Twitch wanted revenge for the pain and humiliation Jane had inflicted on her. But was it possible that the band somehow realized she had the hoof, and were chasing her to get it back? Could they have communicated with Jim somehow?

Jane holstered the Calamity Horn and pulled the hoof from her pocket. Examining it slowed her pace, but running forward into unknown peril was a fool's choice, and the band seemed occupied with the Queen's Rangers anyway.

The hoof was curved like a crescent moon, wide as two of Jane's fingers and thick as one. It was yellowish in the light of the Outer Bounds, odorless and smooth like ivory, like a stone worn from millennia of lying in a river bed.

Except, Jane's fingers found with practiced probing, for one tiny little chip.

Either the power that had smoothed the hoof fragment out—the waters of Dudael, Jane guessed, having been there recently and seen the holding pit of her one-time conflicted antagonist—had missed a tiny divot, or since the hoof's extraction from the waters, someone had cut from the inside a tiny flake, a chip the size of her own pinky's nail.

Which could be how they were following her.

Jane cursed, her words of annoyance shaking dust from the lintel of a doorway under which she passed and sending a scuttling thing like an orange centipede scurrying for cover. She sent some of her precious reserves of ka-force over the clipping where her fingers had been, searching for the connection she guessed must exist—

and there it was. Jane felt it with her ka like a ribbon of water, tenuous, subtle and invisible, stretching away into the maze behind her. It must be the wizard Adrian, she guessed. These thieves feared other criminals, and so they had taken measures to allow them to track the hoof if anyone stole it from them.

She considered briefly how this impacted her plan and decided that it was a good thing. The more noise these loose cannons of rock and roll made, the more likely they were to attract the renegade, which was all Jane cared about. The band was nothing to her, the hoof was nothing, even Azazel was nothing; she just wanted to carry out the task appointed by the Legate and get her reward.

And kill Raphael.

The crow flapped ahead of her in the maze.

It wheeled in front of two figures, who waited before a window in the wall the size of a ladies' compact mirror, or the rear view mirror of a motorcycle. They stood tall, straight-backed and regal.

Jane put the hoof away and drew the Horn.

"You travel cloaked in myth," one of the figures smiled gently. She was a tall, thin woman with pale skin, long hair like spun gold and a crown of oak leaves on her head. She wore a green gown and green slippers the color of dew-spattered grass.

"I bought the coat in Sydney," Jane said. "You supposed to be Mab, then?"

"Am I?" the Queen arched an eyebrow. "Australia is a long way from Kansas, in mortal space." The waves of her efforts to seduce Jane splashed around them all and rebounded off the walls, but Jane was unmoved. It was like smelling rotting meat— she couldn't miss the stink, and she certainly didn't want to take a bite, however widely the person offering it might grin. Even without the quicksilver in her palm, Jane was resistant to the charm of the fey folk, but with it, she was immune. "But I see you travel as one of us."

Jane shrugged. "I get around."

"You must be tired." These words came from her companion, a man of the same height, with jet black hair and an identical crown. "Why don't you rest with us? I'm sure we have a lot to share." He was also dressed in green, in a tailed coat and velvety green trousers and he, too, stank of seduction like fly-blown meat.

"Let me pass."

"You are the Marked Woman." Now his voice sounded wheedling and, ever so slightly, uneasy.

"So that gives you a hint as to why your Glamour doesn't affect me. It should also tell you that you really ought to get out of my way," Jane said. It was hard to be certain, but she thought the gunfire was getting closer. She didn't want to fight, if she could avoid it. The fairies in front of her didn't have visible tails, and each wore a leather belt with a sword hanging from it.

"You are in my lands now," the Queen said.

"More or less," Jane grunted. She turned the pistol so the fairies could get a clearer view of it.

The King nodded solemnly. "As she said, you travel cloaked in legend."

"I don't want to kill you," Jane said, "but I won't have my hand forced."

"You would murder Queen Mab on her own doorstep?" the Queen looked affronted, staring at Jane down her long nose. "Queen Mab and her consort Oberon, Peerless Among the Fey?"

Jane laughed and swore in Adamic. The curse word shook the mirror hanging behind the two fairies askew. "Maybe," she said, "and maybe not." Behind her, she definitely heard the sound of fighting getting louder. "You can't kill me, and I have no people you can retaliate against. Why should I hesitate at the thought of killing Mab?"

"If the occupants of the Mirror Throne were crassly murdered by a Flatworlder," the Queen sniffed, "there would be war between the worlds. Are you so detached from your father's and mother's descendants that you can accept that?"

Jane shrugged her shoulders. "Maybe," she said again, "and maybe not. But I'd sure as *hell* kill a couple of Queen's Rangers stupid enough to dress up in costume and try to fool me. And nobody would go to war over that."

They didn't blink. The King curdled his eyebrows like she'd said something distasteful. "Queen's *Rangers?*" he sneered.

She pointed the gun at him. "Drop your pants," she ordered.

He sneered and did nothing.

Pop! Pop! Whizzang!

The sudden presence of bullets in the air told Jane that the band had caught up to her and she was out of time. If her ka weren't so drained, or her pistol, she'd turn and fight them. On the other hand, if her resources were less exhausted, she could have just blasted these annoying fairies into oblivion. Instead, she raised the pistol and fired a shot into the air.

Bang!

"Two left," she said, pointing the muzzle at Oberon. "I don't miss."

"Stop!" he pleaded, his eyes suddenly serious.

"Oberon …" the Queen warned him.

With quick but trembling fingers, the King undid his belt buckle and dropped his green pants into a velvety puddle around his pointy-toed shoes. A donkey's tail twitched nervously into sight.

"I thought so." *Bang! Bang!* Jane emptied the Model 1910, firing the last two shots into the center of the fake Oberon's chest. He flew back without a sound, hitting the wall and sinking to the floor.

"Give my regards to Mab," Jane snorted. She stepped past the surviving fairy chanting in Adamic, burning nearly the last of her ka-fire in the act.

The gate opened and she flowed into it, her whole body passing through the window, tiny though it was.

"Stop her!" she heard at her back, but then the fracas and the Outer Bounds were gone. The crow, of course, followed her through.

The night outside Dodge City, Kansas, was cool and clear, with a thick cloud cover blocking out the stars overhead. Jane stepped out of the mirror, turned, and plucked it from the saddle strap to which it had been clipped. She dashed it on the roadside gravel. To be sure, she ground it into even smaller shards with her heel.

She had other mirrors with her, but it would take the wizard Adrian longer to find them.

"Easy, girl," she said.

She stood several miles away from Wellman's, at the bottom of the bank below the highway and at the edge of an endless field of sorghum. The bushy grass waved cheerfully at her in the darkness, and before she did anything else, Jane stopped and reloaded the Calamity Horn. She filled the clip with thirty-two caliber Auto rounds and then holstered the gun. The shells were unimpressive, weak as far as modern handgun ammunition went—the gun and its curse were everything.

At the right end of the sorghum field was a two-pump gas station, closed for the night, but automatic pumps and vending machines still meeting the needs of one customer in a red pick-up truck. At the left end was a boxy brick building, the sign at the front of which read *FINE CUTS, INC.*

Jane swung into the saddle easily, though the horse—the Mare—was enormous. The Mare, not domesticated and not friendly but accustomed to bearing Jane, curled back its lips to reveal sharp, feline teeth and pranced sideways a step. The Mare smelled of sweaty beast and smoke; she always did. She snorted thickly in acknowledgement of her rider and Jane snorted back. The Mare was the last of the horses of Diomedes, a brutal, bullish man rumored to have been one of the many sons of the profligate Semyaz. The others had been killed centuries ago by an aimless scoundrel whom minstrels had turned into the hero Herakles. This one seemed to be immortal, and she was a fighter; the Mare would eat other animals, but her favorite food was human flesh.

Like Jane, the Mare traveled in disguise. The wards of seeming on her insured that to any casual passerby she appeared as a long, black, growling motorcycle.

"Come on, girl," Jane patted the huge horse and whistled to the animal to calm it. She pulled a fresh vial from one of the saddlebags and poured her drop of quicksilver into it, tamping it shut and replacing it in her pocket. She checked the hoof to be certain it was secure, then clucked with her tongue and pulled the Mare's reins to turn her around.

"Come on, girl," she said again and headed in the direction of the meat packing plant.

CHAPTER FIVE

ane rode once around the meat packing plant to be sure there were no cars parked on its asphalt skirt, cracked and riddled with potholes. Early in the morning, no doubt, there would be trucks and men to load them with butchered carcasses to be shipped off, a piece here and a piece there, to grocers and restaurants in Amarillo, Oklahoma City, and Wichita. By then, Jane hoped to be finished and gone.

And maybe dead.

She had no way to detect the renegade Raphael, but she guessed that he must be close, and would come quickly when she called.

Jane would have preferred to stave in the door of the plant by arcane means, but her ka was drained and weak. Under the crow's humorless stare, she instead wrapped the Calamity Horn in a saddle blanket to muffle it and shot the lock off the back door. Inside the packing plant, she hit the light switches and looked around while she reloaded.

She stood in a small entry area with pegs on one wall heavy with lined white smocks like lab coats, red hard hats and gloves. Signs reminded employees to wear safety gear and shoes with good soles, and to punch out for any break longer than ten minutes. Human resources gibberish festooned much of the space, and there was one small office with a window that looked into the entry, dominated by a single desk and a horde of pencil stubs.

Too small for her purposes.

Jane passed into the main chamber of the plant, leading the Mare by the reins. The big room was refrigerated, and she pulled her duster closer across her chest against the cold as she looked around at a forest of cattle carcasses. The meat hung headless and shoulders down on hooks in snaking lines, from a door in the corner where Jane assumed the live cows were brought to be punched in the head, along conveyer belts where the meat was cut open and organs were removed and sorted, and finally ended in a thick grove of frozen chests that were fully prepared, and cardboard boxes full of organs and limbs, by a rolling cargo bay door.

The space was big enough for the renegade to move around in without immediately exiting. It gave Jane some cover, and limited entrances to have to watch.

The staircase up to the roof was wedged into a corner of the building between a supply closet and the back of the office. Jane hitched the Mare to a column within reach of plenty of good, if chilly, grazing, and climbed to the top alone.

A light rain was beginning to fall, and the wind picked up, threatening to rip away Jane's hat as it gusted to storm levels. Jane scanned the horizon, noting the small clump of lights that was Dodge City—and Wellman's, just at its outer edge—and the strip of shadow that was the highway, cutting among farm houses, tractor repair shops and a saddler's on its way into town. That was the direction from which the rock and roll band would come, if they really could follow the hoof and they chose to come after her.

Maybe, knowing who she was, they would give up.

The crow cut, swooping, across her vision, becoming visible in the darkness for a moment by virtue of the light it blocked out.

"Still you," Jane said. "Always you. Well, not for long."

The Legate had offered Jane a flare-scroll to get the renegade's attention, but Jane had declined. Such a device would only alert her prey that he was hunted, and she knew how to contact the Messengers. It was a skill she had learned from her Father—though not one he'd ever meant to teach her.

Her ka was beginning to recover from her exertions at the bar and in the Outer Bounds. It wasn't much, but it should be enough—she needed very little. The rooftop itself was covered with gravel, which made it a poor surface for her purposes; the little rocks would make it impossible to draw an unbroken circle. There was a big metal box that housed a generator, though, or something to do with the building's power system. Jane chuckled at the lightning bolt decals on the side of the device, took a Sharpie from her pocket and drew a careful circle, three feet across, on top of the case. Around the outside of the circle she drew a second, meticulously inking in a line that was tidy, perfect, and steadily parallel to the inner one. She filled the space between with Adamic words—a name, single repeated over and over again, and words of calling.

When she was done she climbed atop the box and stood inside the circle. The wards themselves, the words and the circle, generated power, and she rested a moment within them, feeling the warmth as her ka slightly replenished itself. For a moment she was tempted to wait, to sit within such a circle and restore her depleted reserves.

She had been waiting six thousand years; couldn't she wait another day?

But Mab's folk knew what she had, she thought, and they wanted it. And the rock and roll band, ragged and disorganized though its members were, was tenacious and motivated and had proved to hold more than one surprise for Jane. It might hold others still, and it would be coming after her and the hoof.

And fundamentally, she thought, fixing her eye on the black bird that had dogged her vision down the millennia, she didn't *want* to wait any longer. With the Calamity Horn at her side, she didn't think she needed to.

Jane raised her arms and began to chant, not in Adamic, but in Angelic. She knew fragments of the language, in the way that modern American kids all knew oddments of Spanish, because it had been in the air, part of the environment of her childhood. These specific words, the ones she now incanted, were a rhyme she had heard Father repeat every winter, many, many years ago.

Jane's plan was simple. She would summon the renegade Messenger, and when he appeared, she would kill him. Just as she had wanted for a long, long time.

Recently, Heaven had come around to agreeing with her.

◦ ◦ ◦

Three days earlier, sitting in a slowly-cooling bubble bath, Jane had realized that she was paralyzed.

She had smelled the candle smoke in the same moment, with its thick reek of cinnamon and blood, but it was too late to do anything about it. The Legate paced slowly into her hotel room. He held the candle in his hand, its flame sputtering red like a Fourth of July sparkler.

He wore red, as befitted his office. He was dressed at least a century out of style, even for one holding his office, in a half-cape-like mantelletta over white sleeves, and a broad circular galero that almost looked like Jane's own hat, though with a flail-like tail. The similarity in their outfits only repulsed Jane; she wore her hat and duster for utility, and this man wore his garb as a statement of affection for the past.

Jane had lived through the past—nearly all of it there was that a human being could claim to have experienced—she remembered it well, and she felt no longing for it. What she wanted was to move forward, to move on.

The Legate smiled an ageless smile, raised his red candle in one hand and drew out a folded piece of parchment with the other. From where she sat, Jane could see the red sealing wax on the parchment, imprinted with the image of a pair of crossed keys. "I hold a letter," he said, in a voice that was both withered and greasy, like a three-day-old hot dog on a gas station counter.

Jane looked to be sure that the Calamity Horn sat on a hand towel beside the bathtub, in easy reach if she were able to move. Not that she'd need that for the Legate—as far as she could tell, he was a mortal man, though the crow seemed bothered by his presence. The bird had flapped to the furthest corner of the Las Vegas hotel room immediately on the Legate's entrance and had stayed there since. It looked resolutely out the window, like it couldn't bring itself even to acknowledge the Legate's presence.

Nor was she worried that the Legate would steal the gun. Its original enchantment bound it to Jane's will and person, and anyone who fired it without her consent would find it a mediocre handgun, old and small. Jane had murdered the priest whose rendered fat had provided the curse-bearing anointing, and it was Jane's will that activated the terrible, murderous enchantment of the Calamity Horn. He might grab it and run, but she would get it back.

"Fine," Jane said. "I hold a knife." It was true, but it was also a bluff, inasmuch as she couldn't move her limbs or raise the blade that rested in the water under her fingers. She did have emergency resources available if she had to draw on them, but she hoped it didn't come to that.

She didn't waste time wondering how the Legate had found her or gotten into her hotel room—he was the agent of a great power, and he had means.

Besides, she was almost enjoying this soak, with the raised bathtub right in the middle of the suite and the panoramic windows over the lights of the Strip, and she was determined that the man's presence wasn't going to destroy her evening.

The Legate sank with aplomb onto the corner of Jane's bed. He set the candle on the stand beside the mattress and crossed his hands on his own lap, still holding the letter. Maybe, Jane reflected, he wore the mantelletta and the hat to give him more bulk—he was a thin man, to the point of being bony, and Jane calculated she could easily lift him over her head and throw him. He might be self-conscious; a man's size could limit his ability to exercise his charisma.

"The contents of this letter might be of interest to you," he suggested.

That introduction guaranteed that Jane wouldn't let on that she cared at all. "You're fancy, for a mailman," she teased the Legate. "Though I don't see your patch for the National Association of Letter Carriers."

"You show very little deference for the Legate of Heaven," the man frowned. He had a faint accent, which Jane thought might be Lebanese or Armenian or Hittite. She wondered where

Heaven had found this man. He dressed a bit like a Cardinal, but that was mere fashion. He might be a rabbi by background, or a Sikh, or a Qodesh of Asherah. He wore wooden beads on a long string around his neck, but they were beads only, not bearing any other ornament. He thumbed slowly in a circle around the beads with his hands, and Jane saw a tattoo on the back of one hand that might be a picture of a tree, or a many-armed candlestick. "I was warned, but the extent of your indifference surprises me still."

"You people cursed me," Jane pointed out. She could have said it bitterly, but the centuries had pounded the emotional vehemence out her. The facts were the facts, and she endured. "*Indifference* isn't the word I'd choose to describe my feelings. You're lucky I don't kill you right where you sit, with a knife in the eye."

"This letter," the Legate continued, "contains the release of your judgment. It contains your forgiveness."

That caught Jane's attention, but she let no hint of her interest slip.

"This letter contains your death."

Jane trembled, slightly, from the neck up. "Sounds all right to me," she allowed. "Why don't you leave it on the table there, and help yourself to something from the minibar on the way out?"

"Forgiveness isn't free," the Legate shook his head like he had just discovered this terrible truth for himself. "Not for sins as serious as yours." He slowly licked his fingers and snuffed the candle. "But I'm pleased that you're willing to talk."

"Now's the time to hit me up," Jane chuckled to hide her relief at being able to move again, drawing her heels up to her buttocks in the deep, bubble-capped water. She wasn't afraid of death—she longed for it—but she hated being told what to do, and imposed paralysis was someone else telling her what to do. "I put down some mad dogs for the State of Nevada last week and then I hit it big on the Cockroach Road. What do you want, a hundred grand?" Money didn't matter to her, so Jane either had it in buckets or had none at all. She couldn't starve to death and paid no utility bills and the Mare could catch her own provender, so when Jane got money, she spent it. Eat, drink and be merry, might have been her motto, for tomorrow you will certainly not die.

"An eye for an eye," the Legate intoned. "A tooth for a tooth."

"A death for a death," Jane shot at him, and now she did feel bitter. "So why not kill me and get it over with?" Suddenly, she felt the full weight of the millennia at her back, and her heart filled with the pangs of the hundred cities that had burned around her and the thousands of men who had died on her blades. She was tired, she was unspeakably old, and she just ... kept ... *going*.

"You lost your death when you took your brother's life from him," the Legate said dryly, as if she didn't remember. He picked up the candle and tucked it into some hidden pocket beneath his mantelletta.

"What, then?" Jane asked, but in her heart she knew where the conversation was going. She willed herself not to look to the side at the Calamity Horn.

"You can have your death back," the Legate finished, shaking the letter gently like it was a birthday present and he was weighing it to guess what might be inside, "in exchange for the death of another."

"Why don't you do it yourselves?" Jane asked. "You guys aren't exactly averse to smiting, when you get the idea you'd like to do it. Ainok, Sodom and Gomorrah, Atlantis, Pompeii, San Francisco, New Orleans ... why not strike this guy with a good old-fashioned thunderbolt, or a plague?"

She knew the answer, but she wanted the Legate to say it.

"This is a case where discretion will be necessary," the Legate said slowly. "Heaven would rather not attract any attention."

Jane shook soap off her hand. "And you came to me," she said, picking up the FN Model 1910, "because of my reputation for great discretion. Also, because I carry the Calamity Horn, a gun that is capable of wounding and striking down even the children of Heaven. And also because you have something you can hold over me. Here I am in Las Vegas, and Heaven is making me an offer I can't refuse."

The Legate nodded. "All true. And also, we came to you because the target in question is an old friend of yours."

On the rooftop of the meat packing plant, standing on top of the lightning bolt-bearing case, Jane raised her arms to the roiling sky and called the Messenger. Angels didn't have true names, not in the way humans did, because the ka, the *ba*, and the body of an angel were not separate things, needing a name to bind them together and casting a shadow over the space among them. An angel was a unitary creation, a spiritual point rather than a cluster, and it had no secret name. Therefore, she couldn't compel it; so instead, she invited it.

Jane called in Angelic when she could remember the Angelic words clearly, and when she couldn't, she supplied the deficit with Adamic. The two were kissing cousins, anyway, and often shared vocabulary—though Angelic, as far as Jane knew, had no profanity at all. So much the poorer.

She touched the fragment of Azazel's hoof and let the feel of the object drift into and seal her message with its tangibility. She spoke words of offer and negotiation in her incantation, telling the renegade that she had the thing he was looking for, that they could join forces, that together they could have what they both wanted.

They were lies, and a trick, and in her heart she planned murder.

The circle carried her words up into the heavens, soaring through and against the rain that pelted down. Lightning flashed in a chain along the horizon as she finished, and a vortex of silver in the dark clouds absorbed her false oaths, sucked them in and spun them out in all directions like meteorites slung at the far corners of the world.

When she was certain the angel would hear, Jane stopped. Her ka ached within her and her body's wounds, still in the final stages of healing, itched and stung. She dropped her arms and stepped down to the gravel rooftop, duster rustling and hat pounding like a drum from the fat raindrops.

The crow flapped its wings as if irritated at what she had done, and glared at her balefully. If a flesh and blood bird had given her such a look, she would have cursed at it and blown all its feathers off.

A car approached on the highway now, and Jane stepped forward and crouched at the edge of the roof to watch. Light poles were few and far between on this stretch of road, but the vehicle slowed as it passed underneath one, in front of the saddler's, and she got a clear look at it. It was a brown van, hammered as only the van of a bottom-feeding rock and roll band can be, and she knew instantly who was inside. She was impressed, though, that they'd caught up with her so quickly. The van killed its speed and then its lights, and then it disappeared in the shadow of a small copse of trees.

She needed Azazel's hoof to bait the trap for the renegade angel, but that was surely what the band must be after. Jane considered her course of action for brief seconds, and then jogged down the stairs.

She needed to hurt them, slow them down, keep them out from under her feet. And she had no fire left in her ka.

The Mare stayed where she had hitched it, razor teeth bloodied by its contented grazing on chilled beef. She pulled the beast away, earning an irascible snort of protest, but no more—decades ago, she and the animal had had it out over which one of them was to be mistress, and they both knew that Jane was the rider and the Mare was her mount.

She left the lights in the plant on. If the band really was following the hoof, they wouldn't believe she was still in the building. But maybe, if she left the lights on, the band would *think* she was trying to lure them into an ambush. That might at least keep them off balance.

She led the Mare out the back door of the plant and swung into the saddle easily. She kicked the beast into a canter and headed for the edge of the lot, where the boundary between the meat packing plant parking lot and a furrowed field of tall, storm-quaking sorghum was marked by a rail fence.

The Mare easily jumped the fence, plunging into the tall cultivated grass without fear or hesitation. Jane watched the road as she progressed, trying to spot the musicians' van—trees cut across her field of vision ahead of her, shading a lane through the planted space, and she thought a creeping darker-than-dark mass under the trees might be the van. Whoever was driving, slow as they were going, must have great night vision. Jane bent low over the Mare's neck and looked for an appropriate tool.

She found it quickly, where the crops gave way to a flat, hard aisle of dirt. There was a medium-sized tractor, and the sight of it gave her momentary pause.

It had been several millennia since she had tilled the soil, but the scent of a moist, broken clod, or the sharp, fertile promise of a gleaming agricultural tool, still pierced her to the center of her heart. For an instant she was again Qayna of the young earth, who loved plants and taught them to love her back. The tall sorghum grass could have been the barley or emmer of her youth, and under the clouds and rain the land around her could have been practically anyplace, including the valleys to the east of Eden.

A flash of lightning on the horizon, and an answering glint in the trees ahead that might have been a reflection on metal, brought her back to herself.

Jane dismounted beside the tractor, whistling to the Mare an instruction to stand in place. She unscrewed the gas cap on the tractor's tank and soaked a spare shirt in the flammable liquid. Tearing the gas-reeking cloth in half, she stuffed one half into the open tank, letting it drape wetly down the side of the tractor. The other half she wrapped around a fist-sized rock she picked up off the ground.

Through the glass of the tractor's cab, she saw the brown van pull to a stop under the gloom of the trees. Its door opened and men piled out.

It was then that she spotted the raptor that could only be Twitch, the silver falcon with the long, incongruous horse's tail trailing behind it, soaring above the trees and headed in her direction. Her wards of seeming and dissembling should hide the truth from the fairy at least for a moment, but Jane knew she needed to hurry.

She repeated her *stay* whistle to the Thracian Mare, wedged Azazel's hoof fragment firmly beneath the saddle, and retreated to the sorghum, holding in her hand the gasoline-soaked rag wrapped around a rock.

Stepping a cubit's length into the sea of grass, she pulled out a cigarette lighter and waited.

The Mare stood calmly beside the tractor, ignoring the thick reek of gasoline and the band. That was a reflection of the Mare's impressive discipline, and her centuries of training—her sense of smell was so acute that she had led Jane across three States on the trail of the brown Dodge van and never lost the scent. The falcon overhead cried angrily, and the Mare ignored that, too.

Jane drifted a couple of yards to one side to get a better view; at a fence on the far side of the dirt aisle, she saw the rock and rollers climbing into the field.

The men all carried weapons, and they approached the tractor with deliberate steps, fanning out like the fingers of a groping hand. Even in the storm-confused dim light of night, Jane could see that Adrian was in the middle of the line, holding some kind of machine pistol in one hand and looking down into the palm of his other. Jim walked beside him, sword drawn. Mike and Eddie came forward on the wings, holding pistols.

She knew that what they saw must be the tractor, and beyond it, a parked motorcycle. Then the wizard hissed something and they all halted. He dug into a pocket and came out with a piece of glass that he held up to one eye like a monocle.

"Son of a bitch!" he spat.

Jane raised the lighter to the gas bomb in her hand—

and the sky exploded into flame.

CHAPTER SIX

Qayna raced under the spires of Ainok as the trails of flame hurtled earthward. She knew that each burning meteorite, bright despite the noon sun overhead and dragging behind it a plume of black and yellow smoke, must be a Swordbearer. She should be hurrying to get out of the city, she knew, but instead she ran toward its center.

She wanted to warn Azazel; she owed him that much.

The crow flew on ahead, just beyond her reach.

Other Ainokites heeded the more sane imperative, though, and she struggled to push through them. Women and men of her own kind—not quite her own kind, but her kin, at least—rushed in a thick and burbling stream toward the gates of the city, and she had to push fiercely to force them to part and let her upstream.

The Fallen were fewer, easier to see and avoid, but much more dangerous. They towered above their mortal subjects, and though Qayna had become accustomed to their appearance, the beast heads and limbs were still terrifying when they rushed at her at full speed. A towering Fallen with the lower body of a horse, Ezeq'el, trampled people who might have been her servants, or even her lovers; a giant with the face of an octopus or a squid dragged shrieking bodies with him as he plunged into one of Ainok's great canals, finding it a more expedient route to the exits;

a corpulent man with long yellow tusks jutting from his face and spikes growing from his back and shoulders lowered his head and charged through the crowd, leaving behind him a trail of mangled corpses and blood.

These were Qayna's people now, and they were destroying themselves in their flight.

The towers of Eden, Mother had told her, were observatories. She and Father had climbed within them to the platforms at their heights to watch the Messengers in flight above them, when they had been Eden's lord and lady. The spires of Ainok, for the most part, were merely spikes, but they were enormous, fingers jabbed in accusation at the sky or daggers pointed at the throat of heaven. Their heights were not platforms—other than on the one, central tower—they were the sharp points of spears.

Whether it had something to do with the spires or not, the Bearers of the Sword burned in their inexorable paths toward points outside the city.

At Ainok's center were the Grand Plaza, the Palace and the Tower. The Plaza was a wide space where the Fallen gathered to debate and, when the Council could not reach peaceable decisions, to shed each other's blood. The Palace sprawled along its western edge, all white stairs and green rooftop garden and blue water; the central source of Ainok's canals were the mighty springs beneath Azazel's home, and they burst forth from the mouths of statues of mutilated Messengers, irrigating the many acres of his private garden-like Palace before radiating out in all directions into the city. The Tower, higher, Azazel boasted, than any of the towers he had left behind, was solid inside and had an enormous staircase winding up around the outside of it to the broad circular platform at its apex.

The Plaza, the Palace, and the Tower were all made of the same gleaming white stone, not native to the hills surrounding the city. Azazel had told her once that he summoned the stone with his sorcery, from a quarry thousands of miles away. Somewhere, there was a gaping hole in a mountainside that sparkled white. The center of the city, even more than the rest of Ainok, was liberally speckled with mirrors. These were the gates of Mab's people, who were not residents but who came and went freely, and trafficked with Ainok's citizens. Azazel hadn't built the city center with wizardry, though, or with the help of the fey folk; Azazel's slaves had done the work. For himself and his own subjects, Azazel insisted on freedom. The followers of Heaven and its Messengers, he insisted, had already chosen slavery and deserved no better. Now the white stone ran red with blood, shed by slaves and citizens alike, trampled under the feet of their Fallen overlords.

Women streamed from the Palace as if its bowels also concealed a spring of concubines. Qayna drew her knife, a weapon almost long enough to call a sword, and fended the rushing women aside. Some of the women—fey or sorceresses, and in that moment Qayna envied them both—leaped into mirrors and disappeared. Those who couldn't rushed down the avenues toward the fires.

Qayna saw Azazel standing atop his Tower. The leader of the Fallen was majestic, even though the animal parts he had grafted onto himself with his own hand, and something else, some streak of wrongness, prevented him and all his kind from being truly *beautiful*. His goat-like legs were crooked, but he held his back erect, and the crimson- and black-streaked fur of his lower half was clean and shone in the sun. His wings, only two of them, were now the wings of an enormous bat, but they still cloaked him with something like majesty. He stood tall and looked about him at the horizon as the Swordbearers touched down.

So he knew. But he wasn't running.

Qayna cupped her free hand around her mouth and yelled up at him. "Azazel!"

The former Messenger looked her way instantly, and laughed a laugh like rolling thunder. He spread his wings like flexing arms, snapped them once, and sailed into the air and in her direction. He was graceful in flight despite his enormity, and when he touched down, Qayna saw that he held a child in his arms. His son, Jacob.

Azazel set the boy down between him and Qayna, and Jacob looked up at her with bright blue eyes. This boy, tousle-headed, pale and small, but with sturdy shoulders and determination in his eyes, was his heir. His father was majestic, powerful and graceful, but Jacob looked like a mere beautiful boy. He looked as human as Qayna.

And how human was that? She thought.

For all his many women, Azazel had only managed to get one living son, and that had been done with the aid of great sorceries. The seed of the Fallen, apparently, did not grow well in the furrows of Eve.

"You must take Jacob and flee," Azazel told her.

"The Swordbearers are here!" Qayna said, waving her weapon in a big circle to indicate that they were surrounded.

Azazel smiled gently, but there was a flash of irritation in his eyes. "Must I repeat myself?" he asked. "I took you in when you had no place else to go, Qayna. Will you not repay the favor?"

Qayna nodded heavily and grabbed Jacob by his hand.

With a heavy *CRACK!* another of the Fallen crashed to the stones behind Azazel and all three of them turned to look.

It was Semyaz. His own beast-assumed attributes included a boar's head and a long tail like a lizard's, which now flicked across the white stones of the Grand Plaza. He had wings, too, like an eagle's, feathered white and gold. The last fleeing concubines scattered, steering wide of the enormous Fallen warlord.

"Azazel!" the Fallen roared. "Your policies have failed!" With a rasp that Qayna thought must be audible outside the city, he drew a wide-bladed falchion from its scabbard at his belt and advanced on Azazel.

Suddenly, Azazel, too, was armed, his long, flaming whip appearing in his hand as if it had been there all along and Qayna had simply failed to notice it. He snapped the weapon in the space between him and the other giant, and Semyaz hesitated.

"I will happily debate the issue with you," Azazel snarled, "the next time we meet in Council!"

Semyaz straightened his back and bellowed at the trails of smoke in the sky. "I challenge you!" he roared.

Azazel cracked his whip again, but Semyaz didn't retreat. "You never had any patience for procedure, did you?" the ruler of Ainok laughed. "You can challenge me the next time the Council meets!"

Qayna dragged Jacob back, though the boy resisted. Around the edges of the Plaza, she now saw gathering others of the

Fallen. They stood jittery, or they prowled with knees bent. She wondered if some of them had expected this contest.

"There is no Council, you fool!" Semyaz hissed, spraying slobber from his rubbery boar's lips. "If we do not act now, there is nothing!"

The boar-headed Fallen charged. Qayna saw the upraised scimitar and thought Azazel was doomed to die with his great city, but at the last second, the leader of the fallen cracked his whip a third time. It lashed Semyaz on his shoulder and coiled around the giant's thick, piggish neck. Then Azazel leaped aside, yanking his rival with him—

and Semyaz crashed head-first into the base of the Tower.

He sank up to his shoulders in the white stone, plowing right through a wide mirror and shattering it instantly into glass dust. The stairs above the Fallen's head shattered into gravel, and a huge crack split the rock.

"*This* to your challenge!" Azazel roared, and rammed his shoulder into Semyaz's back. He drove the other Fallen into the base of the Tower like a nail, as Semyaz squealed and wiggled but couldn't get away. More mirrors fell.

The Fallen around the Plaza hopped up and down, hissed and stared at each other. They were agitated and uncertain. Qayna pulled Jacob's hand and tried to leave down a colonnaded avenue, but a huge Fallen with a serpent's head blocked her way, tongue flicking in and out of his mouth. Qayna raised her sword, but didn't dare attack the giant creature.

"The Council is here!" boomed another of the Fallen. He was a bull-headed giant whose body was covered with scales. In his hands he hefted an enormous club, like the trunk of an entire tree with twisted metal spikes shoved entirely through it. "Semyaz has made a motion, we must vote!"

Others of the Fallen stepped forward, and Qayna jogged out of the way with the child. The serpent-headed giant kept his beady eye on her, though, and she was careful not to give the appearance of fleeing.

Around them on all sides, at the edges of the city of Ainok, smoke and fire rose in sheets. The Swordbearers were setting about their work of destruction.

Qayna's crow circled the Tower, wings stiff.

Azazel stepped into the center of the Council, whip trailing behind him on the stones. He smiled, and Qayna was reminded how majestic he was—how powerful and moving they all were, setting aside the part-animal forms. They weren't beautiful, but something in them stirred her soul.

"I apologize, Semyaz," he purred. "I didn't hear your motion. Could you repeat it for me?"

The Fallen Semyaz kicked his legs and *murmmphed*, his head still stuck in the base of the Tower. The crack split wider and crawled further up the stone.

"Semyaz questioned your policies," Bull Head growled. "He's not the only one of us who thinks you've been too soft on Eden."

Azazel arched his eyebrows and nodded slightly. "What Semyaz did," he said slowly, "was issue a challenge." He looked around at the other members of the Council. "Does anyone else here ... wish to issue me ... a similar challenge?"

There was a heavy silence. The ring of fire surrounding the city of Ainok was through its gates, Qayna thought, and burnings its way closer. She could hear screams, far outside the Plaza, and smell scorched flesh.

"I thought not."

Azazel turned in a flash and kicked his goat-like hoof into the posterior of his rival. Semyaz bellowed in anger, the sound muffled by the stone around his head, and was pounded deeper into the rock.

Semyaz could stand the blow, but the Tower couldn't. The widening crack became a fissure, and suddenly Qayna could see daylight through the middle of the Tower. She dragged Jacob back and away at a sprint, and this time Snake Face was too busy watching out for his own skin to get in the way.

CRASH!!!

Great blocks of masonry rained down around the Grand Plaza, crashing to the ground like falling stars and smashing up the smooth white stone. Mirrors exploded into fragments and dust, forever shattering the gates they contained. Azazel stood still, eyes flashing at his rivals as they cowered in the tumult.

Qayna managed to get behind Snake Face and then several more of the Fallen, and their bodies intercepted big chunks of rock that would have flattened her and the boy. Glass shards and gravel shrapnel still tore their skin and stung them from head to toe.

Then the Tower was flat and a cloud of white dust slowly settled over them all. Several of the Fallen lay bruised and bleeding in the wreckage, but Azazel stood tall in the center. With a single flap of his wings, he snapped the dust off his own person and the ground beneath him.

"Look at that," the founder of the city of Ainok said, glancing down at his own hoof. "You've made me split a nail."

Bull Head sneezed dust and mucus onto the stone and shook his shoulders. "The city is taken, Azazel," he rumbled, staring at his leader with yellow eyes and lowering his club. "We must do something."

"I will." Azazel dropped his whip. "I will do it now. And what you should do ... all of you ..." he didn't look at Qayna, but she realized he was talking particularly to her, hidden as she now was back among the ranks of the Fallen, "is flee."

Azazel, leader of the Fallen, turned and walked through the rubble of his Tower toward the main avenue of the city. In passing, he took the opportunity to kick Semyaz once more, in the belly. Semyaz grunted.

"Do not forget this day," Azazel intoned deeply. "I am yet your leader."

Qayna squeezed Jacob's hand tighter and slipped away. The Fallen around her let her go, probably didn't even notice that she was there. They hesitated only a moment, and then they turned and ran like she did, loping and scurrying and stampeding for the walls.

She didn't mean to, but Qayna found herself following a path parallel to Azazel's. She tried to turn left and move perpendicular to him, expecting that his course would take him into the heart of the action and the danger. Her way was blocked almost immediately, though; at the end of a short alley, she ran into one of the Swordbearers.

He was a giant, as they all were, and he wore the eyeless, visorless helmet of his office. He was wingless, because the

Bearers of the Sword didn't fly, they merely fell to earth to wreak their devastation. Flame erupted about the Swordbearer in a column, fire dripped like burning oil from his arms and sheets of flame trailed behind his enormous weapon. He swung his sword left and right, not like the blinded creature he appeared to be, but as if responding to some inner dictate that had nothing to do with the inputs of his senses. The weapon must be twelve feet long, Qayna thought—she had heard many stories of the Bearers of the Sword in her youth, told by the Bearers of the Word and repeated by her parents, but she had never before seen one and she felt awed. The weapon shattered wood and stone with equal facility, leaving smoking and shattered ruins behind with each blow.

One of the Fallen rushed to get past the Swordbearer, crab-like lower body scuttling with all its power and humanoid arms raising a shield and spear defensively. The Swordbearer's back-handed swing sliced through shield and spear alike, melted the crab carapace merely by passing close to it, and chopped entirely through the Fallen's torso. The Fallen burst into flame and collapsed.

The Bearer of the Sword stepped over the smoking body and moved in Qayna's direction, weapon raised.

Qayna ran. Around another corner, she found herself on the tiled edge of a canal. To one side, the collapsed rubble of several buildings blocked her way, so she yanked Jacob's hand and rushed in the other direction, her eternal crow flapping at her shoulder.

Ahead of her, and on the other side of the canal, she saw Azazel walking forward, his back turned to her. She wondered what he was doing, and so did the boy.

"Papa," he said, and pointed.

"Yes," Qayna agreed, and dragged him faster.

Azazel stopped in a broad square, surrounded not by his Fallen compatriots now but by four of the Swordbearers. He stood upon the trampled bodied of dead men and women and Fallen alike, in a sea of blood, with his city burning around him. The Bearers raised their flaming swords.

"Stop!" Azazel thundered, and the Swordbearers hesitated. "Where is your leader?"

There was no answer from the blind swordsmen of Heaven, but they didn't attack, either.

"Raphael!" Azazel yelled. "Where is the sniveling rat?"

"I'm here, traitor!" Raphael stepped into view among the smoking buildings, and his beauty took Qayna's breath away. It had been years since she had seen one of the Messengers, Bearers of the Word, and she had forgotten how stunning they were. The Fallen retained majesty and some of their beauty, but the tinkering they had done with their own forms marred them.

Raphael flapped his six wings and drifted forward.

Though the Bearer was the more beautiful of the two gigantic figures facing off, Qayna preferred the leader of the Fallen. The mere sight of Raphael, even after so much time, made her skin burn. She felt she was being punched to the ground again to have her sins tattooed upon the scroll of her body.

She shuddered and looked away.

Ahead of her, the way was blocked by a mob of people. Not fleeing citizens of Ainok, but men with swords and spears, coming her direction. Perhaps, she thought, she could bluff her way past them. "I may pretend you are my prisoner, boy," she whispered to Jacob. "Don't be frightened."

The boy nodded.

"Have you come to spout more defiance?" Raphael demanded.

Qayna tried not to be distracted and kept marching along the canal.

"What defiance?" Azazel raised his empty palms in a shrug. "I am defeated, and I have come for punishment. Only leave the others be. They harm no one. They only wish to be free."

Qayna knew that the leader of the Fallen couldn't possibly care very much about whether Semyaz or Bull Head or Snake Face were hurt by the champions of Heaven. He was more than willing to hurt them himself, brutally, in struggles for the leadership of Ainok and its people. What he must care about, she realized, was his son. He couldn't entrust the boy to any of his rivals, so he had given him instead into Qayna's care. He had given Qayna a place and people when her own had thrown her out, and now he counted on her to pay the debt.

Qayna gritted her teeth and ran faster.

She ignored the scene of the surrender across from her. One of the Swordbearers stood on the other side of the canal now, so there was no way she could cross it. To her left was a high wall with no entrance, other than the few unshattered mirrors that still hung on it, and they were no gate to Qayna. Her only way out was through a wall of armed and armored men, faces grim behind metal helmets.

She dragged Jacob towards them, yanking his arm to look fierce and pointing her dagger at him. Ainok had been her only place of refuge, and she owed it to Ainok's founder to try to save his son, if she could.

"I've seized this boy prisoner," she bluffed. "Where do I take him?"

Swords and spears bristled in her direction. The men's armor was bronze and covered in swirling letters not too dissimilar to her own tattoos. Horsehair brushes rose from their helmets, and they wore white, hip-length capes. Qayna stopped, trying to keep the grim, confident look on her face.

The leader of the armed men only stared.

"Well?" Qayna demanded, shaking Jacob by the shoulder. "I think he's someone important."

"Do you think we don't recognized the Marked Woman when we see her?" the leader asked. His voice sounded familiar and he poked his sword at her in a very unsubtle and threatening gesture. "Do you think all the sons and daughters of Adam don't know to recognize the Marked Woman on sight?"

Qayna held her position, mind racing. "Do you mistake me for one of the Fallen?" she snarled.

Out of the corner of her eye, she saw Raphael and other Messengers wrapping enormous chains around Azazel, who knelt in the square alone with his head bowed. The Swordbearers stood motionless and alert around him.

The leader of the soldiers sheathed his sword and wormed the helmet off his face. "Do you think I would not recognize my own sister?" he asked.

It was Shet. Older, bearded, a man now, but unmistakably her brother. His face was cold and bitter.

"Shet ..." she whispered.

"Take them both," Shet muttered to his men, and stepped aside. "Kill the boy."

Qayna dove into the water, dragging Jacob with her.

Immediately, she clamped her mouth over the boy's and breathed the air from her lungs into his. She knew from experience that drowning wouldn't kill her, any more than fire would, or falls, or bleeding.

She had tried them all.

Jacob kicked, but she wouldn't let him go. She dropped the sword. The bottom of the canal was thick with weed and heavy garbage and she kept to it, kicking down with her legs and pulling herself along with her free hand.

Spears stabbed into the water, and arrows, but they missed. Twice, the flaming swords of the Bearers scorched through the canal about her, making the water bubble with heat and the sudden inrushing of air, but the Bearers missed her, too, and Qayna kept swimming. Jacob bit her hand, and still she wouldn't let him go.

Qayna's lungs burned, but she ignored them, knowing that she could not die. She was under the city wall, still kicking, when the weapons of her enemies disappeared and she finally felt she and the child had come to safety. Arms and legs exhausted, skin scratched and chilled, feet hammered from running across the stone, she dragged Jacob from the river outside Ainok's burning walls. In a small grove of gnarled trees, she threw him into the grass and finally sucked air into her lungs, coughing out the water she had inhaled during the long submersion.

She slapped Jacob on the chest in camaraderie, sloshing water from both their bodies. "Well, boy," she laughed. "We made it."

He didn't answer.

And then she realized that the child beside her in the trees was still and cold.

She was still pounding on his chest and trying to force air from her lungs into his when the first chunks of Ainok's masonry, charred and burning, tore from the earth and rose into a heaven thick with smoke.

CHAPTER SEVEN

F*HOOM!*

Jane lit the rag-and-stone missile in her hand and it erupted into a fireball. She ignored the pain. In that instant, her wards of dissembling became inadequate, and all five rock and rollers saw her.

"Carajo!"

Jane whistled sharply. The Mare leaped away from the tractor in her direction, and she threw the stone.

Bullseye.

KABOOM!

The tractor exploded. The flames and force of the explosion engulfed the crow, but Jane didn't bother hoping. The bird would emerge from the wreckage unscathed, as it always had.

She grabbed the rain-slick saddle with burned fingers and hurled herself onto the Mare's back. The Mare whinnied and Jane drew the Calamity Horn.

The men on the ground rolled to their knees and tried to recover dropped weapons, but the fairy dropped at her from above, shrieking a falcon war cry.

Jane aimed high and fired, *bang! bang!* forcing the falcon to drop lower—

and then urged her mount forward with her knees—

the Thracian Mare bit at the fairy with sharp teeth, chomping wing and tail and scattering a bright spray of red blood.

Twitch hit the dirt hard, in female shape, shrieking and clutching her hip.

The Mare reared up, aiming to plunge down upon the fey drummer and shatter her with implacable hooves, but Jane pulled the animal's reins and turned her back into the sorghum furrows, galloping fast. There was no particular reason to save the fairy, but neither was there any time to waste. In a wide circle around her, beyond the planted fields and the meat packing plants and the highway, she saw the burning white columns that could mean only one thing: the Bearers of the Sword had come to Dodge City.

And that was profoundly wrong.

Raphael was absent without leave. Heaven had sent her after the renegade. They had not sent their own minions, the Legate had said, because it was a case for discretion, which had made sense. If the Bearers of the Word were again disobeying orders and making decisions for themselves, Heaven would be seen as weak, as disunified. What believer could trust in a fragmented Heaven?

So why send the Swordbearers now? Had Jane failed?

Or had the Legate lied to her?

All of Jane's instincts screamed at her to *run*, and she did. She spurred the Mare into the performance of its long and turbulent life, racing for the highway, where she planned to turn and head for Oklahoma, back the way the rock and roll band and come and the opposite direction from wherever it was they were going. She wanted, as they said in the old movies, to *get the hell out of Dodge*.

But as she raced for the strip of asphalt at the end of the field, the Bearers of the Sword raced for it, too. Ahead of her, two of the fiery giants emerged from charred and smoking sorghum stalks, swords raised and ready, masked faces unreadable.

They were after her.

A law enforcement vehicle of some sort—Jane couldn't see the writing, but she saw the flashing lights on the rooftop and heard the siren—pulled to a screeching halt before the Swordbearers and two officers jumped out. As Jane veered to race back into the sorghum, she saw one of the Bearers slam his blade down like a drill, through the center of the police car's roof. The flashing lights, the roof and the entire car disappeared in a column of bright, oily flame, and the two cops scattered left and right.

Then Jane's back was turned and she lost sight of them. "Faster, girl!" she urged the Mare, and pointed her nose through the wind and the rain in the direction of the meat packing plant. This wasn't a problem, she thought. She might lose the Mare, which was a shame, but she had an easy escape route and she wouldn't look back.

Part of her wanted to turn and stand. Not fight, just stand still, in the hopes that the Swordbearers could accomplish with their titanic flaming weapons what she herself had been unable to achieve with blade, bullet, drowning, suffocation, fire, poison, curse, acid, falling, or any other of her uncounted attempts. Maybe the Bearers of the Sword could kill her.

But she didn't trust Heaven to be that merciful. If they'd wanted her dead, the Legate could simply have given her the death letter in the Las Vegas hotel room. They could have revoked the curse, or never have cursed her in the first place. Her original punishment could have been merciful execution, instead of condemnation to an eternal pilgrimage with no destination and no reward for piety.

No, Heaven wanted something, and they weren't going to ask nicely.

Racing across the furrows towards the plant, Jane tracked several things. She noticed the cordon of the Bearers of the Sword closing in. She saw the two policemen, puffing along the highway in the direction of the plant, one of them occasionally turning to fire at the flaming angels of punishment. She spotted a scarlet sedan chair approaching at a quick shuffle-step pace from the opposite direction. All of them converged on Fine Cuts, Inc.

Also closing in on the packing plant, juddering across the furrows like a spoon over a washboard, came something that almost made Jane smile: a rusted, dented, cracked, scratched and beat-to-hell brown Dodge van. Not that they were her friends; in fact, they were after her. But she admired scrappiness, and she felt akin to the down-at-the-heels, held-together-by-duct-tape-and-spit rock band. They were wanderers, outlaws and loners, just like she was. Just like she had always been.

Also, Jim was Azazel's son.

Jane considered jumping off the Mare and escaping right in the middle of the field. She'd have done it, except that she wasn't sure she had the strength. The burning fire of her ka was measured by art and intuition, and not by metric science. She knew she was recovering her strength, she thought she probably had the power to pull off now what she had planned, but she couldn't be sure.

And failure would mean capture.

Jane leaped the Mare effortlessly over the rail fence just as the sedan chair from one end and the cops from the other stumbled up to the plant. One of the officers looked panicked and out of his mind; the other was surprisingly calm, holding his fire with his pistol in its holster. She couldn't see the sedan chair's occupant through the hanging red curtains, but it was such a silly and medieval affectation that it just had to belong to the Legate. It was carried, two in front and two behind, by men who were too large, muscular and blank-stared to be normal humans. Golems, she thought. Or professional wrestlers. Given the kilts they were wearing, most likely the former.

The Bearers of the Sword were further away. They swung their swords like harvesting sickles, burning the sorghum to the ground and incinerating trees, buildings, and anything else in their way.

Behind Jane, a *crash!* told her that the brown Dodge van had smashed through the rail fence.

The potholes were full of rainwater now, end even more treacherous. A lesser animal might have broken its ankle; the Thracian Mare charged over and through the hazards without complaint.

She urged the Mare up the concrete steps on the back side of the plant and ducked, holding on to her hat. The mighty beast rushed through the back door in a single kick of its hind legs, scattering papers, jackets and rubber gloves left and right as it breezed through the entry and into the cold room.

Jane pulled the reins and the Thracian Mare skidded to a slow stop, hooves clattering across concrete. Jane tumbled off the horse, grabbing her saddlebags and slinging them over her own shoulder. She made extra sure she had the hoof fragment, tucked into her duster pocket. She wanted out, and she wasn't sure she wanted to go after the rogue Bearer of the Word anymore, not right now, but if others wanted the hoof, then it might become a valuable bargaining chip.

"Thanks, girl," she patted the horse on the rump, and then whistled the command most welcome to her mount. "Give 'em hell."

The Mare snorted jets of steam in the crisp cold of the plant, bared cat-like teeth and galloped for the back door.

"*Chingón!*"

Sudden gunfire filled the meat packing plant. The metal walls made the plant a natural reverb unit and the raucous explosions banged back and forth infinitely. The Mare took hits but didn't slow her charge, and then the entry room collapsed into total chaos, a storm of kicking hooves, chomping teeth, and flying lead.

Jane considered the bathroom doors and almost went inside, but decided against it at the last moment. If she was wrong and her ka failed her, she didn't want to be trapped in a dead end, not by the scruffy rock and rollers any more than she wanted to be trapped by the police or the Legate and his Swordbearers.

And where was Raphael in all this, after all?

Instead, she headed for the stairs, swallowing against the deafening racket of the gunfire.

As she kicked open the door she looked back and saw that she was followed. It was the singer, Jim. He ran with a bloody saber bared in his fist, crashing between the swinging beef carcasses like a freight train rushing along its cleared track through the trees of the forest, knuckles swinging and breath blasting in his nostrils.

She slammed the door in his face and raced up the stairs.

Oh, for more ka, she thought, or more time. But she'd rather be caught by the handsome singer than by the Legate—it was hard to imagine that he could do very much to her, other than cut her or inflict some transient physical pain. Heaven, on the other hand, could really hurt her. She knew that because it had.

His boots crashed into the stairwell behind her as she reached the door at the top.

She hesitated a moment, wondering if she would open the door to find a flaming sword thrust into her face. It probably wouldn't kill her, but it would hurt.

She forced herself to throw open the door and charged out onto the rooftop.

It might as well have been noon, the sky was so bright. Directly overhead, in a tiny circle, she could still see stars. They twinkled like will o' the wisps at the bottom of a deep, black well. A circle of white light blanched out the host of heaven around that bottomless well, and then streaked and blurred, in some places almost imperceptibly, into a ring of fire giants standing still and ready around the plant. There were seven of them, and they stood with swords help upright, fire dripping down to further scorch the ruined fields and mar the asphalt and gravel. The furnace blaze of their fire dried the air up, so that the wind gusting across the rooftop was arid and no rain fell.

Jane cursed, the Adamic imprecation blowing a small crater in the gravel at her feet.

She slammed the door shut behind her, wishing she could know exactly how much ka she had, so that she could throw a ward of sealing onto the exit. It didn't matter, she was almost gone, anyway. She couldn't see the sedan chair or the policemen from where she was, only the implacable giants, faces visored shut and angelic bodies still and ready to pounce.

She heard gunshots, though. Lots of gunshots, and the fierce, blood-drinking whinny of the Thracian Mare.

She raced to the circle she had left on the lightning-bolt-bearing box; it was intact. Jane dropped her saddlebags to the rooftop and clambered atop the metal casing. The circle was not exactly the one she would have preferred, either to regenerate the heat of her ka or to strengthen her gate-opening incantation. Its glyphs were written in Adamic, though, which gave it power and would reinforce her in anything she did; it would have to suffice.

Jane pulled a small round mirror from the saddlebag and set it on the metal at her feet without looking at it. She kept her eyes on the burning giants, ready to leap into action if they tried anything. She had the Calamity Horn, after all; one bullet per Swordbearer was terrible odds and a gamble, but at least she could make them think twice about trying to take her against her will.

She heard the rooftop door smash open, and she turned to face Jim, the singer. He came rushing across the gravel with his sword in hand, but he didn't move like a fencer, cautious, one foot in front of the other. He sprinted, head down and glaring like a bull.

Jane incanted the words in Adamic and felt the fire of her ka flow from her. She waved good-bye at the charging rock and roller, smiled, and stepped onto the mirror—

nothing happened.

She looked down, and saw that the reflective glass had gone dull and gray. Jane cursed again, not meaning to, and the glass cracked.

Jim stabbed at her—

Jane stepped sideways, but a little too late. The burning in her side where his saber cut into her flesh jerked her back to full wakefulness and attention, and Jane dropped backwards off the generator box, drawing her knives.

Jim stabbed again, and a third time, but the box was in the way. He stepped forward and executed a neat shoulder roll across the top of the metal—

Jane stepped in slashing, but was forced back by the heavy heels of his boots before she could land a good blow, and then he pressed her again.

Something bowled into the small of Jane's back, knocking her forward. Frantically, she crossed her long knife blades in front of her and caught Jim's saber blade in them. She pushed, trying to shove the blade out of the way—

and instead, she impaled herself on it. The sword sank into her belly, up to the hilt.

Jane fell heavily, dragging Jim's weapon with her. With confused vision, she saw a white horse flashing red, and for a moment she imagined that the Thracian Mare was coming to her rescue, but then she remembered that the Mare was black, and she realized that the horse she was seeing was the fairy Twitch; that the flashes of red were Twitch's blood where Jane herself had caused injury.

Then Twitch the horse kicked Jane in her head, throwing her body sideways and slamming her to the roof again.

Jane tried to think as she dragged herself away. The band wanted Azazel's hoof back. Did Heaven want the hoof as well, was that what this was about? The angel caretaker of Dudael had failed, and Jane had been sent to recover what had been stolen?

But then why not tell her as much?

"Stop," she croaked. Twitch kicked her again, still in horse form, and smashed her flat to the gravel. "I'm not sure we're enemies." She dribbled the words from her lips with a thin stream of blood.

Jim lifted her off the ground far enough to grab the hoof clipping in her pocket and extract it in a single tug.

"You can't trust her, Jim," the fairy said, and Jane saw her leather boots, with neat rows of shiny metal spikes running up past the ankle on the outside of each boot. *Crack!* She punched Jane in the back of her head with one of her wooden batons.

Ouch. Jane needed to stop getting hit. She raised one arm, and when the fairy's next blow came down, she caught it on the flesh of her forearm and managed to wrap her fingers around the wood.

"Stop," she ground out through the hot blood in her mouth.

She heard an animal scream, and guessed it was the Mare. She felt surprisingly bad for having led the beast to its death. She'd killed and betrayed so many of her own kind, it struck her as incongruous that she should feel like shedding tears for a flesh-eating horse.

She rolled away on her shoulder, dragging the long steel blade with her free hand until it fell out of her body with a wet *pop*.

Jim stood to one side. He held the hoof and looked vaguely puzzled.

"Oberon's tail," Twitch gasped, staring at Jane and stepping back. "You hear a thing a thousand times, but you don't believe it until you see it."

Jane spat blood onto the muddy gravel and lay back. She couldn't breathe now; felt like she was drowning and she was sure it was blood in one of her lungs. It didn't matter. She knew it wouldn't kill her, and in a few moments, the pain would pass. She spat out blood again. "Oberon doesn't have a tail."

Twitch snorted. "And God doesn't have teeth, but that didn't keep anyone from swearing by them for a thousand years, did it?"

Jim bent and slowly picked up his sword. He looked around.

Jane sat up. The Swordbearers loomed large and not far away. A collective step forward, Jane thought, and they could bring their swords down together and reduce the meat packing plant to charred brick and burned ribs. Why weren't they attacking?

And what had happened to her mirror?

And what was really going on here?

"How do you know God doesn't have teeth?" she asked.

"Ah," the fairy sighed, "how do you think? Hadn't you heard he was one of us?"

Jane dragged herself to her feet. The blood had stopped gushing down her chest, but she felt weak and her ka was all but gone, a dim pulsing within her barely worthy of the name. "If God really is one of the folk of the Mirror Queendom," she cracked, "that would explain why Heaven always seems to get everything backward."

"Sir?" a voice elsewhere on the rooftop called. "Sir, this is a … this is a crime scene, and I have to ask you to leave."

Jane turned and saw the Legate, in his mantelletta and galero, stomping her direction across the rooftop. Behind him came two of his big sedan slaves, and now Jane saw that they were indeed golems; they breathed heavy, with their mouths open, and she could see the Hebrew characters tattooed on their tongues.

After the Legate came two law enforcement officers, Sheriff's deputies, Jane now saw. The younger man, with buzzcut hair and a thin mustache, walked in front. He called out to the Legate, asking the red-caped man to stop and getting a cold shoulder in return. Behind him came an older, heavier deputy, with a beard and a paunch and his hand resting on the butt of a gun at his hip.

"And you there," Mustache continued, pointing at Jim. His finger trembled. "Drop your sword, sir, so we can have a polite conversation about what's going on here." The deputy looked around at the Bearers of the Sword that surrounded the building. "A polite conversation that also made some damn kinda sense would be a nice bonus."

Jim tightened his grip on his sword, but frowned like he didn't understand the Deputy's words. Jane was sure she had seen him somewhere before, though not recently.

"Thank you, Qayna," the Legate said. He stopped and sat on the metal casing of the generator. "You've done exactly as we'd hoped."

"Funny," Jane bluffed. "So have you. It's over."

"Everyone here should consider himself under arrest!" Deputy Mustache insisted, pointing his pistol at the ground beside the Legate. "You with the sword, put it down … now!"

"Raphael," the Legate said, and his voice sounded old. "Can we end this?" The golems lurked behind him like exclamations marks waiting to jump onto all of his sentences.

Deputy Beard drew his pistol, a large-caliber revolver. "You heard the man." He raised the gun.

"Thanks, pard," Deputy Mustache glared at Jim.

"It's over," Beard said.

Bang!

Deputy Mustache fell to the ground, bleeding from the back of his head.

"Thank you, Rafi," the Legate said. "Now, let's get down to a little business, shall we?" He removed from under his mantelletta a familiar piece of sealed and folded parchment, and waved it until it caught Jane's attention.

Raphael and the Legate were in cahoots, Jane realized.

She'd been set up.

CHAPTER EIGHT

There never was any renegade," Jane said calmly. The mirror gate must not have worked because the Legate, or someone working with him, had pinned it shut. She looked at Jim, blinking and shaking his head like he had water in his ears, and wondered if the Legate had done something to the singer, too.

"No, there wasn't," Beard agreed. He held his gun with antsy hands, and not with the sure calmness of an experienced shooter. "Or rather, there hasn't been one yet. Soon, there'll be many."

He laughed, and the Legate laughed with him.

"Jim?" Twitch asked, but got no answer.

Jane's curse-driven powers of recuperation were kicking in, and she was starting to feel stronger.

"This has all been a trap," Jane added, ruminating.

The golems growled an objection in unison.

"No," the Legate objected, showing his palms in protest and waving back his sedan team. "What trap? This has all been an invitation. We wanted to arrange a meeting of certain key people." He waved the letter again, tantalizingly. "I assure you that I have only the best of intentions."

"You wanted us to meet you under guard," Jane pointed out, nodding at the Swordbearers. "And stoned."

The Legate waved a hand and muttered something under his breath; that he was a sorcerer came as no surprise, and Jane wondered how good he was. Jim shook his head, his eyes suddenly cleared. He raised his sword an inch or two and took half a step forward, but then halted at the Legate's upraised hand.

"Please, James," the Legate said. "I had to be sure you wouldn't run. But as a sign of good faith, I've cloaked this entire building with wards of silence. Please feel free to join the conversation. I *want* to hear what you have to say."

Jim narrowed his eyes and flared his nostrils.

"Oh, you shouldn't imagine me using the unreliable, spotty, flaring wards of your erratic little wizardling," the Legate assured him. Then he laughed. "Believe me, I'm just as anxious as you are not to be heard by His Lowness at this moment. We'll talk to Lucifer when the time is right, but not before."

"Call off your dogs," Jim rumbled. His voice had something of the trumpet in it, and reminded Jane of the voices of the Fallen. The golems growled at him as if prompted, but the Swordbearers remained impassive and still.

"You must understand me clearly." The Legate's eyes were serious. "We are going to have a conversation now, and that conversation *will—absolutely* and *without question*—go the way I want it to. The Bearers are just here to see to that."

Deputy Beard holstered his pistol and sneered at Twitch. "Miaow."

Twitch hissed at him through her teeth.

Jane stared at the Deputy. His true identity—the name and nature of the being that lurked inside the Deputy's body, animating and controlling him—was still sinking into her consciousness. "Raphael," she said softly. "It has been a very long time."

"Qayna," he nodded.

"I don't usually go by that name." Jane itched all over. It felt like the ink of her tattoos crawled under her skin at the sight of the person who had first etched them into her. She spat on the gravel.

"There is war coming," the Legate intoned. "War in Heaven. Michael and his angels against the dragon."

"The Revelation of John," Jim said. "The refuge and comfort of every crackpot for the last two thousand years." Something burning behind his eyes suggested to Jane that he didn't quite believe his own words.

"War is inevitable!" Raphael shot back. "You can't build a kingdom on lies!"

Jane disagreed: "I'm not sure you can build a kingdom on anything else." She was recovering from the shock of realizing that she was again seeing Raphael, and now she felt anxious to shoot him.

If not for the fact that her own death was in play, a golden worm baiting a tiny hook, she'd have shot him already.

"Cynic!" Raphael was shocked.

Jane shrugged, not meeting the Messenger's eyes. "I've been around too long to be an idealist. What are you going on about?"

"Accept for the moment that war is coming," the Legate said. He shrugged. "Accept it because, if nothing else, I will start that conflict myself. The questions you should be asking yourselves are *what do I want out of the coming and unavoidable conflict?* And *how am I going to get it?*"

"The war between Michael and the dragon." Jim raised his eyebrows. "You're planning to invade Hell?"

"The dragon is a poetic image." The Legate folded his hands piously in his lap. "Perhaps *I* am the dragon."

"So Michael throws you to the earth," Jim followed the logic dubiously, "and you become Satan. You have strange aspirations, Legate. Even my father didn't *want* his fate."

Jane stared hard at Jim, wondering how much he knew, and wondering whether it was true that Azazel hadn't wanted his throne.

"Poetry!" the Legate hissed. He composed himself again.

"Who knew that the titles of the head of the Infernal Council were poetic?" Twitch laughed skeptically. "The Infernals, anyway, seem to take them very seriously."

"It might have been the title," Jim muttered to the fairy, "or it might have been the fart jokes."

Jane felt as nonplussed as the Legate looked.

The man in the mantelletta shook off his confusion. "Forget the Bible. Here's the point. Each of you is carrying a bargaining chip. I will not deceive you or play the coquette—I want what you have, and I will pay."

"*We* want," Raphael corrected him, but the Legate ignored the angel.

Jane looked around at the Swordbearers, gigantic and fiery, immobile in the clouds of smoke that their burning threshed out of the sorghum around their feet. "In other words," she said with deliberate impudence, "you want to kill me, and in exchange, you'll let me torture and kill Raphael first."

The Angel-Deputy chuckled, but turned a little pale. Jane stared him down with an eye full of thousands of years of constantly nurtured hatred.

The Legate fixed her with a stare. "I want the Calamity Horn," he said. "The gun capable of killing even immortals."

"Except me," Jane pointed out. "To my grave disappointment."

"Forgive the pun," the fairy snapped out reflexively.

"I never forgive puns," Jim grunted. "They remind me too much of what I'm missing by holding my tongue all the time."

The Legate smiled patiently. "So you don't need to fear handing it over. Besides, you already know that your death is within my gift." He waved the letter at her. It was so close that Jane could *smell* the parchment and the sealing wax.

Jane's crow settled beside the Legate on the metal box.

Within his gift. That sounded right; the Legate wasn't trying to kill her outright, but was offering her the chance to be able to die. He was doing more than offering—he was selling it, pretty hard.

"I don't fear much of anything at this point. Still, I'm curious." Jane squinted at the big singer. "You must be invading Hell, right? I mean, there are precious few beings this gun is capable of hurting that you couldn't just take down with the Swordbearers. But even the Fallen, they can be beaten with flaming swords." She glared at Raphael, remembering the obliteration of Ainok. "So why the gun?"

"And seven priests," the Legate said in answer, "bearing seven trumpets of rams' horns before the ark of the Lord went on continually, and blew with the trumpet."

Jane snorted. "You don't need to quote me chapter and verse on this stuff. I was there for most of it."

"There for what?" Twitch asked. "I don't know either the chapter or the verse. I'm not much of a reader."

"Joshua's priests blew seven horns and the walls of Jericho came tumbling down."

Jim looked at her with a curious smile. "What was that like?"

"I was on the wall." Jane shrugged. "It hurt like hell, but I survived."

"And I saw the seven angels which stood before God; and to them were given seven trumpets." The Legate's eyes twinkled.

"Back to Revelation? Seven priests with trumpets before the ark, seven seraphim with trumpets before the throne." Jim shrugged. "Sort of a match, I guess, but lots of things come in sevens. Seven sages of Greece. Seven colors in the visible spectrum. Snow White and the seven dwarfs. So what?"

A long spate of gunshots ended in an abrupt equine scream.

Jane frowned. "Seven bullets in my gun is so what," she realized out loud.

"The first angel sounded," Raphael quoted, "and there followed hail and fire mingled with blood, and they were cast upon the earth: and the third part of trees was burnt up, and all green grass was burnt up."

"You'd like that, wouldn't you, you son of a bitch?" Jane remembered the fields of her youth, the moist, firm feeling of earth between her fingers. She almost yanked the pistol out and started firing.

"You think the seven bullets in her gun," Jim pointed at it to underline the insanity of the idea, "are the seven trumpets of the apocalypse? This is what I'm hearing from the Legate of Heaven?"

"Ah, I hate this stuff," Twitch muttered. "Jehoshaphat begat Arad who begat Shem, gobbledy-gobbledy, can't we just skip to the part where we start shooting? Why is life on this side of the mirror always so tedious?"

"Maybe," Jim said, "just *maybe*, we can avoid the shooting this time."

"I doubt it." Jane stared hard at the angel who had tattooed her body, thousands of years ago.

"Gavrilo's Horn," the Legate said. "Don't you see?"

Raphael continued; spittle flecked his chin. "And the second angel sounded, and as it were a great mountain burning with fire was cast into the sea."

"Prophecy is prophecy." The Legate nodded. "It will be fulfilled, whatever I do. I am merely trying to discover a way to fulfill it … advantageously."

"And the third angel sounded, and there fell a great star—"

"Shut up!" Jim snapped.

Raphael arched his eyebrows and closed his mouth.

"Bat-shit crazy." Azazel's son shook his head. "Give me one reason why I shouldn't walk away from you and your madness."

"Because I will give you what you want, James."

Jane looked into the singer's eyes and saw the truth: he was curious, and he was tempted.

At that moment the rooftop's door opened and the other rock and rollers staggered out. Eddie led the way, sawed-off shotgun in his hands, and behind him followed Mike holding a two-by-four and Adrian squinting through his sorcerer's lens.

The golems turned to look at the newcomers and raised their fists defensively, but didn't attack.

Jim raised a hand, palm out, to stop the band's advance.

"Careful!" Adrian shouted back. "There's all kinds of crazy warding and hexes on this building!"

Jim nodded slowly.

"We had this conversation before, Raphael," he said.

"No. I tried to have this conversation, and you refused."

While they were looking at each other, Jane carefully slipped the edge of her duster aside, to be sure she had a clean draw when she needed it.

"What do I want, then?" Jim asked.

"Jim, don't do it," Twitch urged his friend.

"Whatever you want," the Legate told him, "you can get it with power. Power brings all good things. Power, and money, which is the same thing."

"That's true!" Adrian called out, and Mike elbowed him in the chest.

"I could have any woman I wanted," Jim suggested.

"They'd line up." The Legate smiled a pimp's greasy grin.

"Hey!" Mike threw in. "Share!" Adrian elbowed him back.

"Wealth." Jim grinned. "The kingdoms of this world. All I have to do is bow down to you."

"All of them could be yours. And you don't have to bow down to anyone, including me. You'll never have to bow down to anyone ever again."

"I could finally afford to fix the leaky radiator on the van."

The Legate's smile became uncertain. "You could have any car you wanted."

Jim's smile disappeared into a flat, hard line. "I want the damn van."

Raphael shrugged. "So keep the van," he said.

"He's saying *no*." The Legate frowned.

Jim raised his sword and shook its basket hilt at the Legate's galero. "I'm saying you don't know me from Adam," he growled.

"Tell me what you want."

"No!" Jim snapped. Suddenly, he seemed huge, and his voice echoed over the rooftop so loud that even the Swordbearers appeared to stir a little at the sound. "You tell me what *you* want, Legate! What are you doing chasing me down in the middle of nowhere? What do you want, the hoof, is that it? All this for a toenail clipping?"

The Legate and the angel were both silent. Jim towered taller than either of them with his naked sword in his hand, threatening and dangerous.

"If it's just a toenail clipping," the Messenger said slowly, "why don't you give it up?"

Jim barked a short "ha!"

"What is Heaven?" the Legate asked.

"You're asking the wrong guy," Jim snarled. "I've never been."

"Heaven is a palace." The Legate sniffed. "It has gardens, like any palace. The air of Heaven is delicious with the tinkle of fountains and running water. It has a staff, with servants who perform different functions. Some are guards and warriors, others clerks and scribes, still others guides and major-domos."

"And presumably some gardeners," Twitch added. "Won't anybody think of the poor plants?"

The quip cut through all the tension and endeared the fairy to Jane, and she winked. Twitch arched an eyebrow back, in surprise and maybe fear.

"At the center of the palace complex is the audience chamber," the Legate continued. "Here the angels keep burning the eternal fires, maintain the perpetual cloud of incense, and so forth."

"Get to the point."

"Beyond the audience chamber lies the throne room," the Legate continued, unperturbed. "But within the throne room, and at its veil, stand the seven seraphim."

"I remember these guys," Jim agreed, and nodded in Raphael's direction. "Your boy was making fun of them, last time we met."

Raphael shrugged.

"The seven are great and terrible," the Legate went on. "One for each of the seven lights on the great golden tree, they are nameless, faceless beings of eternal fire."

"And beyond them is the throne, and on the throne sits God," Jim finished the Legate's account.

The Legate was silent.

"Did I miss a step?" Jim pressed. "Did I forget the bottle-washing angels, or the shoe polishers, or the angels who wax on and wax off?"

The Legate shook his head.

"Maybe I left out the legions of tortured sufferers," Jim suggested. "Hanging on racks in the kingdom of Heaven to suffer until Judgment Day because their mortal lives weren't suffering enough! Oh, wait, no, Heaven doesn't want *those* people … it sends them away, to somewhere more fitting for them."

"Is that what you want?" the Legate asked slowly. "You want to free the damned souls in Hell?"

"What I *want*," Jim roared, so loud and fierce that Jane took a step back and her hand strayed close to her gun, "is to be *left alone! By you*, by my *father*, and by *everyone else!*"

He looked like his father in that moment, and it took Jane's breath away.

He also looked like Jacob, whom she had killed without meaning to.

"I don't care *who* sits on that throne," Jim bellowed, "so long as he leaves me in *peace!*"

"*No one* sits on the throne!" the Legate charged to his feet, veins popping out in his head.

Jim checked his tirade.

"No one?" Jane asked.

"No one." The Legate sank back to his seat.

"Who runs Heaven, then?" Twitch asked. "You can't have a kingdom without a king, can you?"

"No one," the Legate said again.

"The seraphim." Raphael said it with conviction, and liked the sound of it so much that he said it again. "The seraphim. It has to be."

"You're right, child of Mab," the Legate agreed. "A kingdom with no king is an abomination. It's a ship without a captain, and must run aground. We have to end this terrible situation."

"How do you know there's no captain at the wheel?" Twitch asked. "What did you do, sneak a peek when nobody was looking? There's not even a little man behind the curtain, pulling on levers, no one?"

The Legate ignored the questions.

"You're not going to invade *Hell*," Jane clarified. "You're going to invade *Heaven*. And you need the Calamity Horn so you can shoot the seraphim with it."

"Then why do you need me?" Jim demanded. "Take the gun. Kill her. She wants it. Look at her, you can see it in her eyes. Only leave me alone! I am not a part of your revolution, I have nothing to do with my father."

"Is that how your father sees it, too?" the Legate asked softly. "Does he have nothing to do with you?"

Jim said nothing.

"We need your father and his hordes." The Legate spoke quietly, but with a note of finality in his voice like he was pronouncing sentence.

"You have the Swordbearers," Jim said.

The Legate shook his head. "They are here to execute a Writ, and only because Qayna was good enough to put Raphael's life in danger."

"I'll be better than that," Jane muttered.

"We have sympathizers." The Legate smiled. "The third part of the host of heaven, I believe, is the traditional figure. But they won't take up arms unless they are confident of victory. We need the Horn, and we need your father's help."

"I want nothing to do with it," Jim insisted.

"If you refuse," the Legate said deliberately, "then we will have to kill you, and use your father's hoof as a lever to involve him anyway. I can't have you running around free with this knowledge, James."

"Kill me."

The Legate arched his eyebrows, nodded, and turned to Jane. "Kill him," Heaven's rebel emissary told her, "and the death letter is yours."

"Go to Hell." Jane laughed. "Pun intended." Lightning flashed across the well of darkness overhead, and the rain picked up, heavy enough now to pummel its way down through the ring of fire and splash Jane in the face.

The Legate's eyes flashed with irritation. "Raphael—" he began.

The golems stepped forward.

Jane's fingers brushed the butt of the Calamity Horn. "Go for your gun, you angelic son of a bitch." She stared at Raphael, eyes boring through the puppet-mask of the Deputy's body and imagining the six-winged Bearer of the Word within. "I'm begging you, *please*, as a personal favor to me, go for your gun."

CHAPTER NINE

Fat drops of rain spattered Qayna's face as she dropped down from the ridge and into the open mouth of Hell.

The slope was muddy and she fell more than once on the way down, coating her doe-skin tunic in gray slime. Her nostrils rebelled against the stink of the crater and her eyes shied away from the multitude of dead and dying birds that lay floating in it. Her own crow circled above the hole in the ground, indifferent to whatever killed all the other fliers. The mud was not the result of the rain—it and the few scattered drops were the after-leavings, the remnants, the stirrings in the wake of the flood.

The *Flood*, Qayna knew that Shet's descendants would forever after call it. The windows of heaven had opened and the fountains of the deep had ruptured and everything Qayna had ever known had been obliterated by choppy water.

Qayna had drowned.

Only it hadn't killed her. And after several long days of painful torture, being dragged about by the currents of the deep and gnawed by one strange, eyeless monster after another, she had admitted to herself that, whatever the Flood might do to the Fallen and their children, it wasn't going to end her existence.

She'd armed herself with weapons that wouldn't weigh her down: knives. Then she'd swum to the top, flung herself upon the gnarled, beheaded floating trunk of a tree and begun coughing mud and brine from her lungs. She was still hacking up black ooze when Nuh's boat had passed her by, old Nuh (white bearded and bent over, though he was hundreds of years younger than Qayna—Father and Shet and everyone she had known in her youth all long dead, other than the Fallen and Raphael) oblivious to her, standing on the deck of his bowed, air-tight ship and scratching the long neck of a giraffe.

Qayna hadn't bothered to try to get his attention.

After the Flood had come the monsters. The storm and high water had wiped out the people—the many—who had loved the city of Ainok and embraced its rule, but they also guaranteed that anything that survived them, anything that didn't come off Nuh's weird floating wooden chest, would be preternaturally tough.

Things already living in the deep had survived the hammering of cold water and crawled out hungry and pissed. The ugliest, strongest, most misshapen experiments and progeny of the Fallen had also made it through forty days and nights of rain and the slow receding afterwards. Qayna had been glad to be armed—she had pricked more than one monster into leaving her alone, and used her knives to hack her way to freedom after learning that even the digestive juices of a scabrous, six-legged land whale weren't enough to free her from Heaven's curse.

Most of the Fallen had also survived. Other than Azazel, Raphael and Shet and their army hadn't taken prisoners, and once they had razed Ainok to the ground they had lost interest in pursuing the fleeing survivors. After the Flood, Qayna had more than once hidden in a mud-strangled copse or under a shattered roof or in a festering pile of dead bodies to avoid attracting the attention of one of Ainok's rebel lords.

Bull Head had nearly stepped on her.

Weeks later, the higher ground had begun to dry out—like Ararat, where Nuh and his people had settled—but most of the face of the land was still a mud flat, pocked with ruins and the few trees tenacious enough to have hung on through the devastation. And, on the trail of a rumor she found hard to believe, Qayna returned to Ainok.

To find it a gaping hole.

And at the bottom, with yellow light flickering from it, an opening.

Qayna scrambled to her feet in a thick, fetid pool at the bottom of the crater. This might be exactly the spot where the Grand Plaza of Ainok had once been, she thought, though it was hard to be sure with most of the local landmarks obliterated. As if to confirm her guess, she stubbed her toe on a block of white stone the size of her torso.

"Password?" The voice was slithery-huge, a serpent's hiss, and Qayna recognized the snake-headed giant who had hemmed her and Jacob in when she had tried to escape the Plaza before. He wore a kilt and sandals and stood in front of a cavern entrance vast enough to hold a small town, smoke and light and movement enlivening the space behind him vaguely. She chuckled. It pleased her sense of irony that this same Fallen who had tried to keep her trapped would now try to keep her out.

"It isn't funny," Snake Face protested. "Tell me the password, or I'll kill you."

"I don't have a password," Qayna said. "But I'd like to be polite about this. How about you let me in because I'm an old friend of Azazel's? Or at least, could you tell him Qayna is here? I used to come in and out of Ainok freely."

"Those were more trusting times." The Fallen snatched her from the mud with both hands and sank his long fangs into her belly and chest. Qayna quivered and jerked, but tried not to react, letting the long saber-like teeth completely impale her. She burned as her veins filled with venom, and her limbs shook.

Then the giant threw her to the mud. She hit with a loud *splat!* and bounced. There she lay still a moment, letting the fire raging in her veins cool a bit.

"Fool," the serpent-headed colossus hissed, and resumed his station in front of the cave mouth.

Qayna climbed to her feet. "That's just what I was going to say."

The Fallen gaped.

"You could bite me again," Qayna said. "It would hurt me again. But it still wouldn't kill me." She drew her longest knife and held it ready. "And this time, I'll stab you back, right in the soft tissues inside your mouth."

Snake Face hissed in irritation, but he snapped his mouth shut and he stepped aside. The crow led the way.

The mephitic stink of the crater was even thicker inside the cave. Qayna's lungs ached, but it was less painful than being buried under the Flood.

The vastness of the cavern shrank but it never became less than huge, a rough-hewn, rock-ribbed tunnel descending at a steep angle into the bowels of the earth. It never fully dried out, either, though the air became warm and the moisture consolidated into a reddish trickle of a stream in one corner of the passage, leaving crunchy footing on the rest of the floor. Light came from sputtering red torches set irregularly into brackets in the wall.

At least the dead birds were gone.

Qayna walked forever. When she had finished walking, there was a gate. Beside it waited a giant figure in breastplate, greaves and kilt, leaning on a spear. He looked totally human, other than the scabby bird-like talons that jutted into the gravelly earth under his greaves. Under long, white hair, his face was mostly grave, with just a tiny hint of a smile playing around his lips.

"Again?" she asked.

The giant shook his head. "I am Baraqyel," he said. "I'm not going to bite you."

"Stabbing me with a spear won't work, either. Trust me."

Baraqyel ignored the joke and turned away. "I am to bring you to the meeting of the Council."

Qayna followed him, through the enormous doors, which opened at his slightest touch. "Does that mean it's true?" she asked. "Azazel has returned, and is once again Head of the Council?"

"Azazel has returned," Baraqyel agreed. "Whether he is to preside is the issue that is now before the Princes."

Beyond the gates, chaos reigned. Gibbering, moaning howls filled Qayna's ears, and her eyes were unwillingly stuffed full of the spectacle of torture. A mob of people—humans, people of her stature—ravened and tore at each other, impaled each other on spikes, pummeled and clawed at each other's faces and tore each other limb from limb.

She felt sick.

With his spear, Baraqyel carved a path through the bodies. As she walked among them, Qayna looked into the eyes of the writhing tortured torturers and saw bottomless need and black despair.

"What's wrong with them?" Qayna asked her guide.

"They are dead," he told her, "and unhappy."

Qayna looked over her shoulder as she followed Baraqyel out of the cavern and up a spiral stair on the other side. Maybe, she thought, she shouldn't be so eager for her own death.

Another long corridor, full of arches and grated windows, erupted at its end out of the rough face of a jagged stone wall, and became an arching bridge. Over her shoulder, she saw that the wall both dropped and climbed out of sight, apparently infinite.

Qayna followed Baraqyel out along the slender catwalk until it terminated in another door, this one in the side of a ponderous, impossibly huge stalactite. Creatures guarded the door, hunchbacked, slithering things whose claws scratched on the stone and whose long tongues waggled suggestively at Qayna.

Her guide battered them aside with the butt of his spear. "Wait here," he instructed Qayna, and then he entered the door, shutting it behind him and leaving her alone with the creatures.

One ogled her with mismatched eyes, one enormous and the dark yellow color of a sick man's urine and the other wide and almond-shaped, with a green pupil like a cat's. The other rubbed four filthy, long-nailed hands together, scratching at its own bleeding knuckles and snickering.

"I bite," she warned them, and spat on the floor.

The door opened again and Baraqyel whisked her inside. "Keep quiet."

The interior of the stalactite was a single room dominated by a circular table, its surface above Qayna's head. One seat at the table was larger than the others, a throne, and the space before it was slightly raised. It was vacant. The other seats were filled with the princes of the Fallen, most of whom Qayna knew by sight only. There was tusked Semyaz, there was Bull Head, there was Ezeq'el the centauress. Their faces, where Qayna's view wasn't blocked by her poor angle, wore expressions of fear, surprise, disgruntlement, confusion, anger, malice, greed, and fatigue.

Azazel sat among them and smiled.

"Again I object." Semyaz glared at her with his piggish eyes and flapped his eagle's wings once.

"You object for the wrong reasons," Bull Head rumbled. "Don't object just because Azazel made a motion."

"Is no one allowed to object to anything Azazel says?" Semyaz snorted pig slobber onto his own chest and the table. "Has he become our lord and master without discussion?"

Bull Head stomped to his feet and pounded the table with his knuckles. "You waste my time, Semyaz! And you look like a petulant child!"

"Enough!" Azazel shouted.

Bull Head opened his mouth to say something and Azazel cut him off with a flick of his hand.

"Enough, Yamayol."

Bull Head nodded slightly and dropped himself back into his seat.

"She has no right," Semyaz sulked.

"She is the Marked Woman." Azazel slowly stood. "She was present at the beginning, and I think she will be present at the end. She has every right. She is the witness. Besides," he smiled again, and Qayna almost felt charmed by the titanic bat-winged and goat-legged Fallen, "we have already voted on this point of order, Semyaz, and you have lost."

Baraqyel shepherded Qayna into a corner. There was nothing in the room but the table and its seats, so Qayna assumed she was condemned to *witness* from an impossibly bad vantage point, but Baraqyel stooped without a word, lifted her and placed her on his shoulder. His white hair covered her legs like a cloak.

"I call for the question," Ezeq'el announced. With her horse's body, she stood beside the table rather than sitting in a chair. "Enough yammering. Our situation is clear, our choices are simple."

"Second," Bull Head lowed.

"The question has been called for," Azazel said. "All in favor."

A ragged unanimity of hands approved the motion.

"The candidates for President of the Infernal Council," the bat-winged Fallen continued, "bearing the titles Lucifer, Satan, the Adversary, Moloch, the King of Hell, are Semyaz ..." the boar-headed giant grunted and raised a hand in acknowledgement, "Belial ..." a mass of tentacles and scaly flanks at the far end of the table shuddered, "and Azazel ... that's me.

"All in favor of Semyaz ... Belial ... Azazel."

Hands rose in three waves, Baraqyel voting for Azazel along with many others, and then Semyaz jumped to his feet bellowing. "A tie! Deadlock! No ruler, or a triumvirate!"

"Vote again!" "Kill one of them!" "No!" An explosion of animal noises and yelling dominated the chamber for long moments.

"Silence!" Azazel roared one word, and the racket cut off. He looked across the Council chamber at Qayna. "Do you abstain, then?" he asked her.

Qayna almost fell from her perch. Her crow settled slowly on the back of the empty throne and stared at her. "Me?"

"It's a trick!" Semyaz howled, and his supporters pounded on the table with their fists and stamped on the floor with their hooves. "He's cheating!"

"Point of order!" Belial shrieked. The voice from the mass of tentacles sounded like metal grinding on metal, but somehow it formed intelligible words. "All parties present vote." Something like a beak, beneath something like a golden eye, shoved its way forward through the tentacles and fixated on Qayna. "He has done you hurt, woman. I have not."

"All parties present vote," Bull Head agreed.

"No!"

"She is the Marked Woman," Azazel repeated. "She's practically one of us."

"All parties present vote," Ezeq'el agreed.

They all stared at Qayna. She stared back, wondering whom she would offend if she said anything. She didn't mind the thought of being killed, but she balked at the idea of being trapped in the torture-orgy below.

"No!" the boar-headed Fallen Prince roared, and his hand fell to the hilt of the falchion at his belt.

The table froze. Somewhere under the table, a claw scratched nervously on stone.

"Do you challenge?" Ezeq'el drawled slowly.

Semyaz's eyes flitted around the table, counting his friends and enemies.

"No," Yamayol rumbled.

For a long moment, Jane wasn't sure Semyaz agreed.

Then Semyaz took his hand away from his weapon. "Call for a new vote!" he growled, banging the table again. "New vote!"

"Point of order," Ezeq'el said calmly. "This vote isn't over until all participants have indicated their vote."

"New vote!"

"Point of order!"

Azazel smiled.

Ezeq'el, the centauress, fixed Qayna squarely in the eye and arched one eyebrow.

"Put me down," Qayna said, and Baraqyel did so.

Some of the Fallen stared at her, but most of them stamped, bellowed and shrieked at each other.

"But ... the vote," Baraqyel said gently.

"Yes," she agreed. "The vote."

And then she turned and left the room.

She crossed the bridge at a brisk walk, forged her way through the passages and found herself standing over the field of mutually-abusive dead, staring at their pain and wondering what she had done, and why something seemed to be missing.

Then Azazel joined her, calm and quiet, with her crow on his shoulder.

That was it, she thought. For one brief moment, the crow hadn't followed her.

"You tried to use me," she accused him. She couldn't look at him, just smelled the goatness of his presence by her side. "That was unkind."

"Was it?"

There was a pause, but any silence there might have been was shattered by the shrieks of the sufferers below.

"Did you win?"

"The vote is suspended." Azazel laughed. "Semyaz and his friends are poring over the rules looking for a way out. You've set us back quite a bit—I think we're going to have to start over with a re-write of the rules from scratch."

"But you *will* win."

"I must."

"What about them?" She pointed at the sufferers below.

Azazel nodded agreement. "They are the reason why I must win."

"Baraqyel said they were the unhappy dead."

"They are. Heaven has coined a new word for them, in fact. They are the *damned.*"

"How are they damned?"

Azazel sighed. "It means they have done terrible things in their earthly lives, and now that they are dead, they have to work it out."

"What does *work it out* mean?"

"I don't know." Azazel's eyes got a far-away look. "I haven't worked it out yet."

"Must they suffer?"

"They chose suffering themselves. What they need is someone to make their suffering worthwhile."

"Are you saying you're going to save them?"

Azazel stamped one hoof on the floor. "I definitely won't save them, nor will I save anyone else. I am not the saving kind. What I'm saying is that pain can be healing. Pain can unlock what is inside a person, it can release him of the burden of greater pain and set him in the path of recovery. Pain can, for instance, bring remorse. And I am very definitely the pain-inflicting kind."

A splash of water on the floor at her feet startled Qayna. She looked up to see tears glistening in the giant's eyes.

"I killed your son." She felt she had to say it.

"We killed him together. We both wanted to save him."

"Is that why you want to help …" Qayna gestured without looking at the twisting pile, "these people?"

"Someone must do this work," Azazel said. "I … it has been decreed that I shall be the one to do it."

"That sounds like a commission. Like a trust."

Azazel laughed a single short laugh, like a bark. "It is what it is."

"What happened to you?"

"I was tried. I was sentenced. I was condemned."

"You escaped."

"Here I am."

"Can *I* escape *my* punishment?"

Azazel sighed. "Ah, Qayna, I don't know. I think not. I think your life will last as long as this world's."

"And then?"

"And then a new heaven, and a new earth, and who knows what may be possible?"

Qayna felt tears in her own eyes now. "I think I'd better go," she said. "I don't think I'll come back this way again."

Azazel nodded slowly. "I will escort you out."

CHAPTER TEN

"Stop!" the Legate commanded.

From under his mantelletta, he produced a short stub of candle, burning red. Jane smelled cinnamon and blood, and froze in place where she stood.

"Adrian!" Jim shouted. He couldn't move, either.

"I'm working on it!" the wizard called back. He mumbled furiously under his breath, but without the ability to move his hands, write glyphs or do anything other than speak, Jane knew the organ player's arcane powers would be limited.

Only Jane's crow was unaffected. Bored, it flapped its wings and circled the rooftop among the various actors.

"Listen to me!" the Legate of Heaven hissed. "Stop struggling. We are on the same side!"

"Let me go, and we'll test that proposition." Jane struggled with the spell that bound the muscles of her body in place, but her ka was too weak to shatter the magic directly, and she couldn't reach anything in her saddlebags or her pockets.

"Piss off!" Jim phrased it more succinctly.

"I will leave you alone," the Legate said to the rock and roller. "I cannot promise what your father will say or do, but join me, and we will negotiate with him together."

Jim growled like a dog confronting a trespasser. "You think I'm an idiot, don't you?"

The Legate turned his face to Jane. "Give me the gun." His voice and face were soft. "You have walked a long and a hard road, Qayna, and I have the power to release you from it." His two golem sedan-slaves towered over him, and the Swordbearers towered over them all.

"I don't care to go to Hell," Jane said. "That seems like it would just be more of the same, with less variation in the scenery."

"Oblivion," the Legate promised. He nodded to his own frozen hand that held the sealed sheet of parchment. "You countersign the death letter, and you will cease to exist. Only give me the gun, so I can face the seraphim."

Jane's heart pounded in her ears so loud that she almost didn't hear the man's last words. This was a moment she had dreamed of for thousands of years, now, literally, within her grasp. She could lay down her heavy burden and just sink into nothingness. All she had to do was what the Legate asked. It wasn't even obedience to him, not really, it was just a trade like any other. She didn't think he could even use the gun anyway, though maybe … maybe he had some magic up his sleeve that would make him the Horn's wielder.

"Can I kill Raphael first?" she asked.

"Qayna, please," the angel protested. He couldn't move, either. None of them could, below the neck, until the candle burned out.

The Legate looked closely into her eyes. "Do you really want to?"

"Yes," she said. "Yes, I do. But I'd prefer he get the Hell treatment, rather than oblivion."

"I can't do it." The Legate shook his head. "But I can promise you that in one minute, if you give me the gun, you won't care anymore. You won't care, you won't worry, you won't remember. You won't anything. You will simply vanish."

Jane wanted it. She wanted it really, really bad.

But in her heart of hearts, she knew she couldn't take the offer. Instead, she cursed.

Her Adamic swear-word snuffed out the candle, and she shot her hand for the Calamity Horn.

Raphael went for his gun.

The golems rushed forward.

Jane grabbed the Calamity Horn, knowing that she had only moments before the Legate re-lit his candle and also certain that the Messenger would clear leather first. That was fine with her. She never dished out what she couldn't take.

Bang! Bang!

The angel in the Deputy's body got off two shots and Jane felt them both hit, two mule-kicks to the chest. Then she had the Model 1910 in her hands and began firing, only not at Raphael—she shot at the Swordbearers.

She threw the first bullet over Raphael's shoulder, right at the chest of the Bearer behind him. More of Raphael's shots struck her as she fell spinning, shooting arm extended and throwing out thirty-two caliber rounds like a centrifuge of madness and spiritual plague.

Jim shrieked and staggered away, wrestling with the sounds in his head, and gunfire exploded from where the rest of the rock and roll band stood. Twitch burst into falcon form and sprang away from the meat packing plant.

The Bearers of the Sword were gigantic, imposing, more like towers than like men. That made them virtually impossible to miss. Jane focused on each shot as she took it and not on the damage the preceding shots had done, but she couldn't miss, out of the corner of her eye, the bright red streaks that appeared in the flaming white persons of the Swordbearers. Nor could she miss the shattering shrieks of indignant pain.

The Bearers of the Sword weren't used to being hurt.

For Ainok's sake, she enjoyed their surprise and indignation.

As Jane fired the seventh and final shot, she crashed to the gravel. Another of Raphael's bullets hit her in the shoulder and she grunted in pain, and then a bright red spark kicked the Legate's candle again into flame.

Flat on her back, Jane froze again. A few feet to one side, she heard Jim screaming. The Legate's kilt-clad golems hulked over her, eyes dull and fists clenched and raised to punch her.

"Foolish!" the Legate snapped at her. "Do you know what you risk?"

Jane coughed blood into her mouth and spat it at him.

Then the first of the Bearers' swords crashed down into the rooftop of the building. Chunks of concrete and steel, and bushels of wet gravel, exploded in all directions. In the violence of the suddenly-thrashing air, the candle snuffed out once more.

"Stop!" the Legate shouted.

Jane whipped a knife straight up into one golem's face, rolling to the side as she did. It collapsed backward with a wet murmur, and she came up with a second blade in her hand, which she snapped into his companion's face. She holstered the Calamity Horn and stepped past the magical creatures. She moved briskly; she'd taken them by surprise, but not seriously injured the golems.

A circle of flaming white and red closed in on Fine Cuts, Inc. The Swordbearers' faces were hidden behind their blank helmets, but they expressed their surprise and anger—or perhaps their mechanical, reflexive self-defense instincts—admirably with their upraised weapons.

Jim struggled to his feet, gripping his head between his hands. He hadn't lost his grip on the hoof, which was good. Raphael ejected a spent clip from his gun and fumbled to slot in a full replacement.

"Stop!" the Legate cried again. He incanted something, raising his hands against the advancing Swordbearers. In one hand he held the candle; in the other was Jane's death letter.

Roaring, Jane charged.

She almost tripped over her own saddlebags, but grabbed them on the run. Raphael fired at her again—idiot, he was wasting ammunition—and Twitch, now in her horse form, had clamped her big horsey teeth into Jim's shirt and was dragging him away.

Another flaming sword plunged into the rooftop, this one spiking down like a hammered nail. It missed Jane by several feet and the shockwaves made her stumble. She dropped her shoulder and rammed it into the Legate's belly.

"Oomph!" he barked.

She wrapped her arms around him and kept going.

The rooftop beneath Jane's feet buckled and twisted; she ran faster, gaining strength as she went. Fire at her heels scorched her, and she had no more attention to pay to what the rock and rollers were up to.

She only hoped she had enough fire within her, in her ka, to get where she wanted to go.

The Legate pounded on Jane's back with balled fists. She ignored him, except to squeeze as hard as she could, until she felt soft snaps that might have been ribs giving way. If the man had no breath, he wouldn't be casting any spells on her.

She incanted, murmuring words in Adamic as she reached the lip of the roof. Below her stretched the pocked and pitted asphalt, the water in the craters trembling with the shocks of the violence being inflicted on the building, but reflecting wavering images of the burning columns that were the Swordbearers.

Perfectly serviceable mirrors.

More bullets chomped into Jane's back as she jumped from the building—

arced through the air head-first, squeezing the Legate tight as any girl ever squeezed her teddy bear, saddlebags flopping awkwardly around them—

struck a puddle the size of a small garden pond—

and fell through, slamming to the ground on the hard stone floor of the Outer Bounds of the Mirror Queendom.

"Uuuunnnnnhnhhh," the Legate wheezed in breathless pain.

Jane rolled away from him in the patchy gray light, aching all over from the exertion and from the gunshot wounds. She wondered how many times Raphael had been able to hit her; she owed him that much more revenge, the next time she caught him.

She ejected her clip and groped in a pocket of her duster for bullets.

"You broke all my ribs," the Legate whined.

Jane ignored him.

"Welcome," she heard a cold voice say.

Jane looked up. "Not again." Her words were wet, incomprehensible through the blood bubbling from her lips.

A woman stood before her, tall and slender and fair. Hair like peacock feathers swept back in an iridescent halo from her high forehead. She didn't appear to be dressed so much as to have leaves plastered to her body, all over, and in her right hand she leaned on something that shimmered and was slippery to look at, but might have been a spear or a bolt of lightning.

Between Jane and the woman, and encircling Jane and the Legate, was a ring of fey fighters, leather-clad spear-warriors with animal tails. They all snarled at Jane, and she ignored them, slowly thumbing bullets into her clip.

"You're Mab," she said, when her lungs had cleared of blood enough to talk.

"You are the Marked Woman."

"I'd prefer you let me pass in peace."

"I'd prefer that you not shoot me."

"Fair enough." Jane snapped the clip back into the gun, reholstered it, and stood. She was shaky on her feet, but stayed upright. She found a handkerchief in one pocket and spat blood into it, to avoid spitting on the floor.

No point being gratuitously disrespectful; surely, enough opportunity for genuine disrespect would arrive unaided.

"Idiot," the Legate cursed her. He lay crumpled on the floor, breathing fast and shallow and holding an arm that looked shattered.

Beside him lay the letter. Jane stooped, picked it up, and popped the seal with her finger.

Inside, the parchment was blank.

"Liar," she said, and dropped the parchment on him.

"My cause is just!" he insisted. Shuffling and wheezing, he managed to tumble to his knees. "It's the greatest cause of all."

"You want to be God."

"No, that isn't it!" The Legate's eyes blazed bright. "I want there to *be* a God! I want a Heaven that is compassionate, a God who cares, a throne room that isn't empty!"

"Like I said," Jane muttered.

"Have you no feelings?"

"No," Jane lied. "I did once, and you people stomped them into nothing."

"I can get you a death letter," the Legate promised. "Yes, this one was a fake, but I can get you a real one. I need your help. *We* need your help. The whole *world* needs you. Won't you show mercy? Would you rather that the seraphim run Heaven than me?"

"I would rather," Jane said heavily, "that you stop. If you need a cause, sell cookies for the Girl Scouts."

"You insult me!" The Legate rose, limping to his feet.

"Take him away." Mab gestured with her glittering spear and her soldiers closed in around the Legate.

The Legate's face turned purple with rage as fairy weapons prodded him and fairy hands grabbed. "You insult *Heaven!*" he spluttered.

"That's rich," Jane grunted, and then the Queen's Rangers whisked the Legate away. The echoes and faraway sounds of the arrest continued for some time.

The two women were left with a much smaller retinue of Rangers.

Mab examined Jane closely. "There is fairy blood on your hands," she pronounced.

Jane sighed. "Okay," she admitted.

"I am not familiar with the *okay* defense." Mab frowned. "Do you mean that you rejoice in the death of my Rangers?"

Jane chuckled.

"I am not amused. Do you find it acceptable to kill my people?"

"I rejoice in no death, Your Majesty," Jane said. "Sometimes I get a little tickled by the prospect of my own."

Mab considered this. "I understand."

"Are you going to get in my way?"

"Are you going to attack my people?"

Jane sighed. "I just want out. That's all I've ever wanted."

"Ever?"

"Well, for six thousand years."

Mab shared an expression with Jane that was close to a smile. "I understand."

Jane reached for her quicksilver.

"I was going to make you an offer," Mab said. "I was going to bring you to your horse in exchange for the hoof of Azazel."

Jane arched an eyebrow. "I don't have the hoof of Azazel."

"That's why I can't make you the offer," Mab agreed.

"What do you want the hoof for?" Jane asked. "I thought you people were friends of Hell? Or are you just doing the Morning Star's bidding now?"

"That is not your affair." Mab stared coldly down her slender nose at Jane.

Jane shrugged. Her bleeding had stopped. The crow perched on a stone lintel over her head and stared down at her cruelly.

She felt like she was taking bait, but she had to ask. "Does that mean my horse is alive?"

Mab grinned. "What would it be worth to be led to her?"

Jane tapped the bead of quicksilver into her palm, feeling a small grim note of satisfaction that Mab pulled back slightly at the sight of it. "Nothing," she bluffed. "I'll find her on my own."

Mab laughed a silvery string of bell-like notes. "Very good, Marked Woman." The Queen of the Shadowless Palace beckoned forward one of her Rangers, a chestnut-haired youth with a bushy squirrel's tail. "Take her to the Thracian Mare."

Jane inclined her head politely and then poured the bead back into its vial. "Your Majesty."

"Ride well."

"Enjoy your conversation with the Legate."

Jane followed Squirrel through the Outer Bounds. She wouldn't have admitted it to Mab, but she was grateful for the guide—without it, she'd have spent hours, no doubt, waiting for her ka to recuperate so she could find her way, and then waited hours more at the gate to be able to pass through. In that time, who knows who or what might have come through into the Outer Bounds chasing her? Instead, she slugged calmly through the maze of stairwells, bridges, corridors and chambers with her saddlebags slung over her shoulder, letting her ka heal along with her indomitable body, while Squirrel *chucked* his teeth together and looked at her repeatedly over his slender shoulder.

Through the mirror-gate to which the fairy led her, Jane peered and saw that the Bearers of the Sword had gone. That was enough for her—she nodded to Squirrel, incanted her transition spell and slipped back into the sorghum fields outside Dodge City, Kansas.

She stepped from the rear view mirror of the destroyed deputies' car. The mirror was no longer attached to the body of the vehicle, but lay on the side of the road alone. For that matter, there was no longer a body of the car—just smaller and larger fragments of wreckage.

The same was true of Fine Cuts, Inc., Jane saw as she walked towards it. The enormous swords of Heaven's enforcers had smashed it to rubble and left it burning. Fire was beginning to spread to the adjacent fields, too, and in the distance, Jane heard the wailing sirens of emergency response vehicles.

Jane stopped at the edge of the pocked parking lot and whistled.

After two seconds' delay, the Mare cantered around the back of the plant, baring its predators' teeth at her and whinnying in something that almost sounded like pleasure.

Jane whinnied back and patted the dangerous, violent animal on its face. The horse's flanks were bloody, so Jane left the saddlebags on her own shoulder, took the Mare by the reins and started to lead it down the highway.

"Good girl," she said.

With a guttural coughing, the Dodge van rattled out from the other side of the plant, shocks taking a beating as the driver gunned it over the craters. At the edge of the highway, Jane and the van met, and the rock and rollers braked.

Jane was careful not to be too obvious about it, but she let her gun hand drift down and idle not far from the butt of the pistol.

Jim slid the van door open from the inside. Within, Jane saw Mike and Eddie in front and the wizard, Adrian, in back, squinting at her suspiciously through his sorcerous monocle. Twitch must be flying around under her own power, Jane guessed.

Jim scooted back and made room on the middle seat beside him. He gestured at it invitingly and arched an eyebrow. He looked a bit like his father, Azazel, she thought. But he looked a lot like Jacob. He looked just like Jacob might have looked, if Jacob had ever had the chance to grow up.

Eddie cranked down the window. The guitar player smiled, but in an *I-don't-trust-you-much* sort of way, and he kept his hands out of sight. Jane remembered his pistol and paid attention.

"Thanks," she said. "I'd be more trouble than I'm worth."

"I doubt that," Eddie said, in a voice that sounded like he believed her totally. "You want a lift? We might owe you."

Jane shook her head. "I ride alone. Hadn't you heard?"

Eddie nodded. "Still, Jim has this thing for taking in strays. He likes people with problems. Especially the damnation sort of problem."

Jane frowned. She could hear the sirens closer now. "I don't know whether I'm damned or not. We didn't have damnation when I was a kid, so I don't know where I stand. My big problem isn't that at all—"

"Your big problem is you can't die," Eddie cut her off.

"*Chingado.*"

"Bullseye," she said.

Eddie nodded. "Take care of yourself." He ground his window back up again, Jim nodded, and then they were in motion, rolling onto the highway and away.

Above the taillights of the Dodge, she could make out two birds flying away. One was Twitch, a white-winged raptor with a silver horse's tail; the other was a large black crow.

"Come on, girl." Jane turned and led her mount into the sorghum fields. She didn't have the strength of ka to put together any useful wards, and she could see the lights of the police cars and fire trucks now. She'd feel better after a couple of hours of light walking, and then she'd put together appropriate spells for traveling.

The Thracian Mare neighed a slight protest.

"Don't worry, he'll be back," Jane acknowledged. "The crow will always be back."

About the Author

D.J. Butler (Dave) is a novelist living in the Rocky Mountain northwest. His training is in law, and he worked as a securities lawyer at a major international firm and in house at two multinational semiconductor manufacturers before taking up writing fiction.

Dave writes speculative fiction for all audiences. In addition to his steampunk, urban fantasy, and science fiction novels published with Wordfire Press, he has a forthcoming steampunk fantasy series to be published by Knopf. Look for *The Kidnap Plot* in June 2016.

Dave is a lover of language and languages, a guitarist and self-recorder, and a serious reader. He is married to a powerful and clever woman and together they have three devious children.

Read about Dave's writing projects at:

http://davidjohnbutler.com.

IF YOU LIKED ...

If you liked *Band on the Run*, you might also enjoy:

Quincy J. Allen

Chemical Burn
Blood Ties

Josh Vogt

Enter the Janitor
Maids of Wrath

OTHER WORDFIRE PRESS TITLES BY D.J. BUTLER

City of Saints

Crechling

Rock Band Fights Evil
Hellhound on My Trail
Snake Handlin' Man
Crow Jane
Devil Sent the Rain

Our list of other WordFire Press authors and titles is always growing.
To find out more and to see our selection of titles, visit us at:

wordfirepress.com